Ruins of Empire

Blood on the Stars III

Jay Allan

Also By Jay Allan

Marines (Crimson Worlds I)
The Cost of Victory (Crimson Worlds II)
A Little Rebellion (Crimson Worlds III)
The First Imperium (Crimson Worlds IV)
The Line Must Hold (Crimson Worlds V)
To Hell's Heart (Crimson Worlds VI)
The Shadow Legions(Crimson Worlds VII)
Even Legends Die (Crimson Worlds VIII)
The Fall (Crimson Worlds IX)
War Stories (Crimson World Prequels)
MERCS (Successors I)
The Prisoner of Eldaron (Successors II)
Into the Darkness (Refugees I)
Shadows of the Gods (Refugees II)
Revenge of the Ancients (Refugees III)
Winds of Vengeance (Refugees IV)
Shadow of Empire (Far Stars I)
Enemy in the Dark (Far Stars II)
Funeral Games (Far Stars III)
Blackhawk (Far Stars Legends I)
The Dragon's Banner
Gehenna Dawn (Portal Wars I)
The Ten Thousand (Portal Wars II)
Homefront (Portal Wars III)
Red Team Alpha (CW Adventures I)
Duel in the Dark (Blood on the Stars I)
Call to Arms (Blood on the Stars II)
Flames of Rebellion (Flames of Rebellion I)

www.jayallanbooks.com

Ruins of Empire

Ruins of Empire is a work of fiction. All names, characters, incidents, and locations are fictitious. Any resemblance to actual persons, living or dead, events or places is entirely coincidental.

Copyright © 2017 Jay Allan Books

All rights reserved.

ISBN: 978-1-946451-02-6

Chapter One

Epheseus System
Ten Light Minutes from the Hystari Transwarp Portal
309 AC

"C'mon, c'mon…just a few seconds more," Jake Stockton muttered to himself as he pursued his enemy. His eyes were focused tightly on the small screen, following the Union fighter's every move. He'd taken out three enemy craft already, but that wasn't enough to hang on to his status as the fleet's leading ace…Dirk Timmons had five kills, and that left Stockton two behind his rival.

Stockton's mind was fully on the mission, on his almost feral need to destroy the Union ship in front of him. He knew the enemy pilots had little choice but to fight, that most had found the military to be the only escape from the crushing poverty the masses of the Union endured. But that was too philosophical to interfere with the raw hatred he felt for the foe. He'd seen too many friends die in the year since the war had begun. The faces of his lost comrades stared at him from the darkness of sleep, stoking his need for bloody vengeance.

His hand tightened, the hard rubber of the firing stud smooth against his calloused finger. He'd sent dozens of his enemies to hell, and now he was going to add to that number.

He heard the familiar echo of the lasers firing, the harsh

whine loud in the confines of his cockpit. His eyes remained locked on the screen, even as he fired again.

Damn.

The enemy was angling his thrusters, his pattern almost completely random. The changes to his vector were minimal—he was traveling at nearly 600 kilometers per second, and at that velocity it took a lot of thrust to substantially alter heading. But even the slightest variations from the expected were enough to dodge a laser blast.

Stockton felt his anger heating up. There was respect too, recognition that he was facing another talented flyer. But the admiration was buried deeply, covered over by bitterness, by the pain and death the Confederation forces had suffered in the war to date. Stockton was affable enough aboard *Dauntless*, but when he stepped into his fighter he became something else entirely.

He imagined the thoughts going through his prey's mind. Fear, of course, but also a rapid sequence of panicked deliberations, plots to deal with the danger on his tail. Stockton knew his enemy must have wanted to come about to face him, to meet him in head to head battle instead of giving his tail. But the Union strike force had been gutted, and dozens of *Dauntless*'s fighters were screaming forward, chasing down the few surviving enemy craft. Anything but flight was certain death for the Union pilot…and Stockton was determined that running would not save his adversary.

He fired again…and then again. Near misses. Very near. But misses nevertheless.

Stockton's anger flared. He didn't often run into a pilot who could put up a fight against him, and that was how he liked it. The Confederation forces had been outnumbered since the start of the war. There was no room for closely fought duels, not when there were twice as many enemy birds. Dominance was the Confederation's tactic, facing superior forces with smaller ones and winning the victory anyway.

He swung his ship around, matching his enemy's maneuvers. He hadn't managed to hit the Union fighter yet, but he'd be damned if was going to let the bastard get away. He fired again.

Closer this time, but still a miss. His laser blast had come within twenty meters of the target, which even at close range was considerably more precise than threading a needle. But a miss was a miss.

"You need some help with that one, Raptor?"

Stockton frowned as the voice of Dirk Timmons filled his headset. Stockton and Timmons had been bitter rivals for years, ever since they'd attended the academy together, though they'd mutually agreed to leave the animosity behind after Timmons and his squadron transferred to *Dauntless*. The two aces—and prima donnas, Stockton had to admit to himself—had won each other's grudging respect in the grim fighting of the last campaign. He'd made his peace with Timmons, but he wasn't ready to admit he actually *liked* the other pilot. Not yet, at least.

"I've got it," Stockton snapped back, his intensity manifesting as annoyance in his tone.

He fired, but Timmons words had shaken his concentration. Now he focused again, putting everything else out of his mind. There was his enemy…and there was him, and nothing else, not in all the vastness of space.

His eyes narrowed, locked even more tightly on the display. Then, in the face of all the tension, of the fear and strife of battle, he let himself go. He ignored the pit in his stomach, and let his intuition guide him. He tried to envision what he would do, the moves he would make to shake a foe. He could see the enemy ship in his mind, the view from his adversary's cockpit. He *was* the enemy pilot, moving the throttle, trying to escape the deadly hunter on his tail.

His own hand moved, angling his throttle as his instinct demanded. He fired, and then again, still missing, but ignoring it. There was no frustration now, no urgency, just the enemy, in front of him. Inside his head.

His finger tightened, the sound of the lasers again filling his tiny cockpit. But this time was different. He knew. Somehow he knew before the scanners reported, before even the deadly weapons fired. This time he had hit his mark.

He felt the rush inside, the excitement at the kill, but for an instant he struggled to check it, waiting for the screen to confirm what his gut was telling him. Then the small icon representing the Union fighter winked out of existence. He had one more kill, one more stamp to place on the exterior of his ship.

"Nice shot, Raptor." The earlier slightly mocking tone was gone from Timmons's words, replaced by honest congratulations. "That looked like a tough one."

"Thanks, Warrior." Stockton hoped his response was as genuine as his former rival's compliment. A decade of bad feelings was hard to erase entirely, but age and long overdue wisdom had come to *Dauntless*'s two hotshot pilots. The pointless conflict between them seemed especially foolish now that they shared an enemy.

"So, Raptor, now that you got that guy, what do you say the Blues and the Scarlet Eagles do something about that battleship...before it gets to the transwarp link and jumps out of here?"

"I like the way you think, Warrior," Stockton shot back, angling his thruster to bring him toward the rest of his squadron. "I like the way you think."

*   *   *

"The Blues and the Eagles are beginning an attack run on the enemy battleship, Captain." Atara Travis looked over from her station, her eyes meeting the captain's, carrying unspoken words. No one had authorized the fighters to engage the enemy mother ship...they had just been sent to pursue the broken Union squadrons.

Barron held her stare for an instant. His own silent reply. *Let it go.*

Dauntless had one of the best fighter contingents of any ship in the fleet. *The* best as far as Barron was concerned. And the core of that came down to his two elite squadrons, Stockton's Blues and Timmons's Scarlet Eagles. Not only were the squadron leaders almost certainly the two best pilots in the fleet, but each of their formations was jammed full of veteran flyers.

The skill of his battleship's squadrons had just been displayed in no uncertain terms. *Dauntless* had been on a forward scouting mission, a quick advance into the "no man's land" between the two fleets…and she had run into her counterpart, a Union vessel executing similar orders. The enemy ship had responded quickly, launched a heavy bombing assault, but *Dauntless*'s interceptors had shot down the attack craft like fish in a barrel. Not a single torpedo-bomber had even reached launch range, and their fleeing escort fighters, those that had survived the first engagement at least, were hunted down by *Dauntless*'s deadly squadrons.

Barron felt pride…and relief. He'd seen his ship battered before, felt the impacts of hit after hit, ripping through her hull, destroying her systems and killing her people. But now, *Dauntless* was like a razor, a war machine of such capability, she was the prohibitive favorite in any one on one fight against a comparable enemy vessel. She'd faced an equal here, at least in terms of tonnage and numbers of fighters, but she didn't have a bit of damage…at least none beyond that she'd brought with her into the system.

He looked down at the screen, at the casualty reports that were, for once at least, far less extensive than usual. No one on the ship itself had been killed. There were two injuries, one an engineer who suffered some burns when a cooling pipe blew, and another who fell five meters from a catwalk.

His squadrons had suffered terrible losses in *Dauntless*'s great battles of the past year, but even in his combat wings, casualties had been far lower than he'd feared. The Blues and the Eagles had only lost one ship each, and the combined toll for all five squadrons was only eight…and at least three of those had managed to eject.

The Blues had been *Dauntless*'s since Barron had taken command, but he'd only gained the Eagles during the fight against the enemy's massive supply base. And he'd had to pull out the Barron name to hang onto them once his ship rejoined the fleet. They'd originally been assigned to the flagship, Repulse, but the shade of Barron's war-hero grandfather was still powerful, and his own reputation was rapidly growing as well. It had taken a little effort, though in the end far less than he'd expected. Admiral Striker was a very different man from Admiral Winston, much less likely to take a stand on staid orthodoxy...and willing to accept the assurance from his most successful captain that *Dauntless* could indeed handle a total fighter complement more than twenty-five percent above its rated establishment.

It had required considerably more work to rearrange his ship's bays so they could carry and support seventy-eight fighters, instead of the sixty they'd been designed to handle. The first hurdle had been Chief Evans, who'd been ready to dig in his heels and oppose the measure, at least until Barron tried a little reverse psychology on the gritty non-com who ruled *Dauntless*'s bays with equal measures of unfiltered competence and pure fear. Instead of pushing the chief to acknowledge that his people could handle the increased load, Barron had told him he'd decided to refuse the Eagles, since it was clearly too much for his bay crews to handle. After that, it had just been a matter of holding back laughter as the chief made an impassioned argument about just how and why his people were more than ready to take on the extra load.

Barron had found his additional squadron to be enormously useful, even more so because the added formation was one of the very best in the fleet. He still rated the Blues just a touch higher, but he'd also admitted to himself more than once that his judgment was as likely the result of old loyalties as cold analysis.

"Let's increase our thrust, Commander. The Blues and the Eagles aren't outfitted for bombing runs, so they could probably use some backup if they're going to take that thing out." Barron knew *Dauntless* had no chance of catching the enemy vessel before it transited. But he was just as sure that Stockton and Timmons were well aware of that fact...and that they would be doing everything they could to degrade or disable the battleship's engines. And he wasn't about to bet against them pulling it off. "Besides, Stockton's and Timmons's people are going to burn up the rest of their fuel, and we're going to have to head that way to pick them up anyway."

"Increasing thrust, Captain." Atara Travis's voice was

relaxed. He'd caught a look at his first officer's display a moment before. Travis, too, had just looked at the casualty figures. And, like he had been, she was obviously relieved at what she'd seen.

Barron felt a slight pressure against his chest as *Dauntless*'s engines roared to life. His people had endured the pain of massive g forces when the ship's dampeners had been damaged or knocked out completely, but they were fully functional now, and the slightly more than 10g of thrust felt like a bit less than 2g. Uncomfortable, but not the hellish torment of 10g.

"Advise Commander Fritz I'm going to want full power for the primaries." *Dauntless*'s deadly main guns were fragile and subject to maintenance issues. But when operational, they were enormously powerful, a massive advantage in a duel with Union battleships and their significantly less effective heavy lasers.

"Yes, sir. Engineering reports primaries intact and ready for action."

Barron nodded. "Very well." He turned and looked straight ahead, into the massive 3D tank in the middle of *Dauntless*'s bridge. His ship was a small blue ovoid in the center of the mostly empty space. There were clusters of tiny pinprick spheres, three of them—Yellow, Red, and Green squadrons—heading back toward *Dauntless*, and two, the Blues and the Eagles, moving up on the red icon representing the enemy battleship.

"Captain, Commander Stockton advises that Blue and Scarlet Eagle squadrons have engaged. They have targeted the battleship's engines, and he reports that enemy thrust has been degraded sixty percent."

"Very well." Barron wasn't surprised that his squadrons had battered the enemy's drives, but even he was a little startled at the rapidity. Stockton's and Timmons's pilots had nothing heavier than lasers, and the amount of damage inflicted in such a short time suggested some crazy fighter tactics, including reckless runs into the teeth of heavy defensive fire. He almost snapped out an order for the attacking squadrons to cool it, to refrain from taking any unnecessary risks. But it was too late for that. His chance had been to forbid the attack altogether, and he hadn't done that.

Because you wanted that ship as much as they did…and you knew damned well how they'd go in. Don't be a hypocrite. Even if they suffer losses, it's worth it if we bag an enemy capital ship. One more step toward winning a war that has already cost millions of lives…

"Cut thrust enough to begin powering up the primaries, Commander. I want them ready to fire as soon as we enter range."

"Yes, Captain." Travis turned and flashed a glance toward his station…and in her eyes he saw the cold killer he knew lived inside her. "We will be in firing range in seven minutes."

Barron pushed aside a shiver at the eagerness in his first officer's voice.

Chapter Two

Epheseus System
One Light Minute from the Hystari Transwarp Portal
309 AC

"Fire!" Barron was leaning forward, gripping the armrests of his chair as he shouted out the command. A few seconds later the sounds of the great primary guns firing resounded across the bridge. All eyes moved to the screens and displays, waiting for the scanning reports to see whether the massive weapons had hit or not. *Dauntless* was still at extreme range, but the enemy ship's engines appeared to be completely offline, and the lack of any thrust capacity made the target's course highly predictable…and easy to target.

"Hit," Travis said, reporting the data as it came in. "Two hits."

Barron just nodded. He'd seen it on the display even as Travis made her report. He realized how his own attitude toward such things had changed. He'd known his people would score a hit. Not expected, but *known*. His gunners might miss a wily enemy running a series of evasive maneuvers, but there was no way they would fail to hit a target on a fixed course and vector, no matter the range. The instant his fighter squadrons had knocked out the enemy ship's engines, they had sealed its fate.

"Recharge primaries," Barron snapped out, unnecessarily, he knew. His people knew their business, as well as any spacers he had ever seen. They'd been good when he'd taken command of *Dauntless*, and he hadn't hesitated to use his family name to secure a few special additions like Atara and Fritzie. But now he truly realized what his people had become. He wondered if they even needed him anymore. They all knew their jobs, and they executed them with almost frightening proficiency.

"Blue and Scarlet Eagle squadrons have disengaged, sir. They report fuel status critical."

"Have them get clear of enemy weapons range and then cut their engines. We'll pick them up after we take out this battleship." The idea that *Dauntless* might fail to destroy its adversary never entered his mind. The Union ship was as good as crippled without thrust capacity. Barron didn't even have to close to its weapons perimeter…he could pick it apart with his longer-ranged primaries. It almost seemed too easy. Indeed, compared to *Dauntless*'s other struggles over the past year and a half, it *was* too easy. His people had been honed in battle with opponents like Katrine Rigellus and her razor-sharp Alliance crew…and behind enemy lines, trapped and outnumbered, running a gauntlet to destroy the Union's main supply base. A one on one fight with a crippled enemy battleship seemed almost like an exercise.

Except you still lost people. Less than usual, but men and women who followed you are dead in this fight.

He felt a wave of guilt at his confidence, and at the relief he felt that casualties were relatively light. No matter how great a victory he won, he'd long ago sworn to himself that he would never forget that the blood of his crew was the currency with which he paid for his triumphs. Even when, very occasionally, one came cheap.

He knew the Blues and the Scarlet Eagles had suffered more losses in their attack on the Union vessel. Battleships relied on their own interceptors to defend them against fighter attack, but they also mounted dozens of small laser turrets. Any attack, even one against a vessel stripped of its defensive fighter screen, would suffer some degree of losses to this deadly fire. Barron deliberately looked away. He didn't want to see, not now. There was nothing he could do about it, not one man or woman he could save by focusing on the losses while the battle still went on. There would be time for that later, when he was alone. When he owed nothing to his crew's morale and he could sit in the solitude of his office or his quarters…and feel pain for those lost. And the guilt for sending them to their deaths.

"Both Blue and Scarlet Eagle leaders confirm your orders, Captain. They have transmitted their positions and vectors."

"Very well, Commander." He still wasn't used to the "Scarlet Eagles" designation. Timmons's unit had been called the "Red Eagles," but *Dauntless* already had a Red squadron, and confusion in battle could get men and women killed. Barron didn't like insisting that Timmons make a change—after all, he knew how superstitious fighter pilots could be about such things—but he did it anyway. In the end, the star pilot hadn't put up much of a fight, just one perfunctory objection. Barron suspected Timmons considered 'scarlet' a synonym for red, and therefore a sop to whatever subconscious concerns he had about tempting the gods of flight by making changes.

"Primaries charged and ready, Captain."

"Batteries are to fire at will until the enemy is destroyed."

"Yes, Captain."

Barron leaned back in his chair, some of the exhilaration he'd felt earlier slipping away. He wished he could escape from *Dauntless*'s bridge, flee to the sanctuary of his office where he could face the conflicting emotions. Part of him, at least, felt less like a soldier, fighting for a cause…and more like an executioner. A murderer.

He knew that was unfair. He would have accepted the surrender of the Union vessel, and he knew any prisoners he took would be treated humanely in Confederation custody. But Union ships rarely yielded. His mind drifted back to the struggle at Santis, the great battle with Captain Rigellus and *Invictus*. Alliance ships never surrendered either, though that was about honor and the codes mandated by their culture. Barron hadn't fully understood the fanaticism of the Alliance spacers when he'd fought that fateful battle out on the Rim, but he'd read all he could since then on the history of the Palatians, and on the militaristic empire they had built in just over half a century.

The ancestors of the Alliance had been subjugated, their world conquered, their people enslaved. They had endured generations of misery, and when they finally threw off the shackles, they built a culture centered in strength. *Never again*...those words became their mantra, and the core of their national philosophy. Barron didn't approve, at least not of the extremes to which their stark society had taken its mandate, but he understood.

The Union, however, was something utterly alien and contemptuous to him. A self-proclaimed egalitarian republic, in reality it was an oligarchy ruled by a rapacious class of politicians, one in which all but the most highly placed lived grim lives of hard work and deprivation. The prohibition against surrender was enforced in a practical and brutal way, by holding the families of spacers responsible for their actions. Any Union personnel yielding would do so knowing their parents, spouses, children, and siblings would pay for the crime with their lives... and few doubted the rapacious efficiency of the Sector Nine intelligence agency in such matters.

Barron detested the Union. He considered it a blot on humanity, a threat to every other nation. Yet the men and women his people killed were little more than slaves. They had no choice, unless you could consider watching everyone you cared about murdered for your own failures a choice. Every Union ship his people destroyed was one small step toward winning this war...and losing it was unthinkable. But each victory also meant more unfortunate human beings slaughtered, people who had been consigned to an unending nightmare, simply because of the misfortune of being born on the wrong worlds.

His eyes never left the main display, even as he wrestled with such thoughts. His people were doing their jobs magnificently, *Dauntless*'s gunners carving up the Union battleship like some kind of roast on a holiday table. It was clean looking, at least on Barron's readouts. Words, numbers, diagrams. He knew the reality was quite different, that on the dying Union ship, men and women were suffering unimaginable fear and torment.

It will be over soon, at least, he thought, listening as *Dauntless*'s primaries fired yet again. Almost as if in answer, the bridge erupted into cheers as the small ovoid vanished from the tank. The enemy ship's reactor containment had failed, releasing the equivalent of a miniature sun inside the vessel. The destruction was complete—there was nothing left of *Dauntless*'s adversary now, save for a cloud of plasma and a blast of hard radiation.

It was another victory, but the thrill was gone for Barron, even the sense of achievement. No matter how many battles his people fought, how many of their enemy they defeated, each struggle just seemed to lead to the next. It seemed war, once begun, had no end. Only more killing, more death.

"My congratulations to the gunners, Commander," he said, trying not to sound as robotic as he felt. "Another outstanding performance."

"Yes, sir." He could hear a hint of something in Travis's tone. Either his first officer was feeling the same conflicting emotions, or she was picking up on his.

Or both…

"Bring us around, Commander. Let's go fetch the rest of our fighters."

"Yes, Captain."

"And send out the recovery shuttles. We've got some pilots out there to pick up before they run out of life support."

*   *   *

"You called for me, Captain?" Atara Travis stood at the open doorway, staring tentatively inside. She wouldn't come in without an express invitation, Barron knew. Not though he'd called for her, nor even because she was his best, most trusted friend. *Dauntless*'s first officer tread an odd and highly specific line with him between discipline and friendship. He'd never been able to quite figure it out, why in some situations she could sit back, call him Tyler, and even once in a while, on those rare occasions when either of them drank, tie one on with her old friend with nary a salute in sight, yet in others she displayed a surprising degree of formality. She was always proper with him in front of the crew, of course, but it was her behavior in private that varied so widely.

"Yes, Atara, come in. Sit down." He waved toward the small counter separating the tiny kitchen in the captain's quarters from the main room. "I just had tea sent up. Pour yourself some if you'd like."

"Thank you, sir." She walked across the room, grabbing the small teapot and filling a cup. She turned around, facing Barron again. Then she walked over, sitting in one of the chairs flanking the sofa where *Dauntless*'s captain, in a surprising display of relaxation, was actually semi-sprawled out. Not lying exactly, but not quite sitting either.

"It's just us here, Atara. You can check the 'captains' and 'sirs' at the door." He smiled, just in case his tone wasn't enough to assure her he wasn't scolding her, just inviting her to relax.

"Commander Fritz reports that all systems are operational…" Travis paused. "But, she also advises…and this is exactly how she put it…that she's got everything taped and glued together and about half the equipment on this ship could fail at any time if somebody so much as looks at it the wrong way." Travis's tone was lighter than it had been, but Barron could hear the worry there too. *Dauntless* had come back from the grueling battles behind the Union lines battered and barely patched together, functional only by the grace of God…and the unmatched skill of her engineering team. She'd desperately needed a full repair and refit in spacedock then, but she hadn't gotten one. Instead, she'd spent an additional six months on the front, there because the Confederation needed enough ships to deter any immediate moves by the Union…and because, for all she'd been through, there had been a backlog of ships even more in need of repairs.

"Well, it looks like her tape and whatever else she used managed to hold up long enough. I just got the orders by direct comm. We're coming off the line. We're to proceed to the fleet base on Dannith immediately for extended repairs…" His smile broadened. "…and shore leave for all personnel." Barron needed a break, he knew that much. He needed time for his head to clear, and a few months with no life and death decisions was just the prescription. And he was certain Atara and the rest of the crew were just much as in need of a rest.

"That's good news, Tyler. The crew will be thrilled. Why don't you make an announcement?"

"I will. It will be good to get her back into top shape again, won't it? We've earned our pay, but the last full refit we had was before we went to Archellia. Since then, every break we've had has been cut short, the repairs underway slapped together half-finished."

"We *really* need it. If we didn't have Commander Fritz, I doubt we'd have a functioning system aboard."

Barron nodded. No one had to tell him what a precious asset Anya Fritz was to his crew…even if she was a terror who drove her staff almost to the point of insanity. Barron had heard half a dozen of the nicknames the engineering crews had for their commander, and he didn't presume to think they'd all made their way to the captain's ears.

His eyes darted back to Travis. There had been something in her tone. Concern? "What is it, Atara?"

"Sir?"

"Something's bothering you. So, spill it."

"It's nothing, Tyler. Really." She paused. "I was just wondering…"

"Wondering what?"

"Well, why would they send a routine order to report for service and shore leave directly to the captain, rather than to me?" She looked up at him. "Was it on the regular line?"

Barron hesitated, tension suddenly weighing on him. "No, it was on the Priority One channel."

Travis frowned. "Does that seem like a normal use of the Priority One channel, Ty? Maybe I'm worrying about nothing, but it seems an order like that would have come in with the normal housekeeping traffic."

Barron stared down at the floor for a few seconds. What she said made sense. He'd written off the Priority One usage to the war, and to *Dauntless*'s proximity to the front. But now he was thinking of other transmissions, ones far more sensitive than this last one, sent on the normal channels.

"Don't mind me," Atara said contritely. "I think the last year or more has me a little edgy. I'm seeing enemies everywhere I look."

A bit of Barron's smile came back. "Well, it's not like there haven't *been* enemies and dangers everywhere, so I'd say your senses certainly have reason to be heightened." He paused. "Still, I don't know what could be waiting for us at Dannith. It's pretty far back from the lines, and unlike Archellia, it's not near any other power. There's nothing across that border but the Badlands. So, unless the old empire is going to rise from the ashes and dust and attack us, I'd say we've got a pretty good shot at a crisis-free refit."

"I'm sure you're right, Ty." Atara was trying to mask her concern, and she would have managed it with anyone who knew her less well than Barron. He knew she was still concerned, and more to the point, he realized he was as well now. "I'll go plot a course for Dannith, if that's all right with you," she continued. She got up, but then she hesitated, waiting for permission to leave. Another mix of casual and formal.

"That's a good idea. We're already cleared to go, so we can head out anytime."

Travis walked toward the door, pausing just before she got there. "It's been a tough year and a half, Ty," she said softly, without turning around. "I think it's got me a little paranoid." Then she walked the rest of the way, the door opening as she reached it and closing behind her as she stepped out into the corridor.

Barron sat unmoving, staring at the hatch for a long time.

Yes, you're paranoid, Atara...but that doesn't mean you're wrong...

Chapter Three

Excerpt from Auguste's Meditations on the Cataclysm

We speak of the Cataclysm frequently, in academia as well as routine conversation. We typically refer to it as a single occurrence, some war or disaster dating to a specific point in time. This is not only incorrect, it is antithetical to a true understanding of mankind's fall, and of the subsequent limited rebirth that has created our Confederation and the reality of today.

The Cataclysm was not one event, not even a lengthy one, as it might appear from the many references that so characterize it. Rather, it was a lengthy sequence of separate disasters exacerbated by the poor decisions of those in power, ultimately resulting in the downfall of most technologically advanced civilizations, and in the complete and utter destruction of thousands of formerly-inhabited worlds.

Even the date we assign to this shattering event owes more to the somewhat arbitrary creation of the calendar used in the Confederation than it does to a quantifiable historical happening. In truth, what we call the Cataclysm extended over many centuries, perhaps the greater part of a millennium, as humanity's civilization began to decline from its peak. The point from which we measure our years is but the final low of that terrible sequence of destruction and decay—the moment Megara lost contact with the remnants of the vast civil polity we know today only ephemerally as the empire.

The empire was vast, of that much we are certain, though we know few details about its history. For centuries before the receipt of the last message that marks the start of our calendar, contact had been sporadic, and actual governance from the imperial capital but a historical footnote well beyond living memory.

The empire spanned a region of space many times the size of that we inhabit today. Our worlds, those of the Confederation and the Union, and all the other nations in this area of the galaxy, were once but a fringe sector of the empire, though they fell away from its control centuries before the final crescendo of destruction. It is the very remoteness of our worlds that allowed them to avoid the great depths of the fall that occurred elsewhere.

Humanity's ancient empire, incalculably more advanced than our Confederation, died a slow and painful death, splintering and crumbling into warring parts, and eventually descending in a final centuries-long orgy of destruction. On world after world, the last survivors succumbed to radiation poisoning and uncontrolled disease. The few machines that had not been utterly destroyed gradually ceased to function, leaving nothing but silent graveyards where once stood titanic testaments to mankind's achievements.

All that remains of this great empire is that region of the galaxy designated Abandoned Space or the Quarantined Zone, and colloquially known as the Badlands. On world after silent world, the technology and knowledge gained during untold millennia of growth were slowly lost to the ages.

Outside the Badlands, on the frontier, some planets, worlds like those of our own Confederation, retained enough technology to support a relatively rapid return to space travel and the rediscovery of the transwarp links left behind by the empire. The hundreds of planets known to us, both within the Confederation and in the surrounding nations, are only those accessible through the remaining Schwerin transit lines. Where that ancient system of transwarp portals has failed, worlds once part of a vibrant and prosperous empire are lost to us, trapped by enormous gulfs of space. Occasional radio signals confirm that some few of these planets remain inhabited, but they are removed from our conception of reality, almost as though they occupied an alternate universe.

We of the Confederation take pride in the wealth and science we have developed, yet here, even on advanced worlds like Megara, the technology we control is but a tithe of that our ancestors possessed. We generally view our growth in optimistic terms, as a rebirth, an upward trajectory from mankind's near doom. We ask ourselves how long it will be before we have returned to the levels of knowledge possessed by our ancestors, before we exceed the heights they had achieved.

But the real question I raise in this work is a starker one, concerned not with soaring advancement or glorious futures, but grim prediction. Is our reality truly the early stage of a recovery from humanity's fall? Or merely a brief upswing on an otherwise relentless descent into a true dark age, one that will last for untold eons?

Free Trader Pegasus
System Z-111 (Chrysallis)
Deep Inside the Quarantined Zone ("The Badlands")
309 AC

"We're getting strange readings from planet four. Definitely some kind of energy output." Vig Merrick glanced up from his workstation, a startled look on his face. "It's not like anything I've ever seen, Captain. The pattern doesn't match anything in the database. I checked it against every known form of fission or fusion generation, even chemical sources. But it's... different."

"Different how?" Captain Andromeda Lafarge sat in the center of Pegasus's tiny bridge. She was clad in her usual costume, black leather from head to toe. A heavy pistol and a small knife hung from a belt strung over the back of her chair. *Pegasus's* crew had an inside joke that their captain took her weapons into the shower with her. It wasn't true, but it was closer to the mark than she was prepared to admit to any of them. The hook on the wall in her small bathroom was within easy reach of the shower stall, and Lafarge's reflexes were lightning quick.

She leaned back in her chair, taking a quiet breath, trying to keep herself calm. Her people had come a long way...and just maybe this was what they were looking for. Her pale blond hair was tied tightly behind her head, and her ice blue eyes focused intently on *Pegasus*'s small main display, watching as the meager data trickled in from her ship's scanners.

"Stronger, for one thing. It's *very* intense. Unless I'm missing something, we're talking about output vastly stronger than even a military reactor."

Lafarge felt a flutter of excitement. Could they *really* have found what they'd been seeking for so long? "Bring us into orbit, Vig."

"Yes, Captain."

Merrick was Lafarge's first officer, and her oldest friend. The two were usually informal, but in tense moments, Merrick reverted to calling her "captain" instead of using her name as most of *Pegasus*'s crew did. Lafarge's parents were long dead, and the only legacy she carried from the mother and father so long gone was the name "Andromeda," a mouthful that was mercifully shortened to "Andi" by those who knew her.

Merrick was the only other person in the cramped control room. There was a third station off to the side, one that would have been manned in a crisis situation, but she'd sent the other seven occupants of her ship to their bunks to catch some sleep. *Pegasus* had been on its hunt for a long time, and nothing would be served by having her crew collapse from exhaustion.

Most of her people had been with her for years, and she knew she had their loyalty. But they'd been chasing shadows for months now, burning through much of the profit they'd earned on earlier expeditions pursuing what she suspected most of those aboard *Pegasus* had come to view as a phantom, an obsession the captain refused to accept was a mirage. But Lafarge's gut had never led her astray before, and she wasn't about to start disregarding it now. She'd been called every synonym for stubborn she could think of—and she saw no reason to shy away from any of those characterizations, not now. Not when she was so close.

Lafarge called herself a free trader, even an archeologist of sorts in her more cerebral moments, but other names had been targeted at her as well. Adventurer, rogue, pirate…though she'd always insisted "pirate" was unfair. Perhaps she paid less attention than the authorities liked to rules and laws she felt were ill-conceived or unreasonable, but she'd never fought any ship that hadn't attacked her first nor taken a cargo by force. She was no thief, no cutthroat. In a weak moment, she might even cop to "rogue," but never "pirate."

The governments might lay claim to the artifacts and relics in the Badlands, but she saw no reason to adhere to such restrictions. Governments were always a bit grabby in her estimation, and as far as she was concerned, none of the relics out in the vastness of ancient, Cataclysmic space belonged to anyone save those with the skill and courage to find them. The Badlands—or Quarantined Zone or Abandoned Zone, as the area was variably designated by international accord—was not part of any nation. By treaty, any artifacts found in the zone were to be shared by all humanity, perhaps the most violated rule in the history of international relations. If the governments were going to ignore their own agreements, she saw no reason to turn over her own hard-won treasures to what she could only see as a glorified tax gatherer.

Lafarge didn't object to any ancient tech she found being shared, of course, not as long as she was paid first. She was no collector, and running a ship like Pegasus was expensive. She wasn't out in the middle of nowhere risking her life for nothing. Andi Lafarge had tasted poverty and deprivation at its bitterest and most soul-killing.

She remembered the crime-ridden streets of Hephaeseus's slums, the pain of an empty stomach and the destitution of her orphaned childhood. *Never again*, she had long ago promised herself, and her career since had been dedicated to ensuring her wealth and comfort. When she retired one day it would be to a planet with crystal clear seas and vibrant blue skies, not the polluted, garbage-filled oceans, dense gray haze, and acid rains of her homeworld. And if the black market was the way she made that happen, so be it. She would let no one interfere. If her wits would serve, that was fine, but she carried that pistol and blade with her everywhere for a reason, and she was ready to use them when necessary.

She'd spent a lot of time prowling these long-abandoned systems, and that had taken a toll on her psyche, and on what little faith she'd ever had in mankind as a species. The Badlands were a constant reminder of the shadow that stalked mankind, of humanity's propensity for self-destruction. Lafarge's outlook was a grim one. She saw corrupt governments everywhere, masses of people willing to believe whatever they were told as they were led to ruin. The wreckage of the ancient empire was a look into the past, of course, but to Lafarge it was also a glimpse of a potential future, one she was far from certain the Confederation and the nations surrounding it would avoid.

There was nothing she could do about that, however, and she had no intention of wasting her time trying. She looked to her own needs, and those of her crew. That was all that mattered to her. The fools inhabiting the worlds of the Confederation, and the sheep enslaved by the Union…they created their own reality. She would live on the fringes, in the shadows, and when she was done with her explorations, she would enjoy the comfort her efforts had provided her. She wished no harm on those who did not act against her, but neither did she accept responsibility for people's folly.

"Entering orbit, Captain."

"Very well, bring…"

"Captain, we're picking up something in orbit. It's big… damned big, just coming around into view. And it's the source of the energy readings." Merrick spun around and stared at Lafarge. "It's huge, Andi…bigger than a battleship."

Lafarge stared at the screen, unable to look away. She and her people were searching for an extraordinary find…but the thing her scanners were picking up was beyond her wildest expectations.

Her mind was racing, and she knew she was getting way ahead of herself. How could she even get this thing back to normal space? And what was it? Some kind of weapon? That would be bad. She wasn't shy about selling trinkets on the black market, even bits and pieces of information tech, but the vast construct looming in front of her ship was something else entirely. Her stomach twisted into a knot, as worries crept in, right on the heels of her excitement.

There was ancient technology to be found out in the Badlands—she'd known that a long time, even before she'd been one of the treasure hunters herself—and fortunes to be gained by those willing to take the risks to discover it, but most of the artifacts retrieved had been small items, or bits and pieces of larger systems.

Until now...

"Bring us in closer, Vig. Slow." She couldn't imagine the thing was fully operational, but the energy readings made her nervous. She'd equipped *Pegasus* well for an adventurer's ship, but if the monstrous thing on her scanners was operational and armed, she didn't doubt it could vaporize her little craft with a single shot.

She tapped the small comm unit next to her chair. "Ross..."

"Yes?" Ross Tarren's voice was soft, his voice still hoarse from sleep.

"Time to get up. Rouse the whole crew. I think we've just found something...well, you'll have to decide for yourself what it is. But I think we need everybody up and alert right now."

"On the way, Andi."

She turned and flashed a glance toward Merrick. "I want the scanners on full power, Vig. Don't take your eyes off the screen, not for a second. If there's any kind of energy spike, any signs at all that this thing is active—and maybe preparing to fire—get us the hell out of here."

"Will do, Captain." Merrick's voice suggested he was as doubtful as Lafarge that *Pegasus* could escape if the artifact turned out to be hostile. "We've got the energy readings—more power than I've ever seen any physical construct generate—but no changes, no increases. It's still just sitting there."

"What the hell is that?" Ross Tarren had just stepped onto the bridge...and frozen in place. He stared at the screen in something that looked like pure shock.

"Well, for one thing, it's proof we weren't chasing shadows. This is by far the greatest discovery made in the Badlands."

Lafarge tried to hide her conflicting emotions. She was thrilled to find something so extraordinary, but she was already beginning to realize it would be a difficult thing to monetize. There was no way to sell something like this in a clandestine manner, even assuming she could get it back to Confederation space somehow. And, while she had less respect than the authorities liked for overreaching rules and restrictions, she wasn't about to sell out the Confederation by allowing something of this importance to fall into foreign hands.

"What the…" Dolph Messer stopped at the hatch and stared onto the bridge.

"What's the problem, you big oaf?" Rina Strand's voice was terse, her annoyance clear in her tone.

Messer moved forward as Strand pushed *Pegasus*'s resident giant onto the bridge. The small woman squeezed between Messer and the wall…and then she too stopped. "Shit," she muttered softly.

"Alright, enough gawking." Lafarge turned and glared at her crew members. "We've found something…something big. I need you at your stations, not cramming onto the bridge, taking up space." She gestured toward the single vacant seat on the bridge. "Ross, at your station. Rina, down in engineering…now." She slapped her hand down on the comm controls, activating the shipwide PA. "Everybody, get to your stations. I don't think we've got a fight on our hands, but we're definitely venturing into the unknown, and we're damned well going to be ready for whatever happens."

She leaned back, her gaze returning to the display. She liked to consider herself a pure mercenary, and she'd often said she would haul loads of grain if it paid as well as ancient artifacts. But that was all show. Lafarge was fascinated by old tech, and now she could feel the rumblings in her mind, the curiosity that, upon occasion, earned her that informal archeologist's designation.

What is this thing?

"Still no change, Captain." Merrick's voice was edgy, but it was clear he was as intrigued by the ancient device as Lafarge.

"It's just orbiting."

"Then bring us alongside, Vig." Lafarge didn't move, didn't let an eye wander from the incredible image in front of her. "And see if you can find a place to dock. If this thing lets us get close enough, we're going aboard to have a look around."

Chapter Four

Inside Abandoned Spacecraft
System Z-111 (Chrysallis)
Deep Inside the Quarantined Zone ("The Badlands")
309 AC

"Vig, are you seeing this?" Lafarge moved forward, slowly angling her head back and forth. She still held the portable lamp in her hand, but now she flipped the switch, turning it off. The corridor had been dark when she and Merrick had first entered, but then the ceiling had begun to glow, some kind of lighting units activating in response to their presence. It was dim at first, but the illumination grew until the area around them was as bright as *Pegasus*'s bridge. She felt a tightness in her gut, a combination of excitement and fear. Whatever it was her people had found, it was still operational, at least to some extent.

"I am..." Merrick turned, reaching out and touching the nearest wall, running his hand over the smooth metal. "It's spotless. No dust, no debris. What kind of material is this?"

"I have no idea." She stepped over to the side of the corridor and put her hand on the wall, following his lead. "It's warm. Some kind of heating system?" She looked over at Merrick, aware as she did that her number two didn't have any more answers than she did.

"Could be." *Pegasus*'s first officer moved his hand along the smooth gray surface. "How can this be in such good condition? It looks like whoever was here left an hour ago."

Lafarge nodded. "I know." She'd spent the last eight years scouring the Badlands. One of her earlier finds had been so substantial it had funded her purchase of *Pegasus*, but even that cache had been nothing but broken bits of advanced circuit boards…certainly nothing functional. Not to mention so large. She'd never even allowed herself to imagine finding an intact ship, much less one that made a Confederation battleship look like a lifeboat.

"Let's see what there is this way." She gestured down what looked like an endless corridor. She'd brought *Pegasus* in at what looked like a docking portal, but she'd still been surprised how easily she'd managed to adapt her ship's own umbilical to the artifact's port. It hadn't been a perfect fit, of course, but as much as Lafarge eschewed the occasional designation as a pirate, her ship bore many marks of a past serving one or more buccaneer captains. The extremely adaptable docking portal was just one of those.

The two walked slowly, cautiously, peering ahead as additional sections of the strange overhead lighting activated at their approach. It was the same everywhere—no visible lighting panels, just a strange glow from the ceiling material itself. She'd never seen anything like it, and she didn't have the slightest idea how it worked.

There were a number of hatches and doors along the way, but they were all locked. Lafarge had paused at the first few, trying to figure out to open them, but she'd given up. There were no apparent locks, just smooth doors almost imperceptible from the walls surrounding them.

She pushed ahead, walking down the corridor, alert, her eyes fixed forward. The hall had to lead somewhere, and that was as likely to be important as whatever lay behind the doors.

"This corridor doesn't end," Merrick said softly.

"Well, the ship's a little over fifteen kilometers long, which is big but still definitely finite, so I'm thinking it will end at *some* point." Lafarge's voice was light, an abortive attempt at humor.

She was trying to control her anxiety, with some at least some superficial success. But inside she was scared to death. About what lay ahead. About what this ancient wonder actually was. And about what she was going to do with the discovery. Her mind had been working around various schemes for selling the find, but she'd discounted each one as unrealistic almost immediately. She was beginning to realize she was in over her head. Deeply.

But if I report this to the authorities, they won't pay me... they'll just take it. And they'll probably harass me about why I was here to boot...

She kept walking, trying vainly to push aside the worries. There would be time enough later to decide what to do. Perhaps she could find some portable items, small artifacts she could remove from the ship, unimportant relative to the massive vessel, but with enough value for all her people to retire on. Then she could make an anonymous report to the naval authorities, and let them worry about what to do with the hulking artifact.

"There's something up ahead, Andi." Merrick stopped, reaching out instinctively, pointing. But Lafarge had seen it already. The corridor ended up ahead at a doorway. An open doorway.

"Let's go, Vig. This is no time to stop." She quickened her pace. She liked to think that she was out in the Badlands chasing after bits of ancient technology solely for the money, driven by nothing more complex than the dedication to remain free of the poverty she'd once known. But she was driven by an intense curiosity as well, and she'd studied every artifact she had found before turning them over to her shadowy buyers. That inquisitiveness drove her on now. She was standing inside the greatest discovery in Confederation history, and the immensity of that fact was beginning to crystalize in her mind. She'd always operated in the shadows, and she liked it that way. But now she was at the center of something that would change history. It was more than she could easily comprehend, and she tried to ignore the implications, focusing instead on what was around her now...and how to proceed.

She stepped up to the door, her hand dropping instinctively to her pistol. The weapon was old, its grip worn smooth from use, but it was in perfect condition. She took it apart once a month with solemn regularity, replacing any parts that showed signs of wear. It had saved her ass more than once, and if she needed it again, she knew it would be there for her.

She peered through the doorway into a vast chamber. The ceiling was close to a hundred meters above the deck, and she could barely see the other side in the gloomy distance. It was the largest room she had ever seen, certainly on any kind of space vessel.

She took a few steps inside, stopping again and looking around. It was a hanger of some kind, that much was apparent. A row of cradles extended in out from where she stood, all of them empty. All save one.

Her eyes fixed intently on the sole remaining craft. It was small, at least by the standards of the giant vessel in which it lay, though as she jogged forward to it, she began to realize it was nearly as large as Pegasus.

A shuttle? Lifeboat?

The absence of any bodies or signs of a crew in any of the corridors began to make sense as she counted the almost two dozen empty docking cradles. Whatever had happened centuries before, the great vessel's crew appeared to have abandoned ship. For all she knew, there were a dozen bays like this scattered throughout the ship, each of them as empty as the one in which she now stood.

She stared at the remaining shuttle. It looked fine, but she knew there were a hundred technical problems that could ground a ship, only a few of which would be readily apparent on cursory inspection. She guessed it had malfunctioned somehow all those centuries before.

"I wonder why the crew left," she said, not really expecting an answer.

"I suppose there could have been a lot of reasons." Merrick paused. "But the ship seems sound, and it's still here after all these years, with functioning life support...so it doesn't seem like it could have been anything dire."

"I don't suppose it really matters. A lot of bizarre things probably happened near the end of the Cataclysm." She turned and looked back at her friend. "This was probably a warship of some kind. Wouldn't you agree?"

"I didn't see any gun emplacements along the hull, but who knows how a pre-Cataclysmic ship was designed. It doesn't look like any kind of freight hauler, so what else could something this big have been? Especially with those energy readings."

"Speaking of which...let's try and find that energy source." She had come to realize she'd have to let the Confederation authorities handle this one...as much as it hurt to give up something so incalculably valuable. But she wasn't about to leave without something. She might not be able to haul back a giant ancient battleship, but she was damned sure going to stuff *Pegasus*'s hold full of anything portable she could find. And if that included anything related to the tremendous energy readings her scanner had detected, so much the better.

Merrick pulled a scanner from his belt, looking down at its small screen for a few seconds. "It's below us, Andi. About two hundred meters. We need to find some way down."

"Okay, let's..."

"Andi..." It was Rina Strand's voice on her comm unit. The instant Lafarge heard the tone, she knew something was wrong.

"What is it, Rina?" she snapped, ripping the small unit from her belt and bringing it to her face.

"We've got a contact moving toward the vessel. Still too far out for positive ID, but I'd bet a good pile it's military. A frigate, maybe."

"Confederation?"

"Too far to tell, but it's not broadcasting any beacon."

Lafarge's gut clenched. The lack of a beacon was hardly conclusive evidence, but Confederation vessels usually followed international protocols. And if that wasn't a Confederation ship out there, that probably meant..."

"Rina, get the hell out of here."

"We can't leave without you, Andi!"

"It will take us too long to get back." She shot a glance over at Merrick. There was fear in his expression, but he gave her a slight nod of agreement. "Get that ship out of here. Before it's too late. Get back to the Confederation and report this."

"Andi…"

"Now! We'll be fine. This is a big damned ship, and we'll find someplace to hide. Go! You've got to get some help."

There was a short pause. "Yes, Captain," Strand finally replied miserably.

Lafarge cut the line, looking again at Merrick. "Shugart sold us out. It's the only answer." Her voice dripped with menace.

"You think so?"

Rolf Shugart was a provider of…information, one with whom she had worked before. He'd come to her with the sketchy data that had led her to this find, and she'd paid him well for the scraps of information he possessed. She didn't trust him, but she was still surprised he would have double dealed her so blatantly…and even more so if that was a Union ship out there as she feared.

Lafarge was a profiteer, certainly, and one who had violated a law or two in her time. But she'd never sell the Confederation out to the Union. And she wouldn't have thought Shugart would either.

"What else could it be? A coincidence? We're twenty transits from the nearest inhabited system…you think that ship just happened by?"

Merrick shook his head. Then he asked, "You think it's a Union ship, don't you?"

"I think there's a good chance…which makes it all the more important for Rina and the others to get away." Lafarge suspected she knew a little more about how the Union handled captives than the rest of her people did, but they all had enough knowledge to generate a healthy fear.

Merrick stood silently for a moment. Then he said, "What are we going to do now?"

"We're going to find a place to hide, my old friend. A damned good place…and then we hope for the best." It wasn't the kind of well-thought out plan she liked. It was far from that. But it was also the only one she had. "Let's go. This ship is huge, and if that's a frigate out there, they only have a maybe a hundred, hundred fifty crew, not enough to search this monster very quickly."

She looked across the shuttle bay. "This way," she said, pointing across the vast open space. "There must be some passages at the other end." She was speculating that the Union ship—if it *was* a Union ship—would dock where *Pegasus* had, probably assuming her people had some knowledge of where to board the ancient vessel. And if they did that, she wanted to head in the opposite direction.

She nodded to Merrick and started across the bay. She wasn't running, but it wasn't exactly a walk either. Time was suddenly a precious resource.

She didn't know what she was going to do yet, except hide. Her mind was working as quickly as possible, trying to come up with a course of action, but the realization was beginning to sink in. She and Vig were in trouble.

She did have one plan, though it wasn't useful, not for surviving the next days and weeks, nor for getting her out of this mess. But if she got back to Dannith, and if she found out that Rolf Shugart had sold the information for which she'd paid him so handsomely to the Union…there would be a reckoning, and that gun she cared for so meticulously would see use. She would put the slimy bastard in the ground for sure.

*   *   *

"The small ship has broken free of its docking, Captain. They're running."

Captain Nicolas Pierre nodded. "Pursue, Lieutenant. Full thrust."

"Yes, sir," replied the tactical officer.

"Captain, a word?"

Pierre turned his head, looking across bridge toward the new voice. Jean Laussanne was *Chasseur*'s political officer. As far as Pierre was concerned, he was also a colossal pain in the ass. Most Union captains viewed their political minders with at least some level of suspicion and disdain, but Pierre couldn't imagine most of his peers had to deal with officers involving themselves as constantly in routine matters as Laussanne did. Pierre would have ignored the fool each time he opened his mouth, but every helpful-sounding suggestion carried the implied threat of *Pierre* being labeled "unreliable" if he didn't offer at least a show of compliance. A few words from a well-placed political officer could derail a naval career. Or worse.

"Yes, Commissar?" It took considerable energy to maintain tone that suggested he gave a shit what Laussanne wanted.

"I don't like to interfere with your command decisions, Captain, but…"

You like nothing more than interfering, you pompous ass…

"Do you think pursuing the small vessel is a reason to move away from the artifact? We have been seeking this find for some time, and the implications are…"

"Commissar Laussanne, I appreciate your perspective…" He didn't. He also knew interrupting the political officer was probably stupid, something that would bite him later, but he did it anyway. "But it's very unlikely this massive structure is going anywhere. It's probably been stationary for centuries, since before the Cataclysm. But allowing an unidentified ship to escape is highly problematic. We need to maintain secrecy until we can get word back to headquarters. I remind you, we are closer to Confederation space than we are to our own. Until reinforcements arrive, we have no chance of moving the artifact…and little hope of defending it against any significant Confederation force." He paused, telling himself he should shut up. But he didn't. "So, unless you think you can fly that thing, we're going to need a lot more resources to get it home with us."

Laussanne glared back at Pierre, his gaze a vague promise of future retribution. But he just nodded his acceptance of the captain's rationale.

Pierre knew this was no time to humor the political officer's pretensions. This was the most important mission of his life.

He hadn't really believed he would find anything…apparently, no one had, or they would have sent a far stronger force to investigate.

You know you'll end up in the sub-basement of Sector Nine headquarters if you end up losing this thing…and no one's going to listen when you say you botched the job doing what Laussanne told you to do…

"Very well," Pierre said simply, trying to mask the disdain in his voice. He turned back toward the tactical officer, who was staring back motionless, like a startled animal unsure which way to run.

"You have your orders, Lieutenant." Pierre's words were terse, but not hostile. He didn't expect a junior officer to have the guts to stand up to a commissar. He barely did himself.

"Yes, sir. Engaging thrusters now."

Chasseur was a frigate, a light escort when she served with the fleet, typically assigned to scouting duty or to supporting one of the battleships in combat. But on a mission like this, there was no capital ship to fall back on, no reinforcements. *Chasseur* and her sister ship had been sent on an expedition that had almost certainly been a waste of time…until suddenly it wasn't. He was still trying to come to terms with how important the mission had suddenly become. The computer was reviewing the scanner data, trying to offer a hypothesis on the massive structure's purpose. But it didn't take an AI's review for Pierre to realize that he had stumbled onto the greatest old tech discovery in history…he'd found a ship of some kind, almost certainly some kind of warship, one that looked very much like it was intact.

As the senior of the two ship captains in the minuscule task force, he'd dispatched *Arbalete* back to Union space to report the discovery. Captain Rouget was a reliable officer, and Pierre knew his colleague would drive his ship to the limit to get home and return with reinforcements. Until then there was nothing he could do. Nothing but stop this freebooter's ship from getting away.

His frigate was more than enough to handle a smuggler's vessel like the one he was pursuing. All he had to do was catch it. But as he watched the scanner, he felt the tightness in his stomach worsen. His prey was an adventurer's ship, probably a modified trader or freighter, scouring the Badlands for scraps of ancient technology to sell on the black market. But the thrust level he was seeing was worrisome. His target had a head start, and she was blasting away with nearly as much thrust as his own ship. Given enough time, he could catch her…but the transit point was too close.

He could follow his target into the next system, chase her down and destroy her. There wasn't much doubt about that. But pursuing a ship across *this* system was one thing. Leaving the artifact entirely was quite another. His rational mind told him the ancient ship would be just fine, as it had for the centuries it had remained in orbit around this silent world. But then his eyes connected with Laussanne's…and he saw flashes of himself in a Sector Nine interrogation cell, answering questions about why he left the greatest discovery in history completely unguarded.

"I want full thrust, Lieutenant." He glared over at the tactical officer. "Take the reactor to one hundred five percent output."

He could hear the uncomfortable silence on the bridge. He knew his Confederation foes frequently drove their equipment beyond rated capacities in battle. But Union manufacturing wasn't the same, and he knew the components that made up his vessel weren't as good as those in the Confed ships. Overpowering his reactor was *dangerous*, with a meaningful chance of catastrophic failure, one he didn't care to try and calculate.

"Yes, Captain." The young officer's reply had come slowly, and when it did, the edginess in it was apparent.

"I want the forward laser batteries ready…they are to open fire as soon as we enter range."

"Yes, Captain."

A hit at long range would be a wild stroke of luck, but he had to do whatever he could. All he could do was hope for a lucky shot, one that disabled the fleeing ship. Then he'd have to return to the planet and take position next to the artifact. And hope the Union forces got there before the Confeds.

Pierre just sat quietly, leaning back in his chair, waiting for the g forces he knew were coming. *Chasseur*'s dampeners and force compensators weren't up to handling the pressure from her full thrust, much less the added acceleration from her overpowered reactor. It would hit hard when it came, but Pierre and his people were veterans, they could take it. He fought back a smile, thinking about the fact that Laussanne would be the one hardest hit. Then the engines kicked in on full, and he felt the force slam into him. It was uncomfortable, painful even, but the piteous sound of Laussanne grunting behind him offset it all…and the grin he'd been fighting to hold back won its way out onto his lips.

* * *

"We can't leave the captain and Vig behind!" Ross Tarren protested.

Rina Strand met his gaze, her intensity not a fraction less than his. She stood on the other side of Lafarge's command chair on the bridge. Neither one of them willing to sit in their beloved leader's place. "I want to get them back too, Ross, but what the hell do you want to do? That's a Union frigate. Even with the upgrades Andi's installed, *Pegasus* wouldn't stand a chance. If we let that thing close enough, it will blast us to slag."

"So, we just abandon them? Run away, and save ourselves?"

Strand fought back a surge of deadly rage, her hand shaking as she held it back from the sidearm at her side. If anyone else had said that to her, she'd have put him down without another word, but she knew Tarren hadn't meant it. He was just distraught, the same as every member of *Pegasus*'s crew.

"And what happens to them if we get *Pegasus* blasted to atoms? Does that rescue them?" Strand felt almost disloyal for being the only one on the ship who was thinking straight. It was just the way she was wired. She felt every bit of the agonizing pain any of her crewmates did, but someone had to hold it together and make good decisions.

Tarren didn't answer. He just stared back at her, a helpless expression on his face.

"We have to get out of here, Ross. We have to warn the Confederation." She paused. "It's what Andi would have wanted. It's what she ordered us to do." She knew that last statement was powerful, her words almost weaponized. *Pegasus*'s crew was a difficult group, rogues and scoundrels who'd never fit in anywhere else. Until Andi Lafarge had taken them in. Every one of them loved her unconditionally, and even the thought of losing her was unthinkable.

She held her gaze on Tarren. Then she said, "The only way we can save Andi is to get help…and the only help available is the navy." She didn't mention that it would be weeks before they could return with aid, and she tried not to imagine what could happen to her captain and friend in that time.

Tarren was still silent, but the defiance was gone from his face. Strand felt the same discomfort she knew he did. *Pegasus*'s crew had always avoided the authorities like the plague. They were outlaws, at least as far as the navy was concerned. There was considerable bad feeling, and they'd dodged more than one naval patrol in their adventures. The idea of running to a navy base asking for help seemed alien. But she knew it was the only thing they could do. And for all their resentment of the authorities, no one on *Pegasus* wanted to see the Union gain control of such a powerful weapon. That would be unthinkable.

No, there was no other choice. They had to run. They had to leave Lafarge and Merrick behind while they went for help. No matter how horrible it felt.

If we even make it. Her eyes moved to the display, watching the Union ship gain slowly. Lex Righter was down in engineering, squeezing everything he could from *Pegasus*'s tortured reactor. But there was a limit to what *Pegasus*'s brilliant engineer could achieve…and running from a military vessel, even a Union one, was no easy feat.

Strand stood where she was, silent, watching the transwarp link getting closer. They had a decent chance of making the jump before the enemy ship blasted them to bits, but if that frigate followed them through…

There was no point worrying about that. Not now. All they could do was try to escape, to reach Confederation space and get some help. She felt a sense of urgency, of obligation beyond just the need to save her friends. Lafarge had gotten them all out of close scrapes before…and letting her down now, when *she* needed *them*, was unthinkable.

We'll be back, Andi…somehow, we'll get you out of this…

Chapter Five

Presidium Chamber
Liberte City
Planet Montmirail, Ghassara IV,
Union Year 213 (309 AC)

"My fellow members of the Presidium, I make this report to you under the highest level seal. I can't stress strongly enough how sensitive this information is, or how vital it is that absolutely nothing said in this room is repeated." Villieneuve's words carried heavy meaning in the laws of the Union. The highest seal designation made it treason to divulge anything spoken of in the meeting.

He wasn't naïve enough to believe that would prevent the leakage of information from his report, of course, but with any luck it would delay it, at least for long enough. Under normal circumstances, he would have proceeded without Presidium approval, but that wasn't an option now. He needed resources that could only be committed by the Union's full ruling body.

"Please, Gaston, proceed. I believe I can speak for all present that the security of the information you provide will be duly preserved by everyone present." The First's voice was heavy with arrogance, but Villieneuve's trained ear heard something more telling. He wouldn't say the First was incompetent, exactly, but he was no genius either.

Villieneuve looked around the room. The Presidium Chambers were plush, elegant, the walls clad in the rarest dark walnut paneling, wood from trees long extinct. The lighting fixtures hanging from the ceiling were intricate designs, works of art handcrafted by the best artists in the Union. The very essence of the room spoke of power and luxury, and the twelve men and women seated there ruled over two hundred worlds and billions of citizens with an iron fist. It was all utterly at odds with the egalitarian pretensions of the Union, but Villieneuve knew even more than most of those present such philosophies were an utter farce, at best fodder to keep the masses under control.

There were always true believers, of course, and no doubt some of those had been among the Union's founders two centuries before. They had been useful, he was sure, to the more power-focused of the Presidium's predecessors, their earnest passion almost certainly beyond value in gaining the support of the people. Villieneuve had no doubts about where those who'd truly strived to create a workers' paradise had ended up. Face down in the dirt, bled out and forgotten. Or deep in the sea, where impenetrable depths and carnivorous creatures had eliminated any trace of their murders.

"Thank you, Honorable First. Your assurances are reassuring." They were not. The Union First was a powerful man, of course, but he was largely a figurehead whose strings were pulled by others, Villieneuve himself not least among them.

The power struggles—even outright civil war—that had followed the death of the previous First had instilled in everyone present a true appreciation for stability. Those who had made their bids for power and ushered in that dangerous period of strife had all been killed in the struggle they'd begun, leaving those who remained, men and women more deliberative by nature, to make the peace...and learn the lesson of caution.

The current First held his position because he was the one choice the others would all support, and his...pliability...had played a large role in that. He seemed happy enough enjoying the pomp and luxury of the top position, without undue resentment of the manipulations from those around him.

That satisfied Villieneuve. As the head of Sector Nine, the Union's dreaded intelligence agency, he had enough dirt on his fellow Presidium members to compel compliance from most of them when he needed it. He was perfectly happy to exercise the considerable level of control he did while maintaining a lower profile.

"As all of you know, our grand plan for defeating the Confederation did not live up to expectations. Our position became untenable when a still inadequately-explained enemy incursion was able to reach and destroy the Supply One station."

At least, it hadn't been adequately explained to Villieneuve's satisfaction. It all came back to Tyler Barron. The same Confederation captain who had foiled Sector Nine's plan to bring the Alliance into the war. It seemed improbable, almost inconceivable, that the same man had returned from his unlikely victory on the Rim to almost single-handedly destroy the Union's irresistible onslaught. And yet the intelligence reports left little doubt. Barron's ship, *Dauntless*, and one other Confederation battleship, had somehow gotten behind the Union lines and defeated every vessel they had encountered. The damage Barron's actions had caused the Union's war effort were almost incalculable. There would be a reckoning, Villieneuve had promised himself, but first he had to win the war. And, at last, he had a way.

"We must consider our next course of action. Though our forces on the front lines remain strong, unless we are able to inject a new stimulus into our war effort, I am afraid we face a steadily deteriorating strategic situation as the Confederation's industrial capacity ramps up to full production. We simply can't match their ability to build new ships, fighters, weapons."

Villieneuve looked around the table again, his eagle-like eyes noting all that could be read from each face. "However," he continued, "I have not come here to speak only of dangers. When this body voted to commence hostilities against the Confederation, we relied heavily on Supply One and on the blitzkrieg campaign we expected that construction to facilitate. Nevertheless, even before that initiative failed, Sector Nine was pursuing other alternatives." The overture to the Alliance had been one of those, of course, but Villieneuve wasn't in the habit of telling the Presidium about his failures, at least not the ones he could cover up.

"May we presume that one of these alternative efforts has borne fruit of some sort?"

"Indeed, Honorable First." Villieneuve looked back at the head of the table for a few seconds before turning back toward the assembled leaders. "You are all acquainted, of course, with the area of space known as the Badlands."

There was no direct response, but Villieneuve could hear a murmur of hushed comments. *That was not what they expected to hear...*

"Sector Nine has long been interested in that area of space, fellow Ministers, and we have sent multiple expeditions to explore those ancient and abandoned worlds. The applicable treaties have prevented us from sending more than small scouting craft, but we have pursued other methods of seeking knowledge on ancient technology. Our intelligence operations have been active for many years in the Confederation ports along the border, and that effort has at last scored a great success."

The room remained silent for several seconds, and then the First spoke. "May we assume you have found something significant in that haunted sector of space?"

"Yes, Honorable First. As we know, all manner of smugglers and adventurers prowl around the Badlands, seeking bits and pieces of ancient technology. Confederation patrol ships have made a moderate effort over the years to police the border and confiscate contraband, in accordance with the provisions of international law. We, too, have sought to intercept rogue traffic, though we have been hampered by our greater distance from the more lucrative regions. Of course, what old technology we have been able to retrieve was retained by Sector Nine and not turned over to international authorities as required by treaty.

"Still, despite the Confederation's best enforcement efforts, more than one tramp freighter crew have come back staggeringly wealthy from an expedition. There is a significant black market for ancient technology in the Confederation, flouting

Ruins of Empire

their laws require that all such items be turned over to the government to be shared with the other treaty signatories."

"Yes, Minister, we are aware of the value of ancient technology. As you know, the Union has purchased more than one item from, shall we say, gray market sources, to support ongoing research and development projects. Indeed, there was ancient technology involved in the design and construction of Supply One, was there not?"

"Yes, Honorable First, you are quite correct."

The First frowned. "However, I have never heard of anyone finding more than fragments or small components of ancient devices. Useful for scientific research, certainly, and worthwhile in the long-term race for dominance perhaps, but something that can be deployed in a timeframe to win the war? Is that really possible?"

"Yes, Honorable First. We believe we have made just such a find."

Now...give it to them...

"If you will all look at your screens, you will see a schematic of our discovery. This data was delivered by one of our frigates, half of an expedition we sent to investigate a lead that we... purchased. Please look at once. For security purposes, the data files on your systems will self-erase in one minute."

He stood at his place, and he raised his hand, warding off the complaints he knew were coming. "Please, my colleagues. This is not a lack of trust in any of you. But if you consider the implications of the...item...on your screens now, you will understand the need for the tightest possible security."

He could see that the other members of the Presidium were still restless—that was to be expected from a group of power-mad egomaniacs—but no one objected further, and their eyes all dropped to the screens.

"This is real, Minister? Your people actually *found* this?" The First looked back, a stunned expression on his face. Every pair of eyes in the room stared at Villieneuve, even as the mysterious images began to vanish from their screens.

"It was found, Honorable First, and my people were able to

intervene and capture the crew that discovered it before they could return to Confederation space. They have been detained and…questioned." That was what *Arbalete*'s commander had reported, at least, though on more…aggressive…questioning, Captain Rouget admitted that he'd returned to report the find before *Chasseur* had actually apprehended anyone. The bit about taking prisoners was based on assumption, not on unassailable fact. Still, it served Villieneuve's purpose to deliver Rouget's unfiltered first statement to the Presidium. As far as he was concerned, that was all they needed to know.

"I am confident that no one other than those in our custody have any knowledge of the discovery. I do, however, fear that the information that led this smuggler's vessel to the artifact has fallen into other hands, and may eventually lead the Confederation navy—and other groups—in search of the ancient vessel. We have an opportunity to seize an insurmountable advantage. But we have no time to waste." Again, a few lies, judiciously utilized. In actual fact, he was very concerned about what knowledge was extant about the ancient ship…and just how much time he had before the Confederation sent their own expedition.

"What do you propose?" The doubt was gone from the First's voice, replaced by greed. Villieneuve knew the fool was imagining himself as the Union leader who finally brought the Confederation to its knees. It was harmless enough, but it still poked at a nerve. If the war was won, it would be Villieneuve's victory, and watching this pompous ass take credit would be difficult.

"First, we must launch a major offensive. The Confederation lies closer to the Badlands than we do, and we must prevent them from discovering our operations and our increased presence there. To that end, we have prepared an intelligence campaign designed to deceive the Confederation forces, to convince them we possess a second mobile logistical base, designated Supply Two."

A murmur of snorts and surprised grunts worked its way around the table. Supply One had almost bankrupted the Union. The thought of another such project, even a fake one, was too much for most of those present to handle.

"Is it reasonable to think they would be fooled, Minister?" The First looked uncertain. "We were barely able to build the first one. How could we possibly expect them to believe we were able to build *another* one?"

"You are correct of course, Honorable First. No normal intelligence campaign could succeed. To sustain the deception and to truly divert Confederation attention to the battle front, we must launch a renewed invasion, just as we would do if we truly possessed a second logistical base."

"Our fleet has not yet recovered from the heavy losses suffered in the initial months of the war, Minister. We are not ready to resume the offensive, and we will not be for some time."

"With all due respect, Honorable First, the Confederation fleet is even more badly damaged than our own. If we strike hard now, it will cause considerable alarm in their high command and their Senate. They will almost certainly focus all of their attention on the front lines…and we will use the opportunity to move into the Badlands in sufficient force to safely remove the artifact and bring it to Union space."

The room was silent. Villieneuve had taken them all by surprise, as he'd intended. He didn't want discussion. He didn't want debate. He just wanted the authorization he needed. There was no time to waste. His people had only discovered the ancient ship because he had agents deployed to the ports on the Confederation's border with the Badlands. They were there mostly to pose as black marketeers and to purchase any artifacts that seemed particularly useful, but this time their presence had paid off in a different way. If he hadn't maintained the heavy surveillance, the Confederation could well have ended up with the artifact…and that would have been an unmitigated disaster.

"If this vessel is what you believe it to be, Minister, it would seem we have little choice but to move forward at once. Not only to harness its power for our own uses, but also to deny it to the Confederation. I must commend your intelligence operation for discovering word of this find and for getting our people there before the Confederation."

"Thank you, Honorable First. The urgency we face is the reason I called for this emergency meeting. I must ask for immediate authorization to proceed, including an order for our forces to attack across the line."

The First looked out across the room. "I do not believe we have any choice. We will authorize Minister Villieneuve to direct our military forces in an immediate full scale offensive. Further, the minister or his designate will have full viceregal authority in the Badlands, and shall act in the name of the Presidium in all actions undertaken in that area of space." The First looked down the polished granite table at the twelve other men and eight women who ruled the Union. "All in favor?" Procedure required calling for the vote, but it seemed unlikely anyone would object. A "no" would be more than a rejection of the motion…it would be a direct challenge to the First, now that he had so forcefully stated his desire.

A few hands rose, followed by others, then all those present. A round of ayes followed. It was unanimous.

"The motion is passed by acclamation." The First turned back toward Villieneuve. "You have your authorization, Minister. You understand the enormity of the authority this body had invested in you, I trust.

"I understand. I assure you the resources you have granted me—and all those possessed by Sector Nine—will be utilized with the greatest focus and forethought." He turned back toward the First. "With your permission, Honorable First, I propose we adjourn this meeting so that I may return to Sector Nine headquarters at once and commence operations."

"Agreed, Minister. If there are no objections…" The First paused, waiting a few seconds before continuing. "The meeting is adjourned. Good luck, Minister Villieneuve. I trust you will keep the Presidium informed as your operations progress."

"Certainly, Honorable First." *I will tell you everything I want you to know…*

Villieneuve stood up and nodded toward the assembled ministers. Then he turned and walked briskly through the heavy bronze double doors and out of the Presidium Chamber.

Chapter Six

The Promenade
Spacer's District
Port Royal City, Planet Dannith, Ventica III
309 AC

Tyler Barron pushed aside the strings of cheap plastic beads hanging down over the entry and stepped into the room. The bar was dark, most of its meager illumination coming from small lamps on the tables. Their reddish glow reminded him a bit too much of *Dauntless*'s battlestations lamps. There was a vaguely unpleasant smell in the air, a disagreeable combination of cheap perfume and spilled liquor, mixed with some highly questionable scents emanating from the kitchen. The establishment looked like just what it was—a place where people came for clandestine meetings—and it by no means served the high end of its particular market.

Barron stifled a frown. He'd seen enough spacer's bars, an unavoidable aspect of his profession, and many of them were far worse than this place. But there was an honesty to a watering hole catering to visiting spacers, even down to the smell of alcohol-tinged vomit and the occasional blood stain on the floor. This place seemed to have pretensions beyond its place in the scheme of things, and that grated on him somehow.

He was wearing a civilian suit, as per the strange request

he'd received, but he still felt out of place. The Barrons were a wealthy family, and while his small non-military wardrobe tended toward the basic and conservative, it was all of extremely high quality, so much so that he suspected he couldn't have stood out more if he'd been wearing a plume of feathers on his head.

He'd have questioned the odd summons that had brought him to this strange place, and probably disregarded it entirely, save for two things. One, it had come on the Priority One line and, two, it had been sent by Gary Holsten.

The Barrons and the Holstens had been acquainted for a long time, and the two families had been involved in a number of business transactions together. But that wasn't why Barron had come. Though he was the senior member of his family's main branch, he'd always been content to allow his cousins to tend to the Barron business interests, focusing almost entirely on his military career. Still, he was sufficiently well-connected to be privy to Gary Holsten's other, far less well-known, vocation. That as the head of Confederation Intelligence.

Barron shared at least a measure of the mistrust of intelligence services so common in the military, but though he'd never met Holsten, he'd heard good things about the man. Details were sketchy of course, but he was fairly certain Holsten had been heavily involved in the replacement of Admiral Winston with Admiral Striker. The move had been one Barron agreed with wholeheartedly, and one to which he almost certainly owed his own life, and the lives of his crew.

Not that his opinion about Holsten mattered. Though the strange message was an abnormal use of the chain of command to say the least, he didn't doubt that the intelligence chief had the authority to demand his presence anywhere, at any time.

"Tyler, welcome." A tall man called softly from a booth in the corner, waving for him to come over. He had a companion seated next to him, but Barron couldn't get a look at the man's face. "I want to thank you for meeting me here. I know it's an… irregular…place for such a conference, and I appreciate your indulgence." The man stood up and took a few steps from the table, leaning in toward Barron and whispering, "Please excuse my familiarity, but I would prefer to keep rank and military status under wraps, if possible. I'm Gary."

Barron took the hand Holsten offered, and he shook it briefly. "I'm pleased to meet you, Gary. I find it a bit surprising we've never encountered each other before."

"That's true, though I don't believe you spend much time on business pursuits. I've met several of your cousins, but I can't say I know them well. I hope the peripheral members of your clan are less dissolute and useless than mine."

"I don't see too much of my relatives, Mr....Gary. As you said, I don't focus much attention on the Barron financial investments. The demands of the service, and all." Barron was less than proud of some branches of his family, as much, he suspected, as Holsten clearly was of his own, but discussing such topics made him uncomfortable. In truth, he hardly knew most of his cousins, but he still felt a vague sense of family loyalty. And he was sure of one thing...Holsten hadn't called him there to commiserate about black sheep relatives. "So, how can I be of assistance to you, Gary?" He tried to be gentle about pushing the conversation back on topic, but after he spoke, he was afraid it had come out a bit abrupt.

"I heard you were no nonsense. I see that's true. So, I'll take your lead. Let's not waste any more time." He gestured toward the table. "Please have a seat."

Barron glanced at the faded red leather of the booth. He felt a hesitancy to touch it, a flash of his own slight fastidiousness, but he pushed it aside and sat down. He tried to slide over, to make room for Holsten, but the leather was coated with years' worth of tacky residue, and he had to shove harder to get any movement at all. He tried to keep the look of disgust from his face, but he wasn't sure he'd quite pulled it off.

"I must say, Gary, this isn't in line with what I'd heard about your tastes." The young patriarch of the Holsten empire was known for his extravagant lifestyle, and his relentless pursuit of every supermodel—and half the attractive married women—in the capital. Barron didn't judge. He'd been somewhat of a ladies' man himself, though the responsibilities that came with the command of a frontline battleship had dulled his ardor somewhat, even before the outbreak of war. He'd become quieter since he'd become *Dauntless*'s captain, more prone to spending his free time alone, reading...or just enjoying the quiet. Still, he had to admit a touch of admiration for Holsten's abilities to juggle both the burdens of the Confederation's spy agency and the needs of an apparently endless parade of beautiful women.

"Well, Tyler, let's just say that some of my reputation exists because it is useful to me...and all this establishment lacks in, well, shall we say, the finer things, it more than makes up for in discretion. We are not likely to be disturbed—or overheard—here. Most of our neighbors frequent the bar for quiet assignations or petty smuggling transactions, and they are more concerned with not being noticed than with paying attention to what others discuss. That serves our purpose well."

"What is our pur..." Barron turned and looked across the table, and as soon as his eyes focused on the other man, he fell silent for an instant. "Admir..."

The third conspirator held up his hand. "Please, Tyler. I'm also relying on the discretion Gary assured me this...establishment...offers. It will serve our purposes well, I believe. Call me Van."

Barron hesitated, caught between surprise at the whole situation and discomfort at calling the officer in command of the Confederation's combined fleets by his first name. At least the intelligence chief was outside the normal chain of command, but calling the top admiral "Van" felt disrespectful, invitation or no.

He'd been nervous before, wondering what scheme Holsten wanted to sell him, but Admiral Striker's presence had just escalated the whole thing. It was not only likely vastly more important than he'd expected, but any chance he'd had of saying "no" was also gone. They could speak as informally as they wanted, but anything that came out of Striker's mouth was an order as far as Barron was concerned. "Very well, Van," he managed to say softly, not entirely successful at hiding his discomfort.

"We have something we want to discuss with you, Tyler.

We've received some disturbing news about Union activity, and while we have no confirmation our source is reliable, it's not something we can afford to ignore."

"Are they planning another offensive?" There was surprise in Barron's voice. Since *Dauntless* had withdrawn for repairs, there had been a few small battles on the front lines, but for the most part, the front had been quiet.

"No, Tyler. It has nothing to do with the front. As far as we are able to tell, things there are static, and are likely to remain so for at least the near future. Neither side has the strength to mount a major attack, nor the supply capability to sustain it if it succeeds."

"Then, if I may ask, what could you possibly want me to do that would require such secrecy?"

The two men exchanged glances, and then Holsten looked back toward Barron. "Have you wondered why *Dauntless* was assigned to Dannith for repairs, Tyler?"

Barron returned Holsten's gaze, a look of dawning realization on his face. "It occurred to me that it was somewhat out of the way, but with the Confederation on a war footing, I just assumed it was the only base that had capacity. We were sent to Archellia last time, after all, and that's even farther out."

"That's true, but unfortunately, we've had many ships destroyed outright since *Dauntless* was bumped to Archellia. Shipyard capacity is not the limiting factor on refit schedules now, Captain, a state of affairs you no doubt have deduced for yourself."

"You're saying that you deliberately ordered us to Dannith?"

"Yes, Tyler. That is precisely what I am saying. You are here because I selected you and your crew, and Admiral Striker concurred. Though when we made that decision, we only *suspected* we would need you here, based on fairly thin evidence. Now, we know…or at least we know with enough certainty to demand immediate action."

"Know what? What is it you want me to do?"

"You have served in the Badlands before, Tyler, have you not?" Striker was speaking now.

"Yes, sir...Van. My second assignment was aboard *Hydra*. We did a year's patrol duty in the near Badlands. But I suspect you know that already."

"Yes, we do." It was Holsten this time. He took a nonchalant glance around the room, confirming that no one had any undue interest in the conversation the three men were having. "*Hydra* spent most of that time patrolling the Restricted Zones. You had several encounters with poachers and smugglers."

"Yes, we did. We confiscated some old tech, but it was nothing all that rare. Nothing that seems important enough to bring me here now."

"You are correct, to a point. We didn't bring you here to chase after old tech trinkets, nor to hunt down unauthorized archeological activity. However, your experience, and your track record of service in the Badlands—as well as your overall performance history and the level of reliability and tactical capability you have shown—were central to our decision. Even the fact that you've had encounters with poachers is useful." Holsten paused. "There's something going on in the Badlands, Tyler, something we fear could impact the course of the war. We need you to go in, to find out if we are right...and if we are, to put a stop to it."

"Find what? Put a stop to what? And what do poachers have to do with this?"

"You mentioned yourself that most of the artifacts found in the Badlands are either small items or scraps from larger ones. Have you ever considered the implications if something more significant was discovered? An ancient weapon, for example... one that may still be operable."

Barron felt a tightness in his gut. He'd have disregarded such talk as rumor and gossip if he'd heard it anywhere else. But the navy's ranking admiral and the head of Confederation Intelligence hadn't brought him here because of vague spacers' tales. "That would depend on the specifics, but I'm inclined to think if one side found and deployed such technology, the impact on the war would be...significant."

"And if the weapon in question was one created during the

final stages of the Cataclysm?"

Barron looked back across the table, wordless at first. Finally, he just said, "It would be a disaster if the Union to gain control of such a weapon. Even if they only had one, if it was beyond their ability to replicate it, such a resource would easily tip the war in their favor. If they *were* able to replicate it, all space in this sector would fall to them."

"You agree with our assessments." Holsten slid a small data chip across the table. "This is a copy of…for lack of a better term, let's call it a treasure map. It was sold to a Union agent… one my people were unfortunately unable to apprehend in time to prevent the transmission of the data. We must therefore assume that Sector Nine has the map, and that they have already dispatched teams to recover the artifact."

Barron reached out and put his hand over the data chip, sliding it across the table and putting it unobtrusively in his pocket. "You want *Dauntless* to go after this artifact?"

"Simply put, yes."

"Isn't that a violation of the Abandoned Zone Treaty? I thought warships over a certain tonnage were forbidden to enter the zone."

"It is a blatant violation. One I suspect the Union has already committed."

"I don't take the violation of international law any more lightly than you do, Tyler," Striker interjected after Holsten had spoken. "But some things are more important to me… things like saving the Confederation from utter destruction, for example."

"Do you believe the situation is really that serious?" Barron was still trying to decide if he thought the whole thing was an overblown panic…or the greatest threat the Confederation had ever faced.

"I do," the admiral replied. "Or, let me say more specifically, I believe we *may* face an almost incalculable danger. We cannot be sure this data is accurate, but neither can we afford to simply assume it's a fraud. The consequences of the Union obtaining such a weapon are simply too catastrophic."

"I must agree with Van," Holsten said softly. "If we are wrong—and we are caught—we risk considerable international condemnation. If we're right, and we do nothing, we face utter and complete defeat. We simply can't afford to wait."

"We want you to take *Dauntless* into the Badlands, Tyler, to the system specified on the map we have provided you. Once there, you will explore every centimeter of the space around the designated planet, and you will confirm if there is indeed a significant ancient spaceship present there." Striker's eyes were fixed on Barron's as he spoke. "And if you encounter Union forces, you are to prevent them from gaining possession of the artifact...*whatever it takes*." The admiral paused. "Will you accept the mission?"

"Of course, sir...Van."

"This is not an order, Tyler...it's a request. Had we known all we do now, we would have pulled more ships back from the line, organized a whole fleet to investigate. But there's no time now. We've already waited too long." Striker's voice was strained. It was clear he hated sending Barron and *Dauntless* into the Badlands alone. "This could be like Santis all over again, Tyler. Your people will be on their own, far from any support. Though this time you may end up facing more than one enemy ship." He paused again, and when he continued his voice was softer, more subdued. "And you *must* keep the enemy from gaining control of the artifact."

He thinks he's sending us on a suicide mission. But he doesn't know just how hard it is to kill Dauntless *and her crew. And he has no idea just how much tougher an Alliance ship under a captain like Katrine Rigellus is than the typical Union line ship...*

"I accept." *As you knew I would.*

"Very well, Tyler. Godspeed. *Dauntless* will be released from spacedock in four hours. I expedited her repairs, but I'm afraid we had to cut the manifest short. She'll be fully-functional, but she's still got some systems I would have preferred to see replaced rather than patched back together."

"Don't worry, si... she's a special ship, and she'll get the job done."

"You're an extraordinary group, Tyler, you and your people. And that ship of yours." A pause. "And this could very well be the most important mission you've ever been on, more crucial even than your grandfather's great struggles."

Barron just nodded. Comparisons with his grandfather always made him uncomfortable, but he knew the admiral had meant it as nothing but a compliment.

"Your people will all receive cancellations of their leaves tonight, along with orders to report by 0700 hours base time tomorrow." Striker looked down at the table for a few seconds. "I will make it up to them when they return, I promise. They had their last well-earned rest interrupted, and I'm sorry to see that happen to them again."

"They'll do their duty, as they always do." Barron's tone waxed with pride. He had the best crew in the fleet, he was sure of that much, and he'd have words with anyone who disagreed.

"I'm sure they will, Tyler. Now, you may go prepare. You'll want to study the contents of that data chip tonight."

"Yes…thank you." He shifted, shoving himself toward the end of the booth, but then he stopped. "I still don't understand what my experience chasing poachers has to do with it."

"Well," Holsten said haltingly, "you know all of this information came from intelligence sources, of course. The map came from a man who sells such…intelligence…mostly to smugglers." He paused, flashing his eyes over toward Striker for an instant. "The source of the rest of the information on that data chip—including purported images of the actual vessel—is a crew of Badlands poachers. They're the ones who claim to have found the ancient ship…and they insist they were driven away by a Union frigate."

Barron stared back, trying to keep the incredulity off his face. "You mean you're sending *Dauntless* into the Badlands in violation of international law on the word of a pack of smugglers?"

"Well…" Holsten looked back at Barron for a second, and then he nodded. "Yes. In a manner of speaking, at least."

"And you feel that's trustworthy?"

"No, not on its own, perhaps. But when you've had a chance

to review the scanning records and physical images on the data chip, you will see why we have no choice but to take this *very* seriously. Their nav records confirm the location. They were *deep* into the Badlands, at least from our perspective, farther than any known expedition has ventured."

"Records can be faked, can't they? Do we have any *real* proof?"

Holsten looked back at Barron, but it was Striker who responded first. "No, Tyler, at least not what you mean by proof. But we've reviewed the data, and it appears to be reliable." The admiral paused. "I can't promise you it is accurate, but answer me this…if there is any chance at all that it is, can we afford to ignore it?"

Barron wasn't completely satisfied, but he shook his head. "No…we can't." He paused. "If there is anything there, we'll find it, and we'll keep any Union forces away from it."

"Thank you, Tyler."

Barron just nodded. He was still uncomfortable with the notion of the admiral *asking* him to do something, and he took the man's every word as a command, whether it was intended that way or not.

"Do you have any questions?" Striker asked, noting the still questioning look on Barron's face.

Barron hesitated. Then he said softly, "Just one…if I may ask."

"Certainly. We may not know the answer, but if we do, we will give it to you."

"Do we have any specifics on this artifact, what kind of weapon it is? Some kind of battleship? A platform with powerful warheads? A fighter carrier of some kind?"

Striker looked over at Holsten uncomfortably, and then back toward Barron. "We have very little data of that sort, Tyler, save for one thing…" The admiral paused, clearly uncomfortable.

"We were able to decipher its name from the sketchy information we have…or at least a colloquialization of its designation." Holsten had taken over when Striker fell silent, but now he too hesitated.

"Planetkiller," he finally said, his voice grim enough that Barron knew immediately he believed what he was saying was true. "It was called a planetkiller."

Chapter Seven

Union Frigate Chasseur
System Z-111 (Chrysallis)
Deep Inside the Quarantined Zone ("The Badlands")
309 AC

"This is growing tiresome, Captain Lafarge. Your ship was docked with the battle station when we arrived. You, and your associate, Mr. Merrick, were aboard the ancient vessel. You knew your way around so well, you were able to elude pursuit for several days." Pierre was leaning down, staring intently at Lafarge. "You could have made this easy on yourself, Captain. You could have told us what we wanted days ago. Cooperation will be rewarded…and I can assure you, continued resistance will be punished, considerably more harshly than it has been to date."

Lafarge stared back at the Union officer, her eyes blazing with defiance. They had starved her—for nearly a week now—giving her just enough water to keep her alive. It was unpleasant, but these pukes had no idea where she'd come from. She'd known worse as a penniless orphan, and it would take more than a little hunger to break her. "I told you," she said, her voice a little hoarse, but the tone still strong, unbeaten, "we just got there a few hours before you did. I don't know anything about that ship, certainly nothing useful." She'd have laughed at the irony if her situation hadn't been so dire. She was telling the truth, but she knew they'd never believe her. And telling them she'd only managed to avoid capture for days on end because the ship was so large, and their cloned soldiers were a bunch of morons who thought like so many computers, wasn't likely to improve their moods.

"Captain Lafarge, let me make something clear to you. I'm a naval officer. Interrogating prisoners is not normally within my range of duties. I neither enjoy it, nor do I think I'm especially good at it. But I can assure you there are other forces on their way here even as we speak, and those ships carry trained interrogation teams." He paused, unable to hide the disgust in his voice. "Please," he finally said, "tell me what I want to know, and perhaps I will be able to intervene, to protect you from what otherwise surely awaits you."

Lafarge didn't respond at first. She was angry, and as anyone who knew her could have attested, she was stubborn, so mind-numbingly pigheaded as to be almost a legend among her small circle of acquaintances. But it was apparent this Union captain wasn't trying to harm her. In fact, she was pretty sure he was uncomfortable with the whole thing. It was the other one, she suspected, who had ordered her food withheld. The political officer. Pierre seemed like a reasonable guy, or at least as close to one as a Union captain could be, but Laussanne was a piece of shit, and if she managed to escape somehow, she'd promised herself she'd slip a blade into his fat gut and slice right up to his ribcage.

"I'm afraid we're in for a long and unpleasant session, Captain, because I told you the truth already. I don't know anything about that ship."

"Then I fear this will be a long session Captain Lafarge, and an unpleasant one…at least for you." The voice was different, not Pierre's. Laussanne stood in the doorway, staring in like a vulture.

Lafarge glared at the commissar, her gaze radiating unvarnished hatred. She already had a dozen bruises and cuts from Laussanne's interrogation sessions. The little shit's efforts were far from enough to break her...but they were more than sufficient to earn her enmity. One slip up, a single moment of carelessness, and she would kill the bastard.

She pulled her arms backward, testing the strength of the bonds holding her in the chair. They were strong, too powerful for her to break free. She pulled one of her arms upward, trying to force her hand through the shackle, to slip out rather than break the plastic ties. But no luck. They were just too tight.

Laussanne walked across the room, stopping right in front of Lafarge. "Captain, we've wasted enough time. Captain Pierre was quite right when he told you things will get significantly worse for you when our reinforcements arrive. So, why not cooperate now, when it can do you some good? Tell us what we want to know, and we will ensure that you are well treated, perhaps even released once we have removed the artifact from this system. You aren't a combatant in this war. There's no need for you—and your comrade—to die in an interrogation chamber."

Lafarge didn't move. She just glared back, nothing in her eyes save rage and hatred. She was scared, of course, but she had no intention of giving this slimy bastard the satisfaction of seeing it. She wouldn't have given Laussanne the information he wanted, even if she'd had it. Even if she'd believed his lies about sparing her. Quite the contrary, she knew the key to her survival rested on holding back, on sustaining their belief that she knew something, that she was worth keeping alive.

She wondered how Merrick was doing, if they had interrogated him as they had her. Almost certainly, she answered to herself.

Vig's strong...he can hold out.

She was sure she had a difficult time ahead of her, and there was no question the ultimate end would be a bullet to the brain or a shove out the airlock. She had to look for an opportunity, any opportunity, to escape.

Hopefully before they bring Vig in here and threaten to blow his brains all over me if I don't tell them what they want to know.

She didn't know what she'd do if that happened. She was confident in her own ability to endure pain, but watching her friend murdered in front of her was something else entirely. She was a little surprised they hadn't tried that already, but she suspected with only two hostages, they weren't ready to sacrifice one of them. Not yet. And threatening to do it and not following through would be worse for their efforts than not trying it at all.

"Okay, Captain…" Laussanne turned away…and then he swung around, bringing his backhand across her face in a savage slap. She gritted her teeth against the pain, but she managed to clamp down on the yell that had wanted to escape. There was no way she was giving that piece of shit the gratification. "Let's talk about *your* ship instead. Where did your people go?"

She felt a rush of strength, if not of real hope. Unless they were making a serious effort to mislead her, *Pegasus* had escaped. She was gratified that most of her people had gotten away. And she drew a morbid satisfaction from the idea that *Pegasus* would warn the Confederation, that naval ships would come here and blast these arrogant Union thugs to atoms. Lafarge hadn't had warm feelings for the navy before. But her disdain for the Confederation government didn't extend to conflicts with the Union. She was patriotic in her own way, and one thing was certain. If she lived long enough to see it, she'd cheer as the Confederation ships flooded into the system.

Laussanne slapped her again. "We will get along much better, Captain, if you answer my questions."

She looked up at her tormentor and smiled. It felt strange on her face, utterly at odds with her emotions of the moment, but she couldn't think of anything that would piss Laussanne off more.

"You hit like my mother." She glared at the commissar, struggling to allow not the slightest hint of pain or fear on her face.

"You think your ship escaped, Captain," the political officer said, trying but failing to contain his anger. "But there are Union task forces all around this system. *Chasseur* did not pursue your friends, because there were ships waiting beyond the transit point. There is little doubt that your vessel was destroyed or disabled by now. If any of your crew survived, they are now prisoners, Captain. And when they arrive back here, they will die, one at a time in front of you. Unless you tell us what we want to know."

It took all her discipline to control her fiery rage. She hated this Union political officer...she hated him with a fury she had never felt before. If she'd been able to work her hands free, she'd have lunged for him, taken her chance to kill the bastard, even knowing the guards would shoot her down.

Calm down...he's just trying to push your buttons. If they had more ships nearby, they would be here near the artifact, not spread out across the Badlands.

She knew her logic was sound, that *Pegasus* had probably found a clear route back to Confederation space. But, despite her anger at herself for allowing it, she had to admit that Laussanne had gotten to her. She didn't believe him, but he'd fanned the fires of doubt in her mind. And worrying about her people would only weaken her, drain her ability to resist.

Her thoughts went to her ship. Her people didn't have ranks, not really. She was captain, and Vig was first officer. After that, the crew was just the crew. Would they work well together without her? Or would they fracture, fight with each other?

Rina will take charge...

Yes, she believed that with all of her heart. Rina Strand was tough, far tougher than she typically let on. She would take command of *Pegasus*, and she would get the ship back to Confederation space. The more Lafarge thought about it, the surer she became.

"Captain...Laussanne, isn't it? You were too slow and incompetent to prevent my ship from escaping, and you're too stupid and weak to force me to do your bidding. So, let's just save some time, and give me another one of those weak little slaps instead of boring me to death." Her eyes darted over toward Pierre. She could see trepidation in the captain's eyes, fear that things would escalate. There was something more there too. Was it respect? Lafarge suspected the Union captain didn't like the political officer much more than she did.

Laussanne's hand struck her face, harder this time, hard enough to almost take her breath away. But she just laughed. It took all she had to maintain the façade, but she did it. Then she looked up, her gaze as cold as space itself.

"Did I say you hit like my mother, Captain? I meant to say you hit like my grandmother."

Lafarge didn't even know who her grandmother had been… she barely remembered her mother. But she was pleased with herself at the barb, and one glance at Laussanne's face, twisted in crazed anger confirmed its effectiveness.

It was worth it, even as she saw the shadow of his hand approaching her again, this time balled into an angry fist.

*   *   *

"Scanners clear, Captain. No contacts." Commander Duroc's tone was crisp, professional, as always.

Captain Eugenie Descartes sat at *Triomphe*'s command station. She was edgy, uncomfortable with the mission…and with the extra contingent of political officers she'd been saddled with. She'd more or less managed to maintain a certain détente with Commander Belgarde over the year they'd served together on *Triomphe*. Belgarde wasn't a bad sort, at least as commissars went. She knew he was there to spy on her, of course, to ensure her loyalty to the state, but at least he didn't seem to question her every decision.

Colonel Cloutier and his people were another matter entirely. They'd arrived with orders to set out for the Badlands, and they'd shut down her questions in no uncertain terms. They were pure Sector Nine, that much she'd been able to tell from the start. There was no question in her mind that, despite the uniforms they wore and the ranks they bore, the new arrivals were agents of the dreaded intelligence agency.

Descartes looked at the main display, at the clear stretch of black between her entry point and the transwarp line to the next system. The stars in the Badlands each had half a dozen designations, numbering systems and names, formally recognized and otherwise, given by the explorers who'd charted them or the bureaucratic bodies that pompously exerted their authority over the dead worlds of mankind's past. She'd ordered the Confederation's numbered designations to be displayed to avoid confusion. The Confeds had done the most extensive survey missions, and their system was the most comprehensive. The last thing she needed was confusion, especially when she already knew so little about the mission.

She sighed softly, wondering if Colonel Cloutier or one of his pack of high-strung aides would see disloyalty in her use of enemy nomenclature.

"Bring us to the Z-89 transit point. Decelerate as we approach. I want a dead stop one hundred thousand meters from the transwarp portal." Descartes knew almost nothing of the mission, save for the fact that she was to link up with two other battleships—one of them *Vaillant*, the pride of the Union fleet—and continue on the course she'd been given. She had no idea what justified such a concentration of force in the middle of nowhere while the fleet was locked in a death struggle with the Confeds. Her repeated requests for more information had been met with increasingly emphatic insistences that she knew all she needed to know. She disagreed, of course, vehemently. She was the veteran captain of a Union battleship, and she didn't like advancing into virtually unknown space blind. But she knew how far she could push with her inquiries, and when it was time to back off.

Descartes was a decorated officer, one who had attained a certain amount of political clout of her own. But she knew better than to take on Sector Nine. Her parents depended on her. Her whole family did. The success she'd attained in her career had taken them all from the desperate poverty they'd endured before. She had no doubts—none at all—that her mother and father would have been dead by now save for the benefits of her rank and career. And she was far from blind to the fact that Sector Nine could return her family to its former squalor, or worse, in a heartbeat.

"Yes, Captain. We should reach the designated point in

forty-seven minutes."

"Very well." Her eyes darted back to the display. There were three other transit points into the system, and there was no activity at any of them.

Where the hell are they?

She didn't like the idea of sitting here and waiting...though the thought of going on alone wasn't much more appealing.

The lift door slid open.

"Captain Descartes..."

She felt her skin crawl as Cloutier's grating voice projected onto her bridge.

"Yes, Colonel, what can I do for you?" Her tone was courteous, verging on obsequious. She knew the smart way to behave, but that didn't stop it from making her sick to her stomach.

"Our mission is of the utmost importance, Captain. If the other vessels do not transit into the system within an hour of our arrival at the transwarp point, we will go on alone. Please make all preparations so there is no delay."

"Yes, Colonel. We will be ready." She almost asked again what was so urgent out in the middle of nowhere, but this time she held her tongue. She'd already asked as many times as she dared. Now, all she could do was wait and see what Cloutier chose to tell her. She didn't like it, but she was experienced enough to know she had no choice.

"Commander, advise the engine room we will be transiting in approximately one hour and forty-five minutes. I want all systems prepped and ready."

"Yes, Captain."

"All weapons stations are to be manned and ready before transit. We will be prepared for anything we find in the next system. Understood?" She was uncomfortable, feeling as though Cloutier was watching, and judging, her every action.

"Yes, Captain." Her exec's tone suggested he was as uncomfortable as she was with the lack of information they had been given. But Commander Duroc was a savvy veteran...and he knew as well as she did when to keep his mouth shut and follow orders.

Then Descartes heard the sound of the lift doors closing, and she confirmed her expectation with a quick glance. Yes, Cloutier was gone.

She let out a deep breath, and her stomach unknotted, partially at least. There was one good thing about Cloutier. He didn't tend to spend any more time on the bridge than was necessary. Even better, Belgarde, who had always had the unfortunate habit of planting himself at a workstation and spending hours watching as her officers executed their duties, apparently felt compelled to attend to the colonel, leaving her bridge blissfully free of political minders for extended periods of time.

She exhaled again, harder this time. She might have the bridge to herself, but she was still moving forward, into the unknown, without the slightest idea of why her ship was there or what it might face.

"Damn," she muttered, a bit less under her breath than she'd intended.

Chapter Eight

From the Personal Log of Captain Tyler Barron

We are in the Badlands as I write this, heading at maximum speed to the supposed location of an ancient vessel, one that may contain sufficient technology to fundamentally alter the power dynamic between nations. It is a crucially important mission, though also one I wish had fallen to someone else. I find these empty systems and haunted lifeless worlds very unsettling. There is the familiarity, of course, recollections of several encounters here during my earlier career, but there is more to it more than that.

I trained my entire life for war. I was born to this destiny, and I followed my birthright to the Academy and through early service as a junior officer to command of my own ship. All that time I prepared for the conflict I knew would come, my generation's struggle with the Union, the same battle my father had fought, and my grandfather, and even the great-grandfather I never knew.

Through all that time, listening to my grandfather's stories, competing with other cadets at the Academy, even on the bridge of my own battleship, I viewed that destiny through a single lens. That of victory. This time we will defeat the Union. The next war will see our final victory, and it will free our children from the need to continue this deadly struggle. I understood danger, of course, but it was theoretical then, a romantic image of empty chairs and toasts to fallen comrades.

Then I actually experienced war. Not a skirmish with pirates or smugglers, but actual combat against other warriors, intense and deadly. Our victory over the Alliance battleship brought me renown and glory of my own—earned rather than inherited—and yet inside it filled me with doubts, with regret. The satisfaction I'd expected never materialized. Katrine Rigellus was a worthy opponent, but moreover, she was honorable, at least according to her culture. There was no joy in killing such an adversary, only a deep sense of waste. My childish pretensions, mindless images of good and evil, black and white, shattered that day.

I was born into privilege, a wealthy family, and moreover, as the heir apparent to my nation's most celebrated hero. My grandfather was famous on every world of the Confederation. Katrine's grandmother was born a slave, her world subjugated by neighboring planets for nearly a century. It is easy to criticize the Alliance, to label them as warmongers. Yet, I think back to fishing trips with my grandfather, and I wonder how my attitudes would be different if he'd told me of servitude instead of heroism, if he'd borne the scars not of his battles, but of the taskmaster's whip. Would I have been that different than Katrine? Would Megara and Corellia have emerged from such a past to found the current Confederation? Or would they have taken the same path the Palatians of the Alliance did?

And now, the war so long expected has come. We have fought the Union for a year, a struggle long expected and yet exceeding even the direst predictions in its horror and devastation. I try to draw comfort from the idea that this struggle is clearer. We fight for our freedom, for our very survival. There should be no ambiguity, no crosscurrents of guilt and uncertainty as we fight this terrible enemy.

And yet there is still doubt. The Union's leadership is indefensible, and their destruction would be a cleansing. But the ships we destroy are crewed by men and women much like those who serve with me. They fight because they are ordered to do so, and worse, because their families are virtual hostages for their obedience. The Union has a simple compact with its spacers. If you fight and die, your families will be cared for, and if you flee, they will pay the price for your cowardice.

I have come to appreciate that there are different kinds of courage. The Union pilot, who sacrifices himself in battle so his wife escapes Sector Nine's torture chambers or his child has enough food to eat...can I hate this enemy or call him a coward? Can I rejoice at his death? I derided the Union, much as my comrades do, but now I see there is depth to this picture, dimensions beyond that which are easily visible. I saw the essence of courage in the Alliance crew my people faced at Santis, yet there is much of that same strength in the men and women who crew the Union vessels. We deride them as sheep, pity them as fools who mindlessly follow orders. But it is easy to speak of defiance, and quite another to actually resist when the only result can be the suffering of those close to you.

The vast, endless reaches of the Badlands bring a strange focus to all of this. The ghosts of our ancestors drain away my thoughts of victory as the ultimate end to war. Who "won" the great conflicts of the Cataclysm? Which pile of unburied dead were the victors? And which the vanquished?

And, most terrifying of all the questions surging forth from my deepest thoughts. Am I looking at our past? Or our future?

CFS Dauntless
System Z-37 (Saverein)
Inside the Quarantined Zone ("The Badlands")
309 AC

"All fighter probes report negative contacts, Captain. Lieutenant Timmons's patrol even flew a pass through the dust clouds along the outer system. Our long-range scanners are also clean." Travis turned and looked over at Barron. "I think we're alone here, Captain." Her tone carried a message of its own, that even she thought he was being overly vigilant.

Barron nodded. "Very well, Commander. Recall scouting patrols and proceed toward the transwarp point. But I want scanners to remain on full active mode." He *had* been more intense than usual, more cautious. He suspected he even looked a little paranoid to his crew. Which was fine…because he *was* a little paranoid. If Holsten's suspicions were real, if the smugglers who had returned to Dannith were telling the truth, the key to total military dominance over humanity lay out there, ahead of his ship, deep in the Badlands.

Barron didn't like relying on the word of smugglers, and

even less having the whole group of outlaws aboard *Dauntless*, their ship docked to the battleship's hull. He knew it made sense to bring along the only people who had actually seen the Union forces, but the whole thing still made him uncomfortable. Still, he had to admit, this particular group had at least presented considerable evidence to back up their claims. There was little doubt that a Union vessel had chased them across the Z-111 system. He didn't like the idea that the enemy was already there either, even if it was only a frigate. His people were late already, and if they didn't get there before the Union battleships—the ones he *knew* were coming—it could be the worst disaster in Confederation history. Indeed, it could very well be the end of the Confederation.

Battleships. Plural. He knew how the enemy thought, how they operated. They'd been ahead of the Confederation on this since the beginning. If Holsten and Striker hadn't ordered *Dauntless* to Dannith before they'd had conclusive evidence, all would already be lost. His respect for the two men grew considerably. They'd acted instead of analyzing, sending his orders when all they'd possessed were vague rumors and sketchy scraps of information. And they'd done it artfully. If there had proved to be nothing to their suspicions, all they had done was recall a battleship for a well-needed refit, perhaps at a system farther back from the front than ideal, but nothing that would have seemed all that strange. Barron would have never known his ship had been sent to Dannith for anything but repairs. But when the smugglers arrived with news of events at Z-111, *Dauntless* was in a position to investigate.

Striker had assured Barron that reinforcements would follow, but *Dauntless*'s captain knew it would be weeks before any ships from the front could reach Dannith, and longer for them to get to his position deep in the Badlands. *Dauntless* would be on her own, for a long while, at least…against whatever the Union had sent to retrieve the artifact. It felt oddly familiar, much like the situation at Santis. But this time the stakes were higher, and he was virtually certain he would be badly outnumbered.

Numbers weren't a consideration, not this time. There would

be no retreat from this mission…there could be none. Allowing the Union to recover an ancient weapon of almost unimaginable power, or even an artifact that *might* be such a weapon, was out of the question. There were only two options…victory or death.

His people would be in a fight for their lives and for the future of the Confederation, a desperate one against the odds. They'd been there before and come through. He was confident they would rise to the occasion, give their very best…and their best was damned good. But this time he wasn't sure it would be enough.

He watched as his people went about their duties, glanced at the display as his fighter patrols began their flights back to *Dauntless*. He was nervous, edgy. He'd never liked the Badlands, the strange haunted feeling of passing by worlds that had once been the home to billions of human beings, but were now graveyards scavenged by freebooters. It was a constant reminder of mankind's self-destructive nature, one that struck a bit too close to home now.

Barron had done duty in the Badlands, and he didn't particularly care for the brand of rogues who operated out in the desolate systems, picking at the bones of the dead civilizations, looking for trinkets of old tech they could sell on the black market. Every scrap of ancient technology that ended up in the wrong hands endangered the Confederation, and possibly killed his people. He didn't doubt for an instant there had been old tech in use in the Union's construction of the Supply One base. The Confederation had come dangerously close to losing the war because of that incredible structure, and he was enraged at the thought that it might have come to pass because some smuggler had cared only for the currency his black-market buyer had possessed, and not the fact that he, she, or it had probably been nothing but a Sector Nine front.

"Captain, we're picking up energy readings from the Z-33 transwarp point." Travis's voice was deadly serious.

"Battlestations, Commander," Barron said, his voice firm, even. "Scramble all fighter squadrons." He had no idea what was coming, but his people were deep in the Badlands, and that meant the chance that anything but trouble was coming was vanishingly small.

"Battlestations, Captain," Travis snapped back. "All squadrons acknowledge." The klaxons began sounding, the familiar call to the almost one thousand specialists and veterans on *Dauntless* to man their stations. They had been there before, many times, and all around there was nothing but the quiet efficiency of a well-oiled machine.

Barron glared at the display, through the red glow from the battlestations lamps, his gaze one of defiance, of determination. *Dauntless* hadn't gotten the full refit he'd hoped she would, but she was a Confederation battleship, one with more than her share of honors. If whoever was coming through that jump point wanted a fight, by God they would get one.

*   *   *

"Launch tubes powered up and ready. All squadrons, you are cleared to go." Stara Sinclair sat in the center of the main console in *Dauntless*'s launch control center. Her screen displayed a series of bars, readiness indicators for the ship's five squadrons. *Dauntless* had been built to carry sixty fighters, but her current complement was seventy-eight. That was a change wrought in the fire, when *Dauntless* and *Intrepid* were trapped behind enemy lines, their fighter ranks swelled by the remnants of squadrons abandoned when the battle line had been forced to retreat. Sinclair had been stunned when Captain Barron had somehow managed to get official authorization to retain eighteen of the extra strike craft, and she'd been pushed to the edge of her wits dealing with the fallout from cramming an extra squadron into *Dauntless*'s launch rotations and maintenance routines.

She watched carefully as the status monitors switched to green. *Dauntless* didn't have enough catapults for a normal launch routine with five squadrons, but Captain Barron had ordered three times the normal number of patrols to scout the system, and that left a lot of open slots on the rotation.

Her hands moved over her keyboard and touchscreen, moving small symbols, issuing go ahead orders to ships in the second and third waves. She had the extra spaces, but they were all over the place, two openings from Blue squadron here, three from Red squadron there. The ships would get out there quickly, that much she could guarantee. The formations would be a mess, but that was the squadron commanders' problem, not hers.

She watched as the ships of Blue squadron ripped down the catapults and into space. Jake Stockton had already launched, and her eyes moved to the display, finding the small icon that represented his ship. She'd had feelings for Stockton almost since the day he'd set foot on *Dauntless*. He'd been all cocky and obnoxious on the outside...but she had seen something else there. His loyalty, his dedication. There was a bit of a performer in Stockton, but it only took one look at how his friends, and his pilots, revered him to know there was a lot more to the man than he let others see.

Still, she'd denied her emotions, and even spurned his advances. She hadn't taken his interest as a sign of any real feelings. Stockton had a reputation, and she'd considered his flirtations nothing more than an acknowledgement that she was female, and perhaps that the hotshot fighter jock liked the way she looked walking down the corridor in her uniform. He wasn't the first overly confident pilot she'd had to shoot down. Her position put her right in the line of fire of the least controllable group of spacers in the fleet, and she'd built a wall around herself. She'd drink with the pilots in the officer's club when off duty, and she was popular enough with the squadrons, but they'd all been trained, more or less, to direct their cocky charms elsewhere.

She'd held her ground until Stockton had a close call, even closer than usual. She'd raced down to the flight deck, unable to hold in her relief that he'd survived the crash landing. All her emotions came pouring out, even as she struggled to put them back in their place. She'd been angry with herself afterward. For letting the professionalism that was her pride slip. And for allowing herself to get too close to Stockton. He was the best pilot she'd ever seen—not that he needed to hear that—but he was crazy, too. He was bound to get himself killed one day, and now that dread had made its home deep in her gut. But there was no way out, not any longer. Not since Stockton had returned from a near suicidal mission to deliver data on enemy dispositions to the fleet and told her he loved her.

The Scarlet Eagles were queued up right behind the Blues. The Eagles were without their squadron leader. Dirk Timmons was still out on patrol, and he'd have to return to *Dauntless* and refuel before he could join his people. Stockton was doubling as their commander now, and she had to stifle a small laugh. Timmons and Stockton had hated each other since they'd been rivals at the Academy, and the fact that they had buried the hatchet—enough, at least, to trust each other with their beloved squadrons—suggested that nothing was truly impossible.

She reached out, tapping the communication unit. "Bridge, flight control reporting. All fighters launched."

"Acknowledged, fighter control." A short pause. "Nicely done, Lieutenant."

Sinclair smiled. Commander Travis was popular on *Dauntless*. She was tough, the captain's disciplinarian when necessary, but she was also energetic, focused, and as far as Sinclair was concerned, outright brilliant.

Her eyes moved back to the display, watching as the fighters shook down into their squadrons, and then their battle formations. She sighed softly, her eyes darting quickly to both sides to make sure no one had heard. She was considered a stone-cold officer, one who maintained her calm in the middle of the fiercest battle and kept the launch control center running no matter what. And that reputation served her well, even if the constant death and destruction of the war had begun to get to her. She worried about Stockton, of course, but her mind was also full of images, the faces of men and women, pilots *Dauntless* had lost in its recent struggles. Captain Barron had pulled his ship from the brink of destruction more than once, but in fifteen months the ship had lost more pilots than the number of its original complement. Dozens of comrades, lost out in the depths of space, dying alone, terrified. Everyone assumed she had ice water for blood, but even that was inadequate to ward off the effects of so much loss and fear.

And more will die today…

Her eyes moved to the other end of the display, to the icon representing the Union battleship that had just emerged. Captain Barron had acted quickly, and Sinclair was confident *Dauntless* could best her foe, at least assuming no additional ships transited. But she's come to realize that no victory was free.

And that price would be paid in the blood of men and women she knew…including those she'd just helped launch.

* * *

Tyler Barron stared intently at the display. He wasn't surprised at the new contact. He'd expected to run into enemy forces by now…even earlier. The only question remaining was whether the Union battleship was alone, or whether more vessels would transit into the system momentarily.

The enemy vessel was launching fighters, and he gazed at the tank, watching the clouds of tiny dots appear. *Dauntless* was facing a powerful vessel, a line battleship with all the tonnage—and presumably fighters—as his ship. But he had gained the edge. He'd put his ship on red alert the instant he'd gotten the report of a vessel jumping into the system, and by the time he'd gotten a clear confirmation it was an enemy warship, half his squadrons were already in space. It was an aggressive maneuver. Most captains would have gone by the book, launched a probe or a scouting party, perhaps, waiting for conclusive data before sending out a full-scale strike.

His actions were unorthodox in other ways, too. He hadn't retained a CSP around *Dauntless*, no last line of defense in case enemy bombers broke through. He'd sent all his ships toward the Union ship—five full squadrons, less the roughly dozen ships he'd already had out on patrol. He'd armed two of his squadrons, Yellow and Green, as bombers, with Olya Federov's Red Squadron flying close support. He was relying on the superiority of his pilots to execute both a powerful strike against the enemy, and to form an effective screen to protect *Dauntless*. It was a lot to expect, but he knew what his pilots could do, especially with officers like "Thunder" Jamison and "Raptor" Stockton in the lead.

"I want active scanners on full, Commander," he said without looking up. If there's the slightest increase in energy output from that transit point, I want to know about it. Even if it's nothing but a chunk of rock drifting through."

"Yes, Captain," Travis responded.

"The incoming patrol ships are to be refueled and refit immediately as they return. I want them formed into a CSP under Lieutenant Timmons and ready to launch as quickly as possible."

"Yes, sir."

Barron wasn't overly worried about the foe *Dauntless* was facing now. But if another ship came through the portal and launched a fresh strike force while his fighters were still engaged...

"Captain, I've been working on the ID of the Union ship. She's not broadcasting her beacon, but I'm pretty sure she's *Vaillant*, sir."

Barron's head snapped around toward Travis's station. "How sure are you?"

Travis turned, and she looked back at Barron. "I can't confirm it, Captain...but I'm fairly certain."

Barron felt his stomach tighten. If Atara Travis said she was 'fairly certain', he took it as an absolute assurance. And that meant trouble.

"I want those patrols back aboard as quickly as possible. They are to employ maximum thrust."

"Yes, sir." Travis spun back around, relaying the captain's orders with her usual quiet efficiency.

"And Atara..." Barron was still looking toward his exec's station. "Advise Commander Jamison that his fighters are likely facing veteran squadrons."

"Yes, sir."

Barron took a deep breath. The Union fighter corps had suffered horrendous losses in their invasion of Confederation space and the subsequent battles along the stalemated front, and most of their battleships fielded squadrons almost entirely made up of new trainees. But *Vaillant* was the pride of the Union fleet, an infamous battleship with a kill record as impressive as *Dauntless*'s…and her squadrons were among the very best in the Union service.

Barron's people were going to have one hell of a fight on their hands…and they hadn't even reached their destination.

Chapter Nine

**550,000 kilometers from CFS Dauntless
System Z-37 (Saverein)
Inside the Quarantined Zone ("The Badlands")
309 AC**

"You've got one on your tail, Talon!" Stockton's voice was raw, testament to just how hard of a fight the Union fighters were giving his squadron. Squadrons. He had the Scarlet Eagles under him right now as well as his own Blues, filling in for a Dirk Timmons who'd been out on patrol when the launch orders had been issued. The Eagles were good, a match for his own Blues, though he'd never have admitted that publicly. But the Union wings they were facing weren't the usual pushovers. Stockton had become accustomed to racking up multiple kills in each battle, but he hadn't taken down a single enemy bird yet, and one or two of them had given him a run for it.

"I can't shake him, Raptor!" Corinne "Talon" Steel was one of Stockton's best, a Blue squadron veteran in every particular. But he could hear the fear in her voice now, the loss of the iron control she usually displayed in combat.

"Keep moving, Talon…don't let him get a lock. I'll be there in a flash." His eyes dropped to his display. Talon's ship was more than fifty thousand kilometers from his, and she was blasting hard along a trajectory leading her farther away. "Flash" was an optimistic assessment, he realized. It was going to take him a while to get there...but nobody else was closer.

"I'll try, Raptor...but he's on me like glue..." Stockton heard the waver in her voice, and his stomach clenched. A fighter pilot relied on confidence, on the self-assurance it took to maneuver without hesitation or delay, to make split second decisions. If she lost that...

"Listen to me, Talon! You're a Blue squadron ace with seventeen kills, not some wet behind the ears rookie fresh out of flight school. Cut the shit now, and break free of this bastard." He knew his pilot—and his friend—was in deadly danger, and he felt guilty for yelling at her. But he had to shake her out of the fatalism that was beginning to take hold. He needed the best "Talon" Steele could give him, and he was going to get it out of her, whatever it took.

He saw a flash on his screen, and, for an instant, he thought Steele's fighter had been destroyed. But the small blue symbol was still there, the menacing red icon on its tail.

He took a deep breath and pulled hard on his throttle, slamming the control all the way back. The engines blasted at full, a deafening roar reverberating through his cockpit as 10g slammed into him before the dampeners could absorb any of the force. It felt like a sledgehammer, and he could feel himself slipping toward blackness, his field of vision narrowing as the intense pressure beat relentlessly against him. But Jake Stockton's fighter was like an extension of his body, and his will was a force to be reckoned with. He struggled against the pain, and he held onto consciousness by pure stubbornness, if nothing else.

Then, the dampeners kicked in, reducing the effective force beating down against him. He gasped for breath as the pressure receded enough to allow him to expand his lungs. He was still feeling the equivalent of 3g—uncomfortable, but a massive difference from the crushing hell of 10g. His clarity improved, and his recovering eyes locked on his display. Talon was still there, but he knew any second could be her last. Her pursuer was closing, and his deadly laser blasts zipped all around her wildly gyrating ship.

He could see he'd gotten to her, though, awakened the veteran pilot inside, and incited her pride and confidence to push back against the fear. Her evasive maneuvers were tighter, faster, more random than they had been. She still wasn't able to break free, but she was giving her tormentor the hardest possible target.

Stockton was getting closer, and he squeezed his finger tight, firing his lasers as he entered extreme range. A hit from so far out would have been the sheerest stroke of luck. But he wasn't trying to hit the Union fighter…he was trying to get the enemy flyer's attention. He was trying to save his friend's life.

His ship shook hard. Confederation fighters were state of the art, the most technologically-advanced small craft in space. But they weren't designed to run at maximum thrust for very long. The fighter's turbos were for rapid repositioning or for accelerating into an attack or out of immediate danger. Stockton ignored that fact, and he held his throttle tightly, pulled all the way back, his engines screaming as they continued to blast at maximum thrust.

The whining sound of his lasers echoed through the cockpit as he fired again and again, struggling to break his target's concentration if not to score a hit at this range. But the Union pilot ignored it and clung to Talon's fighter, following her, matching her every evasive maneuver.

Watch this guy, Raptor…this is capable pilot.

He was tearing through space, right toward the enemy, firing wildly, focused solely on getting the Union ace off Talon's tail before it was too late. But now he began to realize, a pilot this good could turn about on him. If he wasn't careful, he'd save Talon by getting himself blasted.

No…no way. This guy may be good where he comes from, but now it's time to show him who I am…

Another blast came close to Talon's fighter…no, this time it hit. Stockton held his breath for a few seconds, waiting and staring while his scanners updated the display. It looked like one of Talon's engines was out. Her cockpit seemed intact, and even before he commed her, he could tell from the changes in her vector that she was still in control. But she was never going to make it giving the enemy her back. Not down an engine.

"Talon, listen to me. On my mark, I want you to blast hard to the starboard…and then pulse your positioning jets and swing around, firing at the bastard. Once you open up, keep firing until I tell you to stop."

"Sir?"

"No questions, just do it!"

Stockton tapped his throttle, angling his thrust, altering his vector to the other side of the enemy fighter. If Talon did as he'd ordered, they would bracket the Union bird, and they could bring their fire in from two sides. With any luck, it would restrict the enemy's movement enough for Stockton to blast him.

"Talon…three, two, one…mark!"

Stockton angled his controls hard, his own positioning jets moving his thrust vector, applying 10g of acceleration at a sharp angle to his current course. He fired…then again, his laser blasts closing on the enemy. The Union fighter finally reacted to the threat, giving up his pursuit of Talon and spinning around abruptly, sending a volley of laser bolts Stockton's way.

He felt the sweat pouring down his neck, the thunderous pounding of his heart in his chest. The enemy's shots had come close, far closer than he'd expected after such an abrupt change of focus. He'd gotten the bastard off Talon's tail, but now he was locked in a death struggle himself. And the man or woman in that ship was good. Damned good.

The two fighters were facing each other, both pilots firing away. There was no time to maneuver for an advantage, no chance to get behind the target. It was a gunfight, a blazing, no holds barred shootout to the finish. Stockton fired again, but his adversary's evasive maneuvers were as good as his own, and his laser bolts went wide. He'd always had a knack for random zigs and zags, precisely the type of move that confounded targeting computers and pilots alike. But he was facing a foe as unpredictable as he was. And his enemy's shots had been near misses, dangerously near, despite his own best efforts to present a difficult target.

Stockton had talked Talon out of her fear, but now he had to admit, to himself at least, he had to face his own. He was used to being the best pilot in any fight. He'd been outnumbered often, of course, and surrounded. He'd faced death more times than he could count. But the idea of falling here, after all he'd been through…of being killed at last by a single Union pilot, it was more than he could accept. For all his words of encouragement to Talon, he was allowing himself to be distracted by his enemy. Images of Stara flashed through his mind, of the pain she would feel when he didn't return.

No. This isn't you. You aren't a trainee, scared and pissing yourself in the face of the enemy. You aren't a lovesick fool, either. You're Raptor, and you've sent four dozen Union pilots to the depths of hell.

Four dozen and one…

He gripped his throttle tightly, trying to empty his mind, to release the intuition that made him such a deadly warrior. His finger was poised over the firing stud, waiting…waiting. He watched his enemy's moves, even as he put his own fighter through a stomach-churning series of maneuvers, bursts of thrusts in different directions confounding his enemy's own targeting.

He tightened his finger—slowly, steadily. And then the enemy disappeared, the icon winking off his display. He'd been so focused, so intent on battling his foe, he hadn't noticed Talon coming up from behind.

He hesitated for a moment, stunned at what had happened. Then he tapped his comm unit. "Nice shooting, Talon."

"Thank you, sir!" The pilot, so recently terrified and facing death was excited, pumped up by the kill. "Time to get back into the fight," she said, her voice again that of a stone cold predator.

"No," Stockton replied. "You've got an engine out, and this group isn't the bunch of green pilots the Union usually fields. Get back to *Dauntless* now."

"Commander, I can't…"

"Now, Lieutenant. That's an order. I don't have time to

argue with you. If you go back into this fight with a wounded bird, you're as good as dead." His voice came out rougher than he'd intended.

"Yes, sir," Talon replied miserably. "Returning to base as ordered, sir."

Stockton felt a wave of regret, and his hand went to the comm unit. But he stopped before flipping it back on. There would be time to apologize to Steele later. For now, she was heading back to the ship, and that was where she belonged.

He told himself he'd ordered her back solely out of concern for the damage to her fighter, for the increased danger she would face against the experienced Union pilots zipping all around. That was true, to an extent…but he had to admit there was something else at play, something he wasn't very proud of.

He was relieved so capable an enemy was gone, of course, and proud of his pilot for scoring such an illustrious kill. But part of him was also angry. It was irrational, he knew, a foolish resentment. But he felt as though he'd allowed the kill to slip through his fingers, and he was annoyed his pilot had scored the victory. It was nonsense, and he knew he shouldn't care who took down an enemy fighter. But Stockton was driven by an almost relentless competitiveness. As much as he knew it was dangerous, he also realized it made him what he was.

But his ability to focus was as much a part of his essential make up as his unrestrained drive, and now he fell back on that, eyes darting to the display, picking out another target. He still had zero kills, and if there was one thing Jake Stockton was not going to do in a battle this fierce, it was return to *Dauntless* empty handed. Raptor didn't whiff.

And four dozen and one was still out there somewhere…

*   *   *

"Arm defensive batteries…prepare to open fire." Tyler Barron sat in his command chair, leaning forward. As was often the case, his harness was loose, hanging down from the edge of his chair. It was a violation of regs, of course, but worse, he knew, it was a bad example to set for his people. He reached down and grabbed the strap, pulling it into place and latching it.

"All batteries armed and ready, sir."

Barron had been looking at the main display, the large three-dimensional holographic tank in the center of *Dauntless*'s bridge. The enormously expensive and complex device was a technological marvel, but he often found the small screen on his workstation easier to follow. And right now, it showed the problem clearly. Barron had deployed his best fighters to screen against enemy bombers. He'd been sure his crack squadrons would obliterate any strike force heading for *Dauntless*. But his interceptors had been locked in a desperate battle with the enemy's escort fighters. These were no ordinary Union squadrons, they were veteran formations from the most celebrated ship in the enemy fleet. *Vaillant* was in many ways the enemy's counterpart to *Dauntless*, though, unlike his own aging vessel, the enemy battleship was almost new…and half a million tons heavier.

He was still confident his people could hold their own, and eventually gain the edge, but they'd been too tied up in the struggle with the enemy interceptors to do a comprehensive job hunting down the bombers. A dozen of the torpedo-armed craft had gotten through and were heading right toward *Dauntless*. The arrogance of not deploying a defensive patrol was coming back to haunt him.

"Captain, Lieutenant Timmons reports he has five fighters ready. He requests permission to launch."

"Permission granted. He is to launch at once and engage the enemy bombers." The returned scouts were drawn from different squadrons, and more than half of them were still being refueled and rearmed, but he was just thankful he had something left in the bays to deploy against the rapidly approaching attack force. A force of five fighters was vastly preferable to nothing, and when they were led by an officer like Dirk Timmons…they just might pull him out of the fire.

He felt the familiar vibration of *Dauntless*'s launch catapults, and his eyes darted to the screen, checking the range of the approaching bombers. It was close, but Timmons's people would get off a quick attack. They didn't have missiles, he knew that much. He hadn't gotten a specific report to that effect—probably because Timmons didn't want to risk being ordered to wait for full rearming—but there simply hadn't been enough time. Five fighters, each with a pair of missiles, might have obliterated the incoming bomber phalanx, but it would be more difficult business with lasers, and far more time consuming. Timmons might take out half of the enemy ships…but even he would never get them all.

"I want damage control parties ready to go. Advise Commander Fritz, priorities are the primary batteries and the reactors." Barron knew he would have to close and face *Vaillant* before this fight was decided. His own bombers were making their attack run on the enemy ship, and the next few minutes would determine if either or both battleships entered that final fight damaged. If he could hang on to his primaries, he had the edge in the fight. If not, it would be bad business, and even if *Dauntless* was victorious, she'd come out of the battle crippled. And retreat now meant yielding the ancient tech to the Union. That was unthinkable.

"Commander Fritz reports all engineering stations ready, sir."

Barron nodded. Then he looked back to his screen, watching as Timmons's fighters sliced into the bombers.

One down…two. Three…

The fighters were well led, but they were still a collection of pilots from different squadrons. Their formation was loose, and despite Timmons's best efforts, their attack was disorganized. They took down seven of the bombers, but that still left five heading toward *Dauntless*.

The battleship's guns opened up next, the short-ranged anti-fighter lasers tearing through space toward the deadly craft. One down. Then another. But three more made it to launch range, and their torpedoes lurched forward from their bomb bays.

"Target those torpedoes," Barron shouted, but before the words escaped his lips, he saw on the screen that the weapons had already converted to plasmas. The pilots in those bombers were as good as the ones in the enemy interceptors. They'd come in on a line right for *Dauntless*, traveling at such velocity that their warheads didn't need to accelerate further.

"Engines, full thrust port," Barron shouted. Evasive maneuvers were the last line of defense to protect his ship from the approaching torpedoes.

"Full thrust port," Travis snapped back, just as Barron felt the g forces slamming hard into him. The ship was vibrating, the sound of the battleship's engines almost deafening, even on the bridge, more than three kilometers forward of the main engineering spaces.

Barron watched as one warhead zipped by, missing *Dauntless* by less than three hundred meters. Once converted to plasma, the weapons had no ability to exert thrust or alter vectors. He'd dodged that one, at least.

"Cut thrust now!" he roared, his eyes fixed on another of the incoming warheads.

"Cutting thrust!"

The pressure vanished, leaving nothing but the stomach-churning feeling of weightlessness for a few seconds, until the compensators responded and restored the sense of partial gravity to the bridge.

Dauntless had evaded another of the deadly weapons.

Barron's eyes were already fixed on the third, and even as he opened his mouth to shout out a command, he knew he was too late. The ball of superheated plasma was headed right for *Dauntless*...and there was no time.

"Secure for impact," he shouted, but even as he did, the ship shook hard. A shower of sparks flew across the bridge as a ruptured support beam collapsed, tearing apart a heavy electrical conduit as it did. The stations on one side of the bridge went dark, their flow of power cut.

The emergency lamps activated, casting an eerie glow across the space.

Barron was already on his comm, flipping the channel to Fritz's direct line.

"What's it look like, Fritzie?" he snapped, even as he looked around the bridge and realized his ship had taken a bad hit.

He caught a chemical scent in the air, and the ionized smell of electrical fires through the ventilation ducts.

His ship had taken a very bad hit…

Chapter Ten

CFS Intrepid
Hystari System
Sector 3 - "The Front Line"
309 AC

"I'm picking up energy readings, Captain. From the Epheseus transwarp link." Heinrich Nordstrom spoke calmly, without any detectable fear, though everyone on *Intrepid* knew what lay beyond the Epheseus portal. First was an empty, useless solar system of four rocky planets, barely warmed by the waning light of an ancient star. But one jump beyond was Jellicoe, a former Confederation planet that had been controlled by the Union for three generations…and the current base for one of their major battle fleets.

"Active scanners on full, Commander." Captain Sara Eaton sat in her command chair, though "sat" was less than an entirely accurate description of the pose. She had a large cushion—not at all authorized by regs—and she leaned sideways on it, hanging heavily off one side of the seat. She'd been wounded, badly, less than two months after rejoining the fleet, and she'd spent ten weeks in the fleet hospital on Cavenaugh while the surgeons put her back together again from the shattered bits of bone that had been all that remained of her spine.

She'd only been back on *Intrepid* for a week, and she felt

lucky to be there at all. She'd spent every day in the hospital in a near panic that fleet command would assign a new captain to permanently replace her. She was in good standing, of course, decorated for her role alongside Tyler Barron in destroying the enemy's Supply One base. They'd have given her another command if she'd lost *Intrepid*, she didn't doubt that. But she wasn't ready to lose her ship, or to leave her crew behind. They had been to hell and back together, and they were her brothers and sisters…and in a way, her children as well.

She twisted to the side, wincing at the pain from even the small movement. She'd had to talk her way out of the hospital…yell and scream her way out was actually a more accurate description. She had to use virtually every bit of the influence her newfound celebrity as a hero of the fleet afforded her, but she'd finally gotten clearance to return to duty, over the objections of the medical staff. The pain was often bad, and she had to admit she walked like someone fifty years older, but otherwise she was healthy enough.

The surgeons had assured her that, with additional surgeries, they could restore her to her old self, that the pain and difficulty walking would be a thing of the past. But they'd also admitted it would take six months, at least, between operations and rehab periods. And it simply wasn't an option in her mind to be away from *Intrepid* for another half a year in the middle of a war. Six more months of medical leave, and she would have lost her beloved ship for sure.

She promised her doctors that if she survived to see peace, she'd return and take them up on their promises. But now her place was right where she was, in the center of *Intrepid*'s bridge.

"Active scanner reports confirm preliminary data, Captain. We're getting strong energy readings. Very strong."

Eaton shook her head. Something was wrong. All intel reports stated the same conclusion. The enemy fleet was badly damaged, and the stalemate was expected to continue for the foreseeable future. But that reassuring prediction didn't explain what she was seeing on her screen right now.

Epheseus was a barren expanse of space, an ancient, dying

star whose sole significance was it lay between two systems heavily occupied by the warring fleets. It had been a sort of no man's land for the past six months...but the Confederation didn't have any patrols out there now, so anything that came through was almost certainly hostile. The Union knew very well there was a strong Confederation task force in Hystari, so if something was on the way, it was a significant fleet.

Fencing in Epheseus was one thing, testing the enemy, probing...even the occasional battleship duel like the one *Dauntless* had fought a month before. But moving straight through that system, into one as strongly held as Hystari? That could only be a major assault. But how? Why? The enemy couldn't possibly sustain a push forward, so why risk losing capital ships just to outrun its supply sources?

"Get me Commodore Reynard." Eaton didn't like the looks of this, not one bit. But she wasn't the task force commander, and there was only so much she could do by herself. "And bring us to yellow alert. I want all pilots to report to the bays and prepare to launch immediately."

"Yes, Commander." A short pause. "Commodore Reynard on your line."

"Commodore, we are picking up..."

"Yes, Captain...we're reading the same thing. But before we jump to any wild conclusions, let's remember it could be probes or a scouting force...it's not necessarily an assault." Reynard's words said one thing, but his tone another. Eaton could hear the nervousness in the veteran commander's voice, and she knew instantly that he was as worried as she was. That didn't surprise her, but she realized she'd been hoping irrationally that the commodore would offer some kind of explanation that hadn't occurred to her, one that didn't involve an imminent Union offensive.

"I thought that too, sir, but the energy readings suggest a significant number of ships in transit."

"Yes, they do. I'm bringing the fleet to yellow alert, Captain..." He paused for a few seconds. "...though I see you've beaten me to that."

"Yes, sir...sorry Commodore. I thought it was prudent."

"And you were damned right too, Captain. Don't ever apologize for doing the smart thing, whatever officious horse's ass gives you a hard time about it." Reynard had a reputation as a bit of a maverick, one with a penchant for blunt speech...and he rarely disappointed in that regard. "You were right to put your squadrons on alert too...I'm making that a fleet command. Hopefully, we'll both end up being a bit hair-triggered. But if those are enemy battleships coming through, at least we'll be ready."

"Yes, sir," Eaton snapped back. "We'll be ready, sir." She flipped off the comm and took a deep breath. "Order all crews to gunnery stations, Commander. And advise Commander Merton I'm going to want full power on short notice."

"Yes, Captain." Her exec's tone suggested he agreed with her moves. Eaton had been a bit concerned about how Nordstrom would handle moving back to a first officer's duties after months of acting command, but so far it had been as though nothing had changed. The two officers worked well together, just as they always had, and she hadn't detected a hint of resentment at his loss of authority. "Captain...we're getting fresh readings. Ships, emerging from the transwarp link." A pause, then: "Large vessels, mass estimates coming in..." His head snapped up from his station and whipped around to face Eaton. "They're battleships, Captain. Three so far...but energy readings suggest more vessels coming through."

"Battlestations, Commander." She knew the fleet order would come any second, but she saw no reason to wait. The enemy was coming...and they wouldn't be in Hystari if they didn't mean business. Her people had a fight on their hands, she had no doubt about that.

Intrepid's bridge was bathed in red light, and the alarms sounded on all decks. Half her people were already en route to their combat stations, per her earlier orders. But now the entire ship was moving to combat readiness.

"Transmission from *Vanguard*, Captain. The order is, fleet opposed invasion."

Eaton stared at her screen for a few seconds, silent, watching as a fourth enemy ship appeared...and then a fifth.

"Fleet opposed invasion order acknowledged, Commander."

Nordstrom relayed her words on the fleetcom channel. As soon as he had finished, Eaton turned and looked right at him.

Launch all fighters, Commander."

*   *   *

Angus Douglas pulled back on his throttle, accelerating toward the ships deployed in front of the transwarp link. The fleet orders had come through, and squadrons from all six Confederation battleships in Hystari were streaking across the system, heading for the invading Union vessels. There had been five of the enemy monsters when Douglas had set out at the head of two of *Intrepid*'s three squadrons, but now there were nine, plus almost a dozen escorts. The tactical situation had changed considerably, and not for the better. But it didn't matter. Hystari was important tactically, and yielding it to the enemy would compel withdrawals from two neighboring systems, not to mention abandoning almost a million Confederation citizens to Union control, for the second time since hostilities began.

Things were starting to look a little hairy, but Confederation forces were used to being outnumbered by the Union fleets.

Douglas was *Intrepid*'s strike force commander, the senior officer of her fighter wing. He'd left the Longsword squadron behind on defensive duty to protect *Intrepid*, and he was leading the remainder of her wing, thirty Lightning-class fighters, right at the enemy ships. The Gold Shields were half of that strength, formed up fifty thousand kilometers behind and armed as bombers. He was at the head of the Black Helms, equipped as interceptors and assigned to protect the vulnerable attack ships as they moved against the enemy line.

"All right Shields," he said into the small comm unit projecting from his headset, "I know you're all anxious, but you need to stay back at least fifty thousand kilometers. We're going to need time to cut through their interceptors, and if you move up too far, we're not going to be able to keep them off you." Douglas knew his pilots already understood that. But he had a fair number of replacements, men and women he didn't know as well as his veterans, and he wasn't taking any chances. Three or four bombers had already moved ahead of the formation, and he wasn't going to let it get out of hand.

"Roger that, Commander. You heard the orders, Shields. Get the hell back in formation now."

"Stay on it, Gold Leader." Douglas knew Todd Eckert was a good pilot, and an effective squad leader. But he was as excitable as any of his rookies, prone to push too far, too fast without a firm hand directing his actions.

Douglas's eyes dropped to his screen. There were clouds of small dots, coming in waves. Union fighters, hundreds of them. At least six of the Union ships had already launched, and the rest would follow any minute, he knew. His people were badly outnumbered. But their quick launch had forced the invading ships to commit their fighters piecemeal, sending their squadrons out as soon as they were ready, instead of waiting and organizing the entire force for an overwhelming strike. Douglas could see his people were going to be facing at least three times their number, and more if enemy battleships kept transiting. But the first line was almost in range, and that was an even fight, more or less.

Which means we'll cut into these Union pukes like a razor…

He was counting down in his head, watching the front line of dots get closer. It looked like the Union had their interceptors upfront, as expected. The same as always.

Time to show these fools what a dogfight really looks like…

"Black Helms, with me…break and attack!"

The same as always…

*   *   *

Eaton's eyes were glued to the display, watching as her Gold Shields made their attack run. Angus Douglas and the Black Helms had sliced through the Union interceptors so savagely, she'd almost felt sorry for the enemy pilots. Her elite squadron had almost obliterated the first wave, and they'd cut right through the next two, clearing a path for the bombers to attack the nearest battleship.

She knew the way back would be harder, that her people would pay a price when they tried to return to *Intrepid*. They had cut through specific sections of the Union fighter formation, and even now, interceptors were closing in, coming up behind.

Enemy capital ships had continued to pour through the transwarp link, thirteen battleships now, and more than twenty-five escorts. Any chance the Confederation force had of holding Hystari was gone…it was just a question of inflicting as much damage as possible on the enemy fleet before running.

Not a word hinting at retrograde movement had come from the flagship, not yet. She hated the idea of retreating, but she knew it was only a matter of time. Reynard was an aggressive task force commander, known as a tough fighter in the Confederation service. But he wasn't a fool. He wouldn't throw his command away in a battle he couldn't win. The trick would be to hold long enough to recover fighters, and then to execute a fighting retreat. The battleships could escape easily now if they abandoned their squadrons, but that wasn't the Confederation's way. At least it wasn't unless there was no other option.

Eaton could still remember the waves of fighters left behind when the battle line had fled after the fleet's terrible defeat at Arcturon. *Intrepid* had been trapped by the enemy flanking force, and she owed her ship's survival to what she still considered the ignominious tactic of hiding in the system's massive dust cloud.

She'd saved several squadrons worth of fighters then, and for a short time, *Intrepid* had managed to carry more than double her normal complement. It hadn't even occurred to her to try to hang on to some of them after *Intrepid* had rejoined the fleet, but she'd heard rumors that Tyler Barron had done just that. She tried to tell herself she'd have never gotten the okay, that Barron owed his influence to the shade of his grandfather. But whatever the case, it was a lesson in audacity, in going after something, even if it was a difficult target. She'd done that in battle, but then, fearless combat veteran that she was, she had shrunk down before the fleet bureaucracy in a way she had never done in the face of enemy warships.

We could use those fighters now, especially if this is the beginning of a major move. And what else could it be?

"Commander, the Gold Shields are to advance. I want that assault force intercepted well before they get into range. If we hit them a hundred thousand kilometers out, our fighters may have time to come about for a second run before those bombers can launch their torpedoes."

Eaton doubted Reynard would keep the task force in the system long enough to fight the enemy battleships, but she knew *Intrepid* and her sister-ships would at least have to endure multiple bombing runs. The Confederation interceptors had savaged the bombing wings, but they hadn't gotten them all. They were just too numerous…and there were far too many Union interceptors escorting them, peeling off to engage the Confederation fighters.

"Lieutenant Weld acknowledges, Captain."

Eaton watched as the fifteen tiny circles around *Intrepid* began to move toward the approaching bombers. The response time was impressive. Weld was her junior squadron commander, but that didn't mean she wasn't good.

"Gold Shields attacking the lead bomber wave, Captain."

Eaton just nodded…and watched. The Black Helms had hit the enemy force hard, and they'd stripped away most of the interceptor cover from the bombers. The ships coming in were weakly defended, and vulnerable to Weld's attack.

She listened as Weld snapped out orders, splitting her squadron, breaking into three attack groups. Two of them went for the remaining enemy interceptors, while the larger center group flew right at the bombers.

The fight was sharp, brutal, and she watched her pilots taking insane risks, driven by the knowledge that anything that got by them would hit *Intrepid*. She was excited, at first at least, one rush of elation after another as enemy ships winked out of existence all across the line. Then, one of the Shields vanished, and she felt like a deflated balloon. Her squadron was doing well, better than she'd dared to hope, but it still hurt watching her people die.

She watched another half dozen Union birds destroyed…and then she felt as though she'd been punched in the gut.

Sandy Weld's fighter disappeared from the screen. Eaton searched frantically for signs that the squadron leader had managed to eject, or that her fighter had just been knocked out of the data net. But there was nothing…nothing except the yawning pit in her gut, and the grim realization that she'd lost another friend.

Chapter Eleven

Approaching CFS Dauntless
System Z-37 (Saverein)
Inside the Quarantined Zone ("The Badlands")
309 AC

"Form up on me. I want you all in tight. We've got to land quickly, but before we can do that, we've got to match *Dauntless*'s vector." Stockton sat in his cockpit, his vision blurred from sheer exhaustion. He'd been in longer battles, but he couldn't remember any as intense as the one his people had just fought… except perhaps against the Alliance squadrons at Santis. He had a headache that felt as if it was digging a trench right through his skull, and even his hands were sore from gripping the throttle and the controls of his fighter. He reached down and grabbed one of the small ampules in the first aid kit, jabbing into his leg right through his uniform. He felt his head clear almost immediately as the powerful stimulant worked its magic. His vision was sharper too, though he could feel his heart beating in his chest like a drum, and a nervous tension that had him fighting to keep his hands from shaking. Nothing was free, after all.

Right now, however, the battle was still on. His squadrons had managed to get the better of their opponents, but a significant number of enemy craft had survived and broken off, as low on fuel and energy as his own birds. The two sides had fought to exhaustion, and the extensive use of thrusters and turbos in combat had drained both sides' tanks, forcing an end to a struggle that would otherwise undoubtedly have gone to the death.

At least both landing bays were operational. Stockton knew *Dauntless* had taken a hit, but he had no idea how bad it was. The Union ship had also taken a torpedo impact, perhaps two. It was hard to sift through the various comm lines and scanner reports in the middle of battle, especially when fighting enemies as skilled as the pilots his squadrons had just faced.

Stockton had been worried about his lack of kills, but that was no longer an issue. He had three now, and he'd almost gotten a fourth. But there was no sense of triumph this time, nor of glory. Too many of his people had fallen in this struggle, and two of the three fighters he'd bagged had been vengeance kills. Each of them had defeated one of his pilots as he watched, helpless, too late to intervene as he had for Talon. Stockton couldn't describe the rage that overtook him when he watched one of his people killed. He became some kind of avenging angel—or devil—and he went after the victorious enemy with such a single-minded ferocity, he scared even himself. He'd hunted down the enemy pilots, blown them to plasma…but when he was done, nothing changed. His pilots were still dead. The satisfaction he'd once gotten from such things seemed lost to him.

"*Dauntless*, this is Blue leader, requesting permission to land Blue and Scarlet Eagle squadrons." There was no time to waste. Kyle Jamison was bringing up the rest of the strike force, the bombers that had attacked the enemy battleship and Olya Federov's Red squadron escorts. He had to get his people back aboard and out of the way. Jamison's birds would be even lower on fuel than his own, and they would need immediate clearance to land.

"Blue leader, you are clear. To expedite landing operations, reroute the Scarlet Eagles to beta bay and bring the Blues into alpha bay." It was Stara, and he could hear the hint of relief in her voice. He smiled for a few seconds, realizing that a good portion of that tone was a response to his safe return. It was gratifying, but still strange to him. He had friends all over *Dauntless*, and he and Kyle Jamison were like brothers, but Stara's concern felt good in a way that was quite new and different.

But there was something else in her tone too, a concern even her joy at his survival couldn't mask. He'd been worried about *Dauntless*'s status as he'd led his battered squadrons back in, but now he was sure. Everything was far from well on the ship.

*   *   *

"Blue and Scarlet Eagle squadrons have landed, Captain. Twenty-two fighters. Refit and refueling operations are underway."

"Very well." Barron suspected Travis would have preferred to leave out the number of returned fighters, but her fastidious nature would never allow her to make an incomplete report. She hadn't included a reminder that the two squadrons had launched thirty-three craft, but Barron didn't need one. He knew exactly how many ships his two elite forces had sent into the maelstrom, and he was also perfectly capable of doing the necessary subtraction to determine how many of his people hadn't come back.

He also knew any claims of aggressive refitting efforts underway were exaggerations. Red, Green, and Yellow squadrons were on the way in, and they'd commence landings in less than ten minutes. *Dauntless*'s bays were capable of bringing in fighters while equipping others, but conducting the operations simultaneously slowed both down. And the incoming squadrons were flying on fumes. Even Chief Evans's ferocious team leadership would be tested to its limit in prepping the Blues and the Eagles for relaunch while bringing in the other squadrons quickly.

"Captain, with your permission…I'd like to go down to the bays and assist." Travis turned around in her seat.

"Go," he replied. "Do what you can. Even a few extra minutes could help." He knew Travis was as aware as he was just how important a job refitting those fighters was. *Dauntless*'s primaries were down, and its power transmission systems were badly damaged. He knew Commander Fritz was crawling through the guts of the massive weapon system, desperately struggling to get it back online. He considered his chief engineer to be a virtual sorceress, and he'd seen her repair systems he'd thought were nothing but scrap, but his gut told him this time the damage was too extensive. He would have to fight this battle without his heaviest guns, and that meant he needed his fighters. As quickly as possible.

"Yes, Captain. I'll keep you posted." She leapt out of her chair and moved across the bridge at a pace somewhere between a jog and a run, a gait Barron suspected was intended to get her there as quickly as possible without instilling panic in the crew.

Barron hadn't discussed the pending final showdown with his first officer, but the two shared an almost telepathic link, and he was certain she'd been thinking the same thing he had. With *Dauntless*'s primaries out of action, the Union ship had the edge in a close-ranged fight. Normally, Barron might feel he could counter a weaponry and tonnage advantage with expertise and the skill of his crew, but now he was facing the pride of the Union navy. His people might still be better—he'd argue to the end they were—but it wasn't by their usual margin, and he doubted it was enough to prevail if the enemy ship still had its own primaries online.

No, *Dauntless* wasn't going to win a close-ranged duel, or if she did, it would be by the slimmest of margins. She'd be one step out of the scrapyard by the time she gained her "victory." But there was more at play than two battleships blasting away at each other, and Barron suspected whichever ship could refit and relaunch fighters first would prevail.

For all the tactics he might employ, and the skill of his gunnery teams—and the sweating engineering crews struggling to get systems operational—the battle likely lay in the hands of the technicians in the launch bays, and the speed with which they turned the battered fighters around and got them back into space again. And if that was the case, he'd put Chief Evans and his people up against any other launch teams…even the pride of the Union. Especially with Atara Travis breathing down their necks

"Lieutenant Darrow, take Commander Travis's station."

"Yes, sir." The communications officer leapt up, struggling for a few seconds to slip out of his harness. Then he raced across the bridge, his nervous jog exhibiting none of the careful control Travis had just displayed.

Darrow dropped into the seat and turned toward Barron, waiting for orders.

"Get me a status report from engineering, Lieutenant. I need Commander Fritz's updated assessment on the primaries and reactor B."

"Yes, sir."

Darrow spun around, pausing for a moment as he stared at Travis's panel. *Dauntless*'s executive officer was almost as much a legend to the crew as the captain. Travis was unmatched in her ability to follow multiple data streams coming in—like a chess master playing a dozen opponents simultaneously—and she'd had additional screens and keyboards installed at her station. Darrow stared at it all, looking stunned for a few seconds. Then he just dove in, flipping on the comm unit, and yelling out commands, doing his best to emulate his recollections of Travis at work.

"Captain, Commander Fritz reports she is still working on the primaries, sir. No estimate on time to completion."

"Very well. Barron had almost snapped back a demand for a projection, but there was no point. If Anya Fritz hadn't given him a time estimate, it was because she didn't have any idea how long it would take. Forcing her to give him a wild guess was the definition of pointless.

But she didn't say she wouldn't get them back online…and she would have if there was no hope…

Fritz was the closest thing he'd ever seen to a miracle worker, and he knew there was at least a chance she would come through. But until then, he had to assume the primaries were gone. He had to find a way to win the fight without them.

"Chief, we need those fighters ready to launch, and we need it five minutes ago."

"Commander…we're doing everything we can, but the rail systems are damaged. It's slowing the transfer of fuel and weapons to the bay." Evans had a reputation as a hotheaded bully, one who drove his crews mercilessly, but now he was on the defensive. The slim woman facing him not only outranked him, but she was just as "chew through steel girders" tough as he was.

Atara Travis was shaking her head before he even finished. She knew she was popular with *Dauntless*'s crew, but she was just as aware of the stories about her unlikely rise from the slums of a hell world to her current rank and position. Many of those tales involved rumors of bodies left behind, and rather fewer of them actually came close to the truth, but she never debunked any of them. Together they created a useful legend, one she was not hesitant to use to get what she needed. And she was amused by the fact that Chief Evans, the terror of *Dauntless*'s landing bays, was scared shitless of her.

"That's not enough, Chief. The primaries are down, and the only way we're going to win this fight is to launch a fighter strike before the enemy does. I don't care what you do, but I want two squadrons ready to launch in fifteen minutes…and the other three fifteen behind that."

"That's just impossible," the burly chief protested.

"It's impossible if we stand here arguing about it." Travis gestured toward the open area of the bay, just behind Evans. "I don't see you hauling equipment, Chief." She turned and waved her arm behind her. "I brought another sixty sets of arms and legs with me." The men and women lined up against the wall were stewards, scientists…virtually everyone on *Dauntless* who didn't have a crucial battlestations role. "So, put them to work. Put me to work." She glared at him with an intensity that made the big man cringe. "But stop telling me what you can't get done."

Evans stood there for a few seconds, an uncertain look on his face. Travis thought he might object or argue, but then he just nodded. "Yes, sir," he replied, as meekly as she'd ever heard him. Evans was a career spacer, a veteran of the last war, and he normally expected his utterances to be obeyed like the word of God. Even officers who outranked him generally quaked in his presence, but now he had met his match on *Dauntless*. Again. Travis knew Anya Fritz and her people had invaded his launch bay during the fight at Santis, and now she had repeated the engineer's performance, with her own special touches.

"Then let's get to it, Chief. We've only got thirteen of those fifteen minutes left."

Chapter Twelve

CFS Intrepid
Hystari System
Sector 3 - "The Front Line"
309 AC

"We're doing everything we can down here, Captain...but that last hit was bad. Half the power feeds from the reactor are severed. It's fixable, but it will take time." Commander Merton's tone said more about the situation than the report itself, communicating stress and exhaustion more emphatically than mere words.

Eaton shifted in her chair, her anger and tension causing her to momentarily forget her injuries. She winced as a wave of agony shot up and down her back, but she just gritted her teeth and ignored it, even as her eyes moistened from the pain. She was a Confederation captain and a veteran warrior...she wasn't about to let pain distract her. Not when her ship was in danger.

"We don't have that time, Doug," she said, as matter-of-factly as she could manage amid the chaos breaking out all around her. There were fires in the landing bays, compartments blown open and exposed to the vacuum of space, and at least two dozen of her people dead...but the worst problem right now was the engines. They were completely offline, and until she had some kind of thrust capacity, *Intrepid* was stuck in Hystari, watching the rest of the task force withdraw.

Commodore Reynard had given the retreat order, the one she'd known was coming. But now it was beginning to look like it was too late, at least for her and her people. *Intrepid*'s combat space patrol had shredded the first three waves of torpedo bombers, gunning down ship after ship before they'd reached launch range. But a struggle so intense came at a cost, in resources as well as casualties. She'd lost more than a third of her fighters to the enemy interceptors accompanying the bombers, and the rest had been on full turbos for most of the battle. She'd had no choice but to order them to land to refuel and refit, just as fresh waves of bombers approached. Her gunners had done the best they could against the fresh assault forces, but there had just been too many enemy ships.

"I understand, Captain," Merton said, "but that doesn't change reality." He paused, and she could hear the sound of a hard exhale through the comm. "Let me go, Captain…I'll get it done as quickly as possible."

"Go, Doug. I have faith in you." She cut the line. Distracting him wasn't going to serve any purpose.

She did have faith in her engineer. Commander Douglas Merton had seen her ship through crises before, and Eaton always backed her people one hundred percent. They gave her their loyalty, and she gave them hers. Besides, there was nothing else to do. *Intrepid* had twenty minutes, perhaps thirty. After that, she'd either be through the transit point, retreating with the fleet…or the eighteen Union battleships and fresh waves of bombers streaking across the system would be on her.

Intrepid had taken three hits, all of them bad, and one of them nearly critical. It would have been worse, but her assault squadrons returned from their attack run just as the final group of Union bombers was beginning its attack run, no doubt planning to finish off the crippled battleship. The interceptors of Black Helm squadron were almost out of fuel when they reached the Union strike craft, their laser cannons down to their last watts of power. But Angus Douglas had led them on a blistering attack anyway, slicing through the approaching strike force and then coming about and hitting them again. Only two bombers got through, and *Intrepid*'s gunners took those out, a significant feat considering that centralized fire control was out shipwide. It was a bit of shared heroism that just possibly saved *Intrepid* from destruction. But that salvation was temporary, and Eaton knew her ship wasn't out of the woods yet, not by a long shot.

Half of the surviving Black Helms had been forced to ditch as their birds ran out of fuel. She'd sent out the rescue shuttle, but now she was far from sure it would be able to land in time. The bays were in bad shape, and a series of internal explosions had degraded conditions further after the craft had launched.

Whether or not she could get the rescue ship back onboard, a fighter launch was out of the question. There was no way to refuel or rearm the squadrons, not with the fires and the blasted systems in the bays.

Survival was in her engineer's hands now. Either her people would escape or they wouldn't. There was frustratingly little she could do but wait.

She remembered the long hours in the dust clouds at Arcturon, waiting moment by moment for the enemy to find her. She'd escaped detection that time, and it was ultimately her own action that gave away her location, as she launched a massive fighter attack on the enemy ships attacking *Dauntless*. This time was different. If the Union battleships got into range of her crippled vessel, it would be over in minutes. Her primaries were down, and more than half the secondaries too. Much of the damage was repairable, severed power conduits and the like. But when the enemy closed into range, none of that mattered. She would either have weapons to fight or she wouldn't…but *Intrepid* would be overwhelmed either way. The engines—escape—that was her only chance.

Without the engines, every man and woman on the ship was as good as dead. *Intrepid* fresh from the shipyard couldn't have faced eighteen enemy ships alone. And there was no doubt, she *would* be alone. The commodore would torture himself over leaving her behind…but he *would* do it. This was war, and he couldn't risk five ships to save one, not when the battle would still be hopeless. Eaton had no bad feelings about that. She knew she'd do the same thing in his shoes.

"All gunners to operable stations, Commander. We may have to make a fight of it here." It was bravado, as much a way to keep her people busy as to fight off the fear. Eaton would go down fighting, that was a certainty. But with nothing but half her secondaries she wasn't going to do more than a few pinpricks.

If they get close enough at all. They can stop outside the range of our secondaries and blast us to dust with their primary batteries.

"Yes, Captain." Nordstrom relayed the command on the intra-ship comm. A few second later, he spun around, staring across the bridge at her. "Captain, I have Commodore Reynard on the comm."

She grabbed the headset she'd set on the armrest and strapped it over her head. "Commodore?"

"Any progress on your engine repair, Captain?"

"My damage control teams are working on it, sir. That's all I have to report right now."

"Any projections?"

"Commodore…the truth is we have no idea. The damage is fairly extensive and widespread. We might get lucky…we might not. We're in trouble, sir." She paused. "You have to leave us."

"None of that, Captain. The Confederation navy doesn't abandon its personnel."

"There's no choice, Commodore. We're too outnumbered. You can't lose six ships instead of one. You can't save us."

"Abandon ship, Captain. *Vanguard* and *Resolution* are closest. We can pick up your lifeboats."

"Commodore," Eaton said softly. "You know there isn't time. Go, sir, please. Don't let us carry the lives of all the spacers in the fleet with us. The Confederation needs those ships. We don't know what this new attack means, but it's a pretty sure bet we'll need every vessel we can get."

"We will stay until the last possible moment, Captain. If there is anything we can do to assist your engineering crews, you just have to ask."

"Thank you, sir." She knew Reynard had meant what he said sincerely, but also that it was an empty offer. There wasn't time for any of the other ships to come to her aid, any more than there was to evacuate her people from *Intrepid*. She also knew he'd needed to say what he had, and she'd let him do it.

She looked around the bridge, at her people, focused on their stations, not a sign of panic or indiscipline. She felt a sudden touch of guilt. They expected her to get them out of this. They were afraid, but their faith in her was stronger than their fear. They'd been abandoned in Arcturon and as good as lost, but she'd gotten them out of there—and led them deep into enemy-held space to destroy the Union's supply base before she'd brought them home.

She'd had lots of help there, of course. Tyler Barron had been the overall commander, and Eaton was far from sure she could have matched his performance in that role. But the situation now was different. If Merton and his engineers didn't get the engines back online, she and all her people were going to die. There were no tricks, no stratagems that could hold off such a massive enemy force.

"Captain, Commander Merton on your line."

Her hand moved to the side of her headset. "Doug, what is it?"

"We're still trying to get the engines back, but believe it or not, I've got the primaries operable. I can't promise a thing. They might get knocked out by the first hit we take…they might even just stop working. But right now, you've got them both online."

"You're a miracle worker, Doug…but what we really need is the engines."

"I know, Captain. We're doing everything that can be done. Don't give up yet."

"We never give up, Commander. You know that."

That doesn't mean we don't fail. That we don't die.

Her eyes darted to the display. The Union officers knew as well as she did how fragile Confederation primaries were. They would probably assume *Intrepid*'s main guns had been knocked out. She stared at the symbols on her screen. The Union ships were strung out across the system, in the order they'd transited. A cautious commander would have stopped and reordered his fleet, moving his ships into a real battle formation. But obviously, the Union admiral didn't think a crippled Confederation battleship was anything to worry about.

We'll see about that, you piece of shit…

If her people were going to die here, they were going to extract a price first…

"Commander, prepare to jettison five hundred liters of fuel, and ignite."

Nordstrom stared back at her, his face frozen in shock. The entire bridge was silent.

"Captain?"

"You heard me, Commander. I want an explosion. Nearby. I want them to think we're even worse off than we are. And I want to mask the power flow to the primaries. We're going to take that first ship by surprise."

Nordstrom nodded, a look of understanding replacing the mask of confusion on his face. But he still looked a little stunned. *Intrepid*'s fuel was compressed tritium. When Eaton said "ignite" she didn't mean start a fire. She meant set off a fusion reaction…a miniature sun. Right next to the ship.

He turned back to his board, his hands moving across the keyboard and touchscreens. He was running calculations, with the ship's AI checking him every step of the way. He had to know just how far from the ship that cloud of tritium had to be before it was…ignited.

Eaton looked up from her own screen. "We don't have all day, Commander."

"Yes, Captain," he said, sounding a bit flustered. "The cloud needs to be nine hundred meters from *Intrepid*…but that's cutting it close."

"That's what I had as well, Commander. Well done."

The surprise returned to Nordstrom's face as he realized that Eaton had done the same calculations he had.

"Well, Commander?" Eaton said sharply.

"Yes, Captain!" He turned back toward his station, his hands moving again, faster this time, almost a blur. A moment later, he turned back. "We're ready, Captain."

"Proceed, Commander." Her eyes shot back to the screen, checking the progress of the lead enemy battleship. There were half a dozen escorts closer, but she wasn't going to waste the one or two telling shots she had on frigates and scouts. "Begin charging primaries as soon as the reaction ignites."

"Yes, Captain." Stockton flipped a series of small switches, and a few second later he said, "Fuel ejected." Then: "Detonating ignition charge now."

Eaton watched on her screen as the nuclear trigger ignited inside the large canister of compressed fuel. In a fraction of a second, the tritium began to fuse, giving off massive amounts of energy. A yellow circle appeared on the display as her ship's scanner picked up the reaction, and the massive amount of heat and radiation it gave off.

Intrepid's armor blocked most of the harmful radiation, and the tiny sun was just far enough from the ship that the heat didn't melt the hull. But it was close enough to interfere with the enemy scanners, and block detection of *Intrepid*'s reactors as they powered up her main guns.

"Energy to primaries, Commander...now." With any luck, her target would blunder right into her primary range, which was fifteen thousand kilometers beyond the reach of the Union guns.

"Primaries charging now, Captain. Gunnery crews ready and in position."

Eaton took a deep breath. She would surprise the enemy ship, she was sure of that...but the shot would be at long range, and even her veteran gunners could miss. The Union ship was being careless, moving forward on a highly predictable course, seemingly confident *Intrepid* had nothing that could threaten it. She reminded herself never to get cocky, no matter what the situation...assuming she lived more than another ten or fifteen minutes, of course.

"Primaries charged and ready to fire, Captain. Gunnery teams are awaiting your order."

Eaton sat stone still, her eyes fixed on the display.

A few more seconds...let them get a little closer...

She didn't say a word. She just leaned forward, even the pain from her back pushed aside now. She had no thought in her mind except the enemy's lead ship. If her people were going to die, they were going to make the enemy pay for it.

"Captain, we've got it!" Doug Merton's voice erupted in her headset, the normally dour engineer sounding downright giddy. "We've got the engines back online."

"Well done, Commander. You and your people earned your pay this month. Stand by for maximum possible thrust on my command."

"Yes, sir..." Merton sounded confused. Eaton knew why. He'd expected an immediate order to fire up the engines. But she wasn't ready to leave, not yet. She was going to give these Union bastards a lesson in the pitfalls of carelessness, of arrogance.

"Gunners, fire at will...and make it count."

"Gunners, fire at will." Nordstrom nodded to himself. "Make it count," he added, his voice taking on an almost sinister tone.

Eaton sat where she was, her teeth gritted against the pain in her back, her eyes locked on the display, waiting...

The lights dimmed, and the familiar sound of *Intrepid*'s primaries echoed off the ceiling and walls of the bridge. There wasn't a sound after that, save for a few deep breaths. Every eye was fixed on the display, waiting to see what the gunners had wrought.

Eaton could see the enemy ship had not altered its vector at all...and she knew, even before the scanners updated, that her gunners had hit. Her people wouldn't miss a target on a fixed course, not even at the longest range.

"A hit, Captain," Nordstrom shouted, even as her own eyes were fixed on the data streaming in the display.

Two hits...

"Two hits," her first officer said echoing her thought.

"Directly amidships, Captain. We're detecting hull breaches and massive ejections of atmosphere and fluids." Nordstrom paused...then he spun around and said, "Internal explosions... she's hurt Captain. She's hurt bad!"

The bridge erupted into applause, a wild round of cheers. Eaton knew it for what it was. Her people had been under enormous tension. They still were. But with the engines back online they had a chance to survive...and the hit on the enemy ship was a trigger to release the fear and anxiety that had been gnawing at them all. So, she let it go on...but just for a few seconds.

"All right, I know you're all excited, but we're still sitting in the path of a huge enemy fleet, so back to your stations, all of you. Let's get out of here."

She turned toward Nordstrom. "Commander, full thrust if you would. Follow the rest of the task force out of here."

Chapter Thirteen

CFS Dauntless
System Z-37 (Saverein)
Inside the Quarantined Zone ("The Badlands")
309 AC

"Primaries are still down, Captain. We'll be in range of the enemy's main batteries in two minutes." Darrow was tense, clearly edgy at filling in for so towering a presence as Atara Travis, but he was holding his own.

"Very well, Lieutenant. Prepare for evasive maneuvers as we enter range." *Dauntless* was accelerating at 6g, heading straight for the enemy vessel. Barron intended to continue increasing his velocity, at least until his guns were in range. He was going to take everything *Vaillant* could throw at him, a run of roughly twenty thousand kilometers where his enemy's main weapons could hit him before he could return fire with his secondaries. He hated giving the Union vessel—especially one as competently crewed as *Vaillant*—time to fire at him unanswered. He hated the fact that he couldn't get a decent scanner read on how badly his own bomber squadrons had damaged the enemy. He hated just about everything regarding the current situation. But there was nothing he could do. Nothing but gut through it, and rely on his people rising to the task. That, and a little bit of luck.

"Evasive maneuvers locked in, sir. Ready to commence on

your command."

"Captain..."

Travis's voice came through on his headset, just as he was about to acknowledge Darrow's report.

"Yes, Commander?" he replied, holding his hand up, gesturing for the communications officer to stand by.

"We've got Blue and Scarlet Eagle squadrons ready to launch, sir. Awaiting your order."

Barron felt a surge of excitement. It was the first good news he'd had so far in this fight. His eyes darted to the display, to the red ovoid that represented his adversary. There was nothing around it, no clouds of tiny dots, not even one or two specks representing newly launched ships. The enemy hadn't managed to refit and launch any of its fighters. Yet.

"Launch, Commander, now! With all possible speed."

"Yes, sir." Travis cut the connection, and a few seconds later, Barron felt the vibration under his chair, *Dauntless*'s launch catapults hurling the fighters of his two elite squadrons into space.

None of the Blues or the Eagles had been fitted as bombers. There simply hadn't been time to change their configurations. Strafing runs with lasers could damage the enemy ship, especially if there were hull breaches and other vulnerable areas to target. The impact of that kind of attack was not nearly as severe as a successful bombing run, far less likely to be decisive. But it was better than nothing.

A lot goddamned better than nothing...

His eyes darted back to the display. Still no launches from *Vaillant*. He was thrilled to have fighters in space, and he was amazed that Travis had made it happen so quickly, but he was also well-aware *Dauntless* hadn't really gained an edge. Not yet. His two squadrons had to get to the Union battleship and launch their attack before the enemy got their own fighters into space. A dogfight three-quarters of the way to the Union battleship would accomplish nothing, and with his primaries down, the enemy benefited from any delay in fighter attacks.

His squadrons were launching with *Dauntless*'s intrinsic velocity, which meant they would be moving *fast*. That, at least, was a good thing. They'd ultimately have to decelerate to make their runs, but first, they would blast hard with their turbos, accelerating further and closing the distance to the enemy ship rapidly. It gave them a chance of getting there in time. If they didn't, they'd end up in a massive brawl with the Union squadrons. That would take them out of the ship versus ship struggle. And Barron needed those fighters hitting that battleship.

"Entering range of enemy primary batteries in twenty seconds, Captain."

"Commence evasive maneuvers. Random thrust pattern."

"Yes, sir." A few seconds later: "Engine room acknowledges, Captain." Barron knew, even as Darrow made the report. He could feel the change in his ship's thrust, the random blasts that would alter *Dauntless*'s exact location enough to confuse the enemy targeting systems, while generally maintaining its overall vector.

The tension on the bridge was palpable. Most of *Dauntless*'s crew were veterans, and they'd been in tough fights before. But Barron knew from the tightness in his own gut that experience only went so far. Facing a dangerous enemy, fighting at a disadvantage, struggling to stave off defeat…it never got easier.

"Enemy opening fire, sir." Darrow's report was loud, clear, the lieutenant putting his best effort into sounding professional. But Barron could feel the impact of the words, on himself—the sound of his heart pounding in his own ears—and on his crew. He could feel their fear…but something else too. Their eyes were on him, the confidence they in him that went beyond facts. He loved them for their loyalty, but they would never know the weight their faith placed on him. They believed he would get them out of this. And he was far from sure he shared that point of view.

Barron watched as laser blasts erupted on the display, ripping through space exactly where *Dauntless* would have been, save for the last burst of thrust that had taken his ship five hundred meters from the enemy's first shot.

He exhaled hard. His ship would be vulnerable for a little over two minutes before he could return fire. *Dauntless* had to make it through without taking serious additional damage. Then, at least, it would be a fight where the skill of his people would matter.

Time to run the gauntlet...

*   *   *

"Raptor, I'm picking up launch detections." Timmons's voice was as calm as usual, at least to most ears. The Scarlet Eagles' commander was an unflappable veteran, one who rarely let concern or fear show...but it was still clear to Stockton that his comrade knew the implications of the news he reported.

Stockton looked down at his own screen, confirming what his comrade had just told him. *Damn.* It *was* bad news. His people could handle the squadrons now pouring out from the enemy ship in a head on fight, but that wasn't the problem. *Dauntless* needed his people to make strafing runs...and there was no point to his pilots winning the fighter battle only to watch their base ship destroyed. The loss of the battleship would mean certain death for his people. He would never surrender, especially not to the Union, and he was sure none of his pilots would either. That meant the enemy battleship had to be destroyed, whatever it took.

His eyes darted to his scanner again, this time searching for the rest of *Dauntless*'s fighters. Red, Green, and Yellow squadrons were coming, he was sure of that...but none had launched yet. The Greens and Yellows had been outfitted as bombers, and that meant it would take longer to get them refit and back into space—whether Barron had ordered them reloaded with fresh torpedoes or stripped down to interceptor kits. But Olya Federov's Reds would have been quicker to refuel and rearm, and Stockton suspected they'd be ripping down the catapults any minute. The "book" called for holding them until the bombers launched, but he'd have bet his last coin that Tyler Barron would send them out the second they were ready.

But even then, they'll be too late...

"Warrior, those fighters will still be shaking down into formation when we get there…especially if we don't decelerate." The idea just burst into his head. It was crazy, unorthodox for sure. But he thought it just might work.

"How can we engage them if we don't dec…" Timmons's words trailed off, and Stockton knew his former rival had just caught his meaning. "You mean ignore the enemy fighters?"

"That's what I mean. We blast right through them and launch a fast attack on the enemy battleship. Those birds will still be getting themselves set up…they won't be able to hit us too hard."

"You hope," Timmons replied. "We'll be giving them an undefended flank…and if they realize we're not going to turn to face them, they'll be able to ignore defensive maneuvers and be that much more aggressive with their attack." He paused then added, "Even if we get past them, this velocity is hardly optimal for attacking a battleship."

"What the hell is optimal about any of this, Warrior? *Dauntless* is hurting, you know that. We've got to help her win this fight, whatever it takes. We won't be able to do multiple runs, at least not before we can decelerate, but maybe one will do the trick. That crate took two torpedo hits…even if neither was critical, there have to be weak spots, maybe even hull breaches."

"That's probably true, but precise targeting at this velocity? Is that even possible?"

"Sure we can," Stockton snapped back, struggling to hide his doubts. They were moving at four hundred kilometers per second, far faster than optimal for precision strikes. "We can do it because we have to do it. Because that's what *Dauntless* needs us to do." There wasn't a lot of logic in his argument, but it was the kind of thing fighter pilots were prone to say. And in his experience, desperation alone had fueled more than one unexpected success.

"Those aren't rookie fighters coming out of there, Raptor… they're going to hit us hard if we don't engage them. Even a few shots at our flanks and rear are going to hurt."

"But like you said, it'll be just a few shots, Warrior. Their intrinsic velocity is almost opposite ours. They'll whip by us and have to decelerate to come about and re-engage. And by then, we'll be through with our run, and *Dauntless* will be in firing range...and our chance to give the captain an edge will be over. Then we can take down those fighters." They had to hit the enemy battleship, and that was the primary consideration. The only one.

"I'm with you, Raptor." There was a level of camaraderie Timmons's voice that he'd never expected to hear coming through his comm. War had brought the rivals together, and now it was time to show the Union just what the Confederation's two best pilots—and squadrons—could do.

Stockton switched to the wide channel. "All right Blues and Eagles, listen up, I'm going to give it to you straight. We're not going to decelerate...and we're not going to engage the enemy fighters you see popping up on your screens. We're going in fast and hard at the enemy battleship, and I need your best shots. I know I'm asking you all to put yourselves at greater risk, to ignore those birds firing at you, but *Dauntless* needs us, and the captain's counting on his two best squadrons. Are we going to let him down?" He knew he was asking a lot of his men and women. Ignoring an enemy trying to kill you was far from easy...especially when you knew that foe was good enough to take you down. But he believed in his own pilots, and he believed in Timmons's men and women as well.

"You all heard Raptor." Timmons's voice came through the comm right after Stockton's. "I know it's not going to be easy, but that's what we've got to do...and that's all any of us needs to know."

"Warrior is right," Stockton added. "This is what we have to do...and that's all we need to know about it."

He listened to the responses on the comm channel, mostly raucous battle cries he suspected were as much attempts to cover fear as genuine reactions. But whatever they were, one thing was clear. They were with him. They were ready.

"All right squadrons, let's do this..."

Chapter Fourteen

CFS Dauntless
System Z-37 (Saverein)
Inside the Quarantined Zone ("The Badlands")
309 AC

"I want the fighter launches interspersed with evasive maneuvers...that gives a one second window to get each wave of ships out." Barron had been snapping out orders nonstop, obsessing over every aspect of his ship's approach to the enemy. *Dauntless* was in range of the enemy's main guns now, and she was dodging a barrage of fire, seemingly-random bursts of thrust making the battleship as difficult a target as possible. She'd been hit twice, though neither shot had damaged anything critical. But now he had to get Red squadron into space, and if he sent the fighters out while *Dauntless*'s engines were blasting in a random direction, it would take Olya Federov half an hour to get her birds into any kind of useful formation...and that was time they didn't have. Time he didn't have.

"Yes, sir," Darrow replied, trying to sound on top of things, but not quite pulling it off. Barron knew his communications officer was doing a credible job of keeping up with the blistering pace of his commands, but he also knew the young lieutenant was being pushed to the very edge of his abilities. Barron knew how spoiled he was...Atara Travis was the best first officer in the fleet, and he was feeling her absence keenly as the battle approached its climax. She was still down in the launch bays, and as much as he wished he had her on the bridge, he knew her energetic supervision had gotten the Blues and the Eagles—and now the Reds too—out at a speed conventionally considered impossible.

"Alternate, Lieutenant," Barron said, trying not to let his frustration show. If not being Atara Travis was a fault, it was one every officer in the fleet, save the genuine article herself, shared. "Blast the thrusters, and then a one second delay. That's enough for the catapults to launch once. Then another burst of thrust on a different vector...and then one second to launch again."

"Yes, sir," Darrow answered, with more conviction this time. Barron's orders were far from "by the book," mostly because there weren't more than two or three crews in the fleet that could have executed them. But Barron's faith in his people had grown into a pillar of strength, and the longer they'd served together, the more he'd come to know just how much he could expect from them.

Dauntless jerked hard, a particularly strong burst of thrust. Barron had adjusted the AI's proposed sequence of evasive maneuvers, adding a touch of human intuition no electronic intelligence could match. His people were in their toughest fight since the terrible battle out at Santis, and he knew it would take everything he had—everything *all* of them had—to see it through to victory.

The display flickered, four tiny dots appearing next to Dauntless. "Lynx" Federov and three of her Reds. Then the ship shook again, more softly this time as the thrusters fired in almost the opposite direction. Barron was still staring when he saw another half dozen laser shots whip by...and one slam right into his ship.

The bridge shook once, and then again, a few seconds later, as the laser hit was followed by a distant internal explosion. Barron had come to know his ship well, almost like his own body, and he was fairly certain the hit hadn't been critical. Still, supplemental explosions were never a good thing, and damaged equipment and uncontrolled fires would just pull Fritz's people from working on the primaries. He still hadn't given up on getting a shot with *Dauntless*'s powerful particle accelerators. Not quite, at least.

He watched another four tiny circles appear, and then he forced his eyes to the side, toward the enemy ship and his two attacking squadrons. He'd looked away a few seconds before, unwilling to watch as his best pilots willingly exposed themselves to enemy attack…all in an effort to strafe Union battleship, to gain an edge—any edge—for *Dauntless*. It was hard enough watching such self-sacrificial courage, but he'd listened in on the communications, sat stone still on the bridge as Jake Stockton had outlined his plan. Barron knew he could have intervened, ordered Stockton and his people to face the enemy fighters instead of making a quasi-suicidal run past the Union squadrons to strike the battleship itself. But he'd remained silent. He'd let them go in…and whatever happened, it was his responsibility, more even than Stockton's.

The elite formations suffered, certainly, but as he looked again, he realized they hadn't been as badly hurt as he'd feared. Stockton had been correct…skilled pilots or no, the enemy hadn't had time to organize their formations. They had made his people pay a price, but then their own vectors and intrinsic velocities had quickly taken them out of range. And Stockton and Timmons were leading the remaining Blues and Eagles right at *Vaillant*.

He watched as they made their final approach, closing the remaining distance in a matter of seconds. *Dauntless* shook again, even as his attention was fixed on the fighter attack. His people had managed their maneuvers well, but *Vaillant*'s gunners knew their trade. He'd been lucky, at least so far. The Union main guns weren't a match for the strength of his primaries, but they were more than capable of blasting his ship to scrap. One well-placed hit could cripple *Dauntless*.

"I've got Commander Stockton, sir. He reports that Blue and Scarlett Eagle squadrons are making their attack runs."

"On my line, Lieutenant."

"Yes, sir." The communications officer flipped a switched and turned back toward Barron. "Connected, Captain."

"Raptor...Captain Barron here." He used Stockton's callsign instead of his name.

"Yes, sir...we're going in. We lost Hopkins and Klein to the enemy fighters, and Biggs a few seconds ago to defensive fire. Should be about thirty seconds, Captain, then you'll know if we managed to do any good."

"You've got my every confidence, Raptor. All of ours. Do what has to be done." Barron cut the line, just as *Dauntless* heaved again, hard this time. A bank of workstations went dark, and a conduit running along the ceiling fell, a shower of sparks flying all across the bridge. The display tank blinked, a ripple of colors moving through the hologram for a few seconds before it stabilized.

Barron leaned over his armrest, his hand moving to the comm controls. But he stopped.

Fritzie will report anything crucial. Don't take her away from her work...

He turned just as the display snapped back into crisp focus... and two lines of tiny dots whipped by the enemy battleship one at a time. Stockton and Timmons had their squadrons in single file lines of attack, about one thousand kilometers apart. One ship from each of the two forces passed *Vaillant* every three seconds, loosing two, perhaps three laser blasts before they passed.

Barron watched his screen, waiting for damage assessments to begin flowing in. It was all guesswork, the AI's best estimate of what each hit had accomplished. Virtually every shot connected, a testament to the skill and experience of the pilots involved. But most of them struck the battleship's armor, the tiny lasers carried by the interceptors too weak to significantly penetrate the protected areas of *Vaillant*'s hull. Timmons had managed to score a hit where the enemy ship's hull had been breached. Barron knew that laser would have torn through the fragile interior of the Union vessel, but whether it would cause serious damage depended on its location.

He watched, waiting for any signs that *Vaillant* had been badly damaged…reduction in thrust, plumes of air and liquids blasting out into space. But there was nothing. The enemy just kept approaching, accelerating at a constant rate and firing its heavy guns.

"Thirty seconds until secondaries are in range. All gunnery stations report ready to fire."

"Very well…fire as soon as…"

"Captain…" Fritz's voice reverberated in his headset. "…I don't know how, but we've got the primaries online." A brief pause. "At least I think they're online. I've got the power conduits open full if you want to try to crash energize and fire."

Barron leaned back in his chair. *At least I think they're online.* The words repeated again and again in his head. Fritzie was the best engineer he'd ever known…but she was very precise. And her words meant exactly what they said. If she told him she wasn't sure, that meant she wasn't sure.

He felt a rush of indecision, a rare uncertainty. Should he charge up the main guns? If they were actually functional, and if the enemy didn't manage to knock them out again…or the reactor, or the power lines…just maybe he would get in a close-range shot that would cripple his enemy. But if he had the secondaries stand down for several more minutes, and the primaries were unable to fire, his ship and crew were as good as dead.

"Belay that fire order. Charge the primaries." He spit out the command, feeling a wave of uncertainty even as he did. But there was no time to deliberate. He had to make a choice, and he went with his gut. If the primaries came through, he had some hope of getting out of the fight in something close to operable condition. And he had to take that chance.

"Primaries charging, Captain." A short pause. "Sir, Lieutenant Federov reports Red squadron is engaging approaching enemy fighters."

"Very well, Lieutenant." Barron made sure his voice was deep, that the uncertainty he felt stayed deep in his mind. His people needed to believe he was in total control.

"Captain, we've got Yellow squadron armed with torpedoes

and ready to go." It was Travis on his headset. Her voice was hoarse, and the sounds of chaos in the bay were loud in the background.

Barron paused. He had no interceptors to escort the bombers. *If they run into enemy fighters they could be wiped out...*

He looked at the main screen, at the bright red bar that showed the primaries' charging status. *More than halfway...maybe we can do without the bombers...*

But even as the thought went through his mind, he felt the words coming out of his mouth. "Launch, Commander. You have one minute before we fire the primaries."

"Roger that, sir. Commencing launch operations now."

Barron felt the catapults sending the first four bombers into space. He knew there had been no choice, not really. The primaries had been a gamble, Stockton's fighter strike had been a gamble. He couldn't hold back anything now, no tactic or action that could be the difference between victory and defeat.

The floor under his feet vibrated again, another four of Yellow squadron's ships launching. Even as he counted the seconds between launches, his eyes were fixed on the status bar for the primaries.

Dauntless shuddered again, yet another hit. Barron could tell this one had impacted directly amidships, and his breath caught in his throat as he waited, his gaze locked on the bright red bar of light. The next few seconds stretched out agonizingly, as he watched to see if the primaries were still receiving the massive flow of power from the reactors...or it that last shot had severed some critical connection.

Yes!

He could see the indicator still moving. Just another few seconds and the massive guns would be ready to fire. He hoped. The unusual uncertainty in Fritz's report still gnawed at his mind.

He slapped his hand down on the comm controls. "Primary gun crews, this is the captain. I want you constantly monitoring and updating your firing solutions." He paused, just for a second. "You've got to hit," he said. He realized as he did that his people always gave their best, that the very statement was unfair in its essence. But then he repeated himself. "You *have* to hit."

"Understood, sir." The gunner's voice was serious. There was no doubt the man knew what was riding on his crew's performance over the next thirty seconds or so. "We'll get it done, Captain." The strain in the gunnery officer's voice was a testament to just how much pressure he felt.

Barron closed the line, even as he watched the readout hit maximum charge. The guns were ready, at least they were if Fritz's repairs held. He sat stone still, amid the near silence of the bridge. He knew every eye in the large control center was fixed on him, every veteran officer there frozen in place, drawing deep and worried breaths.

He glanced at the cluster of yellow dots, the bomber squadron he'd just launched. They were clear of *Dauntless* and on their way to the enemy. *If* they got past the enemy fighters, and *if* they made it to *Vaillant*, they might cripple or destroy the Union battleship. But Barron knew it would likely be too late to save his ship, that any such attack would be a skeletal hand from the grave, rising to strike the enemy in one last act of vengeance.

No, if the battle is to be won now, it will be Fritzie and the gunners down in the fire control center…

He hesitated, just for an instant, feeling a strange reluctance to give the order. If his people fired and missed, their chance of surviving the battle would drop massively. The same if he gave the fire order and the guns failed to respond, if Fritz had missed some malfunction. He waited, for a brief passing second, savoring the hope the shot would succeed. Then he sucked in a deep breath and took hold of himself, banishing the fears and weaknesses he didn't have time for.

He looked across the bridge at Darrow, wishing once again, unfairly perhaps, that it was Travis there waiting for his command.

"Fire."

Chapter Fifteen

Command Center
Fleet Base Grimaldi
Orbiting Krakus II

"I want those revised transit orders ready in ten minutes, Commander. And send a communique to the shipyards at Gravis. *Honorable* and *Indomitable* are to be released at once for return to duty."

"Yes, sir." The logistics officer was clearly stretched close to his limit. Striker had been at the fleet's main forward base for less than twelve hours, but he'd hit like a typhoon, blasting out a seemingly unending series of orders and demands for information.

"Any word yet from Tantor?" Admiral Van Striker was on edge too, but he carried the burden of knowledge in a much deeper way than his subordinates. The various specialists who staffed the fleet's main forward base tended to focus on their own specific areas of expertise, tracking enemy movements or fleet logistics. Striker was thinking about all of it, every second.

"Negative, sir. The last report stated that Commodore Isaacson was expecting an enemy attack at any time."

Striker nodded sharply and stood where he was. Tantor was the next place the enemy would hit, Striker was sure of it. At least it was the logical target if this offensive was the real thing and not some kind of deception or sick Union strategy to "bleed its enemy white." Tantor was a choke point, a system with connections to four other Confederation systems, each of them leading to strategically crucial locations. If the enemy took Tantor, they would be two transits away from Krakus, which was the next vital nexus they'd have to seize to threaten the Iron Belt and the Core.

If Isaacson was defeated, Striker knew he'd be under immense pressure to abandon Grimaldi base. He looked around at the officers at their stations. They'd fled once before during the initial Union onslaught, and he couldn't imagine the blow to morale a second evacuation would cause. It was a miracle that Grimaldi even still remained. Admiral Winston had not ordered the base destroyed when he'd had to order the retreat, probably because he'd convinced himself he would take it back in short order. Even more amazingly, the Union forces had failed to scuttle the massive orbital platform when they'd been forced to withdraw, a clear deviation from their standard doctrine.

Somebody went out the airlock for that one…

That was two close calls for Grimaldi, but there wouldn't be a third. Striker hated the idea of abandoning the fleet's main operations center, but if he was forced to do it, one thing was absolutely certain. He'd leave nothing behind for the enemy but dust and plasma.

"Admiral, shuttle Omicron has just landed." The officer paused for a second. "You asked to be notified, sir."

"Very well," Striker replied. The added explanation wasn't surprising. He'd specifically told the officer to advise him when the ship landed. No one else on Grimaldi knew that shuttle Omicron was anything but a routine courier ship, and certainly not that Gary Holsten, head of Confederation Intelligence, was its primary cargo.

"I will be in my quarters," Striker said abruptly. He walked across the control center, pausing at the bank of lifts and turning back for a few seconds. "If any reports come through from Tantor, any at all, advise me immediately. I don't care if it's a battle report or a requisition for cleaning supplies."

"Yes, sir. Understood."

Striker turned and stepped into the small car, reaching out and punching one of the keys on the control panel instead of simply telling the AI where he was going. His quarters were on level four, but he had a stop planned on the way...though it was just about as out of the way as possible.

He stood quietly as the lift moved down, past level four, all the way to the shuttle bays, more than five hundred meters below his quarters. The doors finally opened, revealing a massive deck, filled with more than a dozen small craft, shuttles, freight carriers, and fighters from one of the squadrons tasked with defending the fleet base. There was a background level of activity, ships being loaded and unloaded, and service teams working on the fighters. A single man stood in the forefront, alone, waiting quietly, his eyes focused straight ahead.

"Gary, I'm glad you could come." Striker stepped out of the elevator and extended his hand.

"There was no choice, Van. You know that." Gary Holsten took a step forward and grasped the fleet admiral's hand. There were all sorts of protocols for how two such lofty personages were expected to greet each other and converse, but the two had worked closely together over the past six months, and they'd both agreed to dispense with the formality, especially when they were alone.

The intelligence chief and the admiral had collaborated on a number of projects, including the perpetration of a massive fraud that had put Striker in command of the fleet and Admiral Winston out to pasture. It had been done solely out of concern for the Confederation, a move born in desperation during the darkest moments of the war, but that hadn't made it any less risky. The results had been extremely beneficial for the Confederation, and Striker's offensive—a move Winston would never have dared to make—had hit the Union just as the effects of the destruction of their supply base had reached their forward formations. In one move, Striker had driven the enemy forces back almost to the prewar borders, a situation that had held for six months of bitter stalemate. Until now.

"I hope you have more insight into what's happening than I

do, Gary. I'm afraid the enemy's actions make very little sense... unless there's something we don't know. And all the 'somethings' I can think of are quite bad for us."

"Is there a 'Supply Two' base out there somewhere? That *is* what you want to ask me, isn't it?"

Striker hesitated, looking for a few seconds as though he was going to deny Holsten's statement, or at least expand on it. But then he simply said, "Yes."

"That's a question I'd love to be able to answer for you, Van..." Holsten paused and then gestured toward the lift. "Why don't we head back to your quarters? I'm sure the security on Grimaldi is top of the line, but I'd feel better if we were behind a closed door instead of out in the middle of a landing bay. I'd bet there are Union spies on this station, despite our best efforts to root them out."

Striker nodded. "Of course, you're right." He turned and stepped into one of the cars, waiting for Holsten to follow before he said, "Deck four."

The two men were silent as the car moved quickly upward. The door opened onto the fourth level corridor, and Striker stepped out, turning left and walking about thirty meters before stopping in front of a silvery metal door. "Open," he said. The door slid open, and he gestured for Holsten to enter, then he followed after the intelligence chief.

"Lights." Striker walked across the large room. The fleet admiral's quarters were massive by the standards that usually applied in space. Striker was the fleet's senior commander, and Grimaldi was a fortress and an enormous base, not a ship. Still, the admiral had been a little stunned when he'd first set eyes on the suite of rooms. "Whoever designed Grimaldi was looking to kiss up to the admiral," he said, sounding a little embarrassed about the opulence of his quarters.

"Who wouldn't want to kiss up to the fleet admiral?" Holsten smiled, briefly at least. The situation they were together to discuss was a grave and dangerous one, and Striker knew the stress Holsten was under, mostly because he was under it too. "You deserve every square centimeter, Van. Your victories saved the Confederation."

"Most likely I would have led the fleet to its final annihilation, had I not had unexpected help. We both know Captains Barron and Eaton were the real heroes."

"The Confederation is large enough to have three heroes... more even, if accomplishments warrant. I gambled on you, Van, if you will recall, and your success repaid me. Not only by saving the Confederation, but by doing so in such a decisive manner as to make it politically impossible for the Senate to come after me. Presented with the choice of 'blaming' me for the actions that led to victory or taking credit themselves, they chose to pat themselves on the back instead. They backdated more than one resolution that day."

Striker just nodded. "Anyway, we're alone, Gary. So, have a seat..." He gestured toward a large sectional sofa. "...and tell me, *do* they have another mobile supply base?"

"I wish I *could* tell you," the spy said softly. "But the truth is, I don't know. The economists, the number crunchers and analysts...they maintain it is absolutely impossible. They claim there's no possible way the Union had sufficient resources to construct another base of that size and cost." He stared at Striker, and there was doubt in his eyes. "But, of course, they're the same geniuses who had no inkling the enemy had the resources to build the first one...so we must at least allow for the possibility that our esteemed and highly educated colleagues don't know what the hell they're talking about."

Striker nodded, a small grin slipping out. He shared Holsten's disdain for highly credentialed "experts" with little real world experience to temper their conclusions. "So, you think they may have one?"

"Honestly, I don't see how either. They put the original one past us...a brilliant piece of intelligence work, I have to admit. One that made me look like a fool. But over the past six months, we've gone a long way toward rebuilding our assets in the Union. They took us by surprise just before the outbreak of the war, purging a vast number of our agents. Now, we've started to see a greater flow of intel."

"And you haven't gotten wind of any new supply base?"

"Quite the contrary," Holsten said. "We have gotten multiple leads on one."

Striker's face went white. "You have?"

"That doesn't necessarily mean anything, Van. You have no idea how much data we go through, and how little of it actually proves to be useful."

"But if you're getting leads about a mobile supply base…"

"We're almost getting too many leads."

"Too many? What does that mean?"

"It means maybe they do have another base as big and capable as the one Captain Barron's expedition destroyed, or even one of much smaller capability." He paused, looking right at Striker. "Or maybe they have nothing at all…and they just want us to believe they do."

"What would they gain by that? Why launch such a costly offensive if they don't have the ability to sustain it?"

"As a diversion, perhaps?"

"A diversion? For what purpose?"

"That *is* the question, isn't it? Perhaps they're trying to take our attention away from the Badlands."

"They would launch an assault across the entire front just to distract us from the Badlands?"

"What would you do to gain control over an ancient warship, one with technology far beyond anything we have now?"

"So, you think the intel we found is accurate? That Captain Barron is actually going to find an artifact of such power? You did just mention how much useless information flows through your organization."

"I don't know. It's true that only a small percentage of the raw data we analyze leads to anything important. But the lead regarding the artifact seemed credible—enough that I still believe it was worth sending *Dauntless*. That means it's definitely possible that this entire offensive is nothing but an elaborate diversion.

"And it's possible it's a real attack, an attempt to break us before ships start rolling off the Iron Belt production lines. Perhaps they've managed to come up with some kind of logistical scheme to support their fleet. We must be prepared to hold them back, keep them out of the heart of the Confederation."

"Yes, you're right. We must keep them from reaching the Iron Belt worlds. If they're able to destroy our new ships half-built in their spacedocks…" Holsten's voice trailed off. His meaning was clear.

"On the other hand, if you were correct earlier, if the Union is going to such lengths to take our attention away from the Badlands, we can be sure they've got more than one battleship there. So, even if Captain Barron finds what we sent him to locate…"

"He may be overwhelmed." Holsten shook his head. "In that case, *Dauntless* would be destroyed, and the enemy would gain control over whatever is out there."

"So, what do we do? Do we send reinforcements to Captain Barron? I had planned to dispatch *Triumphant* and *Aspirant*, as we'd discussed…but…"

"But?"

"*Aspirant* was destroyed in the initial Union onslaught. And I held *Triumphant* back to support the line."

"So, what can you spare?"

"Nothing, really. I'm not even sure I can hold the line with everything I have."

"So, if we assume the Union attack is a diversion to take our attention off the Badlands, and we dispatch a task force there… if the assault turns out to be real, we may weaken ourselves to the point where we can't hold."

Striker nodded. "And if we don't send aid to *Dauntless*, and the Union invasion *is* nothing more than a deception, we could be doing exactly what they want. We could end up sitting here and watching them seize a weapon of almost unimaginable power."

"If it even exists."

Striker had a pained look on his face. "We could go around in this circle forever. But we believed it existed enough to send Captain Barron and his people to go find it. What of them? Do we abandon them, leave them to be overwhelmed by the enemy?"

"It's as upsetting to me as it is to you...but Captain Barron volunteered for the mission."

"Volunteered?" Striker shook his head. "We may have put on a little farce to that effect, but you know as well as I do there was no way for Barron to decline, not with both of us asking him to go. He took it as an order, no matter what you and I might have pretended. And we promised to send him reinforcements."

"There are, what? A thousand crew on *Dauntless*?"

"Just under. Why?"

"What are the losses along the front since the enemy launched this offensive?"

Striker frowned. He knew where Holsten was going, and he didn't like it. Cold-blooded logic had always been difficult for him, despite his reputation as a fighting admiral. "Considerable."

"My last report has them at over ten thousand, just in the first few days. I have no doubt you have more up to date figures than I do. And none of that includes the thousands—millions—of people living on the worlds we're being forced to abandon." He paused, and Striker could see the pain in his expression. "Or the billions on the worlds still behind us.

"I admire Captain Barron as much as you, Van...he is a credit to his famous family and a true hero in his own right. But we have to make a decision based on far more than one man, or even the crew of one ship. If this is *not* a diversion, it could mean total defeat. Millions dead, billions more enslaved." His eyes were focused on Striker's. "The fate of *Dauntless* and her crew are irrelevant in our analysis. We can only consider the military situation, and the likelihood that there really *is* an artifact of immense power out there. But even if there is, if the line collapses, if the enemy fleets advance into the Iron Belt and the Core...they will capture or destroy the ships under construction...and the Confederation will fall. Regardless of whether there was an ancient ship out there and we sent ships to seize it, it would be too late."

Striker sat silently for a moment. Finally, a look of acquiescence came over his face. "So, the question remains, does the enemy really have a supply base, or is this all an elaborate deception? And what do we do about it?"

"Yes, I'm afraid so. Or, more to the point, if it is real, can you stop them if you send a task force to the Badlands?"

Striker felt cold. "Gary, I'm not sure I can stop them anyway, even if I don't detach any ships. If they can sustain this offensive…we're in trouble."

Holsten frowned, and he took a deep breath. "Do we bet the Confederation that they're bluffing?"

Striker shook his head, not in answer to the question, but simply the manifestation of his uncertainty. He hated the idea of abandoning *Dauntless*. And the thought of the enemy gaining ancient technology was terrifying…but if the Union offensive was real…

The comm buzzed. "Yes," Striker snapped, leaning toward the small unit.

"Admiral, we have received a report from Tantor."

He could hear from the officer's tone. The news was bad. "Yes?"

"Commodore Isaacson is dead, sir." A pause. "His task force is all but destroyed."

Striker felt as though he'd been kicked in the stomach. *Isaacson dead? With most of his force?*

"The transmission advises the enemy is on the move, Admiral. They are coming this way."

To Grimaldi. Of course. If they can take or destroy the fleet base, we'll have to fall back from a dozen systems.

Striker turned and looked at Holsten.

"I think we have our answer," the intelligence chief said grimly. "We have to assume the enemy advance is real, and that they have the means to sustain it. We just can't take the chance. At least until we can stabilize the line. If there is going to be a battle here, it's one we can't lose. No matter what." He stared at the admiral. Striker had a horrified look on his face, but he began nodding his head in reluctant agreement.

"Captain Barron will have to manage on his own…somehow. At least until the fight here is done." Holsten looked as despondent as Striker, but there wasn't a hint of doubt in his voice.

"I agree," Striker said, sounding like death. "We must hold here. God help us…" He paused for a few seconds. "And God help Captain Barron."

Chapter Sixteen

CFS Dauntless
Z-107 System (Melatha)
Approaching Z-111 Transwarp link

"It's called Chrysallis. Informally, at least. It's officially designated as Z-111." Barron sat behind the metal desk in his office, trying to ignore the headache he'd had for a week now. The destruction of *Vaillant*, the victory over the Union's greatest vessel, should have been a cause for celebration. But the cost had been too high…and too personal this time. Discussing minutia like the names of Badlands systems was an effort to keep his mind off things he'd rather not think about…and it had been a stunningly unsuccessful effort.

"Why two names?" Atara Travis sat across from him, trying to act normal, though he could see that she, too, was distracted by thoughts of recent events.

"Badlands systems are governed by international law, at least they're supposed to be. But the ambassadors and other gasbags move at a glacial pace. They managed to implement a numbering system for stars out there, and they're supposed to ratify names as they're submitted. But I suspect the whole thing's actual purpose is to justify a massive number of diplomats and their staffs semi-permanently assigned to the International Tribunal for Administration of Restricted Space. ITARS." He paused. "Amusing, isn't it, that the names governments give to their webs of appendages all seem to form pronounceable acronyms?"

Barron was trying hard to keep his mind off sickbay. He'd been down there half a dozen times, and Doc Weldon had told him the same thing again and again. He simply didn't know if Jake Stockton was going to make it or not.

"He'll pull through, Ty." Travis ignored the quip about governments and went right to the heart of what they were both thinking. Not that she didn't agree about the pointless nonsense produced by pompous bureaucrats…she suspected she was more critical even than Barron, and that was saying something.

Barron just nodded. Travis was smart, capable, the best first officer in the fleet. But blind faith was far from her greatest strength, and her attempt to reassure him about *Dauntless*'s star pilot was almost comically unsuccessful.

"We'll see, Atara." His thoughts drifted back to the final stages of the battle with *Vaillant*. Commander Fritz had gotten the primaries back online…and she'd managed to keep them functioning for two shots before her rushed repairs gave out. It had been a near-miracle that she'd managed to repair the main guns so quickly, and it had equalized the battle, even given *Dauntless* the edge for a few minutes. But then the fight became a slugfest between the two ships…and it went on long enough for the fighter squadrons to come about and make a second strafing run.

Stockton had led his people in, again ignoring the enemy fighters—more of them in space now—driving to point blank range before firing. The veteran pilot had placed his shot precisely, right into a massive hull breach where *Dauntless*'s primaries had hit the Union ship…and the rest of the Blues and Eagles had followed him in. By the time they were done, the pride of the Union navy was crippled, the battle all but decided. But Stockton had taken a hit from one of the vessel's defensive turrets.

He'd managed to get back to *Dauntless*—Barron still couldn't figure out how—but then he'd had to land his stricken ship. Barron had watched his ace pilot make more than one difficult landing…and squeeze through close call after close call. But this time Stockton's skill and luck had failed to meet the challenge. He'd lost control of the fighter as he approached the bay, and his breaking thrusters failed. He came in like a bullet, and slammed into the far bulkhead. His disintegrating fighter had burst into flames.

The struggling fire crews worked feverishly to put out the conflagration and get to the trapped pilot. Stockton was still alive, but almost every centimeter of his body was burned, so badly in some places that the flesh was simply gone, nothing but exposed bone and blackened remains of charred muscle.

He'd been unconscious—thankfully—when they rushed him to sickbay. Jake Stockton would have died almost immediately if anyone else save Stu Weldon had been *Dauntless*'s chief surgeon. The skilled medical officer acted quickly, proving himself once again to be a member of the crew on par with Stockton himself, and Fritz and Travis. He performed emergency surgery, and then he put Stockton into a cryo-tube, placing the wounded man in near-stasis. His report had been blunt, straightforward. If they got the patient back to a base with regeneration capability, he had a chance. But he could only last so long in cryo-preservation. Weldon had left the definition of "so long" frustratingly vague.

It had taken everything Barron had to resist the urge to turn around and head right back to Dannith. To save his friend. But duty was there, as always, overruling personal feelings. Images of ancient vessels slipped into his mind, massive engines of death out in front of the Union fleet, burning Confederation planets to cinders. He'd realized almost immediately. There was no turning back. Not this time. He wasn't sure what he would find when his ship arrived at the designated system, but he knew he had to follow through. Stockton would just have to hang on…somehow. He felt grim, his logical mind telling him there was no way his friend could last long enough. But he'd learned never to count "Raptor" Stockton out, not completely.

He looked up, realizing he and Travis had been sitting quietly for several minutes. He felt like he should say something, but no words came. A feeling of guilt came on him. He was particularly fond of Stockton, despite the wild pilot's tendency to push orders to—and sometimes beyond—their limits, but he reminded himself that almost seventy of his people had died in the fight against *Vaillant*. He'd spent hours reorganizing the duty rosters, struggling to keep his stations fully manned despite the loss of so many veteran spacers. They deserved his thoughts too, though there was little he could do for the dead.

"I wonder what we'll find," he finally said, as much to break the silence as for any other reason. He knew Atara had no more idea than he did if there really was a great ancient artifact waiting for them, or if this had all been a waste of time. A very costly waste.

"I don't know, Ty. You are far more familiar with the Badlands than I am. Do you have a gut feel?"

Barron just looked back at her for a few seconds. He was a voracious reader, at least when things like war and duty didn't lay waste to his private time. He'd read everything he could find on the Cataclysm, but that had proven to be a sparse array of offerings, even for a man of his resources. There was no doubt that the empire had possessed technology far in advance of the Confederation's…but that didn't mean there was a great war machine waiting in the next system.

"I don't know either, Atara. The admiral and Holsten wouldn't have sent us here unless they at least had strong reason to believe it was a possibility. They were spooked by that translation. What is a 'planet-killer' anyway?" He hadn't shared the designation with his people, only with Travis. "Just a scary name for a powerful weapon? Or is it literal? Could there be something out there powerful enough to destroy entire worlds?"

"I guess we'll find out," she answered, just before the comm unit buzzed.

"Yes," Barron said."

"Approaching transit point, Captain. Estimated time to jump, fifteen minutes." It was Darrow's voice.

"Very well…I'll be right there." He looked over at his first officer. "Well, I guess it's time we go find out." He stood up, moving slowly around the desk. "And see if it was worth everything it cost us."

And whatever else it's going to cost before we're done.

*   *   *

Stara Sinclair sat quietly next to the cryotube, in exactly the same place she'd spent virtually every off-duty hour. It was a violation of regs, of course, but she knew Doctor Weldon didn't have the heart to make her leave. He'd begged her to get some sleep, and he'd demanded that she eat something, even making that a condition of allowing her to remain, but otherwise he'd let her be.

She had cried for the first three days, her normal granite resolve failing her, but now there were no more tears. There was just emptiness, and a cold grief the likes of which she'd never imagined. Stockton wasn't dead, not yet, and she tried to hang onto the hope that he would survive, that he would recover and come back to her. But she didn't believe it, and on some level, she knew she was already beginning to mourn him.

She hated herself for giving up, but she'd always been cynical, considering those who could blindly believe in things to be fools. She knew just how badly hurt her lover was, and also that his survival depended on getting back to Confederation space as quickly as possible. And that wasn't possible, not now.

"No change?"

She knew the voice, of course, but it still took a few seconds for her mind to focus, for familiarity to assert itself.

"No, Commander…no change." She spoke softly, almost emotionlessly. Her head hadn't moved, and her eyes remained fixed on the tube in front of her. "Dr. Weldon said there wouldn't be any…not unless…"

Kyle Jamison moved alongside her. "I've known Jake for a long time, Stara. He's a fighter."

"Oh, I know…he's a fighter. Fighting is his life, and maybe now the end of it." She was mostly overcome with sadness and worry, but there was anger there too, and it was starting to boil over. "How many times has he done something like this? Again and again...he acts like danger can't touch him, like he's indestructible. I thought for sure he'd never make it when he left to deliver the communique to fleet command, but there he was, waiting for us when we got back. But his luck had to run out..."

"It hasn't run out yet, Stara."

"How long do you think we're going to be out here, chasing whatever we're chasing? Whatever chance he has, it's back at Dannith. Dr. Weldon was clear about that. Time is running out, Kyle, and we're still heading in the opposite direction."

She turned to look at Jamison, one of the few people on *Dauntless*—or anywhere—she'd let see her red, puffy eyes and tear-stained cheeks. "Why is he like this, Kyle? Why did he always take so many risks?" The past tense that slipped out of her lips.

"Stara...that's how he is. But, let me tell you something not many people know. He isn't nearly as crazy as he wants everybody to think. Yes, he's aggressive, and he seems almost insane to those who watch him. But the truth is...he's just that good, Stara. He looks suicidal to most people, because they can't imagine pulling off the stunts he does. But he *does* pull them off. That's the point. People can't comprehend the reach of his ability." He paused for a few seconds. "I consider myself an accomplished pilot, but I can't fly like he does. No one can."

"Except Dirk Timmons," Stara said, almost smiling for an instant as she remembered Stockton's expression when they'd first run into his old rival in *Dauntless*'s corridors.

Jamison nodded. "And that's why they were always such rivals. We all wondered what terrible wrong was the origin of their mutual dislike. But there was nothing...except each one of them had always been unquestionably the best, until they met each other."

Stara did smile this time. It didn't last, but she was surprised to find that talking about Stockton made her feel better. A little, at least.

"I think Jake is the better of the two, not that I ever told *him* that."

Stara nodded. Then she turned back toward the long canister. It looked too much like a coffin for her tastes, though she knew the device was keeping Stockton alive.

"Thank you, Kyle." She was surprised how much talking to Jamison had helped. She wasn't sure if it was real, or if she was just letting herself buy into empty hope, but she knew she wasn't ready to give up. And she had been a few minutes before.

"He loves you, Stara. As gregarious as he can be in a crowd, he's a closed book to most people…but he's like a brother to me. And what he feels for you is the real thing. I've never seen him as crazy about anyone." He paused. "He'll fight Stara, harder than you or I could imagine. He'll do it because that's what he is. And he'll do it to get back to you. Don't give up on him, not now."

Stara just nodded. She could feel the tears coming on again, but she also felt better, stronger. Jamison was right…giving up on Stockton now would be wrong, whatever her cynicism told her. She owed it to him to believe, at least for a while longer. If he could fight, she could fight…and that was exactly what she was going to do.

* * *

"Transwarp insertion in thirty seconds, Captain. All systems green." Travis's voice echoed across the bridge. She'd been a human being in Barron's office, alone there with her friend. She'd voiced her uncertainties, even her fears. But now she was back on the bridge, *Dauntless*'s solid steel executive officer once again, and the very tone of her voice stiffened the spines of those who heard it.

"Very well, Commander. Proceed." Barron admired his first officer, and he nodded to himself, a brief recognition of his good fortune in having her as his second in command. She hadn't been well-known when she'd first transferred to *Excalibur*, second officer to his first, but she was now. *Dauntless*'s adventures had created recognition, and one had to go no farther than her captain to discover that Atara Travis had been vital in helping secure those great victories. Barron had credited her in every report, given her the full due she deserved. He suspected every captain in the fleet envied him, and he'd sworn to himself that he'd never forget everything that she did.

Barron braced for the transit, wondering as he did just what his people would find in Z-111. He'd taken the mission seriously—there was no other way to approach an operation assigned by both the top admiral in the service *and* the head of Confederation intelligence. But he wasn't sure he'd ever really believed he'd find what they'd sent him here to discover. An ancient warship? Intact, or close to it? It all seemed too crazy.

But now he realized his stomach was twisted in knots, his mind going over every detail of what he knew. He realized that for all his skepticism, he *did* expect to find something. Or at least he considered it a significant possibility.

He had the crew of *Pegasus* onboard, their ship docked to *Dauntless*, during the entire voyage…even through the combat with *Vaillant*. Somehow, fortune had smiled on their vessel, and it had escaped damage entirely.

He'd assigned them quarters and seen that their needs were met, but he hadn't spoken to them yet. He didn't think much of the kinds of rogues who scoured the Badlands for ancient trinkets, and since he knew he wouldn't believe anything they said anyway, he didn't see anything to be gained by interviewing them. They'd requested permission to come to the bridge when they'd first come aboard, but he'd ordered them confined to the immediate vicinity of their quarters. He'd heard hardly a peep from them since the fight with *Vaillant*. He didn't doubt they'd seen danger before, but he'd have bet almost anything that none of them had been in a battle like the one *Dauntless* had just fought.

He knew Travis had spoken with them, and of course, he had reviewed their scanning records. They were convincing, he had to admit. Still, it was nothing but data, and he knew data could be easily faked. Some things simply had to be seen to be believed…but, nevertheless, through all the doubts, he realized that in his gut he did believe there was something in the Chrysallis system.

He felt *Dauntless* slip into the transwarp link, the strange alternate reality of hyperlight travel. It was uncomfortable, as always, and he felt disoriented…but he managed to cling to his thoughts, to his imaginings of what was waiting for them.

"Transitioning to normal space," Travis shouted. Movement to and from alternate space tended to affect the senses in strange ways, and spacers often came out whispering or screaming at the top of their lungs. "All systems report green, Captain," she said a few seconds later, her voice returning to normal.

"Active scanners, Commander. Full power." There was no point trying to hide, and no time to play the game of cutting power and sticking to passive scans. Whatever was here, Barron had to know, and he had to know as quickly as possible.

"Active scanners online, Captain."

"You've got the specified coordinates, Commander. Let's see what's there."

"We've got the planet, sir, but we're too far out to pick up orbiting structures."

Barron glanced at the display. The planet wasn't far from the transwarp link. *Dauntless* could be in range in a matter of minutes. "Engage the engines…5g thrust. Take us in."

"Yes, Captain. Thrust commencing now."

Chapter Seventeen

Inside Abandoned Spacecraft
System Z-111 (Chrysallis)
Deep Inside the Quarantined Zone ("The Badlands")
309 AC

"We came in right here...you can see where the umbilical connected." Lafarge gestured toward the spot where *Pegasus* had docked with the ancient vessel, and the rough patch her people had left behind when they'd escaped. She wasn't sure what she was going to do now that she was back aboard the ancient craft. She'd pretended they had broken her, that hunger and thirst—and most of all, the threat to put a bullet in Vig Merrick's head—had driven her beyond endurance. She'd been pretty sure they were bluffing with the threat to kill her friend. They only had two hostages, and they weren't likely to kill either one of them until they got what they wanted. Lafarge's piteous appeal for them to spare her friend was a bit of acting, as were her promises to lead her tormentors to the crucial sections of the ancient ship.

The truth was, it would take more than a few beatings and a little hunger to defeat her. Even more than murdering her friend in front of her. She knew very well they would never let either of them go once they had all they needed. Giving them what they wanted, making herself useless to them, would be a death sentence for both of them. She was sure of that.

There was just one problem. She *was* useless to them. *Pegasus* had docked right before the Union ship had arrived, and she and Vig had just begun to explore the great artifact. She had seen a good portion of the ship when she'd been trying to evade the FRs hunting them down, but there hadn't been time to study anything in any detail. Her concern then had been evading the troopers trying to hunt her down, and she'd hardly noticed anything about her surroundings, save places that looked like likely hiding spots.

She shuddered as she thought of the Union's clone soldiers. She'd heard of them before, of course, but she'd never seen them before now, much less faced them as adversaries. It wasn't so much their combat capabilities, though she didn't doubt those were substantial. They just seemed so cold, so…alien.

"Down this corridor. That's where we found it. I'm not sure it's the control center, but it looked like an important place, with at least a dozen workstations." She knew damned well she wasn't leading them to any kind of critical location. It was some kind of lab, she guessed. But this entire exercise was about wasting time…and once they realized the location wasn't a critical one, she'd suggest another. And then another. She would lead them all over the vessel, from one useless spot to the next, at least for as long as they continued to believe she knew more than she did. Then…well, there was no use worrying about that until the time came…

"The hall is very long, several kilometers, at least. It looks like there was a system of ship's cars to move around the vessel, but I have no idea if it's still operative or how to use it." Actually, she knew very well they were not functional, at least not the ones she'd found. But the slower she gave out information, the better.

"That is no concern, Captain Lafarge. We will walk." Laussanne's voice had become an almost unbearable irritant to her, the nasal whininess mixed with intolerable arrogance almost more than she could handle. She'd always had a temper, and she was usually quick to act on it. But the Union commissar was flanked by FR guards, and her hands were shackled together. Now wasn't the time, but she promised herself she'd kill the bastard the instant she got the chance. *If* she got the chance. Things weren't looking good right now.

She'd passed the time in captivity—between interrogation sessions, that is—imagining herself cutting Laussanne into quivering chunks, staring into his eyes with a smile as his life slipped away. But she would settle for any opportunity. Even a quick shot to the head would be satisfying, though she had to concede it would be disappointing to miss the chance to watch the bastard suffer.

She led them down the corridor. She'd chosen it because it was long, and would take considerable time to traverse. *You're ignorant scum. You have to believe I know something, because you're lost yourselves. You think the answer to every problem is beating cooperation out of someone...or worse...*

She took a bit of solace from her guess that things would go badly for them all if they returned home empty handed.

But that's not likely...not unless the others bring back help...

She wondered again what had happened to her crew. Had they made it back to Confederation space? Had they been able to get help? She had no definitive evidence that they'd escaped at all, but the guards and Laussanne had been careless with their own words. She had excellent hearing, and she was always paying attention. And her captors were clearly concerned about time, about learning what they needed about the artifact as quickly as possible.

She wondered for an instant if, having escaped, her people would return. Would they take the risk of contacting the navy, knowing full well their activities were illegal in the Confederation? Would they really try to persuade the authorities to send help? Their kind—and hers—usually avoided the government forces any way they could.

She pushed the thought from her mind. Her crew was loyal, and they deserved better than her doubts. And when they reached Dannith and delivered *Pegasus*'s scans of the monstrous ancient vessel—and the Union frigate that had taken control of it—the Confederation forces would respond. They couldn't afford to ignore that kind of evidence. They'd have to check, even if they suspected it was fabricated.

She had to buy time, and the best way to do that was to get away from her captors, to find a place to hide, and make them track her down again. She wished Laussanne had brought Vig as well, but the fool wasn't that stupid. Still, if she managed to get away, it would make her friend safer. They wouldn't dare risk killing or seriously injuring their sole captive. As long as they had the two of them, she knew there was still a chance they might actually kill one.

"How long is this corridor?" Laussanne's fatigue was clear in his voice.

She frowned. If it had been possible to think less of the Union political officer, she would have. "I told you it was a long way. I was on the run last time I was here, as you know. I'm afraid I didn't count my steps." She paused then added, "It's at least another kilometer, perhaps two."

She actually had no idea of the distance to the end of the hallway—she hadn't come this far earlier, having turned off into one of the compartments along the way. She'd decided the lab she'd been leading them to wouldn't be convincing enough, that she'd take a chance and see what lay farther down the hallway. And she enjoyed the expression on the commissar's face as she told him he had two more kilometers to go.

She'd been watching, waiting for a chance to make her move. She liked her odds in any straight up fight with Laussanne. She was sure she could put the pompous ass down. She figured even money she could take the junior officer next to him too. But there were two FRs following about three meters behind. They carried assault rifles, and their faces were grim masks, showing no signs of any emotion at all. She figured she had just about zero chance of taking them both out as well as Laussanne and his aide. At least without some kind of distraction.

"Commander Laussanne..."

She heard the voice on Laussanne's comm unit. It was faint from where she was, but she could just make out the words.

"Stop," the commissar commanded. She did as he demanded, trying to look like she was sullen, angry...but actually, she was listening carefully.

"Laussanne here...what is it. I hope it was worth interrupting my..."

"Commissar, our scanners are picking up a Confederation battleship. They have entered from the Z-107 portal, sir." Lafarge wasn't getting every word, but she heard enough to piece together what was happening.

They did it! They brought back a Confederation battleship!

"...heading directly toward the planet, Commissar."

She saw the fear on Laussanne's face. She had to fight a rush of giddiness at the cold terror in her nemesis's eyes.

You gutless coward...it's one thing to face helpless prisoners, to smack them around and act tough. But now you're in trouble...

"You look like you're going to piss yourself, Laussanne." The words just blurted out, before she could rethink them. It was an impulse, a sudden plan with inadequate consideration, but just maybe, if she could get him mad enough while he was already scared and confused...

"*What* did you say?" His words were sharp, angry. She figured she'd made him forget his fear, for a few seconds. But she was confident it would return.

"You heard me," she said, staring at the Union officer with cold intensity. "You couldn't stop my ship." She stared at the commissar's incredulous face. "Yes, I know they got away. I heard you talking about it. You've got a big mouth, you and your trained monkeys. And you wasted weeks, first trying to find me and then questioning me. Now, you're out of time. They're back...with a Confederation battleship." She smiled. "You're going to die, Laussanne...or you're going to spend the rest of your life in a Confederation prison."

"Shut up," he yelled, and he lunged toward her. She could see his balled-up fist coming, but she was much quicker. She ducked, and shoved her own shackled hands upward, hitting Laussanne right in the crotch. He screamed in pain and dropped hard with a thud. Lafarge had already leapt back to her feet, moving toward the junior officer. The man was fumbling for his sidearm, but she barreled into him, and the two of them fell to the floor. She heard the gun hit the deck, her eyes catching it as it skittered about a meter from where she lay.

She spun her head toward the officer. He was conscious, but he seemed dazed. She'd have felt better if she'd hit him again, just to make sure, but there was no time. She knew the FRs were there, that they'd react quickly...and she was well aware they were a far greater danger than Laussanne or his aide.

The pistol...that was her hope. She was betting on surprise, that the FR's would be caught unaware, that it would take them a few seconds to respond. Long enough for her to grab the gun...and kill them both.

She lurched forward. It was difficult, with her hands still shackled, but she jerked hard, and reached out toward the weapon. Then she felt a dull pain, something hitting her between the shoulder blades. Then again.

The FRs...

One of them was standing behind her. She could see his shadow on the wall. He'd hit her with his rifle butt. The other had moved around, and now he reached down and picked up the pistol. She'd known her attempted escape was a long shot, but she still felt a wave of despair. It wasn't the danger, or even the beatings, that wore her down. It was the captivity. She was used to her freedom, and she'd do anything, take any risk, to get it back.

The FR behind her grabbed her roughly and pulled her up, as the other one moved toward Laussanne, helping the still-groaning political officer to his feet. She could see the venom in Laussanne's expression, the promise of payback. But she knew there wasn't time now. Not with a Confederation battleship approaching.

"Commander Laussanne..." Lafarge could hear Pierre's voice again. Laussanne's comm unit had fallen when she'd attacked him, and it was lying on the floor. The political officer gestured for one of the FRs to pick it up.

Lazy sack of shit…

He grabbed it from the clone-soldier and put it to his face. "Captain Pierre…you are to debark all Foudre Rouge soldiers, fully armed and ready for battle. All superfluous crew as well, every man or woman you can spare and still fly *Chasseur*. I want them all armed. We have fleet units on the way, I am certain of that. We must hold this ship until they arrive."

"Understood, Commander."

"Once that is done, Captain, you are to take *Chasseur* and try to lead the enemy away from here, buy as much time as possible. You should have a speed advantage. If you can get them to follow you…those are hours gained for reinforcements to get here."

Lafarge wasn't an expert in Union command structures, but she knew there was an odd dynamic between a ship's captain and its political officer. Technically, the captain was still in command, but the political officer had significant power. As a practical matter, the commissar could relieve the captain by accusing him of disloyalty, and as a result, the political officer could effectively overrule the ship's military commander. Generally, she suspected, with unfortunate consequences, at least in a combat situation.

"Yes, Commander." Lafarge couldn't hear the captain's voice all that well, but she got enough to detect the resentment there, something she realized Laussanne was too arrogant to perceive.

The political officer turned toward one of the FRs. "Take her to the large room where we boarded. Watch her carefully, Sergeant." He glanced back at Lafarge, the hatred still bright in his eyes. "I'm not done with her yet."

"Sir!" the soldier snapped.

Lafarge had known that the Foudre Rouge were clones, created expressly as soldiers. Their accelerated childhoods were little more than training periods, and they were indoctrinated and conditioned their entire lives to obedience. Their sex drives were chemically suppressed, and they had no relationships, no spouses, no children. They served until they were no longer able to do so. But even Andromeda Lafarge, born a cynic and skeptical of virtually everything she'd ever seen, had a hard time believing the rumors that old and badly wounded soldiers were simply euthanized. That was a system so monstrous, not even her mind, one that immediately saw the dark side of everything, could wrap around it. Was it possible that the FRs were so effectively conditioned that they accepted such atrocities? That they still unquestioningly served those who treated them that way?

Laussanne turned and walked down the corridor, back the way they had come. A few seconds later, the soldier shoved her forward, extending his arm and pointing down the hallway. "Go," he said brusquely.

Brilliant conversationalist...

She hesitated for a few seconds, and the soldier pushed her again, harder this time. "Move," he commanded.

She took a deep breath and started down the corridor. The arrival of the Confederation ship had revived her hope. It was possible, likely that the Union soldiers would kill her, even if the Confederation forces managed to take control of the ship... but she was still better off than she had been. Now she had a chance.

Whether they killed her or not, she knew her people had made it back. She wasn't the type to open herself up to close relationships, but her people had been loyal to her, and she'd repaid that devotion with her own. She wasn't done yet...she'd do everything she could to escape, to disrupt things. But if she failed...she preferred to die in victory rather than defeat. And her people escaping, the Confederation taking control of the artifact...those were victories, whether she survived them or not.

She just hoped she had the chance to kill that pompous ass Laussanne, whatever else happened.

Chapter Eighteen

CFS Dauntless
Z-111 System (Chrysallis)
Approaching Z-111 Transwarp link

"It's a Union frigate, Captain. *Chevalier* class, one hundred forty thousand tons. Main armament two five hundred-twenty-five megawatt focused energy lasers. Secondary weapons, six double turreted two hundred megawatt pulse lasers. Crew..."

"Thank you, Commander." Barron interrupted gently. He was constantly amazed at the depths of information Travis stored in that vast and mysterious contraption she called her brain. It would have been yeoman's work for any first officer to look up and recite such a litany of details, but Barron knew—from past experience as well as present observation—that Atara Travis was not looking at any screen as she delivered her report, nor was she relying on anything pulled from *Dauntless*'s massive database.

"Red alert," Barron said. "Scramble Bl...Scarlett Eagle squadron." The Blues were always his default squadron in a tight spot, and as much as he'd wrestled with Jake Stockton's tendency to interpret orders...flexibly...he'd come to rely heavily on the ace pilot and his pack of veterans. But Stockton was down in sickbay, fighting for his life, and somehow it didn't seem right to send his people out without him, not when he only needed one squadron. And apart from Kyle Jamison, who commanded his entire strike force, Dirk Timmons was next in line. And the Eagles were damned near as good as the Blues. *As good*, some would say.

"Yes, Captain."

"I want all secondaries armed and ready to fire."

"Yes, sir…all gun crews report in position and ready. All weapons stations check out…green indicators across the board."

"Very well. Bring us toward the enemy ship." *Dauntless* was in surprisingly good condition, at least on the surface. All her systems were fully-operational, but Barron knew his ship was held together by one patch after another. Her current status spoke, as usual, of the extraordinary skill of Commander Fritz and her engineers…and this time of Jake Stockton as well. Barron understood why Stockton had led that second desperate attack against *Vaillant*. *Dauntless* might have won the fight anyway…the hits from her primaries had been extremely effective. But she would have been gutted in the extended fight. Stockton's run had ended the battle sooner, saving *Dauntless* countless hits. Barron would never have ordered his pilots to make that second attack…but Stockton, as usual, hadn't asked for permission. He'd just done it.

But this time he didn't come through miraculously unscathed.

Barron looked over at the display, at the enemy ship, of course, but also at the hulking thing right behind it. The smugglers had told the truth, their scanning data was accurate. They had indeed found an intact—more or less, at least—ancient ship of some kind. Barron couldn't tell exactly what it was yet, except that it dwarfed his own battleship.

Barron felt the thrust as his ship accelerated toward the artifact and the Union frigate positioned nearby. It was gentle, *Dauntless*'s dampeners absorbing most of the 5g of pressure generated by the battleship's massive engines. He watched as the range decreased…and then he saw movement.

"Captain, the frigate is running. Thrust at 10g…no, 12g."

"Pursue. Engines to full thrust."

"Yes sir."

Barron leaned back in his chair, anticipating the pressure he knew was coming. The dampeners were fully operational, but *Dauntless*'s engines blasting at full would overwhelm them. The battleship's maximum thrust was right around 11g, perhaps 12g if Fritz did her usual magic dance and pushed it right to the edge. But *Dauntless*'s force absorption capability maxed out around 7g.

He took a deep breath, exhaling just as the sensation of five times his body weight hit him. Then he turned his head slowly toward Lieutenant Darrow's station. "Transmit our ID, Lieutenant." His words were forced, and he stopped to take a tortured breath. "Clear channel. Advise the Union vessel we demand they cut their engines at once. They are to surrender, or we will open fire." Barron knew there was some bluff to his threat. The frigate was a light, fast ship…it could out-accelerate *Dauntless*. The enemy was within primary range, but Barron would have to cut thrust and wait several minutes while his main guns charged before he could fire. And all the while, the Union ship would be blasting away at 12g. Almost 14g now, he realized as his eyes moved to the display. Whoever was in command of that ship was pushing it to its limits. It was risky…but it was exactly what Barron would have done in the same situation.

The enemy was just at the edge of the range of *Dauntless*'s secondary batteries. It would take a lot of luck to score a hit before they got away. A lot of luck.

"No response, sir. I'm repeating the communique on a continuing loop."

"Very well."

They're not going to surrender. And we can't catch them if they want to run.

The enemy wasn't heading toward one of the system's transwarp links…in fact, they were moving out into deep space. They'd have to come back within range of *Dauntless* to get to one of the jump points, or at least take a long and circuitous route around.

They can't do much harm out in the far reaches of the system. But Barron still didn't like leaving the enemy out there intact.

"Commander Travis, launch the Eagles. They are to pursue the enemy as far as fuel allows, and then they are to return. If they can catch the vessel they are to demand surrender again… and if there is no response they are to engage. I want that ship crippled, though, not destroyed. Clear?"

"Yes, Captain. Clear." She tapped at her headset. "Fighter control, launch Scarlet Eagle squadron immediately. Orders… pursue enemy contact the extent of fuel supply. Demand surrender and if refused, engage targeting engine systems."

Travis turned toward the command station. "Launch control acknowledges, Captain."

A second later, the familiar feeling under Barron's feet confirmed the launch in a more direct way. Less than a minute later, the confirmation came in. The Scarlet Eagles were on the way.

"Cut thrust, Commander. Bring us around…back toward the artifact."

"Yes, sir."

"I want probes launched, Commander. Three full spreads. Cover the two transwarp points, as well as all approaches to the artifact, five hundred thousand kilometers out."

"Yes, sir."

Barron wasn't taking any chances. It looked like *Dauntless* had gotten there in time, but he had no doubt—none at all—that more Union forces were on the way, ships far more dangerous than a single frigate. He was expecting his own support as well, but he knew how long it would take to pull a task force from the battle lines and get it out to the Badlands. However he figured it, he was looking at two weeks, maybe three…or even longer. And his gut told him the Union would be there first.

He had no idea if the ancient ship was operable, but the prospect of getting it moving under its own power seemed unlikely. At a major base, with legions of scientists and engineers, maybe, but out here in so short a time? He doubted it. And that meant he had to defend it against anything that came this way…until he was relieved.

Hold until relieved. However long that takes. Against whatever comes. Striker and Holsten hadn't put it quite that way when they'd briefed him—when he'd "volunteered" for the mission—but he knew very well that was why he was here. *Against whatever comes...what will that be?*

"As soon as the probes are launched, bring us alongside the artifact, Commander. I want scanners at full power...there's an active energy source inside that thing, a big one." He didn't really expect any attack—after all, the Union ship had been docked to the thing when *Dauntless* first transited, and so had *Pegasus*—but if the power readings inside that thing spiked by so much as enough to heat up a cup of coffee, he wanted to know about it.

"Yes, Captain. Active scanners are operating at full power. No change in readings. Just a steady background power source... but no signs of imminent attack or thrust."

"Very well." *At least as far as we can tell. What we don't know about the technology in this thing could fill an immense database.*

"Power up all assault shuttles, Commander. And advise Captain Rogan I want his people ready to go in fifteen minutes." He paused. "Full combat gear."

"Yes, Captain." A few seconds later: "Captain Rogan acknowledges, sir. He advises his people will be in the bay ready to board in ten minutes."

Barron suppressed a smile. Bryan Rogan was a Marine... as far as Barron could tell, he was as much a Marine as it was possible for a human being to be. Rogan's people had always come through for him, and he had tremendous confidence in them. The Marines were an aloof group, and they tended to keep to themselves. They performed routine security duties on *Dauntless*, but mostly they were there waiting for a situation that required some genuine ground pounders. The artifact wasn't actual ground, of course, but it *was* a boarding action. Barron had no idea what was waiting over there. And he wasn't going to take any chances.

He sat for a moment, his eyes focused on the scans of the massive structure. He was both shocked—and strangely unsurprised—that the find had proven to be real, that the smugglers' claims were true.

"Captain, the...crew of the *Pegasus*...is requesting permission to board the artifact."

"Denied," Barron snapped. He'd virtually confined the small

ship's crew to their quarters, and he didn't want them underfoot now, getting in the way of his Marines. Still, he understood their desire to search for their captain, and he wondered if he'd been too hard on them, if his prejudices had colored his treatment of them. They had reported the artifact…and in a sense, perhaps, they'd helped save the Confederation. Barron didn't know what the ancient ship could do yet, but he was sure it would be a disaster if it fell into the Union's hands.

He shook his head, and even as he did, he felt his attitude toward the smugglers softening. "Advise them we are going to secure the vessel first…and then I will allow them to go over and join the search for their comrades." He knew how Atara would have felt if he'd been missing and she'd been held back from looking for him. Indeed, every man and woman on *Dauntless* would feel that way, and he would about them. He disapproved of Badlands smugglers, but he couldn't fault anyone for loyalty.

"Yes, Captain."

Barron stood up abruptly. He was a creature of duty, and there was nothing in his life as important as his role as *Dauntless*'s captain. But he was a curious man too, one who craved the pursuit of knowledge. It was beginning to dawn on him that this was the greatest discovery in Confederation history, and he felt an irresistible longing to see it. Now.

"Commander, you have the con," he said simply, matter-of-factly. "I'm going over with the Marines."

Travis spun around, a look of undisguised horror on her face. "Captain, I suggest you wait until Captain Rogan's people have…"

"You have expressed your concern, Commander Travis. And I appreciate it. But I'm a big boy, and I can take care of myself." His tone was a little harder than he'd intended. The last thing he wanted was to snap at Travis, especially when he knew she was right. He had no place going over there with the Marines, no place at all. He was *Dauntless*'s captain, and he belonged on her bridge. But he was going anyway.

It's your fault, Atara…I couldn't do this if I didn't have someone as competent as you to leave in command. He held back a smile.

"I'll be careful," he said, his voice softer. "But that thing over there could change history. It is the most momentous discovery in our lifetimes. In ten lifetimes." He paused. Then he smiled at her and turned around, bounding across the bridge toward the lift.

*   *   *

Barron sat on the shuttle, moving around, trying to get comfortable. He wasn't used to body armor, but Captain Rogan had insisted. No, more than insisted. The Marine, who'd followed every order Barron had ever given with almost fanatical obedience, had come closer to mutiny than *Dauntless*'s captain had thought possible, absolutely refusing to proceed unless his commanding officer wore the full combat kit.

Barron knew his presence, armored or not, made his Marine commander intensely uncomfortable. There was little doubt Rogan considered the captain's safety his personal responsibility, one he took *very* seriously. He'd tried to talk Barron out of coming. Then he'd suggested the captain wait until his first wave had gone in and secured the docking area, at least. Barron knew it all made sense, that Travis and Rogan were right. He had no place on the assault shuttle. But that didn't matter…he *had* to go. It was curiosity, yes, the desire to be one of the first to set his eyes on a find of historical significance. But there was more to it than that.

Hundreds of his crew had died since he'd taken command of *Dauntless*, brave men and women, devoted, loyal…killed following his orders. He'd sent so many of his people into dangerous situations, and now again, he'd ordered his ship's Marines to go into the unknown. This time he was going with them. He didn't know if it was Stockton down in sickbay, probably dying, or the nearly twenty pilots he'd lost fighting *Vaillant*, but duty didn't matter now, nor obligation. The truth was, he *had* to be on this shuttle, and so he was. If something went wrong, if he was killed or incapacitated…well, then, Atara Travis would be one of the best captains in the fleet. He didn't have the slightest doubt.

"Commencing docking procedures now. Hold on back there, this might get a little rough." There was an edginess to the pilot's tone. The immensity of the ancient vessel was almost overwhelming. It had been here, deep in the Badlands, undiscovered for centuries. It was impossible not to be intimidated by it.

The shuttle lurched as its deceleration thrusters fired, and again as the pilot hit the maneuvering jets, aligning with his chosen spot. Barron could feel the vibration as the boarding umbilical extended, and then a sharp metal on metal sound as the diamond-tipped blades dug into the ship's hull, aided by short-ranged, high-powered lasers. It took a while, longer than normal for sure. That wasn't a surprise. The ancient alloy was undoubtedly superior to anything used by the Confederation.

Finally, the comm squealed again. "We're in…Marines, you are clear to board."

Rogan jumped up, and he was half way across the room before Barron had managed to undo his harness. *Dauntless*'s captain had to fight back a laugh as he watched the Marine so clearly make sure he was between Barron and the door. He finished fumbling with the harness and shoved the straps aside, getting up and reaching down to grab the assault rifle at his side, something else Rogan had insisted upon.

"Captain, please…let us at least go through and secure the immediate boarding area."

"Very well, Captain Rogan," Barron replied. He gestured toward the hatch with his rifle. "I will follow."

"Thank you, sir." The Marine's tone was heavy with gratitude. "All right," he snapped to the twenty other Marines in the shuttle. Let's move out. Now!"

Chapter Nineteen

Command Center
Fleet Base Grimaldi
Orbiting Krakus II

"Scanners confirm enemy ships emerging from the Landar transwarp point, Admiral. It looks like a dozen frigates so far. No capital ships." Commander Jarravick had been Striker's key aide before the admiral was promoted to command of the entire fleet, and he'd remained at that post, even as the responsibilities attendant to it increased exponentially. Striker knew Jarravick deserved a bump in rank to match the increase in the size and importance of his workload, but it was just something he hadn't gotten around to yet. He made a mental note to revisit the issue when the recent crisis had passed. *And before the next one starts...*

"Very well," he replied, his voice almost robotic. He'd been listening to the reports as they came in, but most of his mind was elsewhere. He'd expected the enemy move against Grimaldi, at least he'd considered it a strong possibility, especially if this new offensive was the real thing. But not so soon. The enemy was advancing from four different jumping off points, and the transwarp network between systems imposed its own timetables, to which even the most aggressive battle plans were subject.

Striker had been sure it would take at least another week to consolidate a combined fleet large enough to take on the main Confederation force *and* its forward base. Grimaldi had ten particle accelerators even heavier than a battleship's primaries, and two dozen squadrons of fighters. It was a formidable target, and it was strongest in a situation like this, backing up the fleet. It would take everything the Union could muster to break through. And no matter how many ways Striker tried to figure it out, he couldn't come up with any way it was possible they could launch that all-out assault now. Not this quickly.

"The picket line is to engage, Commander." He'd deployed a line of his own light escort ships near the transwarp portal, thirty ships strong. They'd be blown to bits by a force of battleships in a straight up fight, but they were more than enough to face the Union frigates…and then maybe to harass any of the enemy's heavier vessels if they started coming through.

"Yes, sir."

Striker stared at the huge 3D display in the middle of the control center. There were twenty-nine blue ovoids in two rough lines, every battleship he'd been able to muster. Almost every capital ship the Confederation still had in space. He'd lost half a dozen of the big ships since the enemy offensive began, and ten more had been forced back to the shipyards, most of them so badly damaged they didn't have a beam hot enough to toast a piece of bread. It would be months before he got any of those ships back, especially since he'd sent them farther to the rear, bypassing the more forward shipyards in danger of being overrun if the enemy broke through.

"Commodore Harris acknowledges, Admiral. The forward line is advancing."

"Put the fleet and the base on yellow alert, Commander." Striker almost ordered full battlestations, but he held back. If the enemy was just probing, his pickets could handle things. His battleships had all seen action over the past few weeks, and their crews were exhausted and depleted by losses. They were here to face a major enemy attack, if it came, not to chase around enemy escorts poking their nose through the portal.

"Yes, sir. All fleet line units to yellow alert. Grimaldi base to yellow alert."

An instant later, Striker's eyes caught the lamps around the control center glowing yellow. New personnel began moving into the control room, as the alert status called more of his people to their duty stations.

He watched as the display updated his forward line's approach to the enemy. The battle began as both sides opened fire. The escort ships were lighter-armed than the battleships that formed the main strength of the fleets, but they were faster and far more fragile. The fight was sharp, quick. His frigates had half a dozen cruisers adding some heft to their line, and it showed. The Union lost eight ships, to only four Confederation vessels, and the survivors turned and raced back at full acceleration toward the transwarp point.

Every instinct in Striker screamed that he should order his line to pursue, especially since four or five enemy vessels were lagging behind, engine damage preventing them from engaging full thrust. But this wasn't a time to ignore caution. Picking off a few escorts wasn't going to change the status of the war, and if he got his pickets too close to the transwarp point, they were vulnerable. A few enemy battleships coming through at the right moment would savagely tear into his light forces.

"Commodore Harris advises his forces are pursuing the…"

"Negative, Commander. Harris is to stay where he is. No pursuit."

Striker could feel the pause, an uncomfortable quiet in the air while Jarravick took the slightest bit of extra time to respond. He knew the aide disagreed…that virtually everyone in the control room disagreed. To them, after more than a year of brutal fighting, it seemed anathema to let Union warships escape. He understood how they felt, but he didn't have the luxury of reacting on pure emotion. Van Striker knew he needed every scrap of force he had if the enemy eventually launched a full-scale assault on Grimaldi. The enemy was playing some kind of game with him. This was the third time Union ships had transited, and still he'd seen nothing stronger than a cruiser.

He hadn't figured it out yet, but he was damned sure going to. The Union had more escorts than the Confederation, and they no doubt considered the light craft far more expendable than their battle line. But what could they gain sending in such forces? They couldn't expect to launch a credible assault on the Confederation fleet base with frigates. Yet no heavier forces had followed.

What are they up to? Is it all just an elaborate scheme to mess with my peoples' heads, to run them ragged before the real *attack? Or is it a diversion?*

And what about Dauntless*?* He'd been looking for a place in the order of battle for weeks now where he could spare a battleship or two…but there was nowhere. His forces had fallen back all along the line. He hated the idea of leaving Barron on his own…and, worse, if there really was some ancient ship out there, he was taking a terrible risk not supporting *Dauntless*.

But if Grimaldi fell…if the enemy really had a way to sustain an offensive, the entire Confederation could be in jeopardy. And even an ancient artifact of astonishing power wouldn't do any good if Megara and the rest of the Core worlds were destroyed or occupied before it could be studied and put to use.

Perhaps the Union can't sustain an invasion the entire way. Maybe they just wanted to push us back to Grimaldi, then take the time to build up their logistics…

Almost on cue, Jarravick turned toward him. "Admiral… report from Commodore Harris…"

Striker turned and met his aide's gaze, and as he did he could almost hear the words before they were spoken.

"Union battleships transiting, sir. Three so far, but energy readings suggest more are in the tube."

Striker took a deep breath and sat silently for a few seconds. Then he said simply, "Commodore Harris is to withdraw his forces two million kilometers from the transit point."

"Yes, sir."

"And bring the fleet to red alert, Commander. And Grimaldi base as well."

*   *   *

Sara Eaton walked across *Intrepid*'s bridge. Her once tidy

control center was a battered wreck. She stepped over the large rubber-coated cable running across the center of the space, a temporary power reroute put in place by her engineers in an effort to replace the shattered conduit that had once run just above the ceiling of the bridge.

There were scratches and gouges on the once smooth and polished floor where the debris had fallen, but at least the damage control teams had hauled away the shattered chunks of the conduit…the one, she reminded herself, that had sent two of her people to sickbay with broken bones and other injuries.

At least no one was killed…in that incident.

She knew that had been a matter of pure providence. If either Lieutenant Dulles or Ensign Colmes had been a few centimeters forward of where they'd stood, both would have been killed instantly. That fortune, though she thought "fortune" was a grandiose term for what her people had experienced over the past few weeks, had not extended to others in different areas of the ship. *Intrepid* had suffered heavy casualties in its recent fights, including an abnormally large number of fatalities. Her people—and she herself—had been hardened in the brutal early months of combat, and even more so in their desperate mission behind enemy lines, when *Intrepid* and *Dauntless* had destroyed the enemy supply base. But the intensity of the fighting over the past month had pushed them all to their limits.

By any reasonable standard, *Intrepid* should be in spacedock, her savaged systems getting the attention and repairs they needed, but there were other ships in worse shape, and Admiral Striker needed her in the line. So, Sara Eaton was going to do everything she could to make sure her ship was ready to do whatever was required of it.

"Status report?" She stood for a few seconds as Commander Nordstrom jumped out of her chair and moved toward his own workstation. She'd been in her quarters when the battlestations klaxons went off, and she was silently cursing herself for leaving the bridge at all. She'd only done it after thirty-six straight hours on duty, *and* after the fourth time Dr. Jervis had practically demanded she get some rest, but as such things tended to go, the instant she'd nodded off, the enemy had decided to make another move. The klaxons had awakened her even before Nordstrom's comm an instant later. She'd leapt up and raced to the bridge, and she suspected her disheveled state was quite the sight to her crew, accustomed as they were to their captain's fastidious nature.

"Four enemy battleships have transited, Captain. Energy readings suggest additional vessels are en route. Admiral Striker has ordered the fleet to assume combat formation Beta-2, ten million kilometers from the transwarp point. I ordered the engine room to engage thrust just before you arrived on the bridge."

"Excellent, Commander. Well done." Even as she replied to her exec, she felt *Intrepid*'s engines kicking in. The dampeners absorbed most of the thrust, but she could still feel the acceleration. "Weapon status?"

"The primaries are online, sir, but the power transmission lines remain fragile. Commander Merton doesn't know how long he can keep them operational without making additional repairs. All secondary batteries are operative, except for numbers four and nine, which were destroyed in Hystari."

"Very well. Advise Commander Merton I want him to do everything possible to keep the primaries online." She knew as the words left her lips it was pointless order. Merton knew how crucial the main guns were. The fact that they were operational at all was a testament to the efforts of his engineering teams.

"Yes, Captain." Nordstrom's tone suggested he felt the same way. But he relayed her comments just the same.

She turned and looked at the display. Seven enemy battleships now. And the power readings from the transwarp link suggested multiple additional vessels in transit. The enemy had been sending small forces through and then withdrawing, but this was looking like the real thing.

Eaton had mixed feelings. She knew a major fight would be difficult and dangerous, that more of her people would likely be injured or killed. But that battle was coming whether she liked it or not, and part of her was relieved to get it underway.

The ignominious flight from Hystari still stuck in her craw, and the engagements that followed had been hardly more satisfying. She hated retreating, watching the Confederation's proud navy falling back before the enemy onslaught. But the Krakus system was a crucial choke point, the last decent place to mount a concentrated defense before the Iron Belt. The Confederation had already lost Grimaldi base once, but that had been when Admiral Winston was in command. She didn't think Striker would yield it so readily, at least not without one hell of a fight.

It's about time…

Chapter Twenty

Inside Abandoned Spacecraft
System Z-111 (Chrysallis)
Deep Inside the Quarantined Zone ("The Badlands")
309 AC

Barron crouched down, cautiously peering around the corner. He could hear the sounds of gunfire up ahead. He'd suspected the Union frigate had landed personnel on the spaceship, and Rogan and his Marines hadn't been aboard more than two minutes before that was confirmed. It only took another ten seconds or so before *Dauntless*'s resident warriors had confirmed they were facing not just some random spacers, but a force of FRs, their hated rivals.

The Foudre Rouge were the Union's elite soldiers, clones, created and raised for a single purpose: to fight in service of the state. They were conditioned, surgically-altered, subjected to endless training and ruthless discipline. To most people in a place like the Confederation, they were considered slaves, the manner of their "birth" and subsequent treatment a crime against humanity. But to the Confederation Marines, they were just the enemy, and a century of brutal warfare had only increased the hatred between the two forces. There was no quarter in a battle between the Marines and the FRs, none given and none requested. A fight between the two was always to the death.

Barron felt a fear he detested. He hated staying back while his people were fighting, but he was also grateful for his place behind the brutal combat. He knew he wasn't a coward. He'd led his ship into some tight spots, and he'd managed to keep it together and bring his people through. But situations affected people in different ways, and Barron was not a foot soldier. He'd bristled at Rogan's insistence he stay back while the Marines secured the area...but he did it anyway. The FRs had strange effects on a lot of people, the almost alien nature of the brainwashed soldiers too difficult for many to understand. And they gave Barron the creeps.

"Captain, I need you to stay where you are...or better yet, fall back to the shuttle. I don't think we've got a huge force here, but they're well placed...and they probably know their way around in here a lot better than us." Barron could hear intense gunfire in the background. It didn't sound like it was very far from the Marine leader.

"Acknowledged, Captain Rogan." Barron wasn't about to retreat back to the ship—he'd have to surrender his Barron DNA if he did that—but he was less than pleased with himself about how willing he was to do as his Marine commander asked and stay where he was.

He heard something coming down the hall, and he spun back around, taking another look down the corridor, his assault rifle at the ready. There was something there. He tensed, his finger moving toward the trigger. But recognition held his hand. It was one of Rogan's people...no, two of them. And both were wounded.

Barron forgot his earlier fear and leapt around the corner, moving toward the two Marines. The first, a woman whose name was hovering just at the edge of his mind, shouted out, "Get back, sir...there's fighting farther down this corridor." He could hear in the woman's voice—*Crane...that's her name, corporal Crane*—that she was struggling, and he kept moving toward her, reaching out and catching her just as she stumbled forward.

She fell into him, and he could see she'd been shot in the midsection. He took a quick guess and decided it wasn't critical, at least not if she got help soon. But Rogan's shuttle hadn't carried a medic, and though the other assault ships had docked nearby, they had come through different entry points, scattering the Marines around a ship where they had no idea what lay twenty meters down the corridor, much less in nearby sections and on the decks above and below.

"Let's go," Barron said, sliding his arm under hers. He looked back at the man behind her. He'd been hit too, and the material of his uniform leg was covered in blood. He was limping, but he was keeping up, more or less.

"I'm good, sir," the Marine grunted, obviously in pain but just as clearly still able to move on his own power.

"Back to the shuttle," Barron said, moving as quickly as he could while holding up the armored corporal. She groaned in pain as he twisted himself, trying to reach under her arm to get a better grip. "I'm sorry," he muttered, as he moved forward toward the docking port.

He leaned his head against his shoulder, tapping the small comm controls on the side of his helmet. "Lieutenant," he said to the shuttle pilot. "I'm heading back with wounded Marines. Come through the umbilical and help me get them aboard."

"Yes, sir," came the almost instantaneous reply.

Barron managed to make it to the opening in the side of the corridor, just as the pilot was moving through. "Grab her shoulders, Lieutenant. You'll have to pull her through." His eyes dropped to the Marine, now semi-conscious and looking back at him with glazed eyes. "This is probably going to hurt, but we've got to get you on the shuttle." He focused on her eyes, trying to decide whether she'd understood him. It came up a coin toss in his mind.

He pushed her up toward the pilot, the lack of any real howl of pain suggesting to him she hadn't understood his words, that she was more out than awake. He suspected she was better off unconscious, at least for now, but he worried about how long she could last without medical attention. "Get the med kit," Barron said to the pilot. "Do what you can for them."

He turned toward the second Marine. "Can you make it by

yourself?"

"Yes, sir." A short pause. "Captain, you're not going to…"

"Get in there as soon as the tube is clear. And do what you can for Crane." His voice was cool, rational…but it didn't invite further comment on his pending activities.

Barron got up, pulling the assault rifle off his shoulder where he'd stowed it. All thoughts of staying around the corner, of letting the Marines secure the place before he stuck his nose out, were gone. He looked down at his armor, covered with a slick sheen of Crane's blood.

No, there was no way he was hiding down the hall, not while his people were fighting and dying up there.

*   *   *

Lafarge stood against the wall, staring at the pair of FRs standing guard over her. The two soldiers hadn't moved, hadn't taken their eyes off her…she could have sworn neither had even blinked in the hour they'd had her in the room.

There had been no sign of Laussanne, but she'd managed to pass the time, for the past fifteen minutes at least, listening to the sounds of gunfire, a broad smile on her face. Rationally, she knew a fight only put her at greater risk. Laussanne wanted to question her further, and he wanted to make her pay for what she'd done earlier, but she had no doubt if the Union forces were desperate enough, the political officer would order his clone soldiers to cut her down where she stood. Still, the idea of Confederation Marines—and who else could have boarded the ship?—gunning down these cold-blooded FRs, was just too good, even for a cynic like her. She couldn't help but think about the Union soldiers being gunned down, and in spite of her situation, in spite of her hard-boiled personality, a wide smile erupted on her face.

"Those are Confederation Marines out there, aren't they? Gunning down your pod mates or whatever you call them." Her voice was caustic, dripping hatred, though somewhere deeper down she viewed the FRs as victims. But that was far too philosophical a thought for the present situation, and she buried it. Such ideas could only interfere with her killing the troopers in cold blood, which was exactly what she was planning to do the first chance she got.

The FRs ignored her. They just stood as they had for the past hour, unmoving, looking unconcerned that enemy—to them, at least—forces had boarded the ship, and were even now killing their comrades. She'd been waiting for them to get distracted, looking for the first chance she had to jump one and grab his weapon. She'd seen their reflexes, and she knew any move would be difficult and dangerous, but it wasn't in her to play the cowed prisoner. If she got an opening—any opening—she would take it.

She leaned toward the closest soldier, trying to look as though she was stretching a sore arm. But the FR snapped his rifle up, pointing it at her head. He didn't say anything, and the same sickly non-committal expression remained on his face. Lafarge didn't know what orders the soldiers had been given, how much effort they would take to avoid killing her is she provoked them. But something told her it would be dangerous to push too far.

She heard hurried footsteps, and her head whipped around toward the doorway. Laussanne and one of the spacers from *Chasseur* stepped into the room.

"You two, go…down this hall and take position." He gestured toward the FRs, and then to the corridor. The soldiers nodded their acknowledgement, and one replied with a sharp, "Sir!" Then they turned and jogged through the doorway.

"Losing, Laussanne?" Lafarge said mockingly. "Can't even spare a couple guards to watch me?"

"I don't need any guards to watch you," the political officer said, raw hatred in his tone. "Your knowledge of this ship is the only reason you're still alive…"

She glared at him. *It's a good thing you don't believe me when I tell you I don't know shit…*

"…but if I'm going to lose control, the last thing I need to do is allow the Confederation to get that information." He looked at her, and she could see in his eyes he was close to killing her.

He'll wait, but only while his people hold out. If—when—the Marines break through, he'll shoot me without a second thought.

Her eyes darted back and forth, scanning the room unobtrusively.

The FRs are gone…I may not get a better chance…

She stood where she was, but she tensed her legs, ready to lunge at the Union officer. She was a little farther from him than ideal, but she didn't have time to waste. She could hear the sounds of the fighting getting closer…and she knew Laussanne would kill her before the Marines rescued her.

The political officer's comm unit buzzed. He pulled it from his belt and held it to his face. She couldn't hear what he was being told, but she could see the tension it was causing.

"You must hold, Lieutenant," he ordered. "There is no falling back, no retreat."

It's always the cowards who expect someone to fight to the death for them…

She leapt across the room, jumping high and bringing her leg around, taking the political officer in the knee. Her move had been quick, savage, and she'd taken the distracted man completely by surprise.

Laussanne howled in pain, and he dropped hard, first to his knees and then forward, shoving out his arms instinctively to absorb the impact. His pistol fell from his hand and skittered across the metal of the deck. She dove for it, reaching out, extending her arm as far as she could, even as she knew the other spacer was pulling his own sidearm. She felt the hard plastic of the weapon's grip…but it was just too far away. It slipped through her closing finger, and slid into the wall a meter away.

Shit!

She was dropping to the floor herself, the intensity of her move for the weapon costing her the balance she needed to stay on her feet. She went with it, swinging her body hard to the side in an effort to give the spacer a tougher target, as she pushed herself toward Laussanne's pistol.

She heard a crack, later than she'd expected it, and then another. She bit down, waiting for the pain of a bullet hitting her. But there was nothing.

He missed!

She ignored the pain of impacting the floor and she slid forward, her hand darting out, grabbing the gun. She swung around hard, bringing up the pistol as she did. There was no time to aim...she had to rely on pure instinct. She felt her finger tighten, even as another loud shot rang out. She felt that one, on the side of her leg. It was a flesh wound, she was almost certain, but it still hurt like hell.

She ignored the pain, and she fired, watching a spray of blood erupt from the spacer's head.

She twisted hard. The spacer was finished, but Laussanne wasn't dead, he wasn't even seriously injured. She brought the pistol around, ready to finish off the miserable bastard. She could feel his death. She ached for it.

But wait...he has a weapon too...

He must have had two pistols.

Her arm was moving, even as his was doing the same. Her mind was racing, trying to figure out which of them was going to win the deadly race...but the best she could come up with was, it looked like a tie.

"Drop the weapons! Now!"

She froze for an instant, but she didn't drop the gun.

"Drop that pistol, *right now.*"

There was something different about the voice. It didn't have the almost robotic cadence of the FRs' speech. She opened her hand, letting the weapon drop the few centimeters to the deck. It was pure instinct, a sudden urge she followed. She'd been ready to fight to the death.

She saw shadows moving into the room, heard hard boots on the metal deck. Then hands reaching down, pulling her up, searching her. Her eyes focused. The room was full of armed soldiers. But they weren't wearing the reddish-brown uniforms of the FRs. The had gray fatigues, with heavy body armor. Confederation Marines.

Her eyes caught Laussanne, held between two giant Marines. The Union officer had struggled for a few seconds, but now he'd given in, and he just stood there, a terrified look on his face. "Commander Jean Laussanne, Federal Union navy," he said in response to the demand of a Marine officer, his voice shaky, broadcasting his fear.

The officer turned and took a few steps toward Lafarge. "And you?"

She stared back silently. She was thrilled at the thought of the FRs being defeated, and glad to see Laussanne in custody—though she was still determined to kill the piece of shit—but her career hadn't been one that particularly ingratiated her to the Confederation's Marines either.

The Marine walked right up to her, staring into her eyes. His expression lacked the cheap cruelty of so many of the Union personnel, but she could see he was deadly serious. She'd always thought of the Marines as jackbooted enforcers, at least on some level, but she had some idea of their camaraderie and esprit de corps. She suspected they had taken losses here, that this officer had watched his Marines die. He'd be in no mood for surly prisoners. But still, she held her tongue.

"I asked who you were," he said, his tone forceful, commanding.

She stood there, looking up, returning his gaze. She was a little scared, but she was determined not to let it show.

"That's got to be Captain Lafarge, Bryan." The voice came from the doorway, from a tall man who stepped into the room as he spoke. "Captain Andromeda Lafarge, I believe?"

She turned and looked over. The new arrival wore body armor as well, but he carried it somehow less comfortably than the others. He wasn't a Marine, she was fairly certain of that.

"Yes, I'm Captain Lafarge," she replied. She was surprised at being addressed as "captain." This man had to be in the Confederation service in some way or another, and even the common spacers tended to look down on what they thought of as Badlands freebooters and scavengers.

She was surprised in another way as well. There was something about him, something she couldn't quite explain. He was good-looking, certainly, but it was more, some kind of charisma. She was normally resentful and suspicious of Confederation naval personnel, but something was different with this one.

"Your crew brought us back here. They managed to make it all the way to Dannith. You have some loyal people, Captain Lafarge."

"Yes, I do…" She paused, looking at him quizzically.

"Tyler," he said, seeming slightly uncomfortable himself. "Captain Tyler Barron."

Chapter Twenty-One

Command Center
Fleet Base Grimaldi
Orbiting Krakus II

"Twenty enemy battleships so far, Admiral. They're beginning to launch fighters." Jarravick was focused on the bank of screens at his workstation. "We've got multiple ships requesting permission to launch their own squadrons."

Striker hesitated a moment. There was something he didn't like, something that didn't feel quite right. There were enemy ships pouring into the system, but they weren't behaving the way he'd expected them to.

The Union forces were moving slowly, their velocities very low as they emerged from the transwarp link. It was ideal—for the defenders—and that made Striker nervous. *Why would the enemy choose a long-ranged fighter action?*

Still, he had no choice but to counter the enemy's action. "Fleet order…all units are to launch fighters."

"Yes, sir. All units…" But Jarravick had jumped the gun. Striker wasn't finished giving his order.

"Hold, Commander. All units are to launch…but I want every ship to hold back one squadron for CSP duties. And I want those patrolling squadrons pushed out, from one hundred to two hundred thousand kilometers from the mother ship."

"Yes, sir." There was confusion in the aide's voice, but he

didn't question the command.

Striker could feel the edginess in his limbs, the tightness in his gut. Why would the enemy hold back their battleships, especially when they were likely to have a substantial numerical advantage when they had completed their transit? A fighter duel didn't favor them, not when Confederation pilots outflew their enemies by a large margin. And Grimaldi base added almost four hundred more birds to the melee, enough to go a long way toward evening the odds in terms of raw numbers. The enemy was playing a game that suited Striker perfectly...and that scared the hell out of him.

"Commander, advise all ship captains, I want them to report anything out of the ordinary. I don't care if they think the Union's changed the paint job on one of their ships...if it seems different in any way, I want to know about it."

"Yes, sir." Jarravick was a veteran and a reliable aide, but Striker knew the commander was completely confused. *It doesn't matter if no one else is picking up that something is wrong. I am, and that's enough.*

"Admiral, we're getting requests from the task forces commanders on the line to advance."

"Negative. All ships are to launch fighters and then hold position." Striker was even considering pulling his battleships back. He wanted to, and he opened his mouth twice to issue the orders, but the words didn't come. A retrograde move would cause confusion among his units, and he suspected it would be bad for morale. He wondered if he was going to be sorry later for holding back...or whether he was just being paranoid.

"Yes, Admiral. All ships to hold position until further notice."

Twenty-three. Twenty-four. Striker watched as more enemy battleships emerged into the system. Within minutes of appearing, each one began launching its full complement of fighters.

His eyes darted to the side, to the clouds of small dots moving toward his battleline. The enemy was sending everything forward, holding nothing back to defend their own ships. He felt a burst of excitement, images flashing in his mind of the havoc his bombers would wreak against the undefended battleships. It was a reckless plan, a foolish mistake.

Too foolish...

He was sure now, more than he'd been before. The enemy was up to something. But what?

The Union battle line stayed where it was, nailed to the stretch of space just in front of the transwarp link, even as the waves of Confederation bombers blasted out into space and began to approach them.

Striker watched as his strike forces moved toward the enemy fighters. He knew this would be a tough fight for his pilots, that if the enemy hadn't left squadrons behind to defend their ships, they must be planning to intercept the bombers on their way. But as he stared at the display he saw the Union fighters continue forward, virtually ignoring the Confederation bombers and interceptors. Striker's escort squadrons tore into the Union birds, killing dozens. Hundreds. But the enemy squadrons ignored it all, returning fire, but not stopping, not even adjusting their courses.

Something *was* wrong. He couldn't understand it, not at first. And then, suddenly, it was clear.

"Commander, the battle line is to withdraw now, maximum acceleration."

"Sir?"

"You heard me, Commander! Now!"

Striker watched as the Union battleships began to move on the display, not toward his ships, but back to the transwarp link. He'd seen it in his mind a moment before, but now there was no doubt. He knew what the enemy was doing. But a glance at the display told him what his gut already understood. He'd figured it out too late.

He watched as more of the enemy ships fired their engines, moving back through the transwarp link, retreating from the system and leaving their fighters behind.

Something was *very* wrong.

"Got another one! That's three already...I think the Union's fresh outta pilots. I don't know who they've got flying these things now, but they don't know what the hell they're doing."

Angus Douglas sat in his cockpit, listening to the excited chatter on the comm lines. His pilots were cutting down the enemy fighters, and they'd suffered hardly a casualty in return. But something wasn't right.

The pilot's words, "they don't know what the hell they're doing," they reverberated in his head, and from the depths of his mind came the response. *They know* exactly *what they're doing.*

His eyes darted to the display, watching the vectors of the enemy fighters. They were making evasive maneuvers, but tight ones, in a very controlled range...and nothing that took them off their direct course toward the battleships.

They're all interceptors...why take such losses to get to...

He looked back at the scanners, zooming in on one enemy fighter, then another, watching their flight, the sluggish way they handled.

These things are interceptors, but they fly like pigs...worse even than bombers...

He did some quick calculations, watching another fighter as it blasted its thrusters, changing its vector to give its pursuers a harder time getting a lock.

His vector's changing too slowly...too predictably...

He punched at a series of keys, running more calculations through the AI. The enemy fighters were seeing about half the normal change to their vectors that would be expected.

But that doesn't make sense. Not unless their mass is...

"Reprogram the scanners," he snapped at the AI. "Projected mass on the nearest enemy fighter."

A second passed, perhaps two. He knew most of that was the time for the active scanners to send a pulse to the enemy ship and read the result, not the time it took his ship's AI to reach a conclusion.

"Estimated mass four hundred twenty-six point one nine tons."

"Reverify."

A few seconds later. "Results confirmed."

But that was wrong, almost double the normal mass of a Union interceptor.

He got a cold feeling inside, and a moment later his eyes caught the long-range scanner. The enemy battleships were withdrawing, leaving the system.

"What the…"

He slapped his hand down on his comm unit. "*Intrepid*, Douglas here. There is something about these Union fighters… something not right at all."

"Commander Douglas, this is Captain Eaton. You are ordered to come about and pursue the enemy fighters…your bombers too. Ignore the enemy battle line. They'll be gone before you get there."

He was surprised to hear the captain on the line, and the instant her tone sunk in, he knew there was trouble. It confirmed what he'd already felt. The enemy was up to something. He wasn't sure exactly what, but it wasn't good.

"Yes Captain. At once." He flipped the comm unit to the main channel. "All fighters, come about immediately and pursue the enemy attack force. Bombers, this means you too. The enemy battleships are retreating…you can't get there in time. We've got to take out these fighters, any way we can."

He angled his own throttle, bring his fighter around. His squadrons had considerable velocity to overcome, and they would have a hard time bringing their vectors around and catching the enemy. He was far from sure his people would make it back before the enemy was in firing range of the Confederation battleships…but all they could do was try.

"Commander, I don't understand…" One of his squadron commanders began to question the order, and he could hear other voices on the main line.

"That's enough…all of you. Just do as you're told, and obey orders." He cut the line, and his eyes darted to the display, confirming they his pilots were doing just that. He could see the fighters blasting their turbos, but the uncertainty had caused a wide variation in timing between squadrons and individual ships.

His strike force was a disordered mess, but there was nothing he could do about it. He was already pressed to reach the enemy fighters in time, and if he ordered his lead birds to slow down and wait for the others to catch up, it would just exacerbate the problem.

He leaned back in his chair, feeling the intense pressure as his thrusters exceeded the ability of the fighter's dampeners to absorb the force. He breathed deeply, as deeply as he could manage with the equivalent of five times his weight pushing against his chest. He gripped the throttle tightly, holding it all the way back, coaxing every bit of thrust his engines had to give. He had to get back and hit those fighters. He *had* to...

*   *   *

"Arm all defensive batteries. Prepare to receive enemy attack." Eaton was leaning forward in her seat, her eyes fixed on the display. Her CSP had engaged the attacking enemy fighters and cut into them with a ferocity beyond anything she could have imagined. They'd taken out dozens, suffering hardly a casualty in return. The enemy ships didn't seem to care about losses. Beyond a rudimentary, and highly predictable, series of evasive maneuvers, they simply pressed on, firing at any of her ships that wandered within their arcs, but making no effort to pursue targets.

The Union fighters were all interceptors, at least the scanners had so labeled them. But they handled as badly as a group of bombers, and perhaps worse. Eaton didn't like it. She didn't like it one bit.

"All defensive turrets report armed and ready, Captain."

"Very well." *Intrepid*'s engines were blasting hard, accelerating away from the enemy attack. It was the right idea, but it had come too late. She could see there was no way her ship was going to escape the enemy assault...no way any of the battleships on the line were going to. There was a cloud of dots in the display, chasing the Union fighters—her own forward squadrons, still following her order to withdraw. There were squadrons all along the line on the way back, but most of them were behind *Intrepid*'s fighters. Eaton had ordered her people back on her own initiative, possibly even in violation of Admiral Striker's existing directives, though the fleet order came a few minutes later. Still, those minutes were looking like a big difference. Her returning fighters might—just *might*—get some shots off before the enemy strike force attacked. Not too many of the other returning wings were going to make it in time.

There weren't many enemy fighters left heading for *Intrepid*. Six, she counted, her eyes locked on the small screen next to her chair. The CSP had done what it could, and its ships were busy decelerating. But they'd never get back in time for another run.

She watched as Commander Douglas's birds came into extreme range, firing as they did. Hits from such a distance would be the dumbest luck, but she'd take what she could get now. And the Confederation birds out-thrusted their Union counterparts, especially these inexplicably clumsy and slow ones.

Intrepid's laser turrets opened fire, and they scored a hit almost immediately.

Five ships left.

There was a flash in the display, and her head shot around, her eyes trying to focus on the source. It was *Nobility*. The battleship had taken some kind of hit. Eaton looked back at her own screen, as the scanner reports were coming in.

No, that's not possible...

The energy released was more than five times that of a plasma torpedo. She stared, unable to move her eyes from it, thinking that it *had* to be wrong.

But it wasn't. Suddenly, she understood. The clunky, robotic maneuvers, the slow, clumsy flight. Those fighters weren't manned by pilots...they were flown by AIs. And they weren't bombing the battleships of the line...they were ramming them.

And by the looks of those readings, they're crammed to the supports with plasma warheads detonating on impact...

"Get me Admiral Striker," she shouted. "And advise Commander Douglas he is to do whatever it takes to intercept those fighters. *Whatever* it takes."

"Admiral Striker is already on the fleet line, Captain."

Eaton nodded, slapping her hand against her headset.

"…the incoming fighters are making suicide runs. They are loaded with plasma warheads and attempting to ram. All ships, full evasive maneuvers. Now."

She could hear the tension in Striker's voice, even fear. She'd already done everything possible, and now there was nothing left but to watch as her squadrons and guns desperately tried to save her ship. One by one, they took out the approaching fighters.

They got all but one…

Douglas himself was on the tail of that ship…but the range was too close. He wasn't going to get there in time.

Then *Intrepid* shook wildly, and the lights went out. Eaton heard a cracking sound as her body was thrown hard forward, into her harness. The pain came an instant later, and despite her best efforts, she cried out.

A shuddering sound echoed on the bridge as every workstation went dark.

She could feel the weightlessness as both *Intrepid*'s engines and dampeners went offline. She leaned back the best she could, gritting her teeth against the pain in her chest. She'd broken a rib…no, more than one. But that didn't matter now.

She reached up to her headset, wincing at the agony of even that small move. "Commander Merton? Engineering?" Nothing. "Sickbay? Gunnery?" She tapped her controls, cycling through every station. But the comm was completely dead.

"Commander, see if we have inter-ship…" Her words stopped dead, just as the emergency lights came on. The bridge was a wreck, half her people poking at their inoperative stations with varying degrees of panic and frustration, while others struggled to deal with injuries ranging from minor to severe.

And on the floor, just next to his station, Commander Heinrich Nordstrom. Or at least what was left of him after the structural support had crushed the top half of his body.

Chapter Twenty-Two

Sector Nine Headquarters
Liberte City
Planet Montmirail, Ghassara IV,
Union Year 213 (309 AC)

Villieneuve was standing behind his desk, poking through the data chips and intelligence reports piled high there. Every few seconds, he took something and placed it in a small bag laying on his chair. The sack contained a grooming kit and a few articles of clothing, in addition to a personal data unit. The intelligence chief was hurrying, and his expression was one of concern, of worried impatience.

Normally, he traveled with a whole retinue, as befitted his station, and several personal aides handled his extensive baggage. But he was traveling light now, and he didn't want to make a spectacle of his departure. In fact, he didn't want anyone to even know he was gone, not for as long as that perception could be maintained.

"You called for me, Gaston?" Ricard Lille walked into the room, pointedly closing the door behind him. Discussions between the two men were, almost by definition, private affairs. Lille was impeccably dressed, in black as usual, but this time he was in sharp contrast to his friend, whose usual smart attire was looking rather rumpled.

"Yes, Ricard. I am leaving for the front…and I need you to fill in for me here. I need you to be acting head of Sector Nine."

Lille looked surprised, a notable change from his usual noncommittal expression. He hesitated for a few seconds before saying, "Of course, Gaston…whatever you need me to do."

Villieneuve knew his comrade was competent enough to handle the job, even to keep the Presidium under control…but more importantly, he figured Lille was the least likely of his top subordinates to stab him in the back and make a play to seize his position, and the almost incalculable power that went with it. He considered the agent to be a friend, certainly, though that was third or fourth on the list of reasons he'd pegged Lille as the safest choice.

Ricard Lille simply didn't crave power for its own sake, not in the way most functionaries in the Union did. Villieneuve knew the agent wanted to live well and to secure his own position, of course, but he also knew Lille didn't want the responsibility that went with high office, nor did he particularly want to become a target for rapacious underlings. He wasn't an administrator by heart. His true love was killing. Lille was an assassin, by trade and by nature, perhaps the best Villieneuve had ever seen.

The head of Sector Nine was far from squeamish himself, nor was he reluctant to fully employ the methods that had made the intelligence agency feared throughout space. But he didn't get the same ecstasy, the pure joy his friend did from the artistry of the kill. Lille was a psychopath, but a very high functioning one, and Villieneuve had always taken steps to ensure the assassin had everything he wanted—wealth, women, and first shot at any prominent kills. It was a relationship that had worked well for years, giving each of them exactly what they needed. That was a much better basis for cooperation than mere friendship, and Villieneuve was well aware he owed some portion of the credit for his current position to his associate's…removal…of obstacles during his rise.

"The front?" Lille added a moment later. "That sounds… unsafe. What prompts you to go there? Bad news?"

"Yes and no. We launched a preliminary attack against the

enemy's fleet base Grimaldi. The attack was simply meant to divert the enemy's attention. We used a novel strategy. Our battleships transited and launched fighters, but the craft were AI-flown and packed with plasma warheads."

"A suicide attack?" Lille made a face. "Well, not suicide, exactly, but still…"

"It was very costly in fighters, feasible only because I was able to expedite shipments of the newer Mark-6 craft to the fleet, leaving the old Mark-5s…available. I'm afraid our logistics will not support a repeat. We may even have trouble replacing normal losses for a while, at least until the production pipeline fills up again."

"Did the attack succeed?"

"Yes. Quite well, actually. Our battleships had all transited back before the assault waves hit, so much of this is conjecture. We left a few scouts behind, but they were only able to collect rather limited data. Still, I'm confident enough to say we caused significant damage to at least ten of their battleships…and possibly destroyed two outright."

"With no losses of our own?"

"None except eighteen hundred fighters…and a good portion of our plasma ordnance. We may have trouble arming a strong bomber attack in the near future."

"Still, that is good news." Lille caught his friend's expression. "Isn't it?"

"Yes…and no. In terms of damage inflicted it was a great victory. But, I'm afraid it has backfired in ways too. The latest intelligence intercepts suggest the enemy is actively contemplating whether the unorthodox attack is a sign that our recent offensive is limited in nature, rather than the type of sustained assault we conducted at the start of the war. They would not be taken by surprise if we were able to launch another such attack—but many in their high command seem to believe that a sustained assault on Grimaldi base is not in the cards. If they lose their concern about an imminent full scale invasion, they may send reinforcements into the Badlands."

Villieneuve rubbed his temples. "The Presidium is concerned now as well, for different reasons. They are worried that our attacks have suffered losses, that we are weakening our position for the long term. They are beginning to question the entire notion of a diversionary invasion."

"They're right, Gaston, aren't they? At least regarding losses. I've seen some of the casualty reports from the engagements. Despite your holding back somewhat, we *have* taken serious damage. And the Confeds aren't stupid—certainly not Admiral Striker. It doesn't take deep calculation to suggest the existence of another version of Supply One is unlikely in the extreme. It will take more than false intel and a few attacks to convince them otherwise. It will take fear."

"The Confederation forces have suffered as well, I will remind you. Our ships aren't shooting blanks, after all. I believe we've created some fear on their end. Despite my concerns, the enemy is still operating as though they expect a full-scale attack on Grimaldi base, and as far as our forward intel reports can ascertain, they have not yet detached significant forces. At least that we know of." Villieneuve's emotions were usually very well controlled, but he realized his words were showing his defensiveness. His plan had been a daring one, and the stress was getting to him.

"That we know of? What are you concerned about? Our attacks have pinned them down well thus far. With any luck, the forces we sent to the Badlands will secure the artifact and tow it back to Union space before the Confeds can react." Lille paused, his eyes darting up, focusing on Villieneuve's. "There *is* something else…what is it?"

The spymaster exhaled hard. "This is not to be repeated, Ricard, not to anyone. Not even the Presidium knows."

Lille nodded. "Of course, Gaston."

"*Vaillant* has disappeared. She is overdue for multiple reports, and she hasn't linked up with the other vessels we sent to the Badlands."

"*Vaillant?*" Lille's normally unreadable tone displayed concern. "Perhaps they had some kind of malfunction. It could be something routine."

Villieneuve looked back at his friend, not thinking for an instant Lille really believed what he was saying. The Union's greatest ship, the pride of the navy, hadn't just vanished. Something had happened to it. And only one thought made any sense.

"You think the Confederation *does* have forces in the Badlands…"

"I think something destroyed *Vaillant*…or damaged it so badly it couldn't make contact with any of the other units deployed there. We have confirmed that the Confederation has not sent a large task force, but we have not been able to account for all of their ships along the battle line."

"They would have vessels out of action, no? Ships sent back for repairs and refit?"

"Yes, but…"

"But?"

"One of the missing ships is *Dauntless*." Villieneuve's voice dripped with hatred.

"Reports stated she'd been sent back for repairs, no? She was in the line for months, Gaston. She saw considerable combat. It's not odd that she would be pulled back for refit."

"No…but I've been able to confirm where she was sent. It wasn't easy, but we managed to intercept and decode a transmission. She was sent to Dannith."

Lille just stared back at his friend for a moment. Then he said, "That's a coincidence. Just because the port is close to the Badlands…" His voice trailed off.

"Can we be sure? How many Confederation ships could have beaten *Vaillant* in a one on one fight? Assuming the Confeds have only *one* ship there?"

"You think *Dauntless* is in the Badlands? That she destroyed *Vaillant*?" Lille still didn't sound convinced, at least not completely so.

"I think it's a possibility we can't ignore. *Dauntless* was ordered to Dannith well over a month ago. That suggests to me at least a chance that the Confederation has some intelligence on the artifact. That they at least considered the potential need to send a ship to investigate."

"You're making a lot of assumptions, Gaston. *Dauntless* could have been sent there for refit, and nothing more. There are a hundred things that could have happened to prevent *Vaillant* from reporting. Don't you think you should wait for more concrete information?"

"What information, Ricard? That the Confederation has seized the artifact, that it's back at Megara being studied by every scientist they have? By the time I have concrete data, it will be too late." He paused. "We must attack Grimaldi base with everything we have. That's the only way to keep the Confederation's attention focused completely on the front. Absorbing heavy losses to take Grimaldi only appears to make sense if we can follow up on the victory. There is nothing else they can deduce from such an assault except that we have another supply base...or some other means to sustain an advance."

He looked intently at his associate. "You know, of course, we can't. Grimaldi itself is at the extreme end of our logistical reach. They know this too…but perhaps a full-scale attack will convince them we do possess that phantom mobile supply base. Still, whether they believe it or not, they will have no choice but to respond with everything they have. Admiral Striker will not yield Grimaldi as Admiral Winston did. Anyone who has studied the man would come to the same conclusion. Even if he is unconvinced about our supply arrangements." He paused. "At least it will take their eyes off the Badlands, if only for a short time."

"Do we have enough force to take Grimaldi if they commit everything they have? We have a lot of ships in spacedock ourselves, and more that were destroyed…and you detached a considerable task force to the Badlands. Attacking Grimaldi and taking it would keep their attention diverted…and it will give us something to show for the cost. Launching an assault and losing, however…"

"We won't lose, Gaston." Villieneuve took a deep breath. "I have committed the strategic reserve."

Lille stared back, a rare look of surprise on his face. "The Presidium authorized *that*?"

Villieneuve just looked back, silent.

"Gaston…you are taking a big chance with this…"

"And if I—we—gain control of a pre-Cataclysmic super-battleship? Imagine the possibilities, the utility. Not just in this war, but in the next. Even internally within the Union. The payoff is simply too great to ignore…and I will remind you of what would happen if the Confederation found that ship and managed to unlock its secrets."

Lille nodded, his expression one of uncertain acquiescence. "You're right, Gaston. But still, what if the artifact isn't what we think it is? All reports suggest that the Confederation's Iron Belt worlds are producing new ships. We're more than a year into this conflict now, with shockingly little to show for it. If the fleet gets blasted to hell, we'll be stuck on the defensive for a year at least…and by the time we can contemplate another move to bring them down, they'll have fresh ships pouring out of their yards."

"It's a risk, Ricard…but what choice do we have? There *is* something out there in the Badlands, and even if it's not the powerful weapon we think it is, there's little doubt it will be packed full of advanced technology. As much as I want to secure it for our own use, it's even more important that we keep the Confederation from finding it. And if Tyler Barron and *Dauntless* are out there…we've hurt ourselves underestimating him before. I don't intend to make that mistake again. If *Dauntless* is searching for the artifact, we need to do everything possible to ensure that the Confeds can't send reinforcements. Our force in the Badlands can handle Barron and his people, by weight of numbers if nothing else, as long as they don't have to deal with anything else. I have sent word to Admiral Villars, warning him that *Dauntless* may be on its way to Z-111. I made it clear he is to gain control of the artifact by whatever means are necessary…and if *Dauntless* tries to interfere, he is to destroy her at any cost."

"Villars has four capital ships besides *Vaillant*," Lille said softly. "Doesn't he?"

"Yes."

"Barron has proven himself to be a dangerous adversary, but there's no way he can take on four battleships." Lille paused. "And if he has indeed destroyed *Vaillant*, it's likely his vessel did not escape that engagement without considerable damage." Lille looked down at the desk and back up at his superior. "But, are you sure we have enough force remaining along the front to win at Grimaldi? You're going to feel the loss of those four ships, not to mention *Vaillant*.

"I think so, Ricard, though not by the margin I would like. I had hoped to distract the Confeds without committing everything, but now I don't think there's a choice. That's why I released the reserve. It's why I'm going up there myself. We need to put everything behind this…or give up the whole thing. And how can we back off, when such a prize is on the line?"

"But if the Presidium finds out…"

"That's the other reason you're here, my old friend." Villieneuve paused. "I need you to keep your eyes and ears open, and if you hear anything, if any member of the Presidium appears to know…too much…I need you to act."

Lille turned and glanced back toward the closed door before returning his gaze to Villieneuve. "Just to clarify, Gaston, by act you mean…"

"Just what you think I mean," he said coldly. "Do what you do best, my friend…"

Chapter Twenty-Three

Inside Abandoned Spacecraft
System Z-111 (Chrysallis)
Deep Inside the Quarantined Zone ("The Badlands")
309 AC

Barron turned away, trying and failing to disguise the abruptness of the move. He'd caught himself looking over at Andromeda Lafarge again. It was the third time...no, the fourth. He wasn't sure what it was. She was an attractive woman, certainly, but she was far from the first he'd seen. Her outfit was provocative, he supposed, form-fitting at least, but again, not excessively so. Still, there was something about her, something he couldn't put out of his mind.

She had a strength...he couldn't place it, but he could feel it. She was a rogue, at least by his fairly straight-laced standards, but leaders came in all forms, and he was sure she was a prime example of one of those. And his gut told him she was smart. Damned smart.

He had come aboard with the Marines, unsure what he would find, if *Pegasus*'s captain would be on the ancient vessel... or in the Union frigate. And, if the latter, he'd been perfectly prepared to blast the thing to atoms, and Andromeda Lafarge with it, if necessary. Barron didn't usually think much of the breed of adventurer that scoured the Badlands for scraps of ancient technology.

But clearly, Lafarge wasn't the normal breed of Badlands rogue. Barron had seen that kind far too many times, dull, cloddish, brutal, trading on their willingness to plunge into the dangers of the Badlands. Andromeda Lafarge was still mostly a mystery to him, but he was willing to bet she wasn't dull or cloddish.

Whatever her previous expeditions had discovered, this time she had clearly found more than 'scraps of ancient technology.' What she'd discovered would change history, and the arrival of her crew at Dannith, more concerned with rescuing her than securing the tech, just might have saved the Confederation from ruin.

Lafarge was on the other side of the room, sitting against the wall while Dr. Weldon took a look at her injuries. A bullet had grazed her leg, a wound that was bloody and looked more serious than it was. And there were contusions, bruises all over her face and back. Barron knew how the Union questioned captives, and he realized that she'd gotten off lightly with a few beatings. But the sight of her injuries angered him. The Marines had taken Laussanne away, to a makeshift detention area they had set up, and Barron knew it was a good thing the Union political officer was gone.

He saw Lafarge stand up slowly, nodding her thanks to the doctor. Weldon had brought a team aboard to treat the wounded Marines. The fight had been a fierce one, as engagements between the Confederation's fighters and their hated enemies always were. As usual, no FRs had surrendered, but nearly a dozen Union personnel had been captured, spacers and support personnel in addition to the commissar himself.

Barron's eyes moved to the other side of the room, to the neat row of tightly zipped bodybags. He'd lost six Marines in the fighting, and another four were seriously wounded and on their way back to *Dauntless* even now. There were seven more lightly wounded, eight if he counted the nasty incision from an FR's knife Sergeant Treves had suffered—a painful looking gash the Marine referred to as a "scratch."

The FRs had lost more than twice that number, all killed, of course, but preliminary interrogation of the captured naval personnel suggested that didn't account for all of them. Rogan had explained that defeated FRs didn't give up, but they often "went feral," disappearing, hiding, pursuing campaigns of harassment against their enemies. Barron didn't relish trying to decipher the secrets of the massive spacecraft with the threat of Union reinforcements hanging over his head, much less having to worry about his research teams being picked off by roving bands of "feral" FRs.

"Captain, I just wanted to thank you again. I've been in danger before, but being captured by the Union was something I'd never even considered among the hazards of my...profession." Lafarge had walked across the room, stopping right in front of Barron.

"My pleasure, Captain Lafarge. I'm glad we got to you before they took you through their full repertoire of interrogation techniques. It's not an experience you would have enjoyed."

"Please...Captain Lafarge is so formal. You know what a mouthful my first name is, but my friends call me Andi." Her voice was hard to fully decipher. Barron suspected she was a complex woman, but the hint of flirtation in her words was unmistakable.

"Very well...Andi." He paused, hesitating for a moment instead of reciprocating immediately. It would be inappropriate for her to address him informally in front of the crew. But then he said, "I'm Tyler," anyway.

"Yes, I know. Your family is very famous...Tyler. And I've seen your own name in the news more than once. It seems to be the perception that you singlehandedly stopped the Union invasion."

Barron shook his head. "Far from singlehandedly, I'm afraid. *Dauntless* played her part, but the entire fleet stopped the enemy...and lost thousands of good men and women doing it."

"I can't imagine what your people have been through."

Barron just nodded. It wasn't something he wanted to discuss. Not with her. Not at all, really, and certainly not in the middle of an ancient ship, with the virtual certainty that Union forces were on the way to try and take it from him.

"So how are we going to get this ship back to Confederation space, Tyler?"

"I don't know," he answered truthfully, grateful for the change of subject. "I'll have a better idea when my engineering team gets here and takes a look around." Barron didn't think it was remotely likely that his people, even Anya Fritz, could get the ancient vessel moving under its own power in any reasonable time frame. It was miracle enough that it was there, structurally sound, with some of its systems still functioning. But it could take years to figure out how to even operate the thing, much less fix any systems that needed repair. And he was far from sure *Dauntless* could tow something this large…and dead certain if she could, it would be at a snail's pace.

"We need to discuss ownership of this thing," she said abruptly. "Or at least some kind of finder's fee from the Confederation."

"I'm sorry…what?"

"My people found this ship, after all. It's only right that we're compensated. Do you have any idea what it costs to bring *Pegasus* out this far? How much risk we took?"

Barron looked back at her, his face hardening. "Do *you* have any idea what it costs to run a ship like *Dauntless*? To travel this far to rescue someone?" He was concerned about the approaching Union forces, about the battle he knew his people faced to even hold on to this amazing discovery. And she was worried about getting paid.

"Tyler, look…"

His comm buzzed and he held up his hand to silence her. She stopped speaking and glared at him.

"Barron here," he said, leaning down toward the tiny microphone. "What is it, Atara?" His tone was rough, abrupt, far more so than Travis deserved.

"Is anything wrong, sir?" Travis couldn't have missed the tension in his voice.

"No, Commander. Nothing I can't handle." He returned

Lafarge's cold stare. "Status report?"

"Yes, sir. Commander Fritz and her team are on their way. They should dock within ten minutes. The Eagles managed to knock out that Union frigate's engines. The ship is disabled and continuing along on its last vector." A brief pause. "If the fighting is mostly finished there, could you could spare some of Captain Rogan's Marines? One platoon will probably be enough. I'd like to send an assault shuttle to match course and speed and board that ship. It's not likely they're going anywhere, but I still don't want to give them time to do repairs." Another short silence. "Better to capture them now, while we still can, sir. We can't be sure what our situation will be in twelve hours… or a day, or a week."

Barron took a deep breath. He knew exactly what Travis meant. His first officer was as aware as he was that they faced a fight here—and probably a hard one—before they would have a chance to move the ancient ship. If they managed to come up with a way to move it at all. But that was Fritzie's problem. His was holding onto the thing for as long as it took for her to work something out, or for the Confederation reinforcements to arrive. And he suspected his job would be as difficult and trying as hers.

"Very well, Commander. Contact Captain Rogan, tell him to dispatch two platoons and sufficient transport. I'd rather hit them with too much than too little. We can't be sure they didn't keep some FRs onboard. And that will leave four platoons here, which should be enough to hunt down a few fugitives."

"Yes, Captain."

He stood silently for a moment. Then he added, "And keep *Dauntless* on yellow alert, with one squadron on patrol at all times. We're close to the transwarp points here…and we don't know what's coming." *And you know something is coming as well as I do…*

"Yes, Captain. Agreed. I also have Yellow squadron ready to go…I'll launch them before I land the Eagles."

"And keep me posted. If the scanners report anything at all, or the fighters detect anything…or if you have a feeling in your gut, even if you're not sure it's not last night's dinner, call me immediately." Barron knew he should go back to the ship. He had no more place staying now than he did coming aboard with the assault teams. But he was mesmerized by the ancient ship, and he was determined to have a look around. A prerogative of command perhaps, but one he was going to exercise.

"Yes, sir. I've got things handled. Take your time over there." He could hear from her voice that she understood...as she usually did.

"Thank you, Atara." He felt a rush of gratitude for having Travis as his exec, as he had so many times before. "Barron out."

He'd been locked in a staring contest with Lafarge the entire time he'd been on the comm. Now he said, "I will authorize a berth on the next shuttle heading back to *Dauntless*, Captain Lafarge." His voice was colder, more professional than it had been before. "Your crew is there, and I am sure they will be very happy to see you." He paused. "I understand your first officer is aboard the Union frigate. You will be glad to know we have knocked out its engines and are preparing to board. With any luck, he will be found and safely brought to *Dauntless*. Now, if you'll excuse me, I'm going to..."

"Don't be like that, Tyler..." Her tone was softer now, as it had been earlier, all traces of the hard-driving mercenary bartering for payment gone. "You have your job to do, and I have mine. But that doesn't mean we can't be friends. She stepped forward and put her hand on his arm.

He felt an urge to pull away, his dislike of Badlands-scavenging rogues fully awakened by their earlier exchange, but he didn't. He was frustrated with himself. He'd dated his share of women, at least during shore leaves and the like, but he'd never had one affect him like this.

"Come on," she said, a sweetness in her voice he wasn't sure he believed, but couldn't ignore either. "I'm the one person here who best knows her way around on this ship. I did manage to hide here for almost a week."

Barron hesitated, unsure what to do for a moment. He'd

been resisting his emotional urge to bring her with him, but her logic was flawless. She did know her way around the ship better than anyone else. He knew he was just excusing himself to do what he wanted to do, but what he knew he shouldn't. But he did it anyway.

"You sure you want to be my tour guide?" he asked, turning back and looking right at her. "I'm afraid it's not a paying position."

He could see the flash of anger, for just an instant before she overcame it.

"You're very funny, Tyler," she said softly, with carefully placed hint of hurt feelings. Then her expression darkened. "It's easy to react as you did, you know. The wealthy and beloved Barron family. Was there ever a day when you had to do more than ask for what you wanted, Tyler? What was the worst thing you ever had to do for a meal? The nastiest torn rag you huddled under to stay warm?" Barron stood and listened, losing track of what was theater, designed to manipulate him, and what was real. And for all his mustered cynicism, he was sure there was truth in her words.

"Maybe one day we'll know each other well enough for me to give you my answers to those questions…but not now. Still, you can be sure it was more than deciding what I felt like eating and ordering it. Or wrapping up in a soft cashmere blanket in front of the family estate's fireplace."

He could see she was really upset, that he'd touched on a nerve. That, or she was the best actress he'd ever seen.

Maybe a bit of both…

Still, despite any doubts about her intentions, he felt ashamed. He had led a privileged life, and many people—apparently, Andromeda Lafarge among them—had suffered terrible deprivation, even in the Confederation. His own first officer was a testament to that. In fact, it sounded like the two had suffered through similar backgrounds.

"I'm sorry if I hurt your feelings." He was sincere, and also a bit defensive. "I may have been born into a privileged life, but I've also fought more than one battle. I've killed, I've been wounded, and I've seen my people die, carrying out my orders. So, perhaps you'll understand it upsets me when I see what seems like a price being placed on patriotism. You may have been born into bad circumstances, but you're damned lucky that place was in the Confederation instead of someplace like the Union. And this thing..." He waved his arms, gesturing to the ship all around them. "...is more than a treasure to be paid for. Any nation that possesses the technology of the ancients will be able to subjugate the others if it chooses. So, unless you want to spend the rest of your life in a Union work camp—or worse—perhaps it's best to save discussions about rewards and payments until later."

He paused, and when he continued, his voice was grim. "Because, sure as hell, we're going to have a fight here before we get a chance to move this thing...and you're probably going to get an opportunity to see more of my people die." He glared at her, his eyes wide, blazing. "And if you complain to me about money again while that is happening, I'll throw your ass in the brig...if not out the airlock. Do we understand each other?"

Chapter Twenty-Four

Command Center
Fleet Base Grimaldi
Orbiting Krakus II

"We have to send help to Captain Barron. *We* sent him there…him and all his people. You know the Union will have dispatched more than a single battleship." Striker sat in his office, in one of the guest chairs next to his desk. Gary Holsten was sitting in the other one, looking back with a pained expression on his face.

"Yes, we did, Van. But that was before the Union launched its assault. If they have a new supply base, and if we lose Grimaldi again, they could advance all the way to the Iron Belt."

"Yes, I know. That's what I've been telling myself. But the fact remains…*Dauntless* is out there. And if the artifact we sent Captain Barron to find does, in fact, exist, and it falls into Union hands…"

"If," Holsten replied. "If it exists, if the Union finds it, if they're able to get it back to their space and decipher its secrets. I understand the danger. But there is no 'if' about that Union fleet, and your scouting reports leave little doubt. There is a large and powerful Union fleet one transit away, stronger even than we'd believed." He looked right at Striker. "Can you guarantee me that you can hold Grimaldi, even with every ship and fighter you have here now?"

Striker paused, looking uncomfortable. "No, of course not. You knew the answer to that before you asked it."

"Are you willing to abandon Grimaldi base? To fall back and select another system to make a stand?"

Striker shook his head. "That was Admiral Winston's mistake in the initial campaign. Grimaldi is where it is for a reason. It's a choke point. However badly Union numbers impact us here, it will only be worse if we give them more room and multiple paths of advance." He paused. "The only reason to consider giving up Grimaldi is if the enemy has no supply base. Then we could trade space for time, knowing they can't get too far too fast. But we very well might be betting the Confederation on that."

Holsten nodded. "My conclusions exactly. So, if you're not sure you've got enough force to win the fight, and you can't or won't fall back…how exactly do we detach battleships from the line to go to the Badlands?" He let the words hang in the air, the image of thousands of men and women dying as their massive warships were battered into rubble.

"And if we lose," he continued, "the Confederation could easily fall even without the enemy gaining ancient technology. We don't have a good choice here, Van. Just a bad one and an even worse one."

Striker exhaled hard, turning and staring at his desk. "You're right," he finally said. "The Union outnumbers us by too much, especially with the extra ships we detected." His head angled back, his eyes locking on Holsten's. "We need every vessel here."

The two men sat quietly for a few minutes. Then, Holsten said, "I feel it too, Van. Tyler Barron is a good man. His crew are among the best the Confederation has. But the cost of this war has already been enormous. If the enemy gets by, if they defeat your forces here and break through…and we have nothing left to stop them, we won't be talking thousands dead or even millions. The toll will be in the billions. Do you think the Union cares how many civilians they kill?" Holsten paused. "You have to win here, Van. You *have* to. And nothing else matters right now. *No one* else matters."

Striker held Holsten's gaze, and then, unable to say the words, he just nodded.

*   *   *

Villieneuve looked out over *Victoire*'s flag bridge. Admiral Beaufort had offered him the command position, volunteering to vacate his chair not once but twice. Villieneuve had refused both times. He needed Beaufort at his station—and at his best—and though the head of Sector Nine had to admit to himself he was as power mad as most of the Union's top officials, he was also far less controlled by his ego…and its companion, insecurity.

Beaufort was a good officer, though not an especially skilled tactician—Villieneuve had to admit he wasn't his predecessor's equal in that regard. But Admiral D'Alvert had been consumed by ambition, so much so that he became too great a danger, if not to the Union, to the careers and positions of other men and women of power. In the end, Villieneuve sent Ricard Lille to "deal with it," thereby effectuating Beaufort's rise to the top field command.

Villieneuve would have preferred someone more imaginative in command of the fleet, but he had to admit, to himself at least, that the Union's system did not encourage creative thinking. Mavericks either rose to the very top—and then only if they were lucky and extremely careful—or they tended to destroy themselves, scaring those who had too much at stake in maintaining the status quo.

At least Beaufort is a soldier, not a hybrid like D'Alvert. The late admiral had been both a senior military commander and a member of the Presidium, an almost unheard of achievement in a system as paranoid as the Union's. It had also sealed his fate. Villieneuve might have let an admiral survive a military reverse, but he hadn't been able to pass up the chance to get rid of D'Alvert.

"The fleet is ready, Minister Villieneuve." Beaufort sounded shakier than Villieneuve would have liked, but he doubted there was an officer in the Union service who would have been steadier right now. The battle in the Krakus system would be a bloodbath, there wasn't a doubt in his mind. The Confederation had yielded their great base early in the war, almost without a fight, but Arthur Winston had been in command then. That aged officer had been among the last to have a pedigree tracing back to service with the great Rance Barron, and he'd ridden it well past his usefulness. Indeed, the fact that a tired old man had commanded the Confederation navy had been a major factor in choosing the time to initiate hostilities. Villieneuve himself had raised that issue in the final Presidium meeting before the invasion, urging his fellows to strike before younger and more aggressive admirals moved into command positions in the Confederation.

But Winston was gone now, and Van Striker wasn't old or a fool. Of all the officers of the next generation that might have succeeded Winston, Striker was the one Villieneuve had feared the most. He was smart, and he was popular among the spacers. He was daring, too. A risk taker, but not reckless. Every report on the man stressed how resolute he was, how deeply he dug his heels in the ground when he deemed it necessary. There was no way Striker would yield Grimaldi as his predecessor had.

Villieneuve knew the base itself would add great strength to the defense. Winston had failed to destroy the facility when he'd abandoned it, leaving it battered but still there for the Union to take. He'd laughed at the foolishness, but then months later he'd seen the Union forces make the same mistake, abandoning the fort, but leaving it mostly intact. That was a mistake he wouldn't see made again. Striker was unlikely to neglect to destroy the facility if he was driven back and forced to abandon it…and even if he did, Villieneuve would make absolutely sure that if the Confeds recovered Krakus, the base would be nothing but radioactive dust.

Villieneuve looked at the display. Forty-four battleships, and over a hundred escorts. Almost all the force the Union still possessed, save for the four battleships dispatched to the Badlands.

Eight battleships…

It had been a gamble, pulling four more ships from Beaufort's battle line, one that few would have understood. He'd analyzed things ten different ways, and he couldn't see how there was more than one Confed ship in the Badlands. But the data—and his gut—told him that ship was *Dauntless*. He'd developed a healthy respect for that ship and her captain…and a seething hatred. Besides, he'd added ten ships to Beaufort's fleet and only taken four away. The Presidium would erupt like a volcano when his colleagues discovered that he'd released the strategic reserve—and forged their approvals to do it—but that was tomorrow's problem, and one he was sure he could handle if his action had gained an ancient battleship.

Four ships had seemed like enough to handle *Dauntless* no matter what. He'd analyzed it every way he could…and then he'd sent the extra ships anyway. Tyler Barron had caused him too much trouble…and it was long past time to blow the man, and his cursed ship, to plasma.

He looked over toward the command station. Then, after a moment of thoughtful silence, he said, "Admiral Beaufort, the faith and confidence of the Union and its people are with you now. Lead your fleet, sir. You may commence the attack."

* * *

Sara Eaton was silent, staring at the small screen on her workstation. She avoided looking out at the main 3D display tank in the center of *Intrepid*'s bridge, mostly because it was hard for her to look that way without seeing the first officer's station out of the corner of her eye.

She'd lost one first officer in the Battle of Arcturon. James Vargus had been her number two since the moment she'd stepped onto *Intrepid*'s bridge, and his loss had hurt her deeply. But, against all odds, she'd become even closer to Vargus's replacement. Heinrich Nordstrom had not only been a top notch executive officer, he'd been a friend. And now, he too was dead.

She knew she had to get a grip. The captain of one of

the Confederation's line battleships couldn't allow the deaths of crew members—any crew members—to interfere with her operations. But it didn't help that, with all the repairs that had to be done, there hadn't been time yet to clean the stain Nordstrom's blood had left all around his shattered chair.

"Longsword squadron has completed their patrol circuit, Captain. They are requesting permission to land."

Taylor Johns was a fine officer, and she was sure he would be an excellent exec…if she could just get to the point where the sound of his voice coming from Nordstrom's semi-repaired station didn't cut into her like a knife in the chest.

"Launch Black Helm squadron first…then the Longswords can land."

"Yes, Captain."

"And tell the bay I want those ships refit and ready in record time. We're on point here, and if Union ships start pouring through that transit point, we'll be the first to engage. We need to be ready."

"Yes, Captain Eaton." Johns had been respectful, almost reverent. Eaton was sure her new second was well aware of her feelings. One of the effects of raw grief was a tendency to be a bit hard on others. She knew Johns hadn't had anything to do with Nordstrom's death, but he'd moved up in rank because of it, and some part of her—one she wasn't very proud of—resented him for it. She knew it wasn't fair, and she was sure she'd get over it…but she couldn't deny that was how she felt.

Nordstrom was a terrible loss, a deeply painful and personal one, but the tragedy could have been even worse. For a few terrible moments after the enemy fighter had rammed *Intrepid*, Eaton had thought her ship was lost. The hit had knocked out power and thrust, and the battleship had been left floating dead in space. But the Union AI had miscalculated, waited a millisecond too long to convert the warheads the fighter carried to plasmas. *Intrepid* took the kinetic impact, and perhaps half the reaction mass converted. Bad, but not as disastrous as it could have been. If the enemy line had been following up the fighter strike, *Intrepid* would have been lost for sure, but there were no Union forces left in the system, and within two hours Commander Merton and his people had restored partial power and enough thrust for basic maneuvering. Over the next few days her people had worked nonstop, and they'd managed to put the tortured ship into something vaguely resembling operational condition.

Intrepid's primaries were so much scrap, and nothing short of six months in spacedock would change that, if the spinal mount system could be fixed at all. Half her secondaries were lumps of twisted and melted metal. But she still carried working weapons, and half her fighters remained. In any reasonable circumstances, she'd have been sent to the rear for repairs, but Admiral Striker didn't have a ship to spare. Not if the Confederation was going to hold Grimaldi. So, the orders had come down for *Intrepid* to remain in the line.

Eaton had felt a moment of resentment, realizing that her people would be in that much more danger in any fight to come. It wouldn't take much to cripple *Intrepid* again, and being helpless in the middle of a major fleet action was decidedly unhealthy. She felt, for a few moments at least, that her crew was being deemed expendable. But Admiral Striker was a good man, and she knew he'd only kept *Intrepid* in the line because he needed her there. Because the Confederation needed her there.

"Black Helms launched, Captain. Longswords commencing landing oper…" Johns's voice stopped abruptly.

Eaton's head snapped around, overcoming her earlier reluctance to look at the exec's station. Something was wrong.

"Captain," Johns said, "we're getting energy readings from the transwarp point." He looked up from his scope, turning back to face Eaton. "Massive readings. If I had to guess, I'd say we've got one hell of an enemy fleet about to come through."

Eaton nodded slowly and took a deep breath. "Red alert, Commander Johns. All personnel to battlestations."

"Yes, Captain. Red alert."

Intrepid's battered bridge was bathed in the red glow of the battlestations lamps. Eaton felt a deep exhaustion, a grinding fatigue at the nightmare of war. For more than a year her ship had been in the thick of the fight, and there was no end in sight. Nothing but more war…and now a battle she had expected, but had somehow hoped to avoid nevertheless.

"Scramble all fighters, Commander. Advise the launch bay I want the Longswords' ships refueled and ready to launch as soon as possible after they land." Her voice was hard, terse.

"Yes, Captain."

Eaton just nodded curtly, scolding herself as she did. *You've got to stop punishing Johns because he's not Nordstrom…*

"And get me Admiral Striker on the comm. Now."

Chapter Twenty-Five

Inside Abandoned Spacecraft
System Z-111 (Chrysallis)
Deep Inside the Quarantined Zone ("The Badlands")
309 AC

"There's a long transverse corridor down this way, perhaps five hundred meters farther down. I think it might run the entire width of the ship, but I only got about a kilometer, and that in just one direction." Lafarge had been leading Barron around for hours, the two of them followed closely by a pair of Marines. Barron had hoped to slip away from the guards, but Captain Rogan had come close to an apoplectic fit at the thought of his commander prowling around the mostly-unexplored and not fully pacified vessel. He'd insisted Barron take a platoon with him, then he lobbied for a squad before he'd taken his final stand at two hand-picked Marines and utterly refused to budge. Barron finally acquiesced, considering it the only alternative to inciting Rogan's first act of insubordination, even outright mutiny.

"You know your way around this ship better than I do... what did you see that seemed most interesting? What looked like it was vital?"

"There's a room down this way, a big room. It's some kind of storage area...I almost passed right through without a second thought. But then I realized there was a lot of functional equipment in there."

"Functional? What do you mean by that?" Barron looked around, at the glow from the ceiling, even perceiving the invisible but breathable air floating around them. It was clear that the artifact's systems were operating, at least on some level.

"Well, everywhere else I went, all the equipment—the workstations, the panels—they all seemed to be shut down. The lighting worked everyplace I went, and life support is clearly functioning. But I didn't see an actual piece of machinery that looked like it was working. Not until that room."

"I think we should have a look. Do you remember how to get there?"

"Of course I remember," she said sharply. Then: "Maybe the canisters in that room are valuable. They'd be a lot easier to move than this entire ship. I could fit a couple dozen in *Pegasus*'s hold."

"Enough," Barron said, his impatience getting the better of him. "We've got more important things to worry about than what bits and pieces you can scavenge here to make a killing."

"A killing? How about recouping my expenses?" she snapped back. "Do you get a bill when *Dauntless* is refit? Because I sure as hell do."

Barron stared back at his companion, and for a moment he was without words. He wanted to dislike her…but he just couldn't manage it, no matter how much she grated on him. She was stubborn—no, pigheaded—and she never seemed to give up on anything she wanted. She might change the subject for a while, but it was always a tactical maneuver, and she'd work her way back to what she really wanted.

She had ignored his earlier warning, paying lip service to it perhaps, but time and time again she brought the topic of discussion back to her claims to the artifact, or at least some portion of it, usually by circuitous means. Her confidence was like nothing he'd seen before, indestructible, no matter what the situation, and her will was as strong as the core of a neutron star. One minute he wanted to throw her in the brig, and the next the two were talking as if they were old friends.

"I'm quite certain the Confederation will pay for any repairs needed to your ship," he finally said. His words started out cold, but somehow they didn't come out quite as scolding as he'd intended. "Now, show me this room you were talking about."

She smiled and nodded, once again exhibiting her instinct on when to back off. "It's this way," she said sweetly. Barron knew it was fake—no, actually he had no idea how sincere it was—but he liked it anyway.

The two walked down the corridor until they reached the perpendicular passage. Lafarge turned right, and Barron followed, the two Marines right behind. They continued for another fifteen minutes or so, until she stopped at a large double door. One side of the hatch was stuck halfway open. She slid through easily, staring back with a smile on her face. "This is it. Do you think you can squeeze through there, Captain?"

Barron reached around, pulling at the body armor vest he wore, loosening the straps and wriggling out of it. The Marines behind him looked nervous, and one of them stepped forward. "Captain..."

Barron turned around. "Sergeant, there is no way I'm going to get through this opening with my armor on...and I *am* going in there. So, unless you know how to open this door, I suggest you stand aside."

The Marine looked on, his expression as helpless as any he'd ever seen on one of the elite force. Finally, the non-com said, "Please, sir...let us go first."

Barron sighed. "Captain Lafarge is in there. Is anything bothering her?" He let the armor slip to the ground. "You can come with me, but I am not about to stand around here and wait. Follow if you'd like." He leaned toward the door, twisting his body and pushing himself through. It was tight, but he made it. He looked back, watching the Marines for a second as they frantically shed their own armor in an effort to keep up with him. He found that kind of thing annoying in the extreme, but he always tried to remind himself it was loyalty at work. The Marines were just trying to protect him. Driving him crazy was only a side effect of their devotion.

He looked around the room, even as his two guards pushed through the narrow opening in an almost comic display. It was immense, extending almost out of sight into the distance. There were racks and racks of large canisters, most piled neatly, but a few clearly dislodged from their normal places and lying on their sides.

He walked over toward one of the closer containers. It was a cylinder, and near the top there was some kind of readout. There was writing of some sort, but it was in an alphabet that was unfamiliar to him. The readout itself was a glowing green bar. He looked around, confirming that the container wasn't connected to anything, that no cables extended out from it. Clearly, the canister had some kind of power source of its own, at least enough to keep that indicator lit for all the centuries the thing had lain there.

"Any idea what these things are?" Lafarge walked up, standing just behind him.

He could feel her breath on the back of his neck, and he found it…distracting. "Umm…no. I have no idea. But I know someone who may." He took a step forward, tapping his hand against the comm unit. "Fritzie, where are you?"

"I'm in the main corridor, sir. Just trying to get my bearings and figure out what's what in here. This ship is amazing. And the engineering…"

"No time for that now, Fritzie. Grab a couple of your people and home in on my signal. There's something here I want you to see."

"Yes, sir. On the way. Fritz out."

Barron thought he heard something, and his head snapped around, his instincts taking over. He stared across the room, his eyes searching for movement, anything. But there was nothing.

He looked for a few seconds more, but then he turned back, first toward Lafarge and then the smooth metal of the canister.

"What is it?" Lafarge asked.

"Nothing. I just thought I heard…" He caught sight of Lafarge, coming at him suddenly. Then he felt her arm, slamming into his back, pushing him forward, even as her other hand grabbed for the pistol at his side.

His mind raced, his usually calm in action deserting him. Lafarge was a pain in the ass, but he'd never expected her to try to attack him. It didn't make any sense.

He tried to swing his body around to face her, but it was too late. She'd shoved him hard and taken him off guard. He tried to regain his balance, but it was too late. He fell forward as she pulled the pistol from his holster.

He slammed down onto his knees, and then forward to the floor, even as he heard the crack of a weapon firing. But it was from the wrong direction, from deeper in the room. Then again, another shot, from closer this time, and a third. He braced for the pain...but there was nothing. He threw himself over on his back, looking up, his eyes focusing on his Marines first. The two of them had leveled rifles, opening up on full auto, firing at something deeper in the room. Then he saw Lafarge, his gun in her hand. She was shooting in the same direction.

He pulled himself up to his feet, turning his head toward the area they were targeting. There were two figures there, one already sprawled out on the ground, and the other falling backwards, riddled with bullets. It only took a second for his mind to catch up, to fill in the blanks.

FRs...

He was angry with himself. He'd been careless...far too careless.

You let yourself get distracted, wandering around this ship like some kind of explorer, uncovering the past. And letting a woman mess with your head. What are you? A schoolboy? You deserved to get shot.

"Captain, we need to get you out of here now, sir." The Marine looked panic stricken, not Barron knew, because of any fear he felt for himself, but because he'd watched his commander almost killed in front of his eyes.

"Calm down, Sergeant," he said, still staring over at the bodies. "It was just a close call. Get on the comm to Captain Rogan...tell him I want a platoon down here immediately. I want every centimeter of this room searched. I don't know what these things in here are, but we're damned well going to find out. And I don't want any more rogue FRs getting in the way."

"Yes, sir." The Marine looked like he wanted argue, but he just hit the com control on his helmet and relayed the orders to Rogan, looking nervous and uncomfortable the entire time. His eyes shot between Barron and the direction from which the attack had come, and his hands were tight around his rifle.

Barron turned and looked over at Lafarge. She was standing still, her arm extended with the pistol. "Thank you," he said, reaching out and putting his hand on her arm, lowering it gently to her side.

"You're welcome," she replied after hesitating for a few seconds. "I guess you *did* hear something after all."

He looked back at her, and then a laugh forced its way out of his mouth. "Yes, I guess I did."

He stood still, and he smiled at her. She was a certified pain in the ass, there was no doubt about that. But she had also just saved his life.

* * *

Atara Travis sat in the captain's place, uncomfortable, as she usually was when Barron wasn't on the bridge. She didn't doubt her ability to do the job. In fact, she suspected there weren't many decisions she would make differently than Barron would. But it just felt wrong not to have him there. The two were a team, and she liked it that way. Her entire career had been one of relentlessly clawing her way upward, farther and farther from the wretched slum where she'd been born. But now that drive had dulled, or at least been tempered by the fact that her next step—to the command to which her entire life had been guided—meant leaving Tyler Barron, splitting up the team they'd created together.

She knew that day would come. With all *Dauntless* had achieved, there was no doubt in her mind that she would be offered her own ship one day soon, probably one of the dozens of new battleships now under furious construction in the orbiting shipyards of the Iron Belt worlds. And even if it never came—or if she refused the offer of promotion—there was no question in her mind that Barron was destined for flag rank, and probably very soon.

They were different in many ways, certainly in their backgrounds, and yet they were the same too, totally compatible. She was an only child as he was, but now she understood what it was to have an older brother. And without him saying it, she knew she was a sister to him.

"Commander, we're picking up energy readings from the transwarp point." Lieutenant Darrow was at her station, doing the job she did when Barron sat in the command chair.

Her stomach clenched. She'd known the enemy was coming…she'd been as sure as she'd ever been of anything so speculative. But she'd hoped for more time.

"Get me Red Leader, Lieutenant."

"Yes, Commander." A few seconds later. "Red Leader on your line."

"Olya," she said coolly, struggling to hide the tension rapidly building inside her. "We've got something coming through the transwarp link. Your people just launched, so your fuel status is good. I need you to move forward. I don't know what's going to come through there, but if they transit and try to launch, I want you ready to intercept." One squadron of interceptors was a small force to send against even one battleship, but anybody coming through a transwarp jump was going to be disoriented at first…and pilots as good as Federov's Reds could tear apart launching squadrons.

Unless this is another ship like Vaillant…

She'd been as surprised as on the rest of *Dauntless*'s crew to discover they'd been up against the pride of the Union navy. She'd allowed herself to become as cocky and careless as everyone else, expecting to run into Union ships and squadrons that weren't even close to a match for *Dauntless* one on one. The fight with *Vaillant* had taught her humility…and caution.

"Understood, Commander." Federov's voice was almost emotionless, as usual. Travis knew that was as much affectation as anything else, the mode she adopted in battle and on patrol. Olya Federov wasn't a pilot cast in the fiery hot mold of a Jake Stockton or Dirk Timmons. She was cooler, more meticulous. But she was far from cold, and she was actually immensely popular, not only with her squadron, but throughout the entire fighter corps.

Travis cut the line and leaned back. Her mind worked quickly, and she'd already decided what to do. But she forced herself to rethink it, to be *sure* before she issued the orders. *Dauntless*'s resources were not infinite, not by a long shot, and she didn't want to waste them.

She felt the urge to contact the captain, to discuss it with him before she took action. But *Dauntless* was eight light minutes from the artifact, and that made any kind of conversation almost impossible. It would be sixteen minutes before she could even get Barron's answer to a question…and whatever was coming through that transwarp link would be there long before that.

Chapter Twenty-Six

Command Center
Fleet Base Grimaldi
Orbiting Krakus II

"We've got thirty-one battleships confirmed so far, Admiral...and over sixty escorts. Enemy vessels are moving in-system from the transit point, accelerating at one to three g's."

"Commodore Flynn reports his forces have engaged. He has launched all squadrons and is moving to intercept the ships on the Union flank."

"Admiral, fighter command advises we are ready to begin launch operations."

Striker sat in the middle of his command center, half a dozen officers snapping out reports to him rapid fire. He'd been almost ready to gamble that the enemy offensive had been some kind of diversion. He'd even drafted the orders to detach a task force of three battleships and six frigates to send to the Badlands. But those orders had not been issued, and now his doubts were rapidly fading. If this wasn't an all-out assault, he wasn't sure what the hell it was.

"Fighter command is to launch all squadrons. I want the entire force to concentrate on the enemy center."

"Yes, Admiral."

He turned and looked over at Holsten, who was standing right behind his chair. "You picked one hell of a time to visit the front, didn't you? You always seem to be right in the thick of things, just when it hits the fan, don't you? I thought spies lurked in the shadows and tapped comm lines, but you seem to be drawn into the fire."

"What can I say? I'm a hands on kind of guy." Striker had come to realize over the months of their close association just how different Holsten was from his reputation. The intelligence chief was regarded as a rich playboy, and even those few who knew about his other role assumed he had gotten it as a payoff for political favors, bought with his family's enormous wealth. Only a very select few were aware of just how sharply intelligent he was...or how devoted to the Confederation.

Striker leaned toward Holsten. "Seriously, Gary...there is still time for you to get out of here. I can have a fast courier ship prepared." He paused. "There is no reason for you to put yourself at risk. This is liable to be a nasty fight."

Holsten just shook his head. "You're right, of course. I probably should go." He looked around the control center of the massive space station. There were over fifty officers and spacers there, managing information flow to and from the fleet. "But I'm not going to. I think I'll see this one through with you, Van." He paused, staring quietly at the admiral. "My gut tells me you're planning to hold here...no matter what."

"I am. We've done enough retreating in this war. I don't know if the Union forces have another supply base, or not. But I do know we're the Confederation navy, and we're going to behave like it. No matter what it costs. We stop them here. Or we die trying."

"I'm with you, Van, all the way." He leaned in, speaking softly next to Striker's ear. "But if you make a stand here and you're defeated, if the fleet is destroyed, it might just cost us the Confederation."

Striker stared back, eyes narrow and focused, expression cold as space itself. "Then we'd better win, don't you think?"

"All fighters launched, Captain." Taylor Johns gave the report with the same professionalism he'd shown since the moment he'd inherited the job as *Intrepid*'s exec, but there was also a hesitancy, a small chink in his veneer of confidence.

"Very well, Commander." Eaton tried hard to soften her words. She knew the hitch in Johns's tone was her fault, that virtually every word she'd uttered to him since he'd become first officer was edged with resentment, even outright hostility. It wasn't intentional. Eaton thought highly of Johns. But she was still trying to get over the loss of Heinrich Nordstrom, and even speaking warmly to her new exec seemed, in some inexplicable way, like a betrayal.

You've got to cut this nonsense. Now. Heinrich was a friend, and a magnificent officer, but he's dead. And you are better than this. You're *Intrepid*'s captain. Act like it.

"Advise the engine room I may want full thrust on short notice." *Intrepid* was under Commodore Flynn, one of the nine ships attempting to move around the enemy flank. Striker had ordered the fleet's main fighter assault to hit the enemy center, along with another of the task forces. Eaton saw the plan, and she understood what Striker was trying to achieve. She liked it… but she knew it was dangerous too, a calculated gamble. Still, what she thought didn't matter. It wasn't her place to critique the fleet admiral's tactics, merely to execute them.

"Yes, Captain." A few seconds later: "Engine room reports ready. Commander Merton advises fifty percent power is the best he can provide."

"Very well, Commander." She struggled to keep her voice a bit softer, friendlier. She'd have liked a moment with Johns, a chance to explain why she'd treated him as she had…but that wasn't an option now. Hopefully, he'd pick up on her change of demeanor. It was the best she could do at the moment.

She was frustrated with Merton too. Her engineer would end up getting her more than fifty percent thrust, she'd have bet on it. Merton was a skilled engineer, one she was grateful to have, but he tended to hold back on his projections, doing his best to ensure he always met or beat what he'd promised. It was a bit of career management, she suspected, and she understood it. But in the heat of battle, she had to know what her engineer *might* be able to do as much as what he *knew* he could do.

"Tell him I want seventy percent, at least for a short burst."

Johns looked a little surprised. He wasn't experienced yet with the game Eaton and the engineer played. But he would get used to it. If any of them survived long enough.

"Yes, Captain."

Intrepid had no place in this fight. Eaton's ship was badly wounded, and the fact that they were still in the battle line spoke volumes about how desperate a struggle the Confederation fleet faced. Admiral Striker was determined to hold, she was sure of that…but Union ships were still coming through the transwarp link, and with each new battleship emerging, victory slipped further out of reach.

She tapped her hand down on the comm unit, connecting directly to Merton. "Commander," she said, her voice deadly serious, "we're going to need everything we can throw at the enemy. I need you to overpower the secondaries…and no holding back on this one. How much power can you give me on the remaining batteries? I need this straight."

The engineer didn't reply quickly, and she knew he was thinking, taking her command seriously. "I can give you one hundred ten percent, Captain." A pause. "Maybe one hundred fifteen."

Eaton was surprised. She'd expected Merton to be his usual cautious self…but it seemed her engineer was as aware as she was what a desperate fight they faced. One hundred fifteen was more than aggressive, it was downright reckless, and it put the gunnery crews at a terrible risk with each shot.

But Intrepid is already a terrible risk, and if we don't get through this fight, none of us will survive…

"Give me one hundred fifteen, Doug." She spoke softly, calmly.

"Yes, Captain…I'll make it work."

She cut the line.

"Captain, we're entering primary range."

"Very well, Commander." Johns was right to report the

range—and Eaton knew the other ships would be opening up, bombarding the enemy vessel before they could return fire—but *Intrepid* was a bystander in this initial barrage. Her primaries might have some residual value as scrap metal and scavenged parts, but the two big guns would never fire again, and replacing them meant stripping her ship down to its skeleton—a year in port at least.

"*Superb* and *Vanguard* are opening fire, Captain…*Colossus* and *Conqueror* also."

"Very well." Eaton didn't like sitting out the opening exchanges, but there was nothing she could do but wait until her lighter weapons were in range.

"Commander Douglas reports the fighters are about to engage. It looks like they caught the enemy squadrons before they could full organize themselves."

"Advise Commander Douglas he is authorized to attack."

The waiting, the cat and mouse game they'd been playing for days now, was over.

*   *   *

"Keep it tight…their formations are loose, and we're here to blow a hole through for the bombers." Angus Douglas knew his people had a chance to hit the enemy interceptors hard, all along the line…but his primary duty was to get the bombers through to attack the Union battleships. He was a pilot, and though he hated to admit it, he knew every fighter in the system was expendable. The Confederation battle line, most of what was left of it, was here, ready to fight to the last. The Union force was larger and stronger, and that meant his people had to hurt those lead ships as badly as they could. No matter what the cost.

"Don't worry, Commander. We'll give you that hole." Lieutenant Jess Korne was one of his best. She was cocky, like so many of his pilots, but she had the chops to back it up.

"Let's make sure we do, Lieutenant." Douglas was a lot more concerned than Korne appeared to be. The Black Helms were the only fighters from *Intrepid* outfitted as interceptors. Both of the other squadrons configured as bombers. The Longswords and the Gold Shields were each around half strength, and Captain Eaton had wanted to hit the enemy battleships as hard as possible. Douglas understood, but that didn't change the fact that he had only nine fighters—including his own—to hold off the interceptors pouring out of three Union vessels.

His eyes dropped to the scanner. Parts of three enemy squadrons were approaching, reacting as quickly as they could to the approach of the Confederation strike force. Their line was ragged, half their fighters lagging well behind. It was far from an ideal formation for facing attacking interceptors, especially a group as good as *Intrepid*'s Black Helms.

"All bombers, stay in right behind us. You're to continue forward no matter what happens. *Intrepid* is counting on you to hurt these battleships. The fleet is counting on you."

He paused, listening to a few replies on the comm, far fewer than usual. His people understood, he was sure of that, and they were grimly focused. It was disconcerting to listen to focused silence from a group as normally boisterous as *Intrepid*'s fighter wing.

"All right, Helms…let's do this." He tightened his hand around the throttle. "Break."

His eyes were fixed on a pair of fighters near the leading edge of the Union attack force. His hand moved to the side, the thrust from his engines adjusting his vector, leading him toward the two interceptors. Taking on two ships at once was tricky, but he was willing to bet he was facing green pilots. He reached down and armed his first missile, his finger poised over the firing stud. He adjusted his targeting, combining his AI's analysis with his own gut feel…then he pressed hard, feeling the ship lurch as the missile launched.

He brought his bird around hard, gambling that his missile would take out the first enemy fighter. It was the kind of cocky assumption he usually tried to beat out of new pilots, but right now he didn't have any choice. There were just too many of the enemy.

His eyes narrowed, focused on the second ship. He had

another missile, but he wasn't going to use it, not yet. Normal doctrine called for firing the heavy ordnance immediately. He knew his fighter would handle better with no missiles, and worst of all with just one remaining in place, but he still hung on to the weapon.

He fired his lasers…then again, just missing his target. He felt a rush—and a bit of relief—when he saw the first Union ship vanish from his screen. His missile *had* found its mark. But he missed the second ship again with his lasers. He was almost ready to launch the last missile, but he took one more shot. This time his lasers were dead on. The enemy fighter vanished.

That's two…

His eyes darted to the long-range display, looking for new targets and checking on his people. The Helms were fighting savagely, but more and more Union ships were blasting into them from all around. The squadrons from *Vanguard* and *Colossus* were covering their flanks, but there were gaps between both, and Union fighters were swinging around, threatening to engulf his tiny force. He'd lost one ship already, and several of his people had their hands full, dealing with multiple bogeys.

He grabbed his throttle, bringing his ship around toward another Union fighter. The enemy ship was coming right at him. He held his hand on the laser, firing as soon as his enemy entered range. But the Union bird evaded, its vector changing wildly as it approached.

This is no rookie…

He fired again, his lasers not even coming close. Then he saw the enemy launch a missile at him.

He was out of time…he had to conduct evasive maneuvers, shake that warhead. But he wasn't about to let his enemy escape, or get on his tail as he fled the missile chasing him. He flipped his weapons control, arming his second warhead. He stared intently, feeling the sweat pool around his neck. He didn't have time to waste…but he couldn't just loose the missile. He had to get a good shot.

He pulled the trigger, relying rather more on his guts than he liked…and then he yanked the throttle hard to the side, pulling it back as the maximum thrust of his straining engines slammed him into his chair.

He'd waited a long time, almost too long…but he was confident, sure he could break free of the enemy missile. He was sure as he banked hard again, putting everything his ship had into its escape. And he was sure a few seconds later…right until the instant the Union warhead slammed into his fighter, blasting it into plasma and dust.

He never knew if his own missile had hit, if he'd gotten the enemy who had killed him.

Chapter Twenty-Seven

Inside Abandoned Spacecraft
System Z-111 (Chrysallis)
Deep Inside the Quarantined Zone ("The Badlands")
309 AC

"Any idea what these canisters contain, Fritzie? They *are* containers of some kind, aren't they?" Barron stood behind his chief engineer, watching as she inspected the cylinders. The room was active now, the hard-soled boots of the Marines rapping loudly against the metal deck. Rogan had taken Barron's close call as a personal failure, a dereliction of his people's sacred duty to protect their commander. In truth, the Marines were driving him crazy now. They'd searched the room...repeatedly. Not so much as an ancient insect could have escaped their notice...but they were still stomping around, checking the same things over and over again.

"If I had to make a guess without further study, I'd say they're magnetic bottles...really advanced ones. They're a lot smaller than anything we've been able to develop...and I'm at a loss for what could be powering them. No battery technology I know of could have lasted centuries, even just to energize these lights on the exterior. And if they're magnetic bottles, it takes considerable energy just to keep them functioning."

"Magnetic bottles? Like in our fusion reactors?"

"Yes. Our reactions take place at temperatures of millions of degrees. No physical structure could hold something like that. We all know what happens when a reactor loses containment and doesn't scrag in time."

"But there can't be active fusion reactions going on inside each of these canisters. That's not possible, is it?"

"Who's to say what is possible, Captain? But no, my best guess is there aren't reactions going on. Again, I don't see any way the limited amount of reaction mass each of these canisters could hold could have lasted centuries…and if the reaction had been powering the readouts and the magnetic field, they would both have ceased functioning when the last of the fuel was gone."

She pulled a small scanning device from her belt and held it against the outside of the bottle. "This material really interferes with our scanners, sir…but I am detecting something that could be a magnetic field. That supports my theory."

"But if there isn't a fusion reaction in there, what could be…"

"No…" Fritz said, staring at the container, and then looking down at the vast rows of stored canisters. "It can't be. It just can't."

"Can't be what, Fritzie?"

The engineer was silent, clearly lost in her thoughts.

"Commander Fritz," Barron said loudly.

"Sorry, sir…but I…well, I was just wondering if these bottles could contain…antimatter."

"Antimatter?"

"Yes, sir…but it seems impossible."

"Why is it impossible? We've produced antimatter."

"Yes, sir…a few grams, perhaps two or three kilograms total in every research facility in the Confederation in a century. The energy requirements to produce it are enormous." She looked out across the massive room again. "If this is antimatter, it's a million times as much as the entire Confederation has ever been able to produce."

"That seems pretty far-fetched, Fritzie." Barron wasn't

doubting his engineer, not quite. But the idea was hard to swallow.

"Though, it makes sense in some ways too, sir."

"How?"

"It explains what might have happened to many of the ships and installations of the old empire. One of the great questions about the Cataclysm is why we've found so little in the way of substantial artifacts like this one. The empire was vast…it must have had thousands of ships. Perhaps millions. How could this be the first one we've found?" Fritz looked down at the canister sitting on the deck at her feet.

"You're saying that we haven't found more ships or bases because they were all destroyed in matter-anti-matter explosions?"

"It is possible. *Any* level of breakdown in containment would be enough, any level at all…even to destroy a vessel this large. Especially from the inside."

"Any breakdown? You mean like one of these canisters ceasing to function?"

"That certainly. Or even developing the slightest leakage. It wouldn't take much antimatter hitting the regular matter of the outer casing to split the thing open and release the rest of the contents. And that would be the end, even of something as large as this vessel."

"*One* canister could destroy this ship?"

"Captain, one gram of antimatter annihilating with a gram of ordinary matter releases more than forty kilotons of energy."

Barron stared back, a stunned look on his face. "One gram?" His eyes dropped to the canister. "And these hold…"

"Guessing at the mass of the casing and the structure of the bottle, I'd estimate each of these holds fifty to one hundred kilograms of antimatter."

Barron didn't answer. He just turned and looked at the rows and rows of canisters in the room. "But that means…"

"If these containers are full of antimatter, and the more I think about it, the more I'm convinced that is highly likely, it offers us a glimpse at the power possessed by our ancestors.

There's more energy stored in this room than all the power generated on every world in the Confederation. In its entire history." Fritz was as shocked as Barron, almost overcome by amazement, even as she described what surrounded her. "No, far more than that. Hundreds of times the energy ever produced in the Confederation, if not thousands. You said there was some conjecture that this vessel was called a planet killer. I can't speak to actually blowing a world apart without far more analysis, but there is no doubt a weapon powered by such quantities of antimatter could destroy all life and every manmade structure on a planet. Easily."

Barron was looking back at her, his doubt slipping rapidly away. Fritz's theory explained many things. "If they were blasting away at each other with things like this…that explains why so little remains, why we haven't had any kind of contact from within the Badlands in over three centuries."

"Yes, sir. It certainly does. If they had this level of mastery with antimatter, the destructiveness of their weaponry almost defies measurement. If they were fighting right up until the end, it is very possible they completely destroyed each other."

Barron shook his head. He'd known the ancient vessel was a valuable prize, technology that simply could not be allowed to fall into Union hands. But there had been a speculative element to that fear, and it was far from certain how quickly Union—or even Confederation—scientists could have made the vessel operational or learned enough from its technology to develop new weapons and systems. But hundreds of canisters of antimatter…that didn't need to be researched. It didn't need to be weaponized. Its very existence made it a weapon. He *had* to protect this ship. He *had* to get it back to Confederation space. Somehow.

"Captain…" It was Rogan on his comm.

"Yes, Captain Rogan," Baron answered.

"Sir, I just heard from Commander Travis. She tried to reach you but was unable. Apparently external communications can only penetrate so far through the hull."

"Yes, what did she have to say?"

"A Union ship, Captain. It just transited into the system. Commander Travis has launched fighters and is moving to engage."

The news hit Barron hard. He'd been hoping for at least a few more days before enemy forces appeared. "Patch me through to Commander Travis, Captain. You can be our relay."

"Yes, sir." A few seconds later: "Captain...are you reading me?"

"Yes, Atara. I've got Captain Rogan relaying the signal both ways."

"So far, we've got one Union battleship in the system, sir. No sign of further transits underway." She paused. "I took it on myself to act, Captain...the squadrons are about to attack."

"You did the right thing, Commander. *Dauntless* is your ship while I'm stuck here...fight her as you think is best. You have my utmost confidence." It was killing Barron to be trapped on the alien vessel while his ship went into battle. But Travis didn't need that extra burden. She was a gifted commander, and he had no doubt she'd lead his ship into battle as well as he could.

"Thank you, sir." There was distraction in her voice, not surprising since she was about to go into a fight. "Captain, I recalled the Marine transports...sent them back to the alien vessel. I don't have fighters to escort them, and if any enemy interceptors get to those shuttles..."

"That's exactly what I would have done, Commander." But it left that Union frigate there, its crew no doubt feverishly working to restore engine functionality. "Just keep a close eye on that ship."

"Yes, sir."

"Captain?"

Barron spun around. Andi Lafarge was standing right behind him. "Not now, Captain."

"But it's about that Union frigate."

Barron felt a surge of frustration. Whatever else Andromeda Lafarge was—and the jury was still out on that—there wasn't a question in his mind she was a pain in the ass. "What?" he asked, not even trying to hide his impatience.

"*Pegasus*. If Commander Travis allows my crew to launch in my ship, they can return here and pick up some of your Marines. We can get them to the Union frigate and board before the crew can effect any repairs. *Pegasus* is armed, unlike your shuttles. If we run into a fighter or two, at least we can fight back."

"Hold for a second, Atara." He stared at Lafarge. "Your ship would have a better chance than a shuttle if she ran into enemy fighters, but you're still talking about significant danger. *Pegasus* isn't a warship, no matter what weapons you managed to sneak on there. You'd be asking your people to take a terrible risk."

"*Pegasus* can bite back, Tyler. You have to trust me on that. And I'd be taking that risk with them…this offer is based on me going too. My first officer is still on that Union ship, and my people stick together. There isn't a man or woman on my crew who won't risk whatever is necessary to save Vig."

"My Marines would be going too. They'd be exposed to the same danger."

"Would you rather leave a Union ship loose in the system, while your own vessel is locked in combat? The Union has engineers too, you know. They just *might* get that ship operational again."

Barron shook his head, a look of doubt on his face. But then he just said, "Atara…release the crew of *Pegasus*. Advise them to bring their ship back to this vessel and dock where they did before."

"Yes, sir…" There was hesitancy in her tone, but she didn't say anything else.

Barron looked at Lafarge, trying to decide if he wanted to thank her or throw her in the brig until the smug look dropped off her face. He was also worried about her. If that frigate had any operable weapons systems remaining, *Pegasus*'s approach could be a hot one. And he found the thought of her being vaporized along with her ship to be a terribly upsetting prospect.

"If any of them question you, tell them Captain Lafarge is waiting for them here. These are her orders. They are to come here immediately and pick her up."

"Yes, sir." Travis didn't sound much more convinced, but she didn't argue.

"Now, take out that enemy ship, Commander Travis. And keep me posted." A short pause. "Good luck, Atara." He cut the line and stood silently for a moment. His ship was going into battle…without him. He and *Dauntless* had been through hell and back more than once. It was *wrong* for him not to be on her bridge now.

"Tyler…"

Barron had sunk deep into thought about his ship, and the battle it was about to fight. He realized Lafarge's hand was on his arm. He turned back and looked at her.

"I know it's hard for you to be here while your people fight a battle…but you have to have faith in them. They will fight it—they will win it—for you."

"Thank you," he said softly. Then, not wanting to discuss it further, he changed the subject. "You be careful out there. We can't be sure that frigate is helpless…her engines are down, but that doesn't mean she can't blow your ship to atoms." He paused, looking at her for a few seconds. He couldn't get a good read on her. One minute he wanted to strangle her, and the next…

He turned abruptly and looked back across the room, deliberately stopping himself from completing that thought. Anya Fritz was about six meters away, hunched over one of the strange canisters. She had equipment and scanners laid out on the floor all around the thing.

*Fritzie…*Dauntless *is going into the fight without her as well…*

His engineer was a miracle worker, one who deserved as much responsibility as he did for *Dauntless*'s victories. *And now my ship has to fight without either of us…*

"Fritzie…" He walked across the deck toward his engineer. She'd been completely lost in her task, and he startled her.

"Captain," she said, "these canisters are fascinating. The nanotechnology in them is centuries beyond anything we have. And I'm convinced now that they *are* antimatter storage devices. In fact, I'd wager they're cartridges designed to power something…a weapon, perhaps. Though any weapon using this amount of…"

"Fritzie," Barron said. "*Dauntless* has picked up a Union ship entering the system. She's moving to engage."

Fritz leapt up, all traces of her former excited curiosity gone. "We have to get back, sir. The primaries, the engines…they're all functional, but they're fragile too. We have to…"

"We're stuck here, Fritzie. I don't like it any more than you do, but we're just going to have to trust our people."

She stared back at him, her expression communicating the helpless tension she was feeling. He knew her mind was racing, trying to come up with some course of action they hadn't considered, some way to get back on *Dauntless* before the coming fight. He knew, because he'd done the same thing…and come up just as empty as the engineer was now.

"Fritzie, I know how upsetting it is to be stuck here, but we can't do anything about that. Still, we don't have to waste our time. This thing…" He gestured all around. "…is clearly still operable, at least to an extent. We've got to figure out a way to move it. If it has lights and life support, maybe it's got engine power too."

She stared back at him, dumbstruck. "Captain…I wouldn't begin to know where to start. First of all, this ship is massive… we've only even explored a small section. Second, I'm like a child playing with a nuclear reactor. This technology is massively beyond anything I've ever seen. I wouldn't know where to even start. It would take a year just to get a good look around and come up with a reasonable guess about how its systems function."

"Fritzie…we've *got* to get this ship out of here. If the Union gets ahold of it…" He let his voice trail off. He was sure Fritz knew exactly what that would mean, better probably than he did himself. "We just have to get it moving. Until we do, *Dauntless* has to face anything and everything that comes through that transwarp link. There is no way we can leave here, not without this ship. Not even if the entire Union fleet pours into this system."

Fritz just nodded. "I'll do what I can, Captain." She looked up at him, a troubled look on her face. "Sir, I've got half the engineering crew here…if *Dauntless*…"

"Let's have some faith in Commander Travis and the others. You left Lieutenant Billings in charge, right? He's a good man. He'll get the job done."

Barron stared at her with what he hoped was a look of serene confidence. But inside he felt the hypocrisy of his words. He could tell Fritz her people could perform without her, and express all the confidence in the universe in Atara Travis…none of it changed the one fact that was eating him alive.

His ship was going into battle without him.

Chapter Twenty-Eight

CFS Dauntless
System Z-111 (Chrysallis)
Deep Inside the Quarantined Zone ("The Badlands")
309 AC

"Steady, Lieutenant…" Atara Travis was leaning forward, her edginess on display despite her best efforts to hide it. *Dauntless*'s fighters had hit the enemy ship hard, the Blues, Yellows, and Eagles following right on the heels of Federov's Reds, gutting and scattering its interceptor formations and clearing the way for Green squadron's bombers to make their attack run.

The Greens had scored three hits, their plasma torpedoes slamming into the side of the enemy vessel, tearing great rents in its hull. The Union battleship was hurt, there was no doubt about that. But it was still functional, and its disordered fighters were regrouping. The fight was off to a good start, but it wasn't over. Not yet. In a vacuum, Travis would have felt good about the state of things. In fact, she had been satisfied…until three minutes earlier, when the scanners picked up fresh energy readings in the transwarp tube.

More Union ships. It had to be. She thought for a brief, indulgent moment that it could be friendly reinforcements, but she knew the situation on the battle lines too well to believe that for long. It would be difficult to pull a task force from the front.

Whatever was coming to *Dauntless*'s aid—if anything was—it wouldn't be there yet.

"Stand by…" she said softly, her eyes locked on the display. The primaries had been in range for almost a minute, but she knew every thousand kilometers closer increased the chances of scoring a critical hit. In normal circumstances, she'd have opened fire the instant *Dauntless* had entered range, but the new contact put her on a time limit. She wasn't going to have time to fight it out. She'd get an initial shot, maybe a second…then she'd have to pull back. She couldn't risk getting caught too close to the transwarp portal if a couple fresh battleships came through.

Darrow glanced back toward her, for about the third time. She could feel the tension on the bridge. Every officer there *knew* that *Dauntless* should be firing. Travis knew the crew trusted her…but she also understood she wasn't Captain Barron. There was some doubt there, some worry—there *had* to be—especially as they blasted toward their target without their beloved captain, guns silent.

Her eyes flicked down to the scanner on her workstation. Energy readings from ships in transwarp space were notoriously difficult to read. The alien environment in the tube had different properties than normal space, and due to the reflections of transit, the energy she was reading on the small screen defied normal mathematical principles. Even *Dauntless*'s main AI could only guess at what was coming, its projection bouncing around, from one ship to as many as five.

Reading the transwarp energy signatures required as much gut feel as number crunching, and Travis was one of the best at it. She couldn't be sure what was coming, but she gradually settled on a range…three big ships, maybe four. And escorts. Too much to hold her ground and face. *Dauntless* would have to retreat.

Pulling back was a brief respite, she realized, not a solution. The enemy ships would blast into the system, chase down *Dauntless*, and seize the artifact. Leaving the system wasn't an option. She had to defend that ancient ship, somehow. But getting blasted right outside the transit point wasn't going to accomplish anything.

"Lieutenant Darrow…primary batteries are to target the enemy's engines." She didn't have time to destroy the enemy ship, but with some luck she could take it out of the fight, at least for now.

"Yes, Commander." She could hear the uncertainty in the communications officer's voice. The range had closed considerably from maximum, but they were still pretty damned far out for targeting specific sections of the ship.

Travis had been watching everything, the enemy's movement, its course. The Union vessel was performing evasive maneuvers, but she thought she was picking up patterns, similarities in the blasts of thrust designed to thwart incoming attacks. If she was right, it might be just the edge she needed.

She punched in the figures she'd been working in her head, and she sent them down to her gun crews. She had every confidence in her people, and she knew they would make the most of what she gave them, without further instruction. It wasn't a certainty, of course, just a better guess. But she'd take anything she could get.

"Lieutenant…primary batteries are to fire at will."

"Yes, Commander." She could hear the energy in Darrow's voice. Her people were in danger in this system, and they were all veterans enough to know it. But it was still one of the hardest things to sit and endure inaction. Striking out, fighting back…it bolstered even the hardest, most grizzled spacer's morale.

She sat quietly, watching, waiting. She'd done all she could, and now she had to trust her gunners. That was the one thing that came hardest to her. Travis had pulled herself up from the lowest of circumstances, and trust had been one of the first things she'd lost. She'd found a new home serving with Tyler Barron and the crew of *Dauntless*, but she'd never lost her almost fanatical self-reliance.

She watched, the few seconds that passed seeming like hours, and then she saw the lights blink, heard the familiar sound of the big ship's main batteries firing.

"Crash recharge," she snapped almost immediately, knowing it wasn't necessary, that her engineering crew would already be feeding power back into the heavy guns as quickly as the conduits could carry it.

"Yes, Commander."

Travis sighed softly. *Dauntless* was not only without her captain, she was also fighting without Anya Fritz, the battleship's almost legendary chief engineer. Walt Billings was a capable officer, one who'd served alongside Fritz—and kept up with her ruthless and relentless demands for excellence. Travis knew he could do the job, though his sometimes clownish behavior made it difficult to remember that at times.

"Hit, Commander!"

She looked back at the main display. Both primaries had hit their target. The AI was still chewing on the data, trying to assess the damage inflicted. Travis knew that would be an estimate at best. Looking from the outside, tens of thousands of kilometers away, was far from a perfect way to detect damage. But she could see the enemy's thrust dropping…to less than half its previous level. That wasn't an absolute certainty—the enemy captain could have cut thrust voluntarily, perhaps even to mislead her—but her read of the Union vessel's earlier moves suggested an inexperienced and unimaginative captain, one unlikely to attempt such a rapid-fire deception.

"Very well," she said, trying to hold back her own excitement. A hit was a good thing, but they were deep in the shit, and she still couldn't see any way out. It wasn't the time for feeling good. "I want the engines ready for maximum thrust back toward the artifact…as soon as the primaries fire again."

"Yes, Commander." Darrow relayed the command to the engine room.

Travis glanced over at the officer sitting at her station. Captain Barron had requested Darrow for his crew after the communications officer had suffered the misfortune of serving under the only Confederation captain in history convicted of treason. The mud from that sorry incident had splashed far, and nowhere more heavily than on the man who'd sat at the guilty officer's communication station.

There had been no proof against Darrow, none at all, but no other captain in the fleet would take him onto his or her crew. Barron's sense of honor had been offended by the injustice of it all, and he'd personally requested Darrow as his senior comm officer. Travis had been against the move at the time, her own past having taught her to invariably expect the worst from people, but now she had to acknowledge the captain had been right. Darrow was a fine officer, and she didn't doubt his loyalty for an instant. *Dauntless* was stronger for his presence, and any suspicions that might have existed about his trustworthiness were long gone.

She looked at the status bar for the primaries. Just over half charged. She slapped her hand on her own comm unit, pulling up Billings's line.

"Yes, Captain?" The engineer was tired, and he sounded out of breath.

"Lieutenant, I need those primaries charged now. You have to push more energy through those lines."

"Captain…the reactors are at full power now. We…"

"Then take the reactors to one hundred five percent…but I need those primaries in thirty seconds. And twenty would be better." She slammed her fist down on the control, cutting the channel before the engineer could reply. She didn't have time for the usual disclaimers on the dangers of overpowering the reactors.

She looked back at her screen, at the energy numbers from the transwarp gate. The first enemy ship would emerge any second, and the others would be close on its heels. She was running out of time to break off. And she wanted that last shot.

*   *   *

"All right, *Dauntless*!" Dirk Timmons shouted loudly, his voice echoing off the bubble of his cramped cockpit. He was racing back to the ship, along with the rest of his Eagles and the Blues, when he saw the first shot of Dauntless's primaries on his scanners. Both weapons had connected, and it looked from what he could tell like both had scored solid hits. And the second shots had been even better placed.

His fighter didn't have the scanning suite to do complex damage assessments, but there wasn't a doubt in his mind the primaries had hurt the Union battleship…on top of the three bombs the Greens had planted in her. He could see the ship's thrust had dropped, that she was accelerating at less than 1g.

He checked his fuel gauge again, and some of the elation slipped away. He had enough to get back easily, at least to *Dauntless*'s current location, but he also suspected the battleship wasn't going to be there by the time his people made it. There was something coming through the transwarp link…and he was almost certain Commander Travis would pull back out of range. That was a sound tactical maneuver, but also one that would leave his squadrons chasing their mothership, burning massive quantities of fuel to catch her and land. And he was far from sure any of his people had enough left.

"Warrior, I need you to bring your people around. *Dauntless* is going to have to pull back, and you don't have fuel to waste." Kyle Jamison had read his mind. Timmons had come to respect Jamison tremendously, both as his immediate superior, and as a man. "Thunder" Jamison was a deadly pilot too, if not quite his equal in the cockpit.

"Roger that, Thunder. I was just thinking the same thing." Both men left a simple fact unspoken. They had no idea where *Dauntless* would go. Commander Travis would give them all the guidance she could, but if, as it appeared, the battleship would soon be evading multiple enemy vessels, he knew *Dauntless*'s first officer would be hesitant to transmit her intentions too explicitly, even in code.

"Bring your people around toward the artifact, say 3g tops. Then, as soon as *Dauntless* breaks, try to follow."

"Roger that, Thunder." Jamison was farther forward, bringing in the last of Yellow squadron. The Reds and Greens had been farther forward. They had already landed.

Even now, Timmons knew, *Dauntless*'s bay crews were frantically refitting those ships, prepping them to launch when whatever was coming through the transwarp link emerged into the system. He knew, probably as well as Commander Travis, what a daunting situation they all faced. There could be no retreat from this battle. Leaving something as awesomely powerful as the ancient vessel to the enemy was inconceivable.

Dauntless was the best the Confederation had. Timmons was sure of that, as was every other man and woman on the aging battleship. But even the best eventually ran into too much. His mind was beginning to cloud with darkness, with the growing belief that he and all his comrades would all die here in this haunted system.

His alarm dinged, and he looked down as his screen. Another Union ship had just emerged from the transwarp point. A battleship, and from the early data coming in, a big one.

Shit…

He could see *Dauntless* now on the scanner, her thrusters firing at something that looked very much like full thrust. She was heading in the general direction of the artifact, as expected. Then he got the recall signal, along with navigational data for his people to return.

"All right, Blues and Eagles…we've got to chase *Dauntless*, and we've got to catch her while we've still got enough fuel to land. That means precise maneuvering. Anybody who is careless is going to end up ditching…" *Assuming we all don't end up ditching.* "…and with the enemy coming up, there's not likely to be a rescue ship coming along before you freeze or suffocate. So, let's stay sharp."

His people were all veterans, and they didn't need to be reminded of what he had just told them. But he'd seen too many experienced pilots make that one mistake at just the wrong time. He wasn't going to let it happen to any of his people, not if he could do anything about it.

"Let's go, boys and girls…back home. Back to *Dauntless*. Engage thrust now." He pulled back on the throttle, feeling the pressure of the increasing thrust slam into him. He angled his head, slowly, painfully, checking to confirm that his squadrons were following. Then he just leaned back, allowing the padding of his seat to absorb as much of the force as possible, his mind drifting to the odds of his people getting back to *Dauntless*.

He figured it at about 50/50. He didn't like that answer, so he went back over the numbers again, this time factoring in every detail he could think of that had a bearing on the squadrons stretching their fuel enough to catch *Dauntless*.

The second time he came up with 60/40. Against.

Chapter Twenty-Nine

Bridge
CFS Intrepid
Krakus System

Sara Eaton stared at the screen in stunned silence. She gasped for air, forcing it into her lungs, even as her eyes clung to the blank spot on the screen, the one where Angus Douglas's fighter had been a few seconds before. There had been no nervous chatter, no sign of fear or distress beyond the norm. One instant, her veteran strike force commander was there…and the next he was gone.

The pain was odd, theoretical. She knew it was there, but it didn't hurt, not really. Not yet. It was just a vague…something. Douglas had been a loyal member of her crew, even a friend. But he was far from the last member of her crew who would die this day.

"All right, we've all got work to do. This battle is far from over, and we've got our orders." She turned her head toward the exec's station. "Commander Johns, I want full evasive maneuvers as we advance."

"Yes, Captain."

She tapped her hand on the comm unit. "Commander Merton, we're about to enter firing range. Are you ready to power the batteries?"

"Yes, Captain, we're ready." A pause. "I'll get you that one fifteen," the engineer added.

"I know you will, Doug." She shut the line and looked over at the display. Her guns would be in range any time.

Her eyes darted around, moving between four red ovals, Union battleships coming into range. *There...that one.* It was closest, and it was also damaged already. *Conqueror* had hit it twice with primaries. Eaton normally rated her ship the equal of any in the fleet, but *Intrepid* was grievously wounded, with nothing save half her secondaries left to face the enemy. She needed a weakened target.

"All batteries, target enemy contact A11. Prepare to open fire on my command."

"All batteries report ready, Captain," Johns replied a few seconds later.

She watched the range counting down, felt the wild jerks as *Intrepid*'s engines did their best to provide a difficult target to the enemy gunners. The Union ships had left her vessel mostly alone, concentrating their fire on *Conqueror* and *Superb*. It made sense to Eaton. Both of those vessels were in far better condition than *Intrepid*.

She was grateful for the respite...but it pissed her off too. In an illogical way, it offended her that the enemy didn't respect *Intrepid* enough to fear her. She was going to make them sorry for that...

"Batteries ready," she said softly. *Intrepid* was well within range now, but as long as the enemy was going to ignore her, she'd use the chance to close to point blank range.

She could see the deadly fight between the four Union ships and *Conqueror* and *Superb*. The Confederation vessels were giving better than they got, but they were outnumbered too. As Eaton watched, *Superb* took a hit, a bad one. The great vessel visibly staggered, its engines shutting down for perhaps ten seconds before kicking back in at half their former thrust. She knew that hit had caused damage...and that it had killed people. But the battleship's primaries were still online, another shot lancing out even as she watched. The massive particle accelerator beam slammed into the enemy ship that had just scored the hit, and repaid it in kind. The Union vessel's thrust stopped entirely, and unlike *Superb*'s, it didn't come back, not even partially.

Eaton felt a rush of excitement, the thrill of the hunt. A ship without thrust was vulnerable, the extreme predictability of its exact location exposing it to enormous damage. She wondered if—it was Captain Wringer on *Superb*, she remembered—Captain Wringer would wait for his primaries to recharge…wait while each second, the crew of that thing frantically tried to get its engines restarted. It was tempting, she had no doubt, to aim the deadly main weapons with enviable precision, and rip deeply into the enemy vessel's hull. But Eaton didn't think she would let so much time go by. No, she would fire her secondaries.

Just as the thought crossed her mind, the display came alight, *Superb*'s entire broadside opening up, raking the wounded enemy ship. Apparently, Captain Wringer had come to the same conclusion she had. The high-powered lasers didn't have the same punch as the deadly accelerators, but they hit hard enough, especially when nearly a dozen slammed into the stricken vessel's hull.

The ship was still now, motionless save for its residual velocity. It didn't respond, not a weapon returning *Superb*'s fire, even as a second broadside smashed into its shattered hull.

Eaton looked back at her own screen, at the ship *Intrepid* had been approaching. *Still no significant fire. They think we're a spent force. They've written us off…*

She turned back toward the drama between *Superb* and its adversary, watching as the Confederation battleship attacked relentlessly, seeking the kill. She felt a burst of raw ferocity, a satisfaction at the impending deaths of so many Union spacers. It was a feeling she didn't dare analyze too closely. This was war, and right now, her comrades were killing the enemy.

Her own ship was closer now…moving into short range. She had to fire soon. The enemy would pick up the energy build up in her weapons from this distance.

"All gunnery stations, lock on."

"All stations locked, Captain."

She glared at the screen, her hands tightly gripping the arms of her chair, fingers white from the pressure. She could see her target, and even as she was looking she knew the enemy captain had realized he was in danger. The vessel's guns had changed their targeting—now they were firing at *Intrepid*. But her evasive maneuvers held, and the laser blasts went wide to the port and starboard.

The range readout dropped further, into the red zone. Not just close, but point blank range. It was time.

"All batteries…open fire."

*   *   *

"Admiral Flynn's task force is pressing forward, sir…but the losses…"

"The losses are not relevant now, Commander." Van Striker listened to his own words, feeling as though they were coming from someone else, a demon devoid of human emotion and morality. But the voice was his, and though he despised what he had just said, he also meant it. He'd drawn a line in the Krakus system, perhaps even staked the future of the Confederation on victory there. Triumph here was all that mattered. No cost, no casualty list, no amount of suffering was too much to endure to attain it.

"Yes, sir." Jarravick's voice had a grave tone to it. Striker suspected his aide understood what was driving him now. *How can he look at me now and not see a monster?*

Striker turned and looked back across the command center, toward the unadorned spare workstation where the head of Confederation Intelligence sat, silently watching. Striker had urged Holsten to leave several times, but all his efforts had been in vain. The spy didn't offer any tactical suggestions, he didn't try to exert any control over Striker or his officers. He just sat quietly. Waiting to see if he and those around him would survive. If the Confederation would survive.

Striker had come to truly like Holsten, a development that had taken him completely by surprise. He didn't think much of spies, and even less of rich scions born into massive family fortunes...but the longer he'd worked alongside Holsten, the more he'd come to realize just how different the man was from most of those with similar backgrounds. He lived a life of almost unimaginable luxury, yes, and he'd dated half the models and actresses on Megara, but on closer inspection, much of that was a façade. Holsten was a creature of duty, as dedicated and resolute in his own way as any who wore the uniform of the navy.

"*Vanguard* is reporting heavy damage, sir. And *Superb* has been bracketed by two Union battleships. Her primaries are down, and she's bleeding air."

"Very well."

He watched the action on the display, listened to the reports. His people were putting up a vicious fight, the instances of extraordinary heroism worthy of decoration almost beyond count. He found himself hoping beyond reason that the time would come when those medals could be bestowed, when some at least, could gather, having survived the nightmare...and pay respects to the thousands lost.

The Confederation vessels were riddling their enemies with hits, blasting massive Union battleships to scrap. But they were losing too many of their own. Entire fighter squadrons had been obliterated, and hundreds of pilots had ditched, floating in the vastness of the system, helpless, waiting to see if their comrades would win the fight and rescue them...or if they would die alone in the frigid blackness of space.

It was a holocaust the likes of which he had never seen before...and there was no sign of an end. The Union pressed on with a comparable disregard for losses, and everywhere they had the advantage of numbers. Every battleship of his that took down its opposite number was engaged almost immediately by a fresh one, and sometimes by two. Reports flowed into station Grimaldi, hot and heavy, each one of them like the shrieking howl of a banshee, speaking of death and torment.

Still, Van Striker had remained in his place, barely wincing even when the report came in that *Fortitude*, his old flagship, the vessel from when he'd commanded Fifth Fleet, had been destroyed. He'd shut his mind down, forcing his thoughts away from his old ship. He didn't have time to think of just how many friends he'd just lost.

He stared at the display, watching the immense battle that had degenerated into scattered struggles all across the system. Battleships dueled each other, smaller escorts made hair-raising attacks at their much larger counterparts. And, all across the system, the fighter squadrons threw themselves at each other and at the battle lines, torpedo attacks and strafing runs exacting a terrible toll. There were great victories, and gut-wrenching defeats, but slowly he began to come to a conclusion, one the AI projections confirmed, one he had feared from the start. His people were losing the fight.

It wasn't by a large margin, but it was a fact nevertheless. Unless the Union forces broke, they would overcome his fleet… and he knew the enemy wouldn't falter. The Union spacers knew too well what awaited any who failed in their duty. The shadow of Sector Nine was everywhere on that fleet, he knew, the culture of fear those spacers had been born into controlling them with a power no less effective than the Confederation's patriotism.

Striker turned again, looking back at Holsten. He could tell the intelligence chief had come to the same conclusion. They were going to come close…but they were going to lose.

Unless we can get more power into the fight. But how?

A small reserve would make the difference, even three or four more battleships. But there were none. He'd already committed everything.

Almost everything.

He looked around the control room. Grimaldi. He'd committed the station's fighters, but most of the combat had been out of range of the fort's other weapons. If he could get the enemy to attack…

Yes, it just might work…

He could pull the fleet back, make a final stand around the station. Maybe…just maybe the extra firepower would make the difference.

No…not enough. But what if…

Yes!

"Commander, fleet order Priority One. All units are to disengage and withdraw at maximum speed toward the Ultara transit point."

Jarravick hesitated, staring back at the admiral with undisguised horror. It was there, on his face, the brutal resignation. Striker had broken, his nerve had failed. He had ordered the dreaded retreat. The Confederation had lost the battle.

"Now, Commander." Striker's voice was sharper, harder.

"Yes, sir." The veteran aide sounded like death warmed over, his words thick with defeat.

Good…if he believes it, maybe the enemy will too. And if they take the bait, we just might have a chance…

Chapter Thirty

Free Trader Pegasus
Approaching Union Frigate Chasseur
System Z-111 (Chrysallis)
Deep Inside the Quarantined Zone ("The Badlands")
309 AC

"Reverse thrust, Rina…now. We want to go in slowly. If that thing's got an operable weapon left on it, I want to know before we're too close to react." *If they've got one of their main guns up, I'll know about it when half of Pegasus gets blasted to slag…*

"Got it, Andi."

Lafarge glanced over at Rina Strand, hunched over the operations console. She knew Rina had always fancied she could be Vig Merrick's equal at backing *Pegasus*'s captain. But now she suspected her friend was realizing the true stress of that crushing responsibility.

"We're inside the range of their main batteries, Andi…still not picking up any energy readings beyond basic life support and ship's operations."

Lafarge just nodded. *Pegasus* was well-equipped for what she was, an adventurer's vessel. But she wasn't up to military standards, not in most areas. And that included scanning technology. She didn't doubt the Union frigate could hide moderate energy generation from her. Things looked to be going as expected, but she knew there was at least some chance she was being suckered in. Not that it mattered. *Dauntless* was engaged in a desperate fight, and there was no way Captain Barron and Commander Travis were going to allow the frigate back into enemy hands. This was Lafarge's only chance to save Vig…and there was no turning back from that.

She tapped the small comm unit next to her. "Lyn, I want you to stay sharp on the laser. If that ship's got any of their point defense turrets active, we can't give it more than one shot at us."

"I'm on it, Andi." Lyn Vetran was the best shot on *Pegasus*, deadly with the vessel's main laser turret.

"Steady, Rina…steady." *Pegasus* had decelerated almost to a stop, and now she was moving forward at barely a hundred meters a second, a virtual crawl in space travel.

She hit the comm again. "Are you ready back there, Sergeant?"

"We're ready, Captain."

"About two minutes. I'll pop the hatch as soon as we're docked."

"Understood, Captain." The Marine's voice betrayed no emotion save cool respect for her position as *Pegasus*'s captain, but Lafarge knew the sergeant disapproved of her and her people. She might have been offended, but she didn't really care what people thought anyway. *Especially not Marines with ramrods shoved up their asses.*

But you care what Captain Barron thinks. Why? Why are you letting him get to you this way?

She shook her head, trying to purge the thoughts from her mind. This was no time for going all soft over some naval officer she barely knew.

She'd been surprised when Barron had sent almost sixty of his Marines with her…and placed them all under the command of a sergeant instead of one of his officers. But she fancied herself a good judge of character, and despite his poorly disguised disapproval, she'd realized almost immediately that Sergeant Hargraves was a steel hard veteran, one who had seen more action than most warriors survived.

"Dolph," she said into the comm unit, "are you and the others ready?"

"We're ready to go, Andi." A short pause. "I don't think the Marines are very happy to have us here, but they can go…"

"That'll do, Dolph." She sighed softly. "Let's at least try to get along with them, okay?" She'd had an argument with Hargraves about her people joining the assault, and Dolph Messer was clearly still pissed about it. Hargraves had been insistent that her entire crew stay on *Pegasus* and leave the boarding action to his Marines. She'd listened to everything he'd said, every reason he'd offered her why his way was the only one possible. Then she'd stared right into his cold eyes and told him that one of her people was on that frigate, and unless he was going to have his Marines turn their guns on her crew and blow them to bloody chunks, they were going. She'd taken Hargraves by surprise—and she fancied she'd even won some small token of respect from the grizzled warrior—but that hadn't been the end of it. The two had continued their battle…until they'd reached a compromise. Lafarge would hold her people back until the Marines got aboard…then she would wait while they secured the landing area before sending her crew in.

She'd lied a bit, seeing it as the only way to get the giant Marine to shut the hell up. She'd let his heavily armed and armored forces board first…that only made good sense. But her people would be right on their heels, and she had no intention of holding them back behind the Marines. Hargraves's mission priorities were different from her own. He was there to secure the ship, and she was there to save her friend. The Marines would rescue Merrick if they found him, of course, but they wouldn't make it a priority. Lafarge understood that, especially considering the overall situation, but none of it mattered to her. She would do everything she could to save one of her people.

"We're beginning out final approach, Andi. Still no sign of energy spikes or any indication of imminent fire."

Lafarge nodded. "That's good news, Rina. But let's get

docked as quickly as possible. The sooner those Marines are in charge over there, the better I'll feel."

"Closing now…"

Pegasus shook, Lafarge gripping the edges of her chair, holding herself in place. Then she heard the sound of the hydraulics, *Pegasus*'s boarding tube moving into place. There was a high-pitched whine, the laser drills burning through the frigate's hull. Her ship's "tube" was leading edge, and it cut through the skins of most ships like a knife through butter. But *Pegasus* hadn't faced military grade targets before, and now she was taking on a Union combat vessel.

She glanced down at the display, at the readings of the drills' progress. *Faster than with that ancient ship, at least…*

The artifact had almost stopped both her laser and crystal-tipped drilling units, requiring her to overload her circuits and pour every bit of energy she could scrape up into the effort. The frigate's skin was tough, but it was giving way far more easily than the ancient vessel's had.

The red light on her workstation turned yellow, and then green an instant later, signifying that the boarding tube had established a spacetight seal. "You're clear to go, Sergeant," she said into the comm unit. "Good luck."

"Understood, Captain," Hargraves snapped back perfunctorily. Then she heard the metal on metal sound of the main hatch opening…and footsteps clanking forward toward the enemy ship.

Hang on, Vig…help is on the way.

But she sighed almost immediately. She was a realist, and she knew there was a good chance the Union spacers had already killed Merrick.

She shook her head, and then she slapped her hand against her thigh, leaping out of her chair and reaching for the pistol belt hanging over the back of the seat.

"You've got *Pegasus*, Rina…I'm going in with the boarding forces."

"But…" Strand turned with a panicked look on her face, clearly ready to argue. But Lafarge was gone already, her friend's stillborn protest barely a sound in the background as she raced down the small corridor that bisected *Pegasus*.

She was going in. Period.

*   *   *

"Chief, I need those fighters refit and launched in record time. Do you hear me?" Travis's voice was raw, cold. She wasn't angry with Chief Evans, but she suspected it sounded like she was. Travis's blood ran cold in her veins, but even she had a point where the stress, the odds…the sheer hopelessness… overwhelmed her ability to cope. And she was close to that point now.

"Commander, there's just no…"

"Do it, Chief!" If there had been any doubt about the sheer rage in her first command, she knew the second would clear that up.

"Yes, Commander…we'll do everything we can."

"Do that, Chief." She slammed her balled fist down hard on the comm unit. She had always deeply respected Tyler Barron, for his abilities, and for the qualities that made him the man he was. But now she felt something different, a true appreciation for the crushing burdens of this chair she occupied in his place.

How did he get through the battle out at Santis? Or the race to the enemy supply base? How could he endure this stress hour after hour? Day after day?

Dauntless was facing four enemy battleships…and at least half a dozen escort vessels. Travis had watched them transit into the system, and her spirits had sunk lower with each one. Two ships, she thought she just might handle, though at a cost. Three was too many…there was just no way. But it wasn't until she saw the fourth one pop onto her scanners that she truly lost hope. The cluster of frigates following behind was nothing more than insult added to injury. The enemy had far more than it needed to destroy *Dauntless*, and they were closing hard despite her best efforts to stay clear, to pull one of the enemy ships from the group and fight it before the others could intervene.

One ship, at least, appeared to be less of a threat. She hadn't had the time to stay and finish the first vessel *Dauntless* had engaged. There wasn't a doubt in her mind she could have blasted the stricken vessel to atoms given a little more time, but she'd had to make a choice…pull out, then and there, or stand and fight all the enemy ships as they emerged from the transwarp link. That had been no choice at all, and the price she'd have paid for the destruction of one enemy vessel would have been the loss of *Dauntless* with all hands…and an open route left behind to the artifact.

She knew what she had to do, hopeless or not. She had to hold back the enemy any way she could, make the fight last as long as possible…and hope beyond hope that Confederation reinforcements would arrive in time.

She looked over at the display. Blue and Scarlet Eagle squadrons were down in the bays now. The Reds and the Yellows, outfitted as interceptors, and the Greens, once again armed with plasma torpedoes, had already launched. She needed every bit of force she could get, but a second's glance at the approaching waves of enemy craft told her all she needed to know. Her people faced a nightmare. The Reds would struggle to stop the enemy bombing waves, one squadron against perhaps eight times their number…and her Greens, with only the battered remnants of Yellow squadron for cover, would do their best to close and launch their weapons.

Dauntless was pulling back, putting as much distance as possible between itself and the enemy fighters. If Federov and her veteran Reds could hold the strike off for a while, buy some time, maybe *Dauntless* could get far enough back to force the enemy fighters to break off and return to base to refuel. But even that was a longshot. If the enemy battleships moved forward, it would extend the range of the bombers. Even now, she was picking up energy readings, as the new arrivals prepared to accelerate toward her ship.

"Commander, we're getting a report from Captain Lafarge."

Not now…I don't have time for this bullshit…

"Put her on." Her voice was tight with impatience.

"Commander Travis, your Marines have taken control of the Union frigate."

That was good news, at least, if largely irrelevant at this point.

"Thank you for the update, Captain." Then, a few seconds later. "Is it possible to get the enemy ship operational?"

"I have no idea, Commander, but I can dispatch my engineer to investigate."

"No, that's not necessary. Is it possible to fit all of the Marines and prisoners onto your vessel?" Then, a few seconds later: "Actually, Captain… please do send your engineer in and report what he's able to manage." Her first impulse had been to disregard the offer of help from the smugglers, but then she realized she needed any break she could get. She didn't really believe the technician from a ship full of ragtag adventurers would be able to get a Union warship functioning when the vessel's own crew had been unable to do it. But she didn't have anything to lose either.

"Consider it done, Commander. Lafarge out."

"Commander, Lieutenant Federov's people are engaging the enemy's lead fighters now. The Yellow and Greens are on a wide arc, trying to get around the main Union force."

"I'm so sorry, Olya…" Travis's words were soft, not meant to be heard by anyone else. She'd sent Federov's people on a near-suicide mission, and it tore at her insides to think about it. She knew Barron had been in situations like this before, and she had been at his side, recommending many of the desperate measures. But it really was different now that hers was the last word. She'd never realized how much psychic comfort she'd derived from the cover Barron had given her, the way she'd clung to the knowledge that, whatever advice she might have given, it had never been her call in the end. Now it was. She did what had to be done, just as she knew Barron would have…but she struggled with it.

She watched as the Reds blasted forward, into a massive cloud of enemy fighters. They were outflanked on all sides, and even as they tore into their enemy, digging great chunks out of the line with their missiles, the Union forces wrapped around, closed from all sides.

Federov's people were clearly more skilled than their adversaries, and they cut down one Union fighter after another. A dozen. Two dozen. More. But they began to take losses too. One fighter destroyed. Then another disabled, its pilot ejecting in time, but to what purpose? The chance of any kind of rescue was beyond remote.

Travis's eyes moved to the side, watching as a group of enemy fighters broke away from the central melee, chasing her bombers and their scant screen of escorts. The Yellows moved out from the strike force, positioning themselves to intercept. They were outnumbered almost as badly as the Reds, but they appeared just as determined to sell their lives dearly. Then she saw it.

Her eyes snapped back to the main display. One of the enemy battleships was moving to the flank, the distance between it and its fellows increasing. She wasn't sure if it was arrogance, carelessness…or just some poorly conceived tactic to support the Union fighter wings. But whatever it was, she saw her chance.

"Lieutenant, I want the engine room ready for full thrust on my command."

"Yes, Commander." Darrow sounded surprised, perhaps a little confused. *Dauntless* had been falling back, hoping to pull the enemy bombers too far from their mother ships and compel them to break off. That *had* been Travis's plan, but now the hunter in her was awakened again. Falling on one of the enemy ships would let her fight on something like equal terms, and if she could defeat the Union battleship before the other two functional ones could react…she just might cut the odds. It was desperation in its purest form. But it was all she had.

"Engine room ready for full thrust, Commander."

"Very well," she said, her voice distracted. Her eyes were locked on the display, her mind racing with calculations. *Yes… yes, we just might have time…*

"Set a course for 302.111.098, Lieutenant." Her eyes zeroed in on the target, and cold resolve took her. "Full thrust…and I do mean everything Lieutenant Billings and his people can coax from the engines. Now."

Chapter Thirty-One

Inside Abandoned Spacecraft
System Z-111 (Chrysallis)
Deep Inside the Quarantined Zone ("The Badlands")
309 AC

"It could be the difference in the fight. We have to move quickly, before *Dauntless* is overtaken and destroyed. But I'm sure it could work."

"I'm not following you, Fritzie. I appreciate there are myriad uses for antimatter, but how is it any more feasible to harness than it is to get the engines operational? We don't have time for months of research. Or years."

Barron stood in the large room, facing Anya Fritz. She'd been all over the ancient ship looking for some way—any way—to get it moving. Finally, she'd come back and told Barron it was a hopeless task. She'd managed to find what she believed was one of the engine rooms, but the discovery had only confirmed her earlier assertion that it would take years and an army of engineers and scientists to get any of it back in working order…or to even figure out how it functioned. Her best suggestion had been to tow the thing, a job she estimated was doable by three, or perhaps four, battleships…at a maximum acceleration that suggested a trip of several weeks just to the transwarp link in the system, and perhaps two years to get back to Dannith. But she'd also suggested with a new idea, a way to hold out in the system until reinforcements arrived.

"Don't you see, sir? These canisters are massive bombs, just as they sit here. All it would take to detonate them is to crack open the container. Not even...just damage it enough so the magnetic field fails...for even a nanosecond."

"But we don't have any delivery vehicles, Fritzie, no way to hit those vessels. Those are Union battleships, a few near misses in space aren't going to take them out."

"I don't think you understand the magnitude of what I'm talking about, Captain." Fritz's tone was cool, but Barron could hear the excitement behind her words. She really seemed to believe her plan could work. And he had long ago learned never to discount anything from his gifted chief engineer.

"What *are* you talking about, Fritzie?"

"We seed the space around this thing with those canisters, each of them equipped with a small charge, enough to crack open the shell. I might even be able to rig up some kind of proximity fuse, so that any enemy ship moving within, say, ten or twenty kilometers triggers a detonation."

"But we've tried to use nuclear weapons in space before... it's just too hard to get close enough to cause real damage."

"For *nuclear* weapons. We're talking about an entirely different order of magnitude here, Captain."

"How different?"

Fritz looked down at the cylinder laying on the floor to the side. "My best guess is that one of those containers contains enough antimatter to generate an eight or nine teraton blast."

"*Teraton?*" Barron stared back at his engineer, his expression one of shock.

"Yes, sir. Assuming total annihilation. And while the near-vacuum of space might present some problems for a pure cache of antimatter finding enough matter with which to annihilate, the outer structure of the canister itself would provide more than enough in this case."

Barron looked down at the long rows of cylinders stacked up in the storage area. "That is why these things are still here, functioning after all these years. But they would have had to develop containment like that, or they could never have carried all of this inside their ship."

"That's true, sir. Any one of these containers failing for a fraction of a second would have reduced even this enormous vessel to plasma. The failure likelihood would have to zero out at least thirty decimals to make antimatter power feasible. To our science, such a level of reliability and durability is a fantasy. But these people—our ancestors—mastered that, and much more." She paused for an instant. "We know so much was lost in the Cataclysm, but to see something like this…"

"I know, Fritzie. What must their information tech have been, their medicine? But we don't have time for any of that now. If you tell me you can make me weapons out of those things, I need you to do it. Now. *Dauntless* doesn't have much time left."

"I can make you bombs, sir…but I can't get the enemy to come to them. And it would take far too long to rig up missiles, even if I could manage to put something together that had a chance of getting through their point defense."

"Don't waste time playing around trying to build missiles, Fritzie…just make me a minefield. And don't worry about getting the enemy here. Leave that to me."

*   *   *

"He's not going to make it. I doubt he'll last the rest of the day." Stu Weldon was staring across *Dauntless*'s sickbay, toward the eerily coffin-like structure that had been keeping Jake Stockton alive for weeks now. The unit's status panel was blinking red, signaling imminent life systems failure. "Unless I do the regen procedure here."

The tall slender woman standing next to him looked up with surprise on her face. "How? We don't have the facilities on *Dauntless*, Stu."

Weldon returned her gaze. Jane Silla was a gifted surgeon, the second ranking medical officer on *Dauntless*, and as educated

Ruins of Empire

a human being as he'd ever met, but she was far more beholden to orthodoxy than he was. Weldon had always been a bit of a rebel, and most of all, he hated to lose any patient he could save. Could even *try* to save.

"He's going to die, Jane. If we don't do something." He paused, his eyes darting back toward the life support pod. "We might lose him, but I'll be damned if I'm just going to stand here and watch him die. We're both familiar with the regen procedure. There's no reason we can't do it here with what we have on *Dauntless*."

"In theory, Stu. But in practice there are…"

"What's the alternative? Do nothing, and watch him die?" Weldon regretted the bluntness of his statement, but it was nothing but the truth. They could try to perform the necessary procedures, violating normal medical procedures to do it…or they could stand by and watch a man die.

Silla nodded grudgingly. "All right, Stu…let's give it a try." She didn't sound hopeful.

"Let's get him prepped."

"Now? What about the fighting? If we lose power…if we take a hit…"

"Will the battle be over in an hour? In two or four? He's got maybe twelve hours left, Jane, and he's getting weaker with every passing moment. We have to do this now."

She just nodded silently.

Weldon looked out across sickbay, calling over to one of the med techs. "I want Commander Stockton prepped for surgery at once." Then he turned back to Silla. "Go get sterilized, Jane. I'm going to need you every step of the way on this."

"We'll do everything we can, Stu." She reached out and put her hand on his arm for a few seconds. Then she turned and walked across the room toward the prep area.

Weldon looked back toward the tube keeping Stockton alive. "We'll do everything we can, Jake. Everything we can. But, I need all you have to…I need you to fight with all you've got." His words were soft, hushed, meant for his ears only. And perhaps, in some inexplicable way, for Stockton's too.

"I'm glad you made it back, Andi." Barron was surprised by the depth of sincerity in his words. He'd been in the makeshift command center Rogan's Marines had set up on the ancient vessel. They had scavenged the AI systems from one of the assault shuttles to create it. He was focused on the battle taking place in the system, on his ship's fight for survival…but the rogue captain had popped into his mind again and again, even as he watched *Dauntless* blast hard back toward the enemy. He'd regarded that maneuver at first with horror, and then a few seconds later with a grim smile as he realized what Atara Travis was up to. It was a gutsy move, and he wondered if he'd have had the grit try it himself. Still, it was a big risk…

Everything is a big risk right now…

For all the distraction and the aching feeling in his gut about his ship, he'd also been worried about Lafarge, plain and simple. The fact that any concern could get through what he was feeling for *Dauntless* and its people was nothing short of amazing to him.

"Yes, given the choice between survival and getting blasted to atoms, I'll take making it out any time." Lafarge smiled. "I left my engineer behind with a squad of your Marines. I don't know if he'll be able to get the frigate underway, but he'll do his best. He may not be a match for your Commander Fritz, but Lex knows his way around an engine. And he's ex-military."

Barron looked surprised. He stared back without saying anything.

"What, stunned a member of your vaunted Confederation navy could sink so low as to sign onto a pirate ship?"

"Now, don't get touchy…I never called you a pirate. A smuggler maybe, or a no-account adventurer." He managed a smile, for a few seconds anyway. "But whatever you are, I'm happy that frigate wasn't nursing an operational battery."

"Yeah," she said, her voice shedding the touchiness of a moment before. "I'm pretty happy about that too."

"Captain…" Anya Fritz walked into the makeshift control room. "I've been working on that…" She glanced at Lafarge suspiciously. "…that project we discussed."

Barron exhaled softly. "I don't think Captain Lafarge is going to sell us out to the Union, Fritzie." He paused for a few seconds. "What do you have for me?"

"I think we can do it, sir. I'll have to scavenge parts from at least one of the assault shuttles...but I think I can get most of what I need from the ship we already tore apart."

"That's good news, Fritzie. At least if any of us are still nursing some thoughts about getting out of here..."

Fritz hesitated, thrown off her train of thought by Barron's dark humor.

"Go on, Fritzie...don't mind me. My brain wanders into dark places sometimes."

"Yes, Captain...ah...well, I think I can rig a proximity fuse pretty easily from some of the systems on the shuttle. That will give us the option of blowing them all at once, or letting them go as enemy ships approach. With a little luck, we might get thirty of these things ready...even fifty. I think I can even work up some hasty ECM to disguise them, at least somewhat. The canisters do half that job already. But we need some time."

"How much time, Fritzie? I'm not sure we've got all that much left."

"A day."

Barron shook his head. "*Dauntless* is heading into battle right now. Even if she's able to defeat the enemy battleship she's facing, and if she can pull back before the other ships bracket her—and those are huge ifs—a day is still a long time." He paused. "Unless she takes off, and doesn't try to defend the artifact."

"But the enemy would take the vessel. They would..." It was Andi Lafarge speaking now, but only because she'd beat Fritz to saying the same thing.

"They'd *try* to take the station. Bryan Rogan and the Marines might have something to say about that." Barron's voice was stone cold. As crazy as his scheme sounded, he was dead serious.

"But Captain," Fritz said, "even one Union battleship carries at least two hundred-fifty or three hundred FRs. Between the casualties they suffered and the forces still on the Union frigate, Captain Rogan couldn't have more than a hundred-twenty Marines left."

"One hundred-twenty-eight, Fritzie. Not great odds, but no worse than *Dauntless* is facing."

"It's no worse if they only send one ship's worth of FRs. What if they land six hundred troops? Or nine hundred?"

"They can't ignore *Dauntless*, Fritzie. My bet is, we've won enough of a rep that they'll send two ships after her, not one. And the one Atara hit before is hurt. Based on the scans we've been getting, she's still near the transit point, limping along with less than 1g acceleration and limited energy output."

"That's a lot of 'ifs,' sir." Fritz looked uncomfortable.

"You have a better plan? If we let them destroy *Dauntless*, they'll come here with everything they have…and Rogan's people will have the same fight, but against even worse odds. I don't see any of our Marines surrendering to the FRs, do you, Commander?"

"No sir," Fritz said. "I don't."

"And even if they defeat any boarding action, once *Dauntless* is gone, what chance do we have to hold out against subsequent assaults?"

"None." Fritz paused. "You're right, sir. There is no option."

Barron frowned. "I have to get word to Atara. My last orders were to stand and defend the artifact. She won't pull back farther into the system, not unless I tell her to. We can't risk a transmission…if the enemy figures out that we're setting up a minefield, we're as good as done for. They'll launch an intensive sweep, enough to overcome whatever ECM you are able to put together. We need some level of surprise to pull this off." He paused for a few seconds. "I'll have to go back…I should be there anyway. I'll take one of the assault shuttles."

"You can't, Captain, for the same reason you didn't want to send the Marines that way. If the enemy detects your course… well, sir, an assault shuttle isn't the fastest or most maneuverable ship out there."

"There's no choice, Fritzie. I'll have to risk it. Meanwhile you get the minefield ready, and we'll see what we can do about setting up a trap for our Union friends. You'll be in charge here once I'm gone."

"Captain…" It was obvious she didn't like the plan…and equally clear she had no alternative to offer.

"No."

Barron turned to face Lafarge, standing right behind him.

"You can't take one of those shuttles. They could catch you in one of those in a garbage scow," she said with more feeling than accuracy. "I'll take you in *Pegasus*, just like we did with the Marines."

"No, Andi…not this time. The enemy frigate was in the opposite direction of the fighting. We'll be heading right toward *Dauntless*, while the enemy ships are all trying to close with her. It's too risky."

"It's a hell of a lot less risky than letting the one man who might get us out of this mess get blown to bits on a shuttle that handles like a snorting pig. Don't underestimate *Pegasus*, Tyler… or me. I'll fly you there myself."

"I insist on that, at least, Captain." Fritz's voice was like iron. "She's right. You'll have a much better chance this way. That ship of hers has jets."

Barron opened his mouth to argue, but then he closed it again. He was between two women who clearly didn't get along, but they were doubling up on him right now. He knew Fritz would risk Andi's life—or throw it away entirely—if it increased his chances of getting through by half a percent. And there was no way to explain, to either of them, why he really didn't want Lafarge to go.

"All right…we'll take *Pegasus*." There was resignation in his voice, and worry. This trip would be far more dangerous than the expedition to the frigate. They would be running a gauntlet through the entire enemy fleet, trying to reach *Dauntless* amid waves of fighters and escort ships…any one of which could blast Lafarge's vessel to ions.

"Good," Lafarge said, looking entirely too self-satisfied to suit Barron. "I'll get the engines fired up."

"Yes, the sooner we get going the better."

She smiled at him—*damn, that is distracting, even now*—then she turned and half-walked, half-jogged toward the door.

He turned back toward Fritz. "Fritzie, you need to gather up everything you need, and move it all with your engineers to some location that seems far from any ingress points. If the Marines are going to have to fight to hold this place, the last thing we want is the enemy getting to your people."

"Yes, sir. I think I found a few spots when I was looking around." She looked behind her. "But we've got a lot of this stuff to move and not much time. And no lifts, no cargo sleds."

"The Marines can help…as long as you move quickly and finish before they have to set up their defense." He took a deep breath, fighting back the stress he felt closing in all around him. He hated being away from *Dauntless*. He hated leaving Fritz and her engineers and the Marines behind. He hated the thought of getting blown to bits in *Pegasus* on the way back, of Andi dying, his people being left without him. He'd been in impossible situations before, but he wondered now if this wasn't the most desperate of all. If it wouldn't be the last.

"I've got to brief Captain Rogan before I go. I'll have him send half his people down here to help your crews."

"Thank you, sir."

"Good luck, Fritzie," he said, realizing the instant the words left his mouth he'd failed utterly to disguise the emotion he felt. Barron didn't give up…it just wasn't the way he was wired. But he knew his chances of seeing his engineer again weren't good.

"And to you, sir." Fritz was just as affected. "It's been an honor serving with you."

Chapter Thirty-Two

CFS Dauntless
System Z-111 (Chrysallis)
Deep Inside the Quarantined Zone ("The Badlands")
309 AC

"Bring us around, Lieutenant...bearing 302.132.289." Atara Travis was gripping the arms of her chair—of Tyler Barron's chair, she reminded herself. *Dauntless* was operating at only thirty percent thrust, but the dampeners weren't functioning properly, and the intermittent bursts of force that resulted were distracting, to say the least. The battle had been hard fought, the Union battleship putting up one hell of a fight.

"Yes, Commander."

Travis could feel the change in *Dauntless*'s thrust as the positioning jets reoriented the engines to the course she'd ordered. She knew she had to pull out...and soon. Her squadrons had done heroic work, and they'd paid the price for it too. Her people had shot down dozens of approaching bombers, but they hadn't been able to turn back the entire first wave. Two bombers had managed to plant their torpedoes in the battleship's guts, and a dozen or more interceptors had raked her hull. Travis knew *Dauntless* had been lucky...she'd taken damage, but nothing critical.

"Port secondaries...lock on to that frigate. Open fire!"

Darrow repeated the command, and an instant later Travis heard the high-pitched sound of the weapons. She imagined the great bursts of focused light, tearing through the twenty thousand kilometers between *Dauntless* and the enemy escort ship. Then she saw the results on the display. The broadside had hit dead on…and the smaller ship stood motionless in space for a few tortured seconds before it split open like an egg, its shattered hull breaking into two large and hundreds of smaller pieces.

There was a round of muffled applause on the bridge. Any kill was a cause for celebration, but picking off a frigate or two wasn't going to get *Dauntless* or its people out of the Chrysallis system. Indeed, as far as Atara Travis could see, nothing could manage that lofty goal.

"Switch bearing to 302.287.102, increase thrust to forty-five percent."

"Yes, Commander."

Travis knew her people whispered behind her back, speaking of her as though her grasp of numbers made her some kind of genius. She'd always had a strong handle on the mathematics of space travel, and her mind worked quickly with complex calculations, allowing her to compute courses that sent other officers to their AIs. But she was far from the savant some of *Dauntless*'s people made her out to be.

If they think I'm more capable than I am, I don't suppose that can hurt right now…

"Starboard guns…ready as we come about…" Her eyes were locked on another frigate, one of the newer, heavier classes. "I want all guns at one hundred five percent, Lieutenant. And I want the gunners to be sure of their lock…we don't have the luxury of missing right now."

"Yes, Commander," Darrow replied tensely, before he relayed the command.

Travis watched as *Dauntless*'s bearing shifted, bringing the enemy ship right into the point-blank range of its broadside. She stood, frozen, waiting…then, "Fire!"

The previous scene was replayed, the sound of the guns, the

silence during the intervening seconds before the AI reported yet another series of direct hits. The frigate didn't break open this time, but it was riddled with deep wounds and bleeding atmosphere. Its energy readings were sustenance levels at best. Whoever was or was not still alive over there, the ship wasn't going to be a threat to *Dauntless* anytime soon.

Travis's eyes moved to the display. The enemy battleship was closing again. The two vessels had passed each other, exchanging all the fire they could manage before zipping by each other to decelerate and return for another run. The Union warship was still dangerous, though it had taken the worst of the encounter so far, but that wasn't Travis's biggest worry. It was the other two ships, closing rapidly, moving to cut off *Dauntless*'s escape. And beyond, nearer to the transwarp link, the first ship, the one she'd hit so hard, was now moving again. It was barely limping along, and she suspected many of its weapons and systems were so much junk, but that didn't mean it was completely out of the fight.

She knew it was time to blast engines full, to swing around, back toward the artifact...to get ready for the last stand. But she wanted one more shot. She *needed* one more shot.

"Cut thrust to twenty percent, Lieutenant. Prepare primary batteries...full crash charge."

"Yes, Commander."

She stared at the enemy ship in the display, watching its thrust, the steady feed of numbers reporting everything from projected energy output to exact thrust angles. She knew her people had hurt that ship, though the kind of critical hit she'd really needed hadn't materialized. Perhaps they had one more chance.

"Status of primaries," she snapped, though her eyes moved at the same time, reading the gauge herself. Just over half way.

"Sixty percent, Commander," Darrow dutifully replied.

C'mon Walt...get me that power flow...

She didn't envy Walt Billings. He had some huge shoes to fill trying to take Anya Fritz's place. She'd always thought the engineering officer was a bit of a clown, though she'd never doubted his skill or intelligence. But he'd come into his own in the past few hours, exceeding all expectations, keeping *Dauntless* nearly fully operational despite two torpedo impacts and at least half a dozen laser hits. If, through some miracle, they managed to survive and get back to the Confederation, she was determined to see him decorated. And she was damned sure going to tell Fritz in no uncertain terms how brilliantly her people had performed, understaffed and without her.

She watched as the indicator moved the final few centimeters. It was time. One more shot…then she had to get the hell out of here.

"Primary batteries, fire."

*   *   *

"I didn't think I could still get space sick after all these years, but now I stand corrected." Barron sat in the third station on *Pegasus*'s cramped bridge. He was monitoring the scanner…and looking a bit greener than was seemly for a naval captain.

"You don't want to get shot, do you?" Lafarge was sitting at the pilot's station, the captain's chair empty. "You said yourself, it's dangerous out here. Well, you were right." She moved the controls hard, suddenly, catching Barron unaware, and shaking him in his chair. "Just make sure you're strapped in, and I'll get you back to *Dauntless*. I'm sorry if we don't have the kind of fancy dampeners you've got on that battleship of yours, but there's a limit to what a pirate like me can afford."

Barron turned back around, and stared at her, willing himself not to be sick. "I never called you a pirate. A crazy person, maybe. Where the hell did you learn to fly this tub?"

"You think this is the first tight spot I've gotten myself out of?"

"We're not out of it yet."

"So little faith…" She brought the ship around again, hard. Barron was beginning to wonder if she was really evading enemy ships…or if she just liked matching the strength of her stomach against his.

"We're almost there. Maybe you should call your ship and let them know it's us. I'd hate to slip by all these Union ships only to get blasted by your people."

"*Pegasus* is in *Dauntless*'s database, and Commander Travis knows your ship. They won't shoot at us."

"But we've still got to dock, and that ship of yours is gyrating like a fish flopping around in a boat." She switched on the main screen. "We've got a scanner feed now."

Barron turned and looked up at the small display. *Dauntless* was there, and then he saw the energy readings spike up dramatically. He knew immediately, his ship had fired her primaries.

At least the main batteries are still online. That's a good sign…

But his eyes caught more than just *Dauntless* and the ship she'd been fighting. There were two more Union battleships, and they were getting dangerously close.

C'mon, Atara…get out of there…

Barron liked to think he had strong nerves, but he'd never seen anything like the stuff that stiffened Atara Travis's spine. If he hadn't known better, he'd have thought she'd scooped it right out of a neutron star.

"*Dauntless*, this is Free Trader *Pegasus*…we are on an approach vector and request permission to dock."

There was a brief delay. Then Darrow's voice crackled through the comm unit. "Negative, Pegasus. We are in combat. You are to pull back at once and stay clear."

Barron smiled. He could hear Travis's words in that response. She'd been more receptive to Lafarge's crew than he had been, but he'd seen her before in combat, the way she clamped down and focused on the struggle at hand. She would have no time for Lafarge's people, not now.

"Lieutenant Darrow, please advise Commander Travis that Captain Barron would like to come aboard." He knew he shouldn't have given his name. In an age of supercomputers and sophisticated AIs, it was always a race between breaking codes and creating new ones. His training had made one thing clear about combat cryptography…always assume the enemy could be listening. And there wasn't much doubt about the effort the enemy would take to shoot down *Dauntless*'s famous captain. But he didn't have time to play games with Atara, and he wasn't entirely sure she *wouldn't* open fire on a *Pegasus* that ignored her command. They were too close for the enemy to intercept them anyway, even if they picked up his transmission. Probably.

"Captain?" It was Travis's voice, and he could hear the excitement in it. And the tension.

"Yes, Atara, it's me. I need to get onboard *Dauntless* as quickly as possible."

"Of course, sir…" There was a short pause. "We're conducting evasive maneuvers. We were just about to pull out of here. As soon as you get within five kilometers, I'll terminate our…"

"You'll do no such thing. You keep dodging enemy fire with everything you've got." He turned and looked across the bridge, a strange grin on his face. "I've got a pilot in here that can dock no matter what you're doing. We'll come in slow. When we get within ten kilometers, transmit us your thrust plan for the next thirty seconds…we'll adjust and dock on the fly." Barron knew he'd just committed *Pegasus* to a maneuver his instructors at the Academy would have called crazy. But the whole situation was crazy.

"Captain, you can't…"

"That's an order, Commander." Then, a few seconds later. "I've got it under control, Atara. Trust me."

"Yes, sir." She still didn't sound happy, but he knew asking for her trust would shut her down. There was no way for her to argue after that.

"Ten kilometers," he repeated. Then he cut the line. He glanced across the cramped confines of *Pegasus*'s tiny bridge, ducking to look under the low riding conduit that partially blocked his view of his companion. "That's not a problem, right?" he said, somehow drawing a bizarre satisfaction from calling Andi on her boasts…even though he was stuck there with her. "Not for a pilot like you…"

"No, it's no problem."

He could hear the unease in her voice. She *was* good, he knew that. But the maneuver they were about to attempt was as insane as any Academy class said it was. He'd never have attempted it, no matter how good a pilot was at the helm...but the only alternative was for *Dauntless* to cut its evasive maneuvering, and that would make his ship a sitting duck.

"No problem at all," she repeated. But he knew she was scared. He was scared too.

*   *   *

Dauntless shook hard, and Stu Weldon struggled to maintain his balance with only his legs. It would have been easy enough to reach out and grab something...except both of his hands were deep inside a man's body, desperately working to save his life.

The operating theater was bright, garish, the lights bathing the sterile whiteness of the room with an almost blinding intensity. Doctors Weldon and Silla had been working for hours, surrounded by four of their staff, trying with all their skill and talent to perform a procedure they had no place attempting in a spaceship's sickbay. One conventional wisdom held was impossible.

Weldon had resolved to make the attempt, no matter what. The only alternative had been to watch his friend die, trapped in the confines of a two-meter-long metal tube. Weldon had a hard time discerning where realism and hope met, whether his belief he had a chance was real, or just a facet of his relentless stubbornness. But he knew one thing. He wasn't going to give up, not while Jake Stockton was alive...or even still revivable.

Stockton had "died" twice already, but both times the resuscitator had brought him back. Weldon had faced a moment of crisis early on, a near-panic that shook his confidence. But he'd quickly pulled himself back together, and for a short time, he'd actually been optimistic. He and his team had made enormous progress, and he'd begun to believe they could actually pull it off. Then *Dauntless* went back into battle.

The ship had been hit multiple times since, and with each one, Weldon's laser scalpel shook in his hand. The lights had blinked in several instances, and, one heart-stopping time, the power had failed entirely for a gut-wrenching thirty seconds. Stockton's life functions had stopped that time, and had only been restored with great difficultly. Even Weldon had been almost ready to call it…when one last desperate attempt was crowned with success.

"Dr. Weldon…we have casualties." The med tech was standing outside the clear wall of the theater, speaking through the comm unit.

"Damn," Weldon muttered under his breath. He'd known it was only a matter of time, but *Dauntless* had gotten through the first part of the fight without taking significant losses. "Serious?" he asked without looking up.

"Yes, sir. Two are critical. We've got radiation burns too, and one serious case of rad poisoning."

"That cuts it, Jane…we can't both be in here." He paused, sucking in a deep breath that was half a need for oxygen and half pure stress. "Go…you handle things out there. I'll finish this myself…somehow." He had no idea how he was going to pull Stockton through without Silla, but he knew one thing for sure…friend or no, he couldn't let *Dauntless* spacers sit out there and die while the battleship's two surgeons were in here fighting a probably hopeless battle to save one man.

"Stu…"

"Go," he said, more harshly than he'd intended. "Go," he repeated, softer the second time.

Silla stood where she was for a few seconds, silent, unmoving. Then she slowly extricated her hands from where she'd been working. She looked like she might say something, but then she just walked out into the airlock that kept the hyper-critical theater sterile.

Weldon looked down at Stockton. The pilot looked like a nightmare, the victim of diabolical torture rather than a man receiving the best care possible. He appeared to have been flayed alive in places, and in others, the film that would hold the regenerated skin as it grew was a ghostly, almost translucent white.

Come on, Jake…you're a strong SOB. Pull through this with me…

Weldon gulped down a deep breath, and he leaned over again, getting back to work as *Dauntless* shook hard once again.

Chapter Thirty-Three

Command Center
Fleet Base Grimaldi
Orbiting Krakus II

"Get me General Ramsay." Striker's voice was raw. "Now."

"Yes, Admiral." A few seconds later. "On your line, sir."

"Mack...I need your Marines in position. The enemy might just blast Grimaldi to scrap, but my gut tells me they want to take it. If they board...well, that makes it your problem. Yours and your Marines'."

"Yes, sir," the officer replied grimly, "it does. Don't you worry, Admiral. If they board this station, they'll have one hell of a fight on their hands."

"I know they will, Mack. And I can promise you we'll give them everything we've got before they board."

"I never doubted that, sir. Not for a second."

"Get your people ready, General. You know all the likely ingress points, and the bottlenecks in the station." He hesitated for a second. "And you know the FRs too, how they think."

"Yes, sir." There was hatred in the general's response, one that spoke volumes of the animosity between the Marines and the FRs.

"Go to it, Mack." He cut the line. Grimaldi had a full brigade of Marines, eighteen hundred strong, and Striker knew every one of them would fight to the death if it came to that...

as he knew it very well might.

He looked over at the display, watching the fleet move toward the transit point. All but Commodore Flynn's task force. His ships were having trouble disengaging. *Superb* was gone now, lost with Captain Wringer and all hands. *Colossus* was a wreck, dead in space and spewing what remained of her atmosphere through half-kilometer long rents in her hull. She didn't have a gun left, nor an engine, and Striker had ordered her abandoned. He didn't know what would happen to the spacers who managed to escape, whether they had any chance of rescue, or if they'd just float in their lifeboats while the rest of the Confederation fleet was destroyed. But they were alive now—almost half the crew had escaped—and Striker tried to focus on that.

"I want those primaries to count, Commander. We'll be taking a lot of incoming fire, so we don't know how many shots we'll get. We don't waste any. I'll skin the man who misses right now." Striker didn't care how unfair his statement was, it was how he felt. Men and women were dying all across the Godforsaken system, and he needed every hit he could get if there was to be any chance those sacrifices had been worth the cost.

"Yes, Admiral."

He'd pulled most of the fleet back. The Union forces had pursued briefly, but now they were doing exactly what he'd hoped they would. They were massing for an attack on Grimaldi. The enemy was battered, almost as badly as his own forces, but they had the strength to take the fortress...as long as they were willing to pay the cost.

And hopefully that cost will be substantial...enough for what I need...

"I think I know what you're planning, Van." The barely audible voice was Holsten's. Striker turned to see the intelligence chief leaning down behind his chair, whispering. "It's a gutsy move, and just maybe one that will work. But you're the commander of the entire fleet, and that means you have no place here when this station is being blasted apart, when FRs are boarding from all sides. You need to transfer your flag."

Striker looked around the command center, clearly uncomfortable having the hushed conversation in front of his officers. "That's not going to happen, Gary. No chance."

"Van…your responsibility goes beyond Grimaldi and the people here."

"No," Striker said, catching himself as his volume grew too loud. "But there's no reason at all for you to be here, Gary. This is my place, my duty. I *have* to stay with my people. But it's foolish for you to remain. We can still get you out of here before we're cut off."

"I'm staying."

"Gary…"

"I'm staying, Van. We'll both see it through to the end."

Striker looked like he was about to argue further, but finally, he just nodded.

"Commander Jarravick, I want all personnel armed and armored. If we have to repel boarders, by God, every man and woman on this station is going to fight."

"Yes, sir." Jarravick still seemed confused, but the raw defiance in Striker's words seemed to energize him. A moment later: "Admiral, Commodore Flynn reports the remnants of this task force are retreating toward the fleet rally point at the Ultara portal. All except *Intrepid*…"

Striker turned his head abruptly toward the display. Sara Eaton's ship was there, a small blue oval surrounded by enemy ships. "What is *Intrepid*'s status, Commander?" He already knew there was nothing he could do, but he had to ask.

"Her engines are down, sir. She appears to have two operable batteries and some minor level of energy generation. A lot of this is guess work. The enemy's all around her, jamming comm signals."

"Get me Captain Eaton!"

The aide hunched over his station, his hands working the communications controls.

"Commander…"

"Sorry, sir…we can't get through. The interference is too great."

Striker stared at the screen, feeling a wave of helpless panic.

Ruins of Empire

He knew there was nothing he could do, even if he could reach Eaton…but it was worse being cut off. Eaton was one of the heroes who had destroyed the enemy's Supply One base, arguably saving the Confederation in the process. Tyler Barron was the other. He'd sent one into the trackless wastes of the Badlands, denying him the reinforcements he'd promised, and now he was going to watch Eaton's ship overwhelmed and destroyed.

"Admiral, the enemy's first line is entering range."

Striker took a deep breath, doing all he could to focus, to purge Barron and Eaton from his mind. He stared straight ahead, his eyes cold.

"Open fire."

*   *   *

"Reroute the power, Doug. I don't care how you get it there, but I want those guns firing." Eaton stood amid the wreckage of *Intrepid*'s shattered bridge.

"Captain, *Intrepid* is done…there's not a system that is more than a pile of half-melted junk." Merton's words were harsh, but she could hear his own pain in them. She loved her ship, but Douglas Merton had crawled through every centimeter of its vast compartments and access tubes. He had nursed her through battle after battle, carefully repairing her damaged systems. And now he was watching *Intrepid* die.

"We've still got two guns, Doug, and that means we're still in this fight. I need that power."

"Captain, the reactors are both down. Unit A is completely gone. B is almost as bad. It would take me a week to get it back online. We've got nothing left but backup battery power…and we're losing that rapidly. We've got fires out of control everywhere. The bays are both gone. Half my engineers are dead. Hell, half the crew is dead. There's nothing left, Captain."

Eaton wanted to scream, to thrust her hands in the air and howl out all the pain and frustration. But she just sat where she was. Her ship was dying…and she was its captain.

But her crew. She was ready to die with her ship, but she had to give her people any chance they had. She reached out, opening the small control panel at the edge of her chair's armrest. There was a red button inside. She'd imagined herself in many situations, but never this one. She hit the button.

"Attention all personnel. Abandon ship. Abandon ship. Immediately…and Godspeed to all of you."

She leaned back in her chair, staring straight ahead, her eyes dull, lifeless. It would be over soon.

"Captain…"

She heard Johns's voice, but it was distant, far off. She was going to die. That was all that mattered now. It wouldn't be long.

"Captain Eaton," Johns said, shouting this time. "We have to go."

"No," she said unemotionally. "You go, Commander. All of you…go!"

"Not without you, Captain." Johns reached out and put his hand on her arm. "Come with us…I'll help you to the lifeboat."

"No," she said, brushing aside his arm. "I'm staying here."

"Then I'm staying too, Captain." He looked up, staring across the bridge at the other officers, who nodded back in turn. "We're all staying."

"No, you're not." Eaton stood up, turning to face her officers. "All of you…abandon ship. That's an order."

They all stood firm, staring back at her. Johns put his hand on her arm again. "Captain, I'll ask you once not to make a mutineer out of me…but if I have to, I'll carry you out of here on my shoulder kicking and screaming." He waved toward the rest of the officers. "And they'll all help me." He paused. "We're *all* going to get out of here…or none of us are."

She looked back, a flush of anger taking her at first, but then subsiding. She understood her people were loyal, that they wanted to help her. Why didn't they understand? She didn't want to survive her ship's destruction.

She felt Johns's hands on her arms. Then another pair of hands, pulling her toward the lift. She fought for a few seconds, struggling to get back to her chair, but then she gave up and let them guide her toward the access tube…and down to the bridge's lifeboat.

*   *   *

"You may proceed, Admiral Beaufort." Villieneuve sat to the side, watching as the Union's top admiral directed his staff. The fleet had pushed the Confederation forces back, compelled them to abandon their vaunted main base for the second time in less than two years. Villieneuve had intended the invasion to be a diversion, but now it seemed as if Beaufort was on the verge of breaking the enemy's back. The Confeds had taken terrible losses. At least ten capital ships had been destroyed, along with dozens of escorts and a number of fighters that defied easy counting. They had made a stand, chosen this spot to hold the line, but now they were broken, fleeing.

"Yes, Minister. At once." Beaufort's voice was hoarse and heavy with exhaustion.

Villieneuve sighed softly to himself. The cost of this "victory" had been almost unimaginable. No fewer than fourteen battleships were gone, and most of what remained were damaged, at least to some extent. Whole fighter wings had been obliterated, and more than forty frigates and other escorts were now radioactive debris. He'd taken a chance committing the strategic reserve—and he still faced a dangerous and unpleasant confrontation when the Presidium discovered what he had done—but those ships had proved to be crucial, the added weight that pushed his forces through to victory.

This isn't over yet. We still have to deal with the base…and then pursue and destroy the remnants of their fleet.

Beaufort had asked if he wanted the base destroyed or taken. He'd felt the urge to shout, "destroy it," to be done with Grimaldi and the whole Krakus system, to push on after the fleeing Confeds. But his intended diversion offered the prospect of so much more now, and if he could capture Grimaldi, it would cut the time to build a forward supply base in half. It was too good a chance to pass up.

Villieneuve knew he'd taken a terrible chance coming to the front, and he'd been scared during the battle, especially when *Victoire* ended up on the front line, locked in combat with a Confederation battleship. He'd felt his mortality there for a few minutes, but then additional fleet units rushed to the flagship's aid, overwhelming and destroying the enemy vessel. But the payoff was beginning to look like a big one. The Confed fleet was on the run…and he had dispatched a second task force to the Badlands, enough power to overcome anything Captain Tyler Barron and his troublesome group of spacers could manage, even if they had somehow escaped destruction at the hands of the first four battleships he'd sent.

He tried to stay focused, but it was hard to keep thoughts of victory from his mind. The coming months could see the long-awaited triumph over the Confederation *and* the recovery of the knowledge of the ancients. The power that technology offered was more even than he could easily imagine. But Villieneuve was a measured man, and he'd learned not to count conquests before they were won.

Even now, his leading fleet units were moving forward, enduring the devastating fire from Grimaldi's particle accelerators. It was a gauntlet they had to run, but once they'd entered their own range the dynamics would shift measurably. The Confederation's base was an awesome construction, but it was basically stationary…and that meant once they were in range, his ships could blast it until its weapon systems were so much scrap. Without the evasive maneuvers that made spaceships so difficult to hit, the massive fortress was an easy target.

"I want all FR contingents on alert, Admiral…all landing craft ready to launch. That thing has a lot of Marines on it, and I want every soldier we have ready to hit it as soon as you knock out the weapons."

"Yes, sir. All Foudre Rouge companies on full battle alert."

Villieneuve watched the main display as the fleet moved inexorably toward the Confederation base. Two more battleships had been gutted by the fortress's weapons, but the rest continued on, and the lead ships were now opening fire.

He watched the fight going on in front of him, but his thoughts wandered, out into the Badlands, to Admiral Villars and the considerable forces Villieneuve had placed at his command. He had some questions, bits of information he longed to possess. First, had Villars found the ancient ship? Had he secured the greatest treasure trove of technology in the history of the Union?

And second…had his forces engaged *Dauntless*? Had they destroyed Tyler Barron and his thrice cursed ship?

Chapter Thirty-Four

CFS Dauntless
System Z-111 (Chrysallis)
Deep Inside the Quarantined Zone ("The Badlands")
309 AC

"Bring us around, Commander Travis. I want full thrust in thirty seconds." Tyler Barron snapped out orders as he stepped out of the lift and onto *Dauntless*'s bridge. "Set a course toward the Z-117 transit point." Barron felt a strange calm as the familiar surroundings of his ship's control center sunk in. He trusted Atara Travis implicitly—at times he even thought she might be a better tactician than he was. But there had just been something...*wrong*...about his ship fighting for its life when he wasn't there.

"Yes, Captain." Travis leapt up from the Captain's chair with an obvious wave of relief. "It's good to have you back, sir." She walked across the bridge toward her station, just as Darrow jumped out of her chair.

"I understand and agree with your tactics, Commander, in trying to finish off this last ship. I'd have done the same thing in your shoes. But there are a few tactical factors that apply now that you don't know about...and they require us to get the hell away from here. Immediately."

Travis paused, looking very much like she might question the decision to leave the artifact undefended, but it only lasted a few seconds. "Yes, sir." A few seconds later: "Ready for full thrust on your command, sir."

Barron plopped down in his chair, pausing for a moment. The situation was as dire as any he'd experienced, but he still felt a rush of satisfaction at being back in his place. The unnatural feeling of helplessness, watching, waiting to see what would happen to his ship was gone. There was still fear, of course, and doubt...but at least he would share his vessel's fate now. There was something about that fact that seemed right to him.

"Andi, you can take one of the extra workstations." His head turned toward the lift, where Lafarge still stood after following him onto the bridge. "Get strapped in, this is likely to be a rough ride."

There were a few surprised looks on the bridge. Barron had been far from solicitous of the smuggler captain and her crew earlier. But *Dauntless*'s team had more to worry about than their captain's attitude toward a few passengers, and they quickly returned their attention to their myriad tasks.

"Fighter status, Commander?" Barron was looking down at his workstation, his finger swiping across the screen, his eyes skimming the damage reports. They were extensive, but nothing that seriously degraded his ship's combat effectiveness. That was a lucky break, he knew.

"All squadrons are in the bays, sir. Refit operations are underway, but they've been slowed by battle damage. Beta bay is in better shape than Alpha...but they're both still functioning. Blue squadron is ready to launch, but I held them back because I was planning to pull back on the artifact." She paused. "Casualties have been high, sir."

Travis didn't offer any numbers to back up her statement, though Barron didn't doubt she knew the exact strength of each squadron. And he didn't ask.

"Very well." He reached down, pulling up the harness and strapping himself into his chair. Then he turned his head, checking that Lafarge had done the same. "Full thrust...engage."

"Engaging, sir."

Barron felt the force of at least five times his weight slam into him, perhaps more. *Dauntless*'s dampeners were normally able to absorb just over half the battleship's roughly 11 g's of thrust, but the pressure seemed heavier than normal, most likely the result of damage to the compensation system. Barron sucked in a deep breath, struggling to force the air into his chest. High g maneuvers were hard on a crew, and no group of spacers performed as well sitting at their stations being slowly crushed. But *Dauntless* needed velocity now more than anything. In a few minutes, he would know if he'd been right, if the enemy was afraid enough of *Dauntless* to send two ships to pursue…as he hoped they would.

Rogan's people had a chance against one ship's FRs, but if two or more of the enemy changed course and moved on the ancient vessel, the fight would be over. The Marines would be overwhelmed and destroyed…and Commander Fritz and her engineers would be killed or captured before they could finish their work. His longshot, the plan to somehow prevail here against impossible odds, would be stillborn.

"C'mon, you bastards…follow us…" He spoke softly, a whisper to himself, as he stared at the display, waiting to see how the enemy ships would react. Then, one of the two battleships that had been closing changed course to pursue.

That's one…

His eyes were glued to the display, his stomach twisted into knots…waiting. Only a few seconds passed, but they seemed like hours, days. Then he saw it. The ship Travis had been pursuing blasted its engines, going after the first vessel. Following *Dauntless*.

Yes!

He looked back on the display, toward the first Union ship, the one Travis and *Dauntless* had crippled. It was accelerating, but still at a snail's pace. Barron didn't know whether the ship's crew would get the wounded vessel truly functional again, but for now it was out of the fight. There was nothing to do but hope that state of affairs continued.

Barron sat in his chair, silent, but inside he was crackling with nervous tension. His plan was working...so far. It was desperate, a wild tactic to save the amazing technology on that ship for the Confederation, and to keep it out of Union hands. The odds of success seemed beyond calculation, but it was the best chance they had. Nothing less than the existence of the Confederation was at stake.

*   *   *

"Sergeant, I want this platoon divided into separate fireteams...and I want a veteran non-com in command of each one. Shift around the OBs if you have to. We don't know where the enemy will dock, and we've got to be ready to react to anything."

"Yes, sir!"

Bryan Rogan had been racing around the vessel, doing his best to prepare a defense. It was an impossible task. The ancient ship was enormous, over a hundred times the mass of a Confederation battleship. Only small sections of it had even been explored. If the enemy boarded in some remote section, they could disperse throughout the ship before his people could respond.

"And I want a tactical reserve placed here." He held out a small tablet, pointing to a spot on the rough map displayed there. "This is where we docked, and there's a good chance they'll come right at us near there." Rogan wasn't sure what he would do in the enemy's situation. Landing in remote locations and dispersing would certainly make it more difficult for his people to clear out the invaders...but the reverse was true as well. If the FRs wanted to gain control of the ship as quickly and effectively as possible, they'd come right at his people, seeking to wipe them out as quickly as possible. The assault shuttles docked to the giant ship's hull were as good as a flashing sign pointing to his Marines' location.

"Understood, sir."

"See to it, Sergeant." Rogan returned the non-com's salute. Then he turned and took a few steps toward the door, stopping abruptly as one of his officers burst into the room.

"Captain, the enemy's coming in. They'll be docking within minutes, sir." Lieutenant Plunkett had joined *Dauntless*'s Marine contingent in a unique way, as one of the few survivors of the force deployed to defend the tritium refinery on Santis. That battle—against the Alliance, not the Union—had been small, but one of the most horrific in the history of the Marines, and there had been no doubt afterward that Plunkett and his few surviving comrades would join *Dauntless*'s detachment. Captain Barron himself had seen to it, facilitating the necessary orders with a little push from his famous name.

"Well, it's as good now as ever." He took a step toward Plunkett. "As soon as we get a solid idea of where they're coming in, I want you to command the forward defense. You know as well as I do, the more we can pen them in, the better off we'll be."

"Yes, sir…but we don't even have a very good idea of where *we* are. If they break out from the area we've got mapped…"

"I know, Lieutenant, I know. We can only do our best." He stared at the other officer. "And we can fight like hell. These are FRs coming…and they don't get past us. It's that simple."

"Yes, sir." Plunkett's tone left no doubt he shared the captain's animosity toward the Marines' old enemies.

"Let's see it done."

Plunkett stared back for a second, his eyes blazing with intensity. "Yes, sir," he repeated grimly.

*   *   *

"Any updates?" Clete Hargraves stood just inside the hatch, looking down at the engineer. Lex Righter was sprawled on the floor, his arms extended halfway into the open panel.

The engineer looked up, his face twisted in frustration. "Nothing. I've tried everything I can to get these engines operational. The fighters who attacked this thing hit it hard. A shipyard might be able to do something, but short of that, I think this ship's flying days are over."

Righter knew that technically the ship *was* flying. It was still moving through space on the course it had been on, and with the velocity it had possessed when its engines went offline… as it would remain forever, or at least until it ran into a sun or an asteroid, or nearby bodies exerted gravitational forces on it to change its vector. That was all well and good for a physics lesson, but the reality was starker. Every second took the ship—along with Righter, Hargraves, his Marines, and their captives—toward the outer reaches of the system…and eventually, interstellar space.

"No chance?"

"None. Sorry…I've done everything I can."

Hargraves frowned. "I think we've got a problem, then. *Pegasus* is gone…sent back to the artifact with the rest of my Marines."

"We should have them send it back before we get too far away."

"That's a no go. Things are too dangerous out there now… too many enemy fighters and escort ships. They'd never make it back. Besides, they've got troubles of their own. The last comm flash said the enemy is about to board the ship."

Righter pulled his arms free, and scrambled up to his feet. "Sergeant, I empathize with what the rest of your Marines are dealing with, but we need a ride off this tub."

"Well, we ain't gettin' one, not any time soon, so you might as well get back to what you were doing and try to figure something out." Hargraves turned around and slipped back out the door.

"Fuuuuuck…" Righter looked back at the panel, and at the spread of control boards and conduit junctions he'd laid out on the floor. There was just no way. He could whip himself up, pretend for a while, maybe, but he was never going to get this frigate underway.

He thought about *Pegasus*, about the tense feeling he'd had watching it leave. Some part of him, the survival instinct of the adventurer, had longed to get on the ship. But his mouth had displayed a will of its own, as it had so often before when he'd gotten in trouble. He could still hear it…his words, volunteering to stay, and try to repair the frigate's engines.

"That'll teach you to keep your mouth shut." He sighed. "While you're drifting through space for the next ten thousand years…"

He froze for a moment. *Wait…*

A shuttle.

A Union frigate had to have its own small craft…a shuttle, or gig or a cutter. Something big enough to get him—and Hargrave's Marines—off this ship. There was no guarantee such a vessel would be operational. The frigate was pretty badly shot up. But it was a chance, at least, maybe something he could fix.

Righter reached down, gathering his equipment into his kit. "So, where the hell is the bay in this thing?" he muttered to himself.

He got up, hoisting the sack over his shoulder. "Where the hell is the bay?" he repeated. He walked out into the corridor. It *was* a chance…and he was going to take it.

* * *

"Keep him in the compensator…and make sure those backup batteries are in place. Ten seconds of these g forces will kill him for sure."

"Yes, Doctor." The med tech looked concerned, her eyes moving over the doctor's haggard form.

Stu Weldon stood against the wall, looking very much like he might fall over if forced to stand without support. His face was drawn, his skin so pale he almost blended in with the stark white of the sickbay walls. The procedure had been the most difficult he'd ever attempted, and he'd had no right to expect any chance of success. He wasn't ready to claim victory yet…there was at least a fifty-fifty chance that Jake Stockton would still die. But that was a damned sight better than the absolute certainty the pilot had faced earlier.

"And get me another shot of stims."

"Doctor Weldon, you've already had triple the maximum dose."

"Then this will be quadruple, won't it?" Weldon stared at his aide with exhausted eyes. "Just get it, Lieutenant. I don't have the time or strength to argue with you. We've still got wounded, right? Should I let them die? Ask them if they'll just wait while I take a nap?" He knew he shouldn't have been so hard on the tech. She was just doing her job, and he knew her concern was real. He also knew a few more stim injections, and his heart wouldn't just stop, it would probably explode. But none of that mattered now. He had a job to do, just like the captain and the others. And by God, he was going to keep going until every wounded spacer on *Dauntless* had been treated.

"Yes, Doctor." The technician turned and walked over toward a bank of cabinets, opening one and pulling a vial from a half-empty rack.

Weldon just stayed where he was. He needed that stim. He wasn't sure he could walk across the floor without it. He turned his head, looking back at the life support pod that once again housed his patient. The regen was in place, the cells and development culture applied to the pilot's body. It was a rough job, sloppy by any textbook standards, but those same books said it wasn't even possible without a full medical facility. Weldon had intended to save Stockton's life. He'd come as far as he could, trading certain death for a coin toss. Much of the rest of it was up to Stockton himself, and Weldon knew that was good news. He didn't know many people tougher than *Dauntless*'s ace pilot.

His eyes caught the red lamp next to the door. *Dauntless* had been at battlestations for hours now. *The crew's going to be needing stim injections soon too.*

He winced as the tech jabbed the syringe into his arm. He'd given thousands of injections, of course, and cut bodies in ways he could hardly describe. He'd performed gruesome rituals, covered in the blood of horribly wounded men and women. But he hated getting shots himself.

"Thank you, Lieutenant."

"Of course, Doctor." He could see the tech still disapproved, but he didn't care. Rules, procedures…they only took you so far. Then people started dying unless someone went rogue. And for *Dauntless*'s battered, burned and broken crew, that someone was him.

He took one last look at Stockton, and felt a passing gratitude for the red alert. At least Stara Sinclair was on duty. The officer, whom Weldon had never known as anything but a pillar of strength, had spent every off-duty second sitting next to Stockton's med pod, her hand resting on the cool glass, a cold, glassy look in her eyes. It was better that she didn't see him right now. Even a few hours would make a difference in how he looked, as the new skin began to grow, making him look at least marginally less like a full-sized anatomy lesson. Assuming he lived.

Weldon shook his head. There was no time to worry about that now. He'd done all he could…for Stockton, at least. Now there were others who needed him.

Chapter Thirty-Five

Inside Abandoned Spacecraft
System Z-111 (Chrysallis)
Deep Inside the Quarantined Zone ("The Badlands")
309 AC

"Pull it back, Fergus. We're trying to draw them forward into the main compartment." Rogan was standing just behind his Marines' forward positions. The gunfire had been intense, the fighting fierce. Rogan had gotten his wish, more or less. The FRs had come right at the Marines. The Union battleship had blasted the Confederation assault shuttles, and then their own craft landed right next to the twisted wreckage of the Marines' ships.

"Fergus is dead, sir. So is Swanson."

"Orrin? Can you get your survivors back?" Rogan tried not to think about how many of his people were down if Corporal Orrin was in command.

"I don't know, sir. They've got the flanking corridor. We're pinned down here. I might lose the rest of the platoon if we make a push to get down that hallway."

Fuck.

Rogan looked behind him. There were two squads lined up against the wall. They were full strength and ready to go, but they were the only reserve he had left. The enemy was pushing in from two directions. Plunkett's people had them stopped, at least for now, but he was still reluctant to commit his last fresh troops.

What passes for fresh, at least...

His Marines had been at it for days now, not full-scale combat save for the past few hours, but hunting rogue FRs and doing what they could to secure the station. He'd rotated them on sleep periods, but tossing aside the bulkiest pieces of body armor and crashing on the floor for a few hours wasn't exactly resting up for combat. Every man and woman in his command was sleep-deprived, and none of them had eaten a meal beyond cold combat rations in days now.

None of that matters...they're Marines...

The thought was reflexive, but he knew it was bullshit. Marines were big on sayings like that, and there were few in their ranks as *Marine* as Bryan Rogan. But pretending his people were as effective tired and hungry as they were rested and well-fed was just stupid. That didn't mean they wouldn't fight like hell... they would. *That* particular piece of Marine lore was spot on. But it did mean they could lose.

"Let's go," he yelled, turning to face the reserves. "We're moving up." He'd considered every possibility. He'd done the math, calculated the probabilities. It was safer to leave Orrin's people on their own. There couldn't be more than a dozen of them left up there, and there were twenty Marines in the reserve squads. He could hit the enemy harder advancing from here than ordering Orrin's people to fall back.

Twenty-one.

Rogan was in command. His place was in the rear, directing the fight. He knew the rationale behind that, he even agreed with it. He was well aware that more men and women were relying on his command ability, that getting himself killed now would only hurt the overall defense. But none of that mattered. Those were his people up there, and by God, he was going to go get them.

The day I abandon my Marines to the bottomfeeding FRs is the day I need a fucking bullet in my head.

"Let's move," he shouted, pulling the assault rifle from his back. "We're gonna go up there and get our comrades…and we're going to send every shit kicking FR we see to hell!"

He heard a lusty cheer behind him as he ran forward, his rifle at the ready in front of him. Then the sounds of hard boots on the metallic deck—twenty Confederation Marines, moving forward like the incarnation of death from a forgotten myth.

"With me, Marines," he yelled, fanning the rage of his small force. "With me…"

*   *   *

"Maintain full thrust, Commander." Barron sat in his chair, and despite the tension, the heart-pounding danger of the moment, it felt like home. This was where he belonged, on his ship, surrounded by his people, and if his skills were to fail him, if luck were to abandon him at last to death and destruction, then this is where he should die too.

"Captain, we've been blasting at full for two hours. The engines…" Barron put his hand up, and Travis let her words trail off. He knew she wanted to remind him about the thrust, but the last thing he needed was a lecture on engine stress factors. Not now.

"I'm aware of that, Commander," he said unemotionally. "Maintain maximum acceleration."

"Yes, sir."

Barron could almost hear the other reminder, the one Travis had caught *before* it had escaped her lips. Commander Fritz was still on the artifact…and that meant Lieutenant Billings and the skeleton engineering team remaining onboard were all that stood between the overworked engines and a catastrophic failure. Blowing out the engines and ending up on a fixed course, unable to conduct evasive maneuvers, would be the end. The Union ships chasing *Dauntless* would finish the job quickly… and all chance of preserving the artifact for the Confederation would be lost.

Barron had considered all of that, but in the end, he'd

decided he would rather depend on faith in his people than any other factor. He'd always liked Billings, and for all the engineer sometimes came off as less than a serious person, Barron was well aware that the lieutenant knew his shit.

He watched the display. The Union ships had lost ground, falling behind as they'd cut thrust to rest their engines. Confederation technology was the superior between the powers, and *Dauntless* could at least attempt to maintain maximum thrust for extended periods. Any Union vessel that tried was almost certain to end up with burnt out engines.

Barron looked back down at his screen, scrolling through the pages of calculations he'd been running. He'd done it all himself, though he'd had the AI check his math. It should work. It *would* work, he'd told himself, with something less than total assurance. It was a maneuver that required precise calculations, but if it was successful…

"Adjust thrust vector to 221.002.115, Commander. Maintain full output." He spoke calmly, his words soft, almost as though he was chatting with a friend instead of commanding his ship in battle.

"Adjusting course, Captain." Travis sounded crisp, broadcasting to all who were listening that she understood exactly what the captain was planning. But Barron knew his first officer well, and the slightly robotic tone to her words told him she hadn't figured it out yet. "We're going to go just by the transit point on this heading, sir, close enough for the gravity well to interfere with our bearing."

"I'm aware of that, Commander. Maintain course and thrust." He was sure it was just a welcome break from the fear and stress, but he was enjoying watching Travis try to figure out what he had in mind.

He leaned back in his chair, trying to hide his own stress. He'd done the calculations, but reading the gravitation from a transwarp link was, at best, an estimate. The faster-than-light connection points were vastly beyond any technology understood in the Confederation, and what scientists didn't know about the amazing constructions could have filled a vastly larger database than what they *did* know. Barron understood that the points gave off waves of gravitation, and that there were generally patterns to the intensity…but he knew he was still guessing.

Dauntless shook as it approached the portal. It was off-course for entering the tube, but far closer than a ship not transiting would normally come. He knew Travis wasn't the only one confused…hopefully the pursuing Union ships had no idea what he was doing. That would be helpful…if his scheme worked, the enemy would have to react quickly, or he would gain the jump on them he wanted.

The ship was rocking hard now as it blasted through the gravity waves at close to one-half percent the speed of light. Barron was counting in his head, his eyes whipping back and forth from the main display to his small workstation screen and the list of calculations scrolling down the page. He hit a small button on his control panel, sending a data file to Travis.

"Lock this nav plan in to the computer, Commander," he said softly. "Prepare to execute on my command."

"Yes, sir." Barron wasn't sure, but he thought he caught the hints of preliminary understanding in her voice. He wasn't surprised. He didn't think he had a chance of fooling her for long. However crazy his plan might be, he knew she'd catch on.

Barron took a deep breath, struggling to fill his lungs. The force of acceleration was hard enough to endure for short bursts, but now every muscle in his body ached. He knew he'd be covered with bruises, as would everyone on the ship. He was also aware that all work on *Dauntless*—the engineers making repairs, the medical personnel down in sickbay, and everywhere else on the massive ship his crew was performing its duties—was proceeding at a glacial pace. There were ways to deal with high g forces, powered exoskeletons and other tools, but it was still difficult to operate under such conditions for so long.

"Execute nav plan," he said.

"Executing, sir."

Dauntless shook again, and Barron could see the ship's vector change on the display as the engine fired at a revised angle and the gravity well of the transwarp point exerted its own force, modifying the continuing thrust from the engines. He squinted, trying to see the new vector as it was recalculated and rendered in the display. His vision was spotty and narrow around the edges—the effect of sustained g forces. But he stared until the image solidified.

Perfect. The course was exactly what he wanted. Directly toward the system's primary…and at the current velocity and acceleration, *Dauntless* would reach the star in less than twenty minutes.

*   *   *

"Any progress?" Hargraves's words had softened somewhat, his earlier suspicious tone toward the engineer moderated considerably. Even a veteran Marine could mellow. And whatever else Lex Righter was, the man had been working his ass off trying to get Hargraves and his people off the Union frigate.

"Some. It's not a total wreck, like the main engines. But it's not in good shape either. It took a lot of damage in the fighting. Worse, I think it must have been hooked into the main power lines when the reactor scragged. There are blown circuits everywhere."

"I'd ask you if you think you can fix it, but I have a feeling you just answered me."

"I can fix it," the engineer said, his pride jumping ahead of his judgment. "I'm pretty sure I can fix it, at least. But it's going to take some time."

"Well, time we've got. We're moving away from the fight, so there's no immediate danger." Hargraves exhaled heavily.

"You want to get back to your comrades, don't you Sergeant? It's killing you to be here while they're fighting."

The old Marine just nodded at first, looking uncomfortable about the entire conversation. But then he said, "I've seen a lot of men and women die over the years, good Marines—and good spacers too. Most of the faces are still with me. I see them at night sometimes." He paused. "I'm not sure what's worse, the ones I remember…or the ones I don't. But nothing cuts deeper than the Marines I knew who died when I wasn't there."

"Are the FRs really as bad as they say?"

Hargraves looked back at the engineer. "Depends on how you mean. In a fight? Yeah, they're tough. But I never met the FR who could take on a veteran Marine. It's more than just combat skill, though. There's something about them…they're not quite human. Being around them gets to you…it wears you down. And they always fight to the death. Always." He paused. "People don't stop to think what war is like when the other side keeps going until the last one is dead. There's no fight against them that doesn't turn into a massacre."

"Do we have a chance, Sergeant?"

"Who? Us here? That's more in your hands than anything. Or the Marines back on the station? If only one ship lands FRs, yes, our people could win. It will cost…I don't even want to think about what it will cost. But we have a chance."

"No, in the whole system. *Dauntless*, the enemy ships, everything. I don't see how we make it out of here."

Hargraves was silent for a moment. Then he said, "I can't tell you about space combat and battleships fighting each other—and I know nothing at all about that artifact over there—but I can tell you one thing. It's not logic, it's not military science…but I believe it to my core." The Marine looked directly at Righter, his eyes boring into the engineer's. "Don't ever count Captain Barron out. Ever. As long as we have him, we have a chance."

Chapter Thirty-Six

Command Center
Fleet Base Grimaldi
Orbiting Krakus II

"Admiral, you need to transfer your flag...now! I can get a company up there to escort you to one of the launch bays, but I can't guarantee we can hold that route open for much longer. If you don't go now, you could be trapped up there." Ramsay's voice was raw, and Striker could hear the sounds of fighting not far from the Marine general.

"General Ramsay, I will not abandon this station. Not under any circumstances." Striker had made his choice. He'd declared that the battle in the Krakus system would be to the finish, and now he'd drawn a line across his control center. He would not be forced back. He would not retreat, leaving the Marines and spacers to fight in his absence.

"Admiral..."

"That's my final word, General. See to your Marines and your battle lines. We are all expendable in the pursuit of victory here, and that includes me."

"Yes, sir." The Marine didn't sound very happy. But he didn't argue either.

"Fleet status, Commander?" He looked over at Jarravick. It seemed strange to see his people wearing helmets and light body armor, but he'd ordered everyone so equipped. The FRs had landed in more than a dozen places. They were all over the station, the battle for control of Grimaldi taking place in hundreds of scattered actions. Anybody on the fortress could end up in a fight with the enemy, and Marines or spacers, engineers or stewards…Striker expected every one of his people to fight to the last.

"All fleet units have fully disengaged. The lead units are approaching the transwarp point."

"Enemy pursuit?"

"Minimal, sir. A line of screening frigates, but it appears all enemy capital ships have taken position around the base."

"Very well." Striker tightened his fists, a passing expression of his satisfaction. The enemy was doing exactly what he'd hoped they would. *Now, if we can just hold out long enough…*

He knew that was a big "if." The enemy had hit Grimaldi hard. There were thousands of FRs moving through the corridors and compartments of the vast station, and Striker was far from certain his Marines could hold off such an overpowering invasion. They would fight, he knew…and if they failed, few would survive. But the end result was most certainly still in doubt.

Time…I need time.

He needed time to get the fleet in position. He couldn't move too quickly. The enemy had to be fully convinced the Confederation navy was broken, fleeing. Then, when he sprang his trap, they would be too committed to respond effectively.

"Status in sectors Epsilon seven and eight?"

"Still under our control, Admiral. But enemy forces are getting dangerously close." A short pause. "The same with Gamma two and three."

Striker nodded. "Acknowledged." The enemy thought Grimaldi was disarmed, that all the station's weapons were destroyed or offline. Exactly what Striker wanted them to think.

The truth was somewhat different. Two large banks of heavy x-ray laser turrets were still operational, along with the reactors to power them. And at the point-blank range of the enemy vessels, they would rip through the Union battleships like an axe through half-melted butter.

Assuming we can hold on to those sections.

Hold on to anything…

Striker knew every part of his plan was a gamble. If the enemy took the station and discovered the functional batteries, he could find the weapons so integral to his plan turned against his own ships, just as they arrived to spring the trap. His scheme to snatch a victory from this carnage in the system could backfire. Success depended on many things now. The officers and spacers in those ships, their morale battered by the losses they had suffered, by the apparent orders to retreat. His people in the control center, focusing on managing the battle, even as enemy soldiers pressed every closer. And the Marines, fighting and dying for meters of corridor, for possession of each wartorn compartment.

It was a nightmare, a horror worse than any he'd seen in fiction or even in the sweat-soaked ravages of his deepest, darkest dreams. It was his creation, and these men and women fought by his order. They would *not* fail; their sacrifices would *not* be in vain. He believed that. He *had* to believe it.

His eyes dropped to the small panel on the side of his chair. He did believe his people could win, but Van Striker was not a man to leave such things to chance. If his Marines held, if the fortress fired its remaining guns, just as the fleet came around and bracketed the Union forces from two sides…the Confederation could win the victory, stop the enemy invasion cold. But if not…he had already programmed the destruct mechanism. If the Marines fell, if the chance of victory slipped away, he knew what his last act would be…what it had to be.

Whatever happened, Grimaldi would not fall into enemy hands again.

*   *   *

Sara Eaton sat in one of the chairs facing the captain's desk. Emilia Crown commanded *Concordia*, and it had been providence of a sort, one flickering ray of light in the otherwise all-encompassing darkness Eaton saw around her, that had put her friend's ship close enough to rescue her people. Some of her people.

Concordia had picked up three of *Intrepid*'s lifeboats, one hundred eighteen of her crew in all. It was a sad fraction of the nearly one thousand men and women that had been her ship's complement, but she was grateful for every life saved. All except one.

Eaton had been ready to die on *Intrepid*'s bridge, and only her crew's emphatic display of loyalty, their refusal to escape if she didn't join them, had gotten her into the lifeboat. There were all kinds of romantic legends, some ancient and others more modern, of captains meeting their ends with their ships. It wasn't something taken seriously—certainly not by the navy, which was profoundly against the notion of losing trained and experienced officers when it could be avoided. But now she understood. She hadn't *wanted* to survive *Intrepid*'s death when she'd sat on her vessel's crumbling bridge, and now, though she'd had time to get more of a grip on her thinking, she still found outliving her vessel to be a painful experience.

The retreat made it worse. Losing *Intrepid* in a victory, holding the line and turning back the invader, would have been one thing. Painful, certainly, but at least the sacrifice would have been worth something. But it hadn't been. The Confederation fleet was in wholesale retreat, the battle a defeat…perhaps even the war lost. It was too much, and the pain was a price that exceeded the value of survival to her.

She took a deep breath. Crown had told her to use her desk, so she could have access to the AI and the scanning suites, but she didn't feel quite right about sitting in that chair. She had always had a great respect for the captain of a ship, and the day she had achieved that great honor herself had been the best of her life. *Concordia* was Crown's ship, and the fact that she and Emilia were friends and former classmates at the Academy didn't change that fact. Besides, she didn't want access to more information. She had no command remaining, no job to do in the fleet. And the remnants of the once-mighty Confederation navy could flee without her help.

She turned her head abruptly. The red of *Concordia*'s battlestations lamps filled the room with an all too familiar glow. Then she felt thrust...significant thrust, probably 8g or more before *Concordia*'s dampeners reduced the perceived effect. That was a lot of acceleration.

She leapt up, old reflexes responding on their own, pushing against the forces slamming into her. She slid around Crown's desk, her fingers moving to the workstation. Had the enemy had some force hidden out here? Some group of ships that had somehow slipped around the retreating fleet?

No...nothing like that. But *Concordia* wasn't heading for the transwarp link, not anymore. She had come about, her engines blasting in almost the opposite direction.

Back toward Grimaldi...

Eaton slid into her friend's chair, all former concerns about it not feeling right gone. Her hands moved over the workstation controls, as quickly as they could with three times their weight bearing down on them. The whole fleet was doing the same, every ship blasting at near full thrust, every one of them now on a course for the beleaguered fortress.

Of course...

She didn't *know* what was going on. There was no way she could. But she had a guess, and with each passing second, she became more and more certain of it. She'd been surprised when Admiral Striker had issued the retreat order. Striker had always seemed like a fighter to her, a man who would battle to the last. The idea of him losing his nerve, cracking and yielding to the enemy—at least while he still had a fleet that could fight—had been alien to her. And now, she realized her earlier assessments had been correct. This had been no retreat, no admission of defeat. It had all been a trap, a plan to get the enemy engaged against the fortress, and then to bring the fleet back, to hit the Union forces and start the final fight.

She felt a rush of excitement. She wanted to jump up, to rush out onto the bridge. But *Concordia* wasn't her ship. She was a spectator in this fight.

Still, she leaned over the desk, her eyes darting back and forth across the formation. She could see the plan. The fleet was splitting into two groups. They were going to hit the enemy on the flanks.

It wasn't over. *Intrepid* hadn't died in vain.

*   *   *

"What in the name of the Eleven Hells is going on here?" Villieneuve glared across the bridge at Admiral Beaufort. *Victoire* was positioned to the rear of the Union fleet, but most of the other battleships were deployed close to the station. The supposedly pacified fortress that was now firing laser blasts from point blank range.

"Minister…there must have been a few emplacements that survived the earlier attack. The fleet will neutralize them before they do much damage."

Villieneuve was staring at the main display, watching as damage reports streamed in from the affected vessels. "That looks like considerable damage to me, Admiral. Do not treat me like a fool." There was real menace in Villieneuve's voice. The Sector Nine chief had a reputation for being less arbitrarily violent than some of his predecessors, but no one thought he was forgiving of failure.

"We will have those guns destroyed in a few moments, Minister."

"You'd better." Villieneuve stood and stared at the screen, watching hit after hit slam into his ships. Then another section of the station opened up, and more laser blasts began ravaging his battleships. He was no master of naval tactics, but he knew the heavy guns on the massive fortress were more powerful than anything on his ships. Beaufort had reported that the station's defensive batteries disabled. Villieneuve had relied on that when he'd ordered the fleet to close to boarding range…but someone had clearly fouled up, overlooked several still-functional weapons the enemy had simply kept silent.

We fell for a trick. Beaufort fell for a trick…and I let him…

"Pull the fleet back, Admiral. At once."

"But, Minister."

"Now, Admiral!" Villieneuve cursed himself silently. He had enough intelligence on Admiral Striker…he should have known the Confederation commander wouldn't have given up, not while his fleet could still fight.

"We're picking up Confederation fighter wings…incoming from…"

Villieneuve heard the rest of the words in his mind before the officer finished the report. *From the Ultara transwarp link.*

Suddenly, it was brutally clear. Striker had suckered them in. He'd never intended for his fleet to withdraw. He'd lured the Union battleships close enough to the station to tie them down. Then he would…

"Confederation battleships heading this way at full thrust."

Villieneuve's hands tightened into fists. He'd been a fool, placed far too much trust in Beaufort. He'd let the Union fleet fall into Striker's trap…and if he didn't get them out now…

"Admiral Beaufort, launch all fighters. All ships. At once."

"Ah…yes, Minister." The startled admiral turned and repeated the order. Villieneuve watched, wondering if the stunned officer would hold it together. He planned to address Beaufort's stupidity, there was no question of that. But not now. There was only one priority at the moment. Extricating what he could of the fleet before it was too late.

The strategic reserve…you committed it all…

He had no idea how he would handle the Presidium… whether he could find some way to escape the doom he had created for himself. But that was tomorrow's problem. Getting out of this Godforsaken system was today's.

"All capital ships are to prepare for full thrust as soon as squadrons are launched."

"Yes, Minister."

Villieneuve walked over to the admiral's chair, glaring at the officer and waving his arm in an abrupt gesture. He'd declined the officer's earlier offer to give up his seat, but the damned fool didn't deserve that kind of consideration now. And Villieneuve knew, if the fleet was going to get out of this mess, he would have to see to it himself.

Beaufort leapt up, rushing across the flag bridge toward another station. He looked back toward Villieneuve, silent, waiting for any orders the spymaster might give.

Villieneuve sat in the admiral's chair, fighting off the rage he felt. He'd underestimated Striker, and he'd placed too much trust in Beaufort. But he could still extricate the fleet—most of it, at least.

"All escorts are to form a line and cover the fleet's withdrawal." His orders were firm, his tone practically daring anyone present to disagree.

"Yes, Minister," Beaufort replied, his voice becoming shakier each time he spoke.

Villieneuve knew what they were all thinking. He was leaving the fighters behind. The FRs. Even the fleet's frigates and escorts. Abandoning them all to destruction…to buy time.

They were all expendable. Every FR in the fleet, every fighter. All of them. The battleships he was struggling to save…they were not. They were all that mattered.

No, not all…

Villieneuve felt a wave of relief as he began to realize he was in time. Just. The battleships would escape. They would lose a few more of their number, perhaps, and many would be damaged even worse than they were now…but the line would escape. *Victoire* would escape. *He* would escape.

He'd allowed his discipline to fail. He'd been suckered in by the seduction of military victory over the Confeds. But all wasn't lost. Far from it. His plan had still succeeded. He had kept the Confeds pinned down, even as he'd dispatched two task forces into the Badlands, more force by far than Striker could have sent.

And even Tyler Barron and Dauntless will be overwhelmed…

The fleet had been badly damaged, and the defeat would shatter what remained of its morale. But none of that would matter, not when he possessed the spoils his people would bring back from the Badlands.

He hid a tiny smile, thinking for a few seconds about what his people would be bringing back. Power. Immense power. The lost technology of the ancients.

And news of the destruction of *Dauntless*.

* * *

"I'm fine, Doctor. There are people here who need your help more than I do." Striker stood in the middle of the control room—or, what had been the control room before the battle that had turned it into a smoking ruin. He pulled away, doubling over and wincing from the pain as he did.

"Admiral, please…sit. Let me have a look."

Striker sighed hard, but he sat. "Just give me something for the pain, Doc."

The doctor sliced Striker's sleeve open with a tiny blade, gently pulling the blood-soaked fabric away. The arm was broken, twisted into an obscene mess. A fragment of bone protruded just above the elbow, and blood was still pouring out.

"Admiral…"

"I will not be moved from here, Doctor, not while any part of this engagement is still in question. So, do what you can and be done with it. I have work to do."

Striker felt a pinprick, and then a wave of welcome relief. The shot didn't eliminate all the pain—he knew nothing that would leave him in working mental order could do that—but it helped. A lot.

"Admiral, I've got to at least straighten this arm out…and I need to put you out before…"

"Not a chance, Doc. If you want to do it, do it here. Now."

"Admiral…"

"I know it's going to hurt. You don't think this hurts already? All of it? How many dead do we have? How many are still fighting? You think I'm going to curl up in a ball over a broken arm?"

The doctor looked doubtful, but he just nodded. He reached out, putting his hands gently on Striker's twisted arm. "I'm just going to get it straight enough to wrap it up for now. We'll operate later."

"Just do it."

The doctor paused for a few seconds. Then he jerked the arm hard, twisting it back into something close to its original shape.

Striker tried to hold it in, but it was too much for him. He yelled, the loud scream echoing off the walls and ceiling of the command center. The pain was indescribable, and he felt for an instant as though he might pass out. But he held on, and the agony slowly receded. It still hurt…a lot. But it was bearable.

"Thanks, Doc," he finally said, his voice raspy, out of breath.

"Just let me wrap it up, Admiral…and get some bandages on your face and neck." Striker had been hit by small shards of metal. He'd pulled most of them out himself, but they had left open gashes all over his upper body and face. He was lucky, he knew. When the blast had first hit him, he'd thought he was done for…but the damage, while ugly and painful, was also superficial. Still, he suspected he looked like hell.

There was something floating around the pain, though. Satisfaction. Relief. His plan had worked…that much was clear. The Union battleships were in headlong retreat. The Krakus system was still in Confederation hands.

His task force commanders had requested permission to pursue, and denying it had been one of the most difficult orders he'd ever issued. But there were still enemy escort craft, and hundreds of fighters, to deal with. And on Grimaldi itself, the battle in the corridors still raged, fed by the desperation of the abandoned FRs and the slow but steady feed of every Marine contingent his own battleships could spare.

His people had done enough, and all he wanted now was to secure the station and the system…and give the survivors the rest they so profoundly deserved.

And dispatch a task force to the Badlands, to *Dauntless*'s aid. He could only hope it wasn't too late.

"Okay, Admiral…I really wish you would let me…"

"This will be fine, Doctor. I know there are others here who need your skills more than I do."

He stood up and walked across the room, stepping over debris and pools of blood as he looked out over his officers. The fight had been the most brutal he'd ever seen. It would go into the books as a victory, and no doubt he would be acclaimed, called the next Rance Barron and similar foolish things. But he felt no sense of glory, no ego-driven satisfaction. The whole thing made him sick. *How could anything like this be called a victory?*

Still, there was cause for relief…and for gratitude to his men and women who had fought so hard here. That fight had not been in vain.

They had turned back the Union invasion. They had held.

Chapter Thirty-Seven

CFS Dauntless
System Z-111 (Chrysallis)
Deep Inside the Quarantined Zone ("The Badlands")
309 AC

"Under ten million kilometers to the primary, Captain." Atara Travis had an odd expression on her face, a partially formed smile. Barron realized his exec knew exactly what he was doing now. Not only did she know, he could tell she approved. He didn't need her to okay his orders, of course, but it was gratifying that the person on *Dauntless* he most trusted and respected concurred with his analysis. Because he himself was far from sure.

Very far from sure.

"Cut thrust to 5g, Commander. Adjust thrust vector two degrees on X coordinate and four point two degrees on Z coordinate."

"Yes, Captain."

Barron felt the relief as *Dauntless*'s thrust decreased within the range of the dampener's ability to compensate. The feeling of something close to Megara-normal gravity was indescribable, and he twisted his sore body, stretching his tortured muscles.

"Five million kilometers, sir."

Barron punched at his own keyboard, running one last set

of calculations through the AI. Yes, everything was still on track. He watched the screen as the numbers counted down the range...and also the gauge displaying the hull's outer temperature. It was over one thousand degrees, much higher than he liked. He was pretty sure his stratagem would work now... unless the hull melted.

"Two million kilometers."

Dauntless was moving at almost one point five percent of lightspeed, an enormous velocity for a manned ship. Barron had taken an immense chance running his engines at full blast for so long, but once again, his aging battleship had come through for him.

He grabbed his headset and put it on. "Attention all personnel. This is Captain Barron. We will be conducting a crash maneuver. I want everyone to strap in, if possible. If not, hang on to whatever you can."

He looked over at Travis. She just nodded.

The ship shook, then again, and Barron felt himself being pulled hard to the starboard. It was the primary's gravity, and if he'd figured everything right, *Dauntless* was about to slingshot around the star and end up on a course almost directly toward the artifact. He'd get there hours ahead of the two ships pursuing *Dauntless*, both of which were now hopelessly out of position.

His body snapped forward as the star's gravity grabbed his ship and pulled it around. He gritted his teeth as the straps dug into his chest. He could hear the shrieking of the structural supports as *Dauntless* was pushed to its limit. But everything held... and Barron's math proved to be sound. The ship was moving away from the star now, its velocity 0.014c, heading right for the ancient spaceship. Where a single Union battleship awaited.

He'd have hours to destroy his solitary opponent...and if he knew his engineer, Commander Fritz would have the antimatter mines ready to prepare a reception for the two battleships now desperately trying to change course and follow.

His people had a chance. It was still a longshot, and everything had to go right for *Dauntless* to make it through. But it was real, and from where things had been hours before, that seemed pretty damned good.

*   *   *

Bryan Rogan fired again, a perfectly placed shot. The FR dropped hard, leaving a spray of blood and other innards hanging in the air for an instant. The Marine captain was a skilled marksman, and as often as not, he only needed one shot. But that wasn't why he'd flipped off his auto fire. His people were running out of ammo…and it was going to be close, damned close, as to whether they had enough to finish the battle.

Dauntless's Marines, at least what was left of its battered contingent, had a real chance to hold out, to repel the FRs invading the artifact. If their supplies held.

The battle had been a bloody one, and half of Rogan's people were casualties. They weren't all dead of course, and the wounded gave those still in the line yet another reason to fight. It was unthinkable to leave their broken and bleeding comrades to the mercy of the enemy, and every Marine still in the fight struggled that much harder to stave off that terrible possibility.

The fighting was vicious everywhere, but right around Rogan, where the largest enemy forces had landed, it was beyond brutal. Men and women had fought to the death with rifle, pistols, knives…even ammunition boxes and makeshift clubs. The dead littered the corridors and compartments, and the smooth metal floors were slick with blood. But still the intensity had not waned. These two forces were blood enemies, and the battle would not end—*could* not end—until one side was wiped out.

Rogan hated the Union, and he detested the FRs with a passion half inherited and half formed by his own experiences. He felt sorrow for the Marines he'd lost in his battles, and he always tried to put their lives first…except when facing the FRs. Defeating the hated enemy was more important than anything, than anyone's survival. Including his own.

He fired again, dropping another of the enemy. He had a good position, one with partial cover and a tremendous field of fire. The enemy had to come around the corner to get line of sight on him…and a Marine like Bryan Rogan didn't need much time. He had three of his people with him, and between them they were holding the front edge of the line.

There wasn't much behind them, save for wounded and the last few crates of ammunition. He'd stripped the rest of his forces, sent them in twos and threes where they were most needed, relying on his ability to hold with a small contingent. The rest, what few remained, he'd sent to Plunkett. The lieutenant was about to launch a final assault, one designed to push the enemy back on their boarding points and bracket the surviving FRs between Rogan's people and the attacking squads. It was risky, and based on an imperfect knowledge of the ship's layout, but Rogan knew his people had to win *now*. They didn't have the strength for a sustained battle, and they damned sure didn't have the ammo.

"Captain, we're ready up here…we just need the word from you." Plunkett's voice was strange, strained and raspy. Rogan knew without asking that the lieutenant had been wounded. He almost said something, but then he held it. Plunkett knew what was at stake. If the officer was ready to lead his Marines in the assault, Bryan Rogan knew he had to let him. Besides, he had no one to replace Plunkett. No one at all.

"Go, Lieutenant. Good luck to you and your people."

"Thank you, sir."

Rogan wondered for an instant how badly Plunkett was hurt. Then he put it out of his mind and whipped his rifle around, firing again. He missed, the FR reacting quickly and dropping back behind the corner just in time. But he didn't have to hit, not really. He just had to hold the enemy back.

Just for a while longer.

* * *

"Careful with that!" Fritz yelled across the room toward a pair of her technicians. The two men had put down one of the canisters more heavily than she liked. "Any one of those things can kill all of us in a microsecond. Those containers have been here for centuries without a single containment failure…at least until you fools rushed in here like a herd of stampeding cattle."

"Sorry, Commander." The lieutenant's voice was haggard, her fatigue clear in every word.

Fritz knew her people were exhausted, that she was being almost impossibly hard on them. But she was just as tired, and no amount of fatigue changed a thing. The Marines were fighting twice their number, desperately trying to keep the FRs from taking control of the station. *Dauntless* was out there playing a deadly cat and mouse game with four enemy battleships. Even Andromeda Lafarge's smugglers had joined in the fight. So, as far as she was concerned, her engineers would just have to dig up the fortitude and energy to keep going.

"Just be careful," Fritz said, softening her voice just a bit. "We've got to get this done. *Dauntless* doesn't have a chance unless we hold up our end." Then she got dirty, pulling out a tactic she knew was unfair. "Captain Barron is counting on us."

"Yes, Commander."

Fritz turned back to her own task, checking the wiring job on one of the makeshift antimatter mines. She was pleased with what her people had managed to do in such a short time. In another two hours, they'd have sixty-one mines ready to go, more than the top end number she'd promised Barron, and each one with a crude proximity fuse as well as an ECM suite she *hoped* would confuse the scanners on the enemy ships.

Everything was thrown together from the materials at hand, and she'd stopped trying to count the things that could go wrong. Besides the obvious worry that one of her people would inadvertently destroy the containment on one of the canisters, killing them all in an instant, she had concerns about the ECM, about the detonation controls…even about whether the charges she'd affixed to blow the things would penetrate the tough shells on the containers.

There was no point in worrying about any of it. They had done the best they could with what they had. And there was no way to test anything. Even if she'd been able to deploy one into space and get it far enough from the station, the explosion would be detectable across the entire system. The warning would put the enemy on alert, and almost certainly dissuade them from blundering close to the artifact, where the mines would have a chance to do their jobs. All she could do was trust in her work, and that of her engineers.

She heard gunfire. It wasn't the first time, but it was definitely closer this time. She'd set up her makeshift production line as far away from the expected hotspots as she could, but there was really no safe place on the entire ship. Not while the battle still raged.

"All right, forget that," she said, looking up. Most of her people had stopped their work and were listening to the shooting. "You've got your jobs and the Marines have theirs. Be glad yours is in here." She paused a few seconds, watching as they all returned their attention—some of it, at least—to their tasks. Fritz took a deep breath. She was a taskmaster and as hard as steel as far as any of her people were concerned, but that didn't mean she didn't feel fear.

They all think I'm immune to it, that I'm some kind of mountain of stone. If they knew how close I was to pissing myself...

But they would never know that. Fritz's reputation was useful, and she'd seen her people driven to almost superhuman feats by the strange combination of fear and devotion they felt for her. And that had saved *Dauntless* more than once. It was too much to lose over a moment of human weakness, at least a visible moment.

The shooting came even closer, and the two Marines Rogan had assigned to guard her people rushed toward the door. One of them, a corporal, turned toward Fritz. "Your people better take cover, Commander." Then she ran closer to the door, dropping to one knee behind a large crate.

"You heard Corporal Quince...now! Find some cover." Fritz slid to the side, behind a large metal box. She reached down to the floor, to the pistol Bryan Rogan had given her. She'd taken it, as all her people had taken weapons, but she hadn't expected to use it. She'd been in as many dangerous situations as anyone in the fleet, but she'd never fired a gun in close combat.

There's a first time for everything…

She gripped the pistol tightly, but her eyes were moving across the room, from one antimatter canister to the next, wondering helplessly just how those metal shells would handle bullets.

Time passed slowly, at least it seemed that way, but a quick glance at her chronometer told her it had been less than three minutes. The fighting was right outside the door now, and an instant later, there was an explosion beyond the closed hatch. The super-hard metal mostly held, but the door was blown from its track. She could hear the sound of boots moving just outside, and then the door began moving inward.

She knew there were FRs just on the other side of that chunk of ancient metal, that they were pushing, forcing the door out of the hatchway. Then it fell with a loud clang, and all hell broke loose.

The two Marines fired from their chosen positions, taking down all the FRs in the front row. Fritz counted four, but she knew there might have been more. Then she saw dark shapes flying in…grenades, she realized.

Two of the explosives landed in open spaces, but one fell just behind Corporal Quince. She saw the explosion, and then the Marine staggered to the side, the rear of her armor and what looked like half her back torn away. There was blood everywhere, and Fritz didn't need Dr. Weldon to tell her the wound was mortal. But the Marine wasn't done yet, and even as blood poured from her grievous wounds, she held herself up for a few seconds, before falling to her knees, still firing, even as fresh shots riddled her now exposed body. Finally, she fell with a sickening thud, as more FRs poured through the door.

"Fight!" Fritz screamed, aiming her pistol and opening fire as she did. Her engineers weren't Marines, they weren't clone soldiers like the FRs…but they were Confederation spacers, and they were fighting for their lives. She felt a rush as she saw one of the FRs go down under her fire. The Union soldiers were better trained and equipped, but they were forcing their way through a narrow opening and her people were under cover. She had no idea how many of the enemy there were, but that didn't matter now. This was a fight to the finish.

She kept firing, even as she saw their second Marine go down. There were at least a dozen FRs dead, more probably, but they were still coming through. Fritz heard a sickening shriek, one of her people, she knew immediately, but she held her focus. "Keep firing," she screamed, knowing they would all run out of ammunition any moment. The Marines had given out weapons, but they hadn't had much ordnance to spare.

She tried to aim, but the FRs were moving forward now, taking cover behind the same boxes the Marines had used. She fired, and again, but the easy targets were gone. There were FRs flanking the doorway, and perhaps seven or eight inside the room, all behind at least some kind of cover.

She wondered what the FRs would have done if they'd known what was in the canisters spread around the room—if they would have pulled back, fearful of causing a catastrophic accident. At least a couple of the cylinders had been grazed by shots, but so far, they had held their containment.

Her head snapped around. She could hear more gunfire out in the hall. Not the high-pitched crack of the Union guns, but the lower sound of the heavier Confederation rifles.

Marines!

She fired, and then again, feeling a burst of hope. Then she saw the FRs in the doorway go down…and a few seconds later, Marines taking their place, firing on the Union troops in the room from behind. It was over in a few seconds, the huge room she had turned into a relatively tidy workspace now reduced to a nightmare of blood and gore.

But the FRs were all down.

Fritz hesitated for a few seconds, until she was sure the fighting was over. Then she stood up.

"Commander Fritz, are you okay?" The man speaking was tall, clad in body armor that she knew was black despite the fact that nearly every centimeter of it was covered with a bright sheen of blood.

"Captain Rogan," she said, unable to contain the distress in her voice.

Rogan looked confused for an instant, and then he gave her a fleeting smile. "No, this isn't my blood, Commander...at least most of it isn't." He turned around toward the Marines behind him. "I want the rest of that hallway swept. Not one of them gets away. Do you understand me?"

"Yes, sir!"

Rogan turned back toward Fritz as the half dozen armored figures jogged back out in the corridor.

"It was a rough fight, Commander." He paused, his eyes dropping to the floor for an instant. "A costly fight. But we won. There are a few FRs still on the loose, but this group that got through here was the last major formation."

Fritz took a step forward, but she didn't say anything.

"*Dauntless* is heading toward us. The captain managed to pull off some kind of maneuver...he left two of the enemy ships far behind. *Dauntless* is going to fight the single battleship here... and then it will be your show, Commander. The captain wants the mines ready in two hours, max."

Fritz nodded, wiping the sweat from her face. "Very well, Captain." It seemed a grossly inadequate thing to say to the man whose Marines had just saved her life, but it was all she had. Then she turned and looked across the room. "All right, all of you...the fight is over, and it's time to get back to work. Now!"

Chapter Thirty-Eight

CFS Dauntless
System Z-111 (Chrysallis)
Deep Inside the Quarantined Zone ("The Badlands")
309 AC

"Launch all fighters."

Commander Travis's voice blared through Stara Sinclair's headset. Sinclair was exhausted, but she was grateful in a way for the seemingly endless stint at red alert. Being at her station, consumed with tasks, helped take her mind off of sickbay. Off Jake.

"Acknowledged, Commander. All squadrons launch." She reached out and flipped a series of switches. The squadrons were all ready to go, the pilots already manning their craft. *Dauntless* had been preparing for this fight through the hours it had taken to travel back to the ancient artifact. Captain Barron's daring move had bought time, a period of hours for the outnumbered battleship to face its adversary one on one…but it would all be for naught if *Dauntless* didn't destroy its enemy and do it quickly.

Sinclair could feel the vibrations moving through the ship as the catapults began to fire *Dauntless*'s depleted wings into space. She scanned her workstation, checking the status of each group of fighters as they cleared the ship.

Sinclair sighed hard as she updated the report status, sending it to the bridge. Her mind wasn't *off* Stockton, just partially distracted. Jake Stockton was the living embodiment of the daring hero fighter pilot, and she was neck deep in fighter ops. It was impossible for her to forget about him, even for an instant. But she was busy, so much so that she didn't have the time to obsess about him.

She knew Doctor Weldon had operated, that he had tried to apply the regeneration treatment that was Stockton's only hope for survival. *Dauntless*'s chief surgeon had taken pity on her, not only telling her what he was going to do, but giving her what she could only assume was a load of bullshit about how well he expected things to go. She hadn't heard anything further for hours, and she'd begun to fear the worst. But then she got the word. He was still alive. That was all. Anything else would have to wait. He'd either live or die now, and there was nothing she could do but see which it was.

She moved her hands over the station, confirming readings, checking the positioning of fighters as they launched. "Yellow Three, you're drifting out of formation. Tighten things up there."

"Acknowledged, Control." Then: "Thanks, Stara."

She knew she was popular with the squadrons, that though she was only twenty-eight years old, she was a sort of mother to them all. Her voice on the Control line was one of the most familiar sounds to the pilots…and for many, her voice was the last one they ever heard. She grieved for every one of her flyers who failed to come back, and she nursed them through their battles with all the power of her scanners and comm suites. But Stockton was something different.

She felt one last vibration, the final four ships of Green squadron. Then she reached out and hit the comm unit. "Commander Travis, Flight Control here. All squadrons launched."

She leaned back in her chair and took a deep breath. They were all out again, all her children.

Once more into the breach…and into the deadly danger and strife of war in space.

And down in sickbay, the best of them all, fighting his own battle for survival, with not an enemy fighter in sight…Please don't leave me Jake…

Don't die on me…

*   *   *

"We're going in hard and fast. There's no time for a protracted fight here. We're gonna clear their fighters away and the Greens are going to get in there and make an attack run. Quick and dirty, and then back to *Dauntless* to refuel and rearm before those other ships get here."

Kyle Jamison was leaning back in his cockpit, angling his throttle even as he sent out his orders to *Dauntless*'s squadrons. He was glad to have the attack to absorb his thoughts. It was better than dwelling on the fact that nearly fifty percent of his fighters were gone…or the that his best friend was in sickbay, fighting against the odds to cling to life. The struggle reminded him of the terrible battle at Santis, except this time *Dauntless* was massively outnumbered. Terrible losses in a victorious fight were bad enough, but suffering grievously and then having to relaunch almost immediately to begin a new battle was just too much.

At least the Union ship's squadrons had suffered even more severe losses. The enemy had sent their ship with the most depleted fighter wing to the artifact, expecting that the other two would engage and destroy *Dauntless*. That was a break for Jamison's people now, but it only increased the importance of finishing this fight quickly and getting back in time to refit for the next battle.

Jamison had ordered his people to sleep while *Dauntless* completed its journey toward the sun and back, but he doubted many had managed it. He certainly hadn't. He'd gone down to sickbay to check on Stockton, and then he'd sat in the launch bay, watching the crew prep and check the remaining fighters.

"Here they come," he said sharply, watching as the enemy fighters moved directly toward his own squadrons. He had four of his units outfitted as fighters, with only the six remaining ships of Green squadron armed as bombers. That was just six plasma torpedoes, even assuming all of them made it through.

The enemy had twenty-one fighters, all interceptors. That was good news. Jamison's people didn't have to worry about screening *Dauntless*, at least not from anything as dangerous as a bombing attack. That meant his interceptors could all hit the enemy wing...and with any luck, wipe it out quickly.

"Break," he snapped into his comm, and he pulled back on the throttle and blasted his ship toward the closest enemy. He flipped up a small lever, arming his first missile, and a few seconds later he launched. He swung his ship around hard, coming down almost behind one of the lead Union ships. He armed and fired his second missile, even as the corner of his eye caught the destruction of his first target. He pulled up again, panning his eyes across the display. Half the enemy fighters were already gone, consumed by his squadrons' missile barrage. His people had only lost one ship so far.

Now it was time to close, time to finish the job with lasers. Then the Greens could hit that ship. Every plasma torpedo that connected was that much less *Dauntless* had to do, that much better shape the battleship would be in when the other Union vessels finally arrived.

*   *   *

"Primaries, fire!" Barron was hunched forward in his chair, his hands clenched into fists. The enemy ship had been putting up a fight. Three of his bombers had scored hits, and *Dauntless* had connected twice with its deadly primaries. Everything had gone exactly how Barron had planned it—but the enemy was somehow still in the fight.

Barron listened to the familiar sound of his ship's main weapons, but before he got the report on whether they'd hit again, *Dauntless* shook hard, the enemy ship's battered broadside connecting with four laser turrets. The blasts hit hard, and Barron knew that where they impacted, sections of the hull had melted and compartments were torn open, exposed to the vacuum of space. He closed his eyes for just a second, imagining men and women blasted out through the jagged gashes, sucked into the frozen, airless void.

"Bring the secondaries online," he roared. The incredibly powerful Confederation primary guns were a mixed blessing. They were the hardest hitting things in space, but they were just two guns, and at closer range, the dozen turrets of *Dauntless*'s secondaries could sometimes do more total damage, especially to a battered target.

Eleven turrets, he corrected himself. One of *Dauntless*'s port secondaries was nothing but a blackened hole clawed out of the ship's hull and a few splotches of melted and rehardened metal. But eleven laser cannons firing together was a powerful barrage, and Tyler Barron knew he had the best gunners in either fleet.

"Fire," he said, his voice tinged with malice toward the enemy. The war had been a hard one, and concepts like honor and respect for an adversary had worn down into a dull hatred. He had sympathized with the Union spacers early in the war, acknowledged that they had no choice but to serve, that they were virtual slaves to their political masters. But he didn't care anymore. The war had become a holocaust, and his thoughts were simpler now, grimmer. They had to die. Every Union ship destroyed, every officer and spacer killed, brought the war one step closer to its end.

Barron watched the display as the damage assessment rolled in. Eight of the lasers had hit the enemy ship, at least two of them in vulnerable spots.

"Maintain fire. All stations, fire at will."

The true edge the secondaries had over *Dauntless*'s main guns was rate of fire. The lasers recharged in less than thirty seconds, as quickly as fifteen if the teams pushed it. The primaries took a solid two minutes, sometimes close to three. That was a long time in a close-range fight.

Barron watched as his lasers fired again. And again. As they did, the return fire lessened sharply. The battle was almost at an end.

"Keep pounding," Barron said, unnecessarily. His people knew their business.

"Captain, Commander Jamison is requesting permission to begin landing operations."

Barron's head snapped around, back toward the display. His squadrons needed to be refit, but they had enough fuel to wait until the fight between the ships was over. He almost told Travis to order them to go into a holding pattern, but then he changed his mind. "Advise Commander Jamison that Beta bay is available. He is to bring as many ships as possible in, and hold the others until further notice." It was virtually impossible to land squadrons on the side of the active broadside. The calculations involved in ensuring none of the fighters came too close to a laser blast were just too precise. But getting half his birds in would help get the refit operation underway. He'd gotten a jump on the two ships that had been pursuing *Dauntless*, but they were still coming...and he wanted his fighters ready before his battered ship faced another fight. At least as many of them as possible.

"Commander Jamison is to prioritize Blue and Scarlett Eagle squadrons." If Barron couldn't have all his squadrons ready, he damned sure wanted his best.

"Yes, sir."

"And that includes him, Commander. Jamison is to land with the initial squadrons. The rest of his people will be just fine." Barron knew, left to his own devices, Jamison would be the last pilot to land. He respected the sense of duty that drove that impulse, but he wanted his strike force commander ready to go when the elite squadrons launched again...especially with Jake Stockton out of action.

"Yes, Captain."

Barron turned back to the display. The readings from the enemy ship were pouring in now. Its energy levels were plunging, its thrust dead, its return fire anemic. A wave of energy jolted through his exhausted body. He was savoring the moment of the kill. Once, he would have been consumed with mixed feelings, overcome with the need to offer surrender terms to his crippled foe. But war had done its job, stripped away his romantic notions of a warrior's honor. Barron was an emissary of death now, and he had only one thought regarding his enemy.

"All batteries, maintain maximum fire. Blast that thing back to the atoms it's made of."

Chapter Thirty-Nine

CFS Dauntless
System Z-111 (Chrysallis)
Deep Inside the Quarantined Zone ("The Badlands")
309 AC

"They'll be in range in twenty-two minutes Captain. Primaries are online, but Lieutenant Billings advises the power lines are badly damaged. He's got several reroutes in place, but…"

"Understood, Commander." Barron hoped his interruption hadn't been too aggressive in tone, but he was just too exhausted to listen to the usual engineer's disclaimer about the power systems and the primaries. His people had done an extraordinary job managing and repairing the damage *Dauntless* had suffered in the past weeks, and he was well aware neither they nor his battered ship owed him a thing. But they were all in the fight together, and there were only two options. Victory or death.

Dauntless would fight. His ship would give its all. If the primaries went down, she would fight with her secondaries. She would battle to the last turret, the last fighter, the last watt of power produced by her straining reactors. If she won the victory, it would be a triumph for all of them, for the fighter pilots who had lost so many of their brethren, for the gunners at their stations and the sweating engineers crawling through the bowels of the ship.

And Fritzie and her people over there...and those contraptions they created...

He had no idea if the minefield would work, no real sense of the power of those devices, save a vague mathematical idea of the power each explosion would unleash. Effective mines were usually highly sophisticated devices, with propulsion units allowing them to close with targets passing nearby. These had none of that, just a simple fuse, and a hodgepodge of ECM devices the brilliant engineer had managed to throw together from bits and pieces of the dismantled shuttles. It was an amazing achievement for the small corps of engineers, and almost unimaginable display of their brilliance and skill. But he had no idea if it would work. If it would be enough.

"Captain, Commander Fritz is on the line."

Barron reached down, grabbing his headset and putting it on. "Fritzie?"

"We're ready, Captain. I've rigged up a...call it a launcher... using the remains of one of the docking tubes. We've run some calculations, and we've set the tube up so we can create velocity, at least enough to launch these in roughly the pattern we want." She paused. "It's crude, Captain, but I've run some calculations. We've got some play on angling the tube, and we can vary the amount of air pressure we use to launch. I've got a rough coverage plan if you'd like to review it."

"No, Fritzie, I trust your judgment." It went against his nature not to check and recheck everything, but he knew there was no point. There wasn't time to change any of the plans, so there was no point in even looking. Fritzie had earned his trust over their time serving together, and he was determined to give it to her. However difficult it was for him.

"Very well, sir. Shall we begin launching?"

"Yes, Fritzie. Get started...and get it done as quickly as you can."

"Yes, Captain."

Barron sighed softly and closed his eyes for a few seconds. He had *Dauntless* ready, her squadrons prepared to launch. His battleship would hit the enemy just as they moved into the makeshift minefield. With any luck, the antimatter canisters would help even the score, make the two on one fight a fairer matchup.

"Captain! We're picking up launches, sir."

Barron was surprised. He hadn't expected the enemy to launch this far out.

"They're from the other ship, sir. The disabled one." A pause. "The one we believed was disabled."

Barron felt like he'd been hit in the gut. The ship Travis and his people had fought first, the one that had been crippled near the transwarp point. He shook his head in disgust. He frequently praised his own engineers, felt gratitude for all the times they'd brought *Dauntless* back from the brink and sent her into the fight once again. Somehow, for all that he'd almost come to expect miracles from his people, it seemed a cold surprise that the enemy had managed to get their wounded vessel back in the fight.

"Bring us around, Commander. Fifty percent thrust, directly toward that ship. And scramble all fighters." Barron suspected the enemy vessel was still in bad shape, that it had managed to get its engines partially back online and at least one of its fighter bays operational, probably only by the barest of margins. But it was coming at *Dauntless* from almost the opposite direction of the other ships.

He couldn't stay where he was, absorb attacks from two sides. That single ship *had* to be badly damaged still, and that meant he could take it out quickly. With any luck, Fritz's mines would hurt, or at least intimidate, the enemy. That would buy time for *Dauntless* to get back. Before the Union ships could land FRs, and wipe out the Marines and engineers still on the artifact.

The plan had been desperate enough before, but now it was hanging by a thread. Barron hated the idea of launching his squadrons now, of risking facing the remaining two ships without them, but the "crippled" ship had launched an impressive strike, one he simply couldn't allow to reach *Dauntless* unimpeded.

They must have gotten both bays operational. Do they have a Fritzie over there?

"Fighter control reports all squadrons ready to launch, Captain. Awaiting your command."

Barron stared out at the display for a few seconds. He almost withheld the order. He knew he was just postponing the inevitable. Even if the antimatter mines worked, the enemy battleships would launch their squadrons long before they entered the range of the makeshift weapons. If both ships were completely destroyed, he'd still have to deal with enemy fighters, trapped and suicidal. But he had to survive this attack to face the next.

"Launch all squadrons."

*   *   *

"Gator, watch out…you've got one on your tail."

"Roger that, Warrior. I'm…"

The voice of his pilot was replaced by harsh static. Timmons's fists clenched in frustration and anger. The Union squadrons weren't a match for *Dauntless*'s, not really, but that didn't mean men and women he knew wouldn't die in the fight. Weren't dying, even now.

The enemy strike force had no bombers. He suspected they hadn't been able to get any of their fighters equipped for anti-ship assaults. It made sense. The plasma torpedoes and their mountings were big, bulky. If the sophisticated rail systems in the enemy bays were out of action, there was no way to get the heavy weapons in place, at least not in any reasonable time. It all made sense. But it also made the whole thing more hazardous for his squadrons in one way. Interceptors were a lot more dangerous to other fighters than bombers.

As "Gator" Simmel can attest…

"All right Eagles and Blues, you're the best pilots in the fleet, but that doesn't mean you don't have to fucking focus! Take your eyes off these people and they will seal your fate. I know you're all tired, but we've got a job to do, and that's all that matters. You've all got stims…take 'em if you need 'em. But I don't want anybody falling asleep at their controls."

His pilots were highly capable—over half the men and women in the two squadrons rated as aces—but exhaustion was starting to take its toll…and that was something he couldn't accept. Dying because you were outnumbered, because the enemy was better, or because you faced overwhelming odds… he understood those. But being killed by an enemy you should defeat, but don't because you're tired? It made him rage inside at the waste of it all.

"I want these squadrons cleaned up, and I mean now. You all look like shit, and this isn't the time for it."

Jamison had left him in command of *Dauntless*'s two elite squadrons, as he led the Greens and the Yellows in an attack run against the Union battleship. "Lynx" Federov and her Reds had been deployed in front of *Dauntless*, a precaution made far unnecessary by the lack of enemy bombers. They were moving up, even now, but Timmons knew he shouldn't need them. Not if he could shake his dazed and exhausted pilots back to their standard level of performance.

"Attack," he shouted into the comm. "All fighters, attack now. It's time to finish this."

He brought his ship around, opening up with his lasers on the Union fighter right in front of him. There were about fifteen enemy ships left, and he was going to see something done about that.

Right now…

*   *   *

"Fritzie, we're about to enter firing range. We'll finish this as quickly as we can, but we're out of range…and out of position too." Barron's voice went silent for a few seconds. "Those other ships are going to get there before we can get back."

"The mines are deployed, Captain. We're as ready as we're going to be. But the fuses are tied to short-range comm units, sir. *Dauntless* is too far away to control them."

"You'll have to do it."

"Captain, I'm an engineer, not a gunner. Not a bridge officer."

"You're a gunner now, Fritzie."

Fritz stood at the portable comm unit, suddenly feeling the weight of the past week's fatigue. She'd been in mortal danger, of course, many times. It wasn't fear of death or defeat paralyzing her. But for all the desperate situations she'd been in, all the times she'd raced against the clock to feed Captain Barron the power he needed or to get a crucial system back online, she'd never stared into the display before, watching the enemy approaching, deciding when and where to attack. That had always been Barron's role. And the stress of it was crushing her now, testing her to her limits.

"I'll try, Captain."

"Do better than try, Fritzie. There's not a doubt in my mind you can do this…unless you convince yourself you can't. Be calm, cool. Watch them approach, and when you think they're as close as they're going to get to one or more of those mines… do it. It might as well be all at once, Fritzie. That ECM you worked up isn't going to hold forever. We've got surprise on our side, but we can't push it too far."

"Yes, sir." Barron's words made her feel better. A little. But she still wanted to crouch down and vomit.

"I believe you can do this, Fritzie…and I need you to believe it too."

"I do, Captain." She hated lying to Barron, but she was far from confident.

"Do what you have to do, Fritzie, just like you've always done before. Barron out."

The line went dead, and Fritz turned toward the display. Like everything else she had available on the ancient ship, it was a makeshift affair, cobbled together from the scraps of their shuttles and other tools. But it worked well enough. If she failed, she knew should couldn't blame the equipment.

The enemy ships were almost there. She had to make this work…she simply had to. *Dauntless* wasn't going to get back in time to prevent a landing. And two Union battleships carried five to six hundred FRs. She knew Rogan's people would fight to the last man. But there were barely seventy of them left, and as good as they were, they had no chance, low on ammunition

Ruins of Empire

and outnumbered eight or nine to one.

Her eyes were fixed on the screen, on the two ovals moving slowly forward, flanked by three smaller icons, the last survivors of the escorts that had accompanied the Union task force when it first emerged into the system. They were getting close…but not close enough. Not yet.

She glanced down at the small control panel, extending an arm out and flipping a series of switches. Everything was ready.

She felt a trickle of unexpected amusement amid the stress and fear. She'd scavenged a button from one of the shuttle dashboards…a large red button. She'd used it as the detonation control

A big red button…to trigger the biggest detonation in history. Recent history, at least.

It was almost cartoonish. *Who says engineers don't have a sense of humor, even if it's inadvertent?*

She put her hand on the edge of the panel. *Not yet…*

Her eyes were narrow, focused. The enemy was coming right toward the minefield. It looked like they still hadn't detected any of her ECM. She couldn't believe it…if the Union ships kept coming, if they didn't detect her mines, it might actually work…

Wait…

Both ships were close now, probably close enough to take some damage if she blew the minefield. But she needed more than that. She needed them to advance right into the maelstrom…and so far, they were doing just that.

She put her fingers over the button, felt the smooth plastic beneath her thumb. Waiting…

*   *   *

"Another hit, Captain. Looks like we took her amidships. I think…"

Travis's words stopped abruptly as *Dauntless* shook hard, her own hit on the enemy ship followed almost immediately by a return blow.

Barron turned his head toward his screen, snapping out,

"Damage report!" to his exec. He knew his ship well, and he could tell by feel that shot had hit hard.

"Primaries down, Captain. Reactor B at thirty percent." A short pause while Travis fielded reports coming in from the various stations. "Lieutenant Billings thinks he can keep it at thirty for a while, but he says he's got to shut it down soon."

"Tell Lieutenant Billings we need every watt, Commander. He is to keep both reactors operational until I order otherwise."

"Yes, sir."

"Secondary batteries, open fire. All gunnery stations, fire at will."

The enemy had scored a lucky hit, but Barron knew his opponent was almost beaten. The Union ship's engines were down again, and that meant she was stuck on a fixed vector. His gunners would pick the thing apart. Already, there were fluctuating energy readings, signs of internal fires and explosions.

The scanners showed huge plumes of atmosphere and fluids blasting out into space, flash freezing like giant stalactites in a dark cave. Barron was sure his ship would win the fight…but the cost had been high. There were still two enemy battleships in the system, and *Dauntless*'s engines were at less than forty percent thrust, and now her primaries were down. *We're not going to make it. Unless Fritzie can actually pull this off…*

"More hits, Captain." There was excitement in Travis's tone, and that told Barron all he needed to know. By the time he'd focused on the display, the damage assessments were flooding in. The Union ship was breaking up, one explosion after another rocking its massive frame. A huge section of its rear structure broke free, and a half-million ton chunk of metal and plastic floated through space, propelled by the explosion that blasted it free.

"Scanner readings?" Barron hunched forward in his chair, his own eyes on the display even as he awaited his first officer's report.

"She looks dead, Captain. No energy readings, no fire. Nothing."

Barron just looked at the screen, reading for himself what

Travis had just told him. The enemy ship didn't seem to have any life support still functioning. No lifeboats either. If anyone was still alive on the hulking battleship, they wouldn't be for long.

"What is Alpha bay's status?"

"Damaged, sir, but Lieutenant Sinclair reports they can land the rest of the squadrons."

"Do it. Immediately."

"Yes, sir." Then, a few seconds later: "Captain, we're getting overload readings on the engines."

"Cut all thrust," Barron snapped back, almost robotically.

"Lieutenant Billings is on it, sir."

"We need those…" Barron stopped suddenly. Every readout on *Dauntless* suddenly went crazy, scanners burning out, even the comm lines blasting out thick static.

Barron's head turned abruptly. There were looks of surprise all around the bridge, stunned expressions on the faces of those uncertain what had just happened. But Barron knew exactly what had caused those readings.

The display was almost offline, the AIs struggling to update the projection, to assess the almost incalculable blast of energy the scanners had just read.

Barron's stomach was tense. It felt like the acid would burn a hole right through any second. Had Fritz done it? Had she managed to damage the enemy ships? Would *Dauntless* face two cripples when it was able to get its engines back online? Or two fully-operational battleships? Barron had tremendous confidence in his people, but he knew his ship had no chance against the latter.

The wait was long, torturous…and then the static began to clear, and a message came through.

"…worked, Cap…mines…ships…"

"Fritzie, do you read me?" Barron had grabbed his headset and pulled it on. "Fritzie?"

"Captain…" The static continued to clear. "Fritz here…the mines…success…"

"The mines damaged the enemy ships? Fritzie…Fritzie…"

"It was...total success...both...destroyed."

"Both battleships were destroyed?" Barron couldn't believe it. Was it possible?

"Yes, sir. Both destroyed...and the escorts. Nothing left of them. Nothing at all."

Barron leaned back and exhaled hard, even as the news disseminated around the bridge. There was a ragged cheer, but he knew his people were too exhausted to celebrate wildly. And he was sure it would take time for the truth to sink in.

"Well done, Fritzie!" Barron said after a brief pause.

"Thank you, sir!" He could hear the joy in the engineer's normally emotionless tone.

"I guess you're a gunner after all!"

Chapter Forty

CFS Dauntless
System Z-111 (Chrysallis)
Deep Inside the Quarantined Zone ("The Badlands")
309 AC

"Lieutenant Billings, your people have done an outstanding job, especially with Commander Fritz and half your number over on the artifact. But I still need those engines. Now." Barron shifted in his chair uncomfortably, reaching out and grabbing hold to stay in place in the zero gravity environment of *Dauntless*'s bridge. The ship's engines were still offline. *Dauntless* had come out of the recent fight with its engines still partially operational. But a few minutes later the ship's engines died abruptly, and it became clear the final shot from the enemy had hit harder than Barron had thought.

"Captain, we're working on them. That last hit cut the main fuel line, and it slagged one of the control units too. The damage is bad. The engines themselves are in pretty fair shape, but actually getting them back online is going to take some time."

Barron was shaking his head as he listened to the engineer's explanation. "Just get them operational," he said. "Every minute matters."

He didn't doubt a word the man had said, but *Dauntless*'s vector was taking the ship hundreds of kilometers farther from the artifact every second. He kept telling himself the Union ships were all destroyed, that it didn't matter if it took a day or two for *Dauntless* to loop back around and return…but he was still uncomfortable.

His people had defeated the enemy task force, a herculean effort that had seemed impossible, even to him. But that still left the battleship out here, alone in the Badlands, and the damage she had sustained had eliminated whatever miniscule possibility might have existed of towing the artifact herself. It was still a waiting game, and the only strategy Barron could think of was to sit and hope the Confederation got here first. He couldn't even defend the artifact, not unless Billings got the engines back online and *Dauntless* was able to get back.

Despite his own tension, he could feel the relief in the air. His people felt as though they'd won a great victory, which of course, they had. But Barron just couldn't share their easy belief that the fight was over. He'd expected Striker to send help sooner than this, and the fact that no Confederation ships had arrived suggested something was wrong. Perhaps the relief force had been intercepted, cut off and defeated. Or, maybe something had prevented the admiral from even dispatching the ships. Whatever it was, Barron's gut told him it wasn't good. And if a Union ship appeared first, he had serious doubts about whether his battered vessel could win another fight.

"Commander Travis, I want a course plotted and ready the instant the engines are back online." He tried to hide the edginess he felt, but he could tell immediately Travis had seen through his façade. And he realized as he looked across the bridge that she shared his concern.

"Yes, Captain. I already computed it. It's locked in and waiting for your order. And for the engines, of course."

"Very well," he said, somehow managing to be surprised yet again by how Travis seemed to read his mind. "Check with the fighter bays as well, Commander. I know everybody wants to let out a deep breath and relax, but I want those squadrons ready to go as quickly as possible." Barron had canceled the battlestations status, knocking the alert level down to yellow. That action had been driven less by a sense that the fight was behind them and more by the reality that his people needed some sleep. The intermediate alert kept increased crew levels at some stations, but it freed up hundreds of *Dauntless*'s people, every one of whom had been ordered to their bunks.

Barron leaned back and rubbed his hand over his face. He wanted to pop another stim, but he resisted the urge. Travis had tried several times to get him to go back to his quarters, or even to his office just down the short corridor from the bridge, but he'd refused. This was where he belonged, and it was where he was going to stay until…

"Captain…"

His blood went cold at the tone in Travis's voice. An instant later, before she even finished her report, his eyes caught the data on the main display. Energy readings…from the transwarp point, the same one *Dauntless* had used to reach the system. The same one the Union task force had traversed.

His first urge was to declare red alert, but he held back. His people were exhausted and their nerves were shot. He would wait…wait until he was sure what was about to come through that transit point.

*   *   *

Anya Fritz walked down the corridor, toward the large compartment the Marines had turned into a makeshift field hospital. She walked inside, feeling a bit like an invader. The Marines hadn't paid the entire cost of the fight to hold the artifact. Two of her engineers had been killed too. But compared to more than fifty of Rogan's people dead, she knew her team had escaped lightly.

The battle against the FRs had been a savage one, and almost half *Dauntless*'s contingent had been casualties. The dead in the brutal combat had far outnumbered the wounded, but even so, more than twenty of Bryan Rogan's people were lying along the wall of the large room atop piles of jackets, clothing, any kind of padding to cushion the hard metal deck. The captain was at the far end of the room, on his knees, hunched over an almost-still form.

Fritz wanted to turn and leave, to flee back into the corridor before Rogan saw her. But she couldn't. She'd received a communique from *Dauntless*, and she had to talk to the Marine. Now.

She walked across the room, hoping Rogan would notice her and turn around without her having to say anything. But the officer stayed where he was, unmoving, even as she walked up right behind him.

"Captain..." She spoke softly, tentatively. "I'm sorry to interrupt."

Rogan stood slowly, a small exhale escaping his lips as he did. "You're not interrupting, Commander. Lieutenant Plunkett is dead."

Her eyes darted to the Marine on the floor beside Rogan. He was lying on a tarp of some kind. The fabric was stained dark red, and there were pools of blood to either side. Plunkett's body was mostly covered, but she could see hints of the grievous wounds that had killed him. She'd only heard secondhand accounts, but it seemed the lieutenant was one of the heroes of the battle. His attack had broken the back of the enemy, and she suspected if his assault had been one bit less intense, Rogan's people would have never arrived in time to save her engineering crews.

And her people wouldn't have finished and deployed the mines...

"He might just have saved all of us, Captain...including *Dauntless*." She wasn't sure if that would make her feel better about a friend's death...he was, after all, still dead, whether he had died for a cause or not. But she'd been around enough Marines to know that sort of thing seemed to comfort them.

"Yes, he died well." There was a fatigue in Rogan's voice, one that suggested some strain in the belief structure that had carried the Marine through his years of duty. A good death, a meaningful death—Fritz had heard the Marines speak of such things—but it was still death as far as she could see. "What can

I do for you, Commander?"

"We just got a transmission from *Dauntless*. Something is coming through the transit point." She paused an instant then added, "It could be our relief." Her tone suggested at least a reasonable amount of doubt about that. "But the captain wants us on full alert just in case."

Rogan nodded. "Yes, Commander. I will deploy my Marines at once and prepare to repel boarders."

Fritz had to respect the "never say die" attitude of the Marines. She was no expert in battles waged in the corridors of spaceships, but she had a pretty good idea that Rogan's people had no chance, not against a fresh, fully-supplied enemy attack force. She knew with even greater certainty that fact wouldn't affect what they did, not for an instant.

"That's not necessary, Captain. I think you can let your people get some rest. It could be friendly forces incoming, and if it's not, we'll have enough warning for your people to get in place."

"Very well, Commander."

"I'll update you as soon as I hear anything." She turned and walked back toward the door.

She wasn't sure if Rogan had truly agreed to wait or if he'd just been humoring her, but she'd done all she could to protect the well-deserved sleep of *Dauntless*'s Marines. If Rogan started rousing them the instant she left the room, her conscience was clear.

Almost.

*   *   *

Barron stared at the screen, struggling to fight off disbelief, despair. He'd watched, waited to see what would come out of the transwarp point, wondering if his ship could handle another opponent. He'd tried to tell himself it was a Confederation force, but somehow he'd known all along it wasn't.

Now he was looking at five Union battleships.

It made things easier, at least in one way. He'd been wracking his brain, trying to come up with a stratagem, some trick of war that would allow him to defeat one more enemy with his battered warship. But this was such an overpowering force, he'd almost laughed when he saw it. All the fighting, the sacrifice… it had been for nothing. These newly arrived battleships didn't even have to engage *Dauntless*. The several hundred fighters aboard could do the job by themselves.

Barron reached down to the comm unit, toggling Lieutenant Billings's line. "Walt, this is the captain. We need that thrust. Whatever you have to do, whatever the risk, you have to get those engines back online."

"Yes, Captain…but if we try to fire the engines before we've gotten all the leaks, we could scrag them for good. Or worse, we could lose the whole ship."

"We're going to lose the ship if we don't have thrust." *We're going to lose it anyway…*

Barron glanced over at the display, at the Union vessels even now moving in-system toward the artifact. He'd had an advantage in the detection game, the probes he'd left around the transwarp point sending him details on the invading task force before the Union scanners could sweep the system. But the enemy would pick up *Dauntless* at any moment. Then they would react.

"Bring us back to battlestations, Commander. Pilots to the bays. I want all squadrons ready to launch."

"Yes, sir." Travis's hands moved over her controls, and the bridge was once again bathed in a glowing red light. Barron could hear the klaxons, on the bridge, but also, in the distance, in nearby compartments. He could imagine his fighter pilots, leaping out of their bunks, rubbing whatever sleep they'd managed to accumulate out of their eyes as they raced down to the bays.

They had launched countless times against desperate odds, but this time Barron knew it would be different. When he gave them the launch order, he would do it knowing none of them would return. This would be his squadrons' last mission, and each of his pilots would fight with the last of their weaponry, the final drops of precious fuel. There would be no attempt to return to *Dauntless*. There was no point. The battleship was as doomed as its pilots.

"Captain, we're picking up fighter launches from multiple ships. It's still early to be sure, but my best guess is they're heading this way. All five capital ships appear to be heading directly for the artifact."

Barron shook his head. He'd known this was coming, though he was surprised the task force commander hadn't detached one or two of his battleships to see to *Dauntless*'s destruction. He felt a reflexive burst of hope, a thought that he could somehow take advantage of this…lapse in judgment. But it faded as he watched wave after wave of fighters launching, over two hundred in all, forming up to attack. It would take the squadrons some time to counter the intrinsic velocity of their launch platforms, and to establish a line toward *Dauntless*. That would buy some time, but not enough.

Barron's mind raced. The prospect of his ship and all his people dying here cut at his soul…but worse even was the thought of the Union gaining control of the artifact, of turning the astonishing technology it held against the Confederation. Against every nation that failed to submit to the tyranny of the brutal regime.

He looked toward the display, the small sphere representing the transwarp link. He imagined the energy readings spiking again, a Confederation relief force this time. But he knew that was impossible. The Union forces showed no signs of concern for any forces pursuing them. That meant whatever small hope he might have indulged was empty. There couldn't be any Confederation ships close enough to make a difference.

"Captain, Lieutenant Billings reports he is ready to restart the engines. He requests your permission to proceed."

"By all means, Commander. At once."

"He advises the attempt will be dangerous."

"Understood, Commander. Proceed." *Anything we do now is dangerous.*

Barron leaned back, taking a breath. He knew the risk involved, and he recalled his words to Billings, his command to go ahead despite any danger.

The ship shook once, so hard that Barron almost fell forward out of his chair. Then he felt the force almost immediately, even as the dampeners kicked in and created a reasonable simulation of normal gravity. It was a relief, in more ways than one. Barron had never liked zero g environments. He'd gotten over the space-sickness years before, but never the sense of discomfort. And the realization that he had engine power back filled him with hope…false hope, he knew, but at least he could do *something*.

"Well done, Lieutenant," he said into his comm unit. "Well done."

"Thank you, sir. We've got the engines back, but only at twenty percent. Perhaps twenty-five for a few minutes…in an emergency."

Barron nodded, to himself as much as anyone. "Understood, Lieutenant. I want you to keep your people at it. I need all the thrust you can give me."

"Yes, sir." Barron could hear in the engineer's tone the unlikelihood of imminent improvement.

He looked down at his workstation, running calculations. He didn't get far before he confirmed what he had expected. Even assuming his people could somehow turn back the enemy fighters, it would take far too long to decelerate and come around, back toward the artifact. The Union battleships would be there long before *Dauntless*…and over a thousand FRs would land and wipe out his remaining Marines.

He couldn't let that happen. The Union simply could not be allowed to gain such a massive technological edge. He had to do something. But what?

He sat, staring at the floor, his mind racing, groping for any strategy. There was no way to get the artifact away from the enemy…and no way to keep the Union forces from the ancient vessel. But perhaps he could still deny it to them, prevent them from using its technology to shatter the balance of power.

"Atara," he said grimly. "Get me Commander Fritz."

"Yes, sir." A moment later: "On your line, Captain."

"Fritzie...I'm sure you've been monitoring the enemy ships moving into the system."

"Yes, sir."

"We can't let the enemy gain control of that vessel, Fritzie."

"No, sir." The engineer's tone suggested she understood completely what that meant.

"Those canisters, Fritzie...can you prepare a time-delayed fuse for one?"

There was a short pause. "Captain...this ship is the most important discovery in any of our lifetimes. In the history of the Confederation. We can't destroy..."

"Commander Fritz, you just told me we can't let the enemy gain control over that ship. Given a choice between destroying it or allowing the Union to gain control of that power, what would you choose?" Barron could hear utter silence around him. He knew every member of the bridge crew was listening, each no doubt with his or her own opinion. But this wasn't a vote. He was in command, and he knew what he had to do. What his grandfather would have done.

"You're right, sir. We don't have a choice." Fritz's voice was downcast. Forcing his master engineer to destroy such a repository of technical wonder was its own terrible cruelty. But it was the only way.

"Do it, Fritzie. Set the fuse for..." He paused, glancing at the display, quickly calculating the shortest time for the enemy to reach the artifact. "...one hour. Then get your people and the Marines off of there."

There was another silence. Longer this time. "Captain, all of the shuttles were destroyed in the attack. I'm afraid that, without *Dauntless*, we're stuck here."

Barron felt a cold horror take him. Anya Fritz, Bryan Rogan...nearly one hundred of his people. They were all stranded.

Dauntless couldn't get back, not with twenty percent thrust. Not in time. The enemy would be there hours before. Slowly, the terrible reality dawned on him. He wasn't just ordering Fritz to destroy a treasure trove of ancient technology. He was ordering her to commit suicide…and kill every one of his people still on that ship.

"I will see it done, Captain. Don't worry about it."

"Fritzie…"

"It's fine, sir. There is no way you can get to us. Please don't make our last sight that of *Dauntless* being destroyed. Go. Save the ship and the rest of the crew. I will destroy this ship."

Barron tried to answer, but no words would come. His crew had suffered losses in the war, bad ones. But seeing friends killed in action was one thing, abandoning them to destruction was quite another. He knew going back would only doom *Dauntless*, and the hundreds still alive in her crew. But he couldn't bring himself to say it.

"I can get them."

Barron turned abruptly, looking to the source of the words. It was Andi Lafarge, standing at the door of the lift.

"That's out of the question. You'd never make it."

"*Pegasus* isn't a match for *Dauntless*, Tyler, but she has her own secrets. And she's a lot faster than your battleship is right now. I can get there before the Union ships and be on the way back… if I leave *now*."

Barron could feel himself being torn in two. He hated the idea of Lafarge putting herself in such danger. But the alternative was abandoning nearly a hundred of his people to certain death, without even an attempt to save them…and that was no choice at all.

"There are almost a hundred of my people there, plus prisoners."

"I can cram them in the cargo hold. It won't be comfortable, and I can't guarantee there won't be some bruises and broken bones, but I'll get them back here."

"Captain, it's too much of a risk. Leave us. You have to figure out how to get *Dauntless* out of here." Fritz had clearly overheard his conversation with Lafarge.

Barron turned toward the smuggler captain. "Andi, I appreciate your offer, but if we're going to get *Dauntless* back to the transwarp point back toward home…"

"You don't have to."

"What?"

"You don't have to get back to the transwarp point, at least not the one you came through." She paused. "I guess my nav data out here is better than yours. There's another jump point, out this way." She waved her arm in a pointless directional gesture. "At least there's one on the map I've got."

"The map you've got?" There was frustration in his tone. "There was no transwarp link on the data your people gave the admiral."

She flashed him an expression he suspected might have been a smile in less dire circumstances. "Let's just say my people like to play things close to the vest. I'll do this to get your people back. I'll do it for you. But don't forget, my first officer is still over there…I'm going for him too."

Barron felt a wave of annoyance. He couldn't figure her out. She was brave, and a good ally…but she was also secretive and suspicious. He'd never met anyone like her. He felt an attraction he found difficult to push aside. But he still wasn't sure if he trusted her.

"Go," he said, blurting it out quickly. "But be careful…and keep your eyes on the scanners. If any enemy gets too close…"

"I understand." She did smile this time, just for a few seconds. "It's nice to know you care, Tyler." She paused for a few seconds, seeming to enjoy Barron's discomfort. Then she turned abruptly and walked across the bridge.

Chapter Forty-One

**Free Trader Pegasus
System Z-111 (Chrysallis)
Deep Inside the Quarantined Zone ("The Badlands")
309 AC**

"Bring us around, Rina...I want to leave plenty of room between us and that flank Union ship."

"Yes, Andi. Engaging positioning jets now."

Lafarge sat in her chair, a place where she'd always felt at home. But the events of recent weeks had been so strange, they had left her feeling...different. She was undertaking an act of altruism, putting herself and her ship at great risk for no material gain. She owed the crew of *Dauntless*, of course. They had saved her, and whatever she was—mercenary, smuggler...pirate—Andi Lafarge paid her debts. She liked to think she would have done what she was doing for that reason alone. But she knew there was more to it.

She'd disliked authority figures her whole life. Her experiences with government in her younger years had been of deprivation, of arrogant bureaucrats who, as far as she could see, always lived better than the masses they "served." She'd crawled out of the squalor into which she'd been born, but she'd had to push beyond the law to do it. Her view of the Confederation's government hadn't improved as she'd gotten older, but it *had* changed, hardened. She and her people had been branded outlaws, at least of a sort, and she'd existed in the shadows, harassed, hunted even upon occasion, by the same navy she was now helping.

It was Tyler Barron. She couldn't come to terms with her feelings for the strange naval officer. He was everything she'd mistrusted her whole life…a strict military commander, utterly obedient to his government masters, a child of privilege, one who grew up in a huge manor house, and not on the streets as she had. But there was something about him…he was all she had always hated, but he was more too. And, whatever she felt for him, it most definitely was not hate.

She hadn't been able to get him out of her mind, not since the moment they had met. And now, she knew, at least on some level, she was here risking her life for Tyler Barron.

"Andi, we've got something on the scanner. It looks like Union fighters."

She turned her head sharply, focusing on *Pegasus*'s small display. *Shit*!

"Captain Lafarge…" Dirk Timmons's voice came through the comm unit.

"Yes, Lieutenant Timmons…"

"We've got Union fighters heading this way. We'll take care of this group, but that's going to pull us away, leaving you on your own. You're going to have to come in on a wider arc toward the artifact, put more distance between *Pegasus* and the Union wings."

"I don't know how much of an arc we can take and still get there ahead of the task force, Lieutenant."

There was a short silence. "I'm leaving two fighters with you, Captain. It's the best we can do and still be sure of handling that group that's coming. But keep your eyes on your scanners. There are a lot more enemy forces out there."

"Understood, Lieutenant. Good luck." She shook her head. She could get to the artifact ahead of the enemy battleships, she was sure of that, but only if she took a fairly direct course. If the enemy fighters forced her too far out of her way…"

"Course adjustment, Rina. Bring us another half million kilometers away from the Union formations."

"On it, Andi." A short pause. "That's going to cut our time margin down to almost nothing."

She took a deep breath, struggling against the g forces. She knew the maneuver would leave almost no time to load Barron's people...and that she might very well face a dead run back to *Dauntless* with enemy forces on her tail. Her eyes moved back to the display. But those Union fighters were too close. She needed to put some distance between *Pegasus* and them.

"Do it, Rina. See if you can coax a little more from the engines. Anything at all would help." She knew that was a risk too, especially without Lex Righter. She hadn't come to terms yet with the loss of her engineer...and her friend. Righter hadn't come back with Vig. For some reason she hadn't been able to fathom, he had decided to remain on the Union frigate, to try to get its engines back online. But the battered ship had remained right where it was, much too far away to reach. If Righter wasn't dead, he soon would be...or he'd be a Union prisoner. Which was probably worse.

"Andi, we've got more Union fighters. They're on a vector to cut us off. We've got to go around."

Lafarge stared at the screen, running calculations in her head. But even before she had the hard numbers, the cold reality hit her. It was over. Her desperate rescue mission had failed. There was no way *Pegasus* could get around the new group of fighters, not before the enemy battleships reached the artifact.

Her hands balled up in frustrated fists. Her mind raced, but there was nothing. No way at all. She felt sorrow for the doomed Marines and spacers...more than she'd ever thought she could. And for Vig, for whatever hope she'd held out that her first officer was still alive. But most of all, she felt as though she'd let Barron down. And that cut through her like a blade.

* * *

"We're coming up on the artifact. I'm going to try to dock

at one of the existing entry points." The pilot's voice was edgy. Righter might even have gone as far as to call it shaky. Ensign Lorne seemed like a decent guy, and a capable officer, but the junior pilot had never flown a Union ship before, much less one barely functional and patched together in a manner Righter himself, the architect of it all, could only call "half assed."

"Do your best Eugene." *Just like I did my best. It might not look like much, but it got us this far. And Lorne will get us docked. Even if it's a little rough.*

"Hang on," the pilot said.

Righter watched as the massive ancient ship filled the forward display. The shuttle moved slowly, steadily toward a docking portal that looked very much like one of Union design. His eyes darted toward the control panel, and the dead comm unit. He'd tried like hell to patch something together there, but it had been to no avail. The shuttle had basic scanners, and engines that functioned—as long as Righter kept an eye on them, at least—but that was about all. Even the life support system was *just* working.

The ship shook, hard, and Righter could hear the sound of metal hitting metal. Too hard. For an instant, he thought they had crashed, that the shuttle he had so carefully restored to working order had gotten all the way to the artifact, only for them to die smashing into its hull. But then he realized they had stopped, and Lorne turned around, pale as a sheet, but with a smile on his face. "We're docked."

Righter exhaled loudly, only then realizing that he was soaked in sweat. He looked down at his still-shaking hands, and then he got up and turned back toward the hatch. "Well done, Eugene. Incredible."

"And to you," the young officer replied, "for getting this thing back into space."

The two men walked to the airlock, stopping to double check that the seal was sound and the tube was pressurized.

"So, we made it." Clete Hargraves walked up behind the two men, the shadows of several of his Marines in the short corridor behind him. "I'm not sure I would have bet on you guys pulling it off," the Marine said, in the coolly matter-of-fact way only a veteran like Hargraves could manage without sounding insulting. "We don't know what's been going on here since we left," he said, just as emotionlessly, despite the implications of his words. "I think my people and I should go first."

Righter nodded. He had no problem with that. He stepped to the side. "By all means, Sergeant."

Hargraves nodded, and he pulled the assault rifle from his back. "Squad," he yelled, looking behind him as he did. "Prepare to board."

Righter stood where he was, watching the Marines move forward, crawling through the tube. He'd been so worried about getting the shuttle functional—and keeping it that way—he hadn't even considered what they would find on the artifact. The small ship's scanners were badly damaged, but he'd gotten enough data to piece together that a major fight had been going on in the system. Had they come all this way just to end up as Union prisoners?

Righter waited, his earlier relief dissipating, giving way to new concern. He half expected to hear the sounds of gunfire at any second, but there was nothing.

Finally, one of Hargraves's Marines came crawling back through the tube. He poked his head through and said, "Mr. Righter, Ensign Lorne…the sergeant wants you both to come aboard. Right away."

Righter could hear the urgency in the Marine's voice, but he hadn't seen nor heard any signs of fighting. What could it be?

He looked at the pilot, noting the young officer wore the same confused expression. They nodded to each other, and then they followed the Marine back through the tube.

* * *

Lafarge watched the shuttle moving toward *Pegasus*. She'd been nothing short of stunned when she'd gotten the transmission from Commander Fritz. She'd been about to contact *Dauntless*, to face the unpleasant task of telling Tyler Barron she'd been unable to get to his people as she'd promised to do. She had dreaded that task, for reasons she only partially understood. The communique had saved her from that...but it had put her and her ship into greater danger. The personnel from the artifact had somehow all crowded onto the captured shuttle, but now she had to link up with them, and the neighborhood was getting decidedly unhealthy.

She'd watched Timmons and his pilots on the display for a few moments. The Scarlet Eagles had torn into the Union squadron with a vengeance, destroying half the fighters in a matter of moments, and sending the rest fleeing back to reorder. The lopsided victory had gained some time, but it had been won against a tiny advance guard of interceptors, less than a tenth of the Union birds loose now in the system. More fighters were coming, even now, and Timmons's people, as good as they were, would soon be outnumbered fivefold.

The shuttle was almost there. She could see from the variation in its vector that its engines were barely hanging on. She'd almost been ready to give Lex Righter up for dead, but instead, she found out her engineer had saved not only the Marines left on the Union frigate, but also everyone on the artifact.

She had been more than impressed by Tyler Barron and his people, deciding without a doubt that the stories about them had, if anything, understated the truth. But her people had done their share as well, and she knew part of the victory—if destroying such a wondrous discovery and then fleeing could be called a victory—belonged to *Pegasus* and her crew. She wondered if the Confederation authorities would come to that conclusion... or realize that without her involvement, the Union would have gained control over the artifact without opposition. Relying on the good sense—or gratitude—of government went against her every instinct. But she didn't see any options.

She watched as the shuttle approached. She knew its comm was down. Fritz had told her that in the communique from the artifact. She'd suggested Fritz bring the portable unit, but the engineer didn't seem to have done that.

No room, Lafarge realized. There were over a hundred people crammed on that shuttle, including the Union prisoners the officers had insisted on bringing. Lafarge didn't have a doubt she'd have left the enemy spacers behind, and she suspected she was seeing Barron's honor code once again at work.

It would be a miracle if the life support held out and no one was crushed or trampled. There was no room for superfluous equipment. And no room for Union prisoners to her way of thinking.

And there was one prisoner there with whom she had a score to settle…

She looked around behind her. Pegasus would be better than the shuttle in terms of space, but not a lot. Her cargo hold and compartments would be bursting at the seams. It would be fine if she was able to get right back to *Dauntless*, but if she had to make evasive maneuvers, or if it took too long to return, she was going to make evasive maneuvers, or if it took too long to return, she was going to have injuries back there…or worse.

She didn't like sitting and waiting for a ship to dock with hers, with no communications. Intellectually, she knew her friend and engineer was on that ship, but it still felt strange. If the shuttle malfunctioned, if anything unexpected happened this close to *Pegasus*, the consequences could be disastrous. She tried to tell herself she was being paranoid, but that was just how she was. Her life had taught her to watch out for the unexpected, for all the things that could go wrong at any time.

The ship shook lightly, and a loud clang rang out a few seconds later. She looked down at her screen, at the row of green lights that meant one thing. The shuttle had docked safely.

She looked over at Rina Strand. "Go down, and open the docking portal. I want everybody onboard immediately." Strand was the only other member of *Pegasus*'s crew onboard. Lafarge would have taken all her people, but she'd known she would need every bit of space she could get. Besides, she'd figured the odds of making it back at around 50/50, and there was no reason to subject more of her friends to that risk.

"I'm on it, Andi." Strand leapt out of her chair and across the ship's tiny bridge. Then she slipped out into the corridor and down toward the airlock.

Lafarge stood just inside the metal door of the airlock, looking out through the small window into the velvety blackness, and the grayish-white metal of the artifact beyond. She was still savoring the image of Laussanne's face as she'd slammed the airlock door shut before he'd gotten through the tube. She'd looked into his eyes, drawing near ecstasy from the panic in his expression as he began to understand. She had promised to kill him…and Andi Lafarge paid her debts.

She only regretted there hadn't been time to truly allow the bastard to reflect in the error of his ways for longer before she'd cut the docking seal…and watched her former tormenter sucked into the frozen blackness.

But now her mind moved on. She'd saved Vig and Lex… her entire crew had somehow made it through this nightmare… assuming *Pegasus* got back to *Dauntless*, and the battleship managed to flee the system.

She raced back toward the bridge, knowing there was no time to waste. Killing Laussanne had been a luxury, but it was the only one she could afford. It was time to get the hell out of here…before the enemy got here. Before Fritz's bomb set off an explosion beyond anything she could imagine.

She slipped into the chair, looking over toward Strand. "All right, Rina…let's move it!"

*   *   *

"We've got them, Tyler. We've got all of them. We're on our way back." *All except one…*

Barron felt relief as Lafarge's words blared through his headset. Partial relief, at least. His Marines, his engineers…all his people he'd been about to give up for dead, were on the way back. And Andi was coming back too. He wanted to feel joy at the news, to let the fear and tension that had twisted him into knots dissipate into nothing. But it wasn't over yet. *Pegasus* was still out there, as were his fighters. And enemy forces were all around, five battleships closing on the artifact and squadrons of fighters dueling his wings, chasing his fleeing vessel.

His scanners had picked up strange energy readings that *might* be the transwarp link Lafarge had claimed was out in the depths of the system. They just might pull this off. *If* that portal was there, and *if Pegasus* made it back and was able to dock. *If* Fritz's timed fuse worked and destroyed the artifact…and *if* his fighters were able to disengage and land.

And if those battleships don't chase us through whatever portal is out here…

He was pretty sure *Dauntless* would make it out of the system before any of the hulking Union vessels could catch her. But they could track his ship easily enough, and chase her into whatever system lay ahead. Andi Lafarge had made some hazy comments about being able to "find the way" home from this new system, but her choice of words had filled him with something less than supreme confidence.

"Send the recall, Commander. All fighters are to break off and return to base."

"Yes, Captain." Barron had been watching the hit and run battles Jamison and his squadrons had fought. *Dauntless*'s fighter commander had conducted a masterful campaign to delay the enemy, preventing them from organizing a major pursuit of the ship. But they were out of time. They had to come back now… or they'd risk not making it. Barron had *almost* had to abandon dozens of his people, but now he'd made one decision he was going to stick to…he wasn't leaving anyone behind.

He glanced at the display, starting to count the number of fighters responding to the order. But he stopped himself. There wasn't time now. The dead would still be dead later. Right now, he was worried about the living. About keeping them alive.

"Captain, scanners are detecting enemy ships moving into range of the artifact."

Barron felt his stomach tense. Had Fritz's fuse failed to work? Had she mistimed it? No, he couldn't believe that. If there was one person he trusted to be utterly fastidious, reliable beyond question—save perhaps Travis—it was Fritz.

He waited, his eyes darting to the screens, checking on *Pegasus* and his squadrons. It looked like they'd all make it back in time, and far enough ahead of their pursuers. He'd run the calculations already. *Dauntless* would barely outrun the fighters on her tail, getting just far enough that the Union wings would have to turn back or risk not having enough fuel to return. As long as the engines held out, and his people managed to land the fighters and dock with *Pegasus* without cutting acceleration.

He pushed those concerns to the back of his mind. He was confident his crew could handle all of that. He was beginning to believe *Dauntless* would escape, that his people would live to fight another day.

As long as that antimatter charge blows...

Barron didn't relish being the man who had destroyed the single greatest discovery in history, and he knew it was something that would eat at him for the rest of his life. But he knew one thing for sure. He'd prefer that by a considerable margin to being the man who'd allowed the Union to gain the power to dominate all of mankind.

He was too tense now to know just how he'd feel, too exhausted, too twisted into knots. Maybe once *Dauntless* was out of this place, when he'd had time to mourn the dead and put things in perspective. Perhaps then he'd have a clearer point of view.

He was staring right at the display, becoming more worried with each passing second, when every instrument on the bridge went crazy.

The display itself went dark, the hologram simply vanishing. Every scanner on the ship overloaded in a microsecond, and the AI struggled to calculate what its inputs were reading. Barron knew, of course. He understood exactly what had happened. Fritz's bomb had gone off...and in releasing billions of kilotons of energy, it had vaporized the hundreds of other canisters on the ship, setting off an almost incalculable chain reaction of matter-antimatter annihilation.

Dauntless was far away, of course, too far to be affected in any way save instrument failure and higher than normal gamma rays hitting the outer shielding. But the Union vessels weren't so fortunate. Petawatts of raw energy blasted outward, slamming into the approaching vessels. Two of the battleships were destroyed outright, vaporized by the massive energies unleashed. The other three were farther out. They survived with varying degrees of damage.

Dauntless's scanners were too scrambled, too far away, to get a solid reading, but Barron knew in his gut that none of the enemy vessels would be pursuing his ship.

He stared at the center of the bridge, where the display hologram was slowly rebooting. He knew what the system would show when it had fully recovered. An area of dissipating heat and intense radiation where once the ancient vessel had been. A planet, devastated in ways he could only imagine, by the almost unimaginable explosion that had taken place in its orbit. Its atmosphere would almost certainly be gone, and perhaps much of its crust along with it. It would be a sight to see, he had no doubt, but there was no time. *Dauntless* had its chance at escape, and Barron intended to make the most of it.

A wondrous bit of technology was gone too, a vessel that had survived the near-destruction of the race that had built it, that had remained in an undisturbed orbit for centuries.

Another victim of this war…and all the good that might have come from that tech…

Barron exhaled hard. Then, Travis's voice pulled him from his thoughts. He welcomed the distraction.

"Captain, Red and Yellow squadrons requesting permission to land, sir. All other wings will be back within fifteen minutes." She paused. "And *Pegasus* is approaching. Captain Lafarge reports some casualties from high g maneuvers, but nothing life-threatening." Travis turned toward Barron, a crooked smile on her face. "She requests that I tell you she'll be back on board in less than thirty minutes."

Barron tried to hold back his own grin, but he knew it had slipped out. "Very well, Commander. Let's get everyone back onboard and get the hell out of here."

Chapter Forty-Two

CFS Dauntless
System Z-46 (Styria)
In the Quarantined Zone ("The Badlands")
309 AC

"I heard you actually looked human again, but I just couldn't believe it without seeing it." Barron walked into *Dauntless*'s sickbay, his eyes moving right to his ace pilot.

Jake Stockton was lying in bed, propped up, looking about a sickly as any human being Barron had ever seen. But he was alive…and according to Stu Weldon, he was going to stay that way. The pale, almost snow white skin covering his body would eventually look just like the ruddy flesh he'd had before his crash, or at least so Doc Weldon had insisted.

"Captain…it's good to see you, sir." Stockton's voice was weak, but Barron could hear the old resolve buried in there somewhere. In that instant, he fully believed Weldon. Jake Stockton had somehow pulled through his ordeal.

"I see you have a party going on down here." Barron looked side to side. Stara Sinclair was in her usual spot, of course. Nothing but combat duty had served to pull her away. But now Kyle Jamison was there too, along with what looked like most of the exhausted but cheerful survivors of Blue squadron.

"Just a few friends, sir. It gets boring down here, you know."

"Well, you could always quit milking this and report back to duty. I'm sure I could dig up a patrol for you." Barron paused and smiled. "Though we'll have to dig up a new fighter somewhere. I've never seen a ship that actually landed in such bad shape." Barron stared right at the pilot. "Seriously, Jake. We lost enough of our people in the last few weeks. I'm damned glad you're still with us."

"Thank you, sir. And I hear Dirk did a good job filling in for me."

Barron didn't respond right away. He just stood there and looked back at Stockton.

"No worries, sir. All that is behind us. I can't think of anybody who can take better care of the Blues for me than Warrior." He laid back for a few seconds, taking a deep breath. "I'd sure like to get out of this thing." He moved his arm, gesturing toward the plastic barrier that separated him from the others. "Maybe you could talk to the doc, work something out. Just a walk."

"Like you *could* walk. You'd fall on your face in two seconds if you even tried to stand." Stu Weldon came walking across the floor. "Not to mention the fact that you'd be a walking, talking invitation to every microorganism on this ship. That new skin of yours is only half grown, and you're not getting out of there until it's one hundred percent. You are my masterpiece, and I will not have you destroying my handiwork." Weldon walked up next to the bed and looked down at the readouts. "And if you give me a hard time again, I'll put your complaining ass back in that medpod, where I don't have to listen to your bitching."

"All right, let's go. All of you." Barron smiled and gestured to the small crowd. "Back to the officer's club…assuming that establishment still functions without Jake there. The first round's on me." He turned and looked back at Stockton, and at the woman sitting next to him. "I think Lieutenant Sinclair can keep an eye on Raptor here, don't you Kyle?" He glanced at Jamison.

"Yes, Captain. I do believe she can handle it."

"Then let's go…all of you. This is sickbay after all. The real party will have to wait until Jake here is released."

Barron stood and watched the group of pilots file out into the corridor, followed—and to an extent, herded—by Kyle Jamison. He paused for a few seconds himself, and he looked down at Sinclair. "I'll leave you here with him for a while, Stara…but I want you to promise me you'll get some sleep."

She looked up and nodded.

"Don't force me to make it an order."

"I won't, sir. Just a little longer, then I'll go. Doctor Weldon wants him to sleep anyway."

Barron just nodded. Then he turned and walked out into the hall.

*   *   *

"I want to thank you for what you did back there." Barron stood in the corridor, facing Andi Lafarge. "I know you went back for Vig, but I also know that wasn't the only reason."

She looked back and smiled. "Well, let's just say you're someone who inspires people. It's clear your crew would follow you to hell."

"Let's hope we don't have orders to that effect waiting for us when we get back." Barron was trying to hold back a grin, but it slipped out anyway.

"What is it?" Lafarge said, looking at him quizzically.

"I was just wondering."

"Wondering what?"

Barron's grin widened. "Well, I just consider it impressive that you managed to get everybody on the artifact crammed aboard *Pegasus* in a matter of minutes, and you still…"

Lafarge's face hardened, her smile gone. "I still…?"

Barron laughed. "You know you're busted, and you still can't help yourself. You've got to play it out to the end, don't you?"

Lafarge just stood there, silent, looking back.

"How did you do it? How did you manage that…with only minutes to spare, without anyone catching you? How did you sneak an antimatter canister onto your ship?"

She looked back. Barron could see the softness in her expression. He knew she was working him, but it didn't matter. He didn't care. He wanted to be angry with her, but he just couldn't do it.

"I'm resourceful, Tyler. I told you that."

Barron shook his head, the grin still affixed to his face. "It took my people two days to figure out what they were picking up on the scanners." He paused for a few seconds. "You know I can't let you keep it, don't you?"

"Even if I say please?"

Barron laughed again. "Yes, I'm afraid so. Even if you say please." He smiled again. "Though I won't enjoy rejecting your request. You do realize that's more antimatter than every bit that has been produced in the entire Confederation in its history? It will do wonders for research. You managed to save at least something of our lost glimpse into the future…or the past, to be more accurate."

"That doesn't pay my bills, unfortunately."

"Do you know what a pain in the ass you are?"

"If that's your idea of a seduction, I'd say your technique needs some work." She reached out and put her hand on his arm.

He glanced down at her fingers, and then he looked back at her and smiled. "Is that so? Maybe you could offer me some advice?"

"Well, you could stop talking for one thing. It's likely to just get you in trouble. Just take me to your quarters. I hear fleet battleship captains have nice cabins…though I can't say I've ever seen one before."

Barron put his hand on hers. "Well, then…it's long past time we remedied that, isn't it?"

*   *   *

"Tyler, I wanted to apologize to you personally. I sent you out there, promised you support, and that support didn't arrive until you were on your way back. I don't take that lightly. I've reviewed the reports, and I have to tell you, I still can't fathom just how you managed to defeat four enemy battleships. It was an amazing display, Captain. Just amazing." Admiral Striker sat opposite Barron, looking across the table at *Dauntless*'s captain. Striker's arm was still in a sling, and his face was covered with partially-healed gashes. He'd recovered from his wounds, somewhat, but he still carried the marks of the terrible battle at Grimaldi, the desperate fight to the finish that had stopped the Union offensive cold.

"Thank you, sir. I appreciate your words. And my people were all involved. I wouldn't have accomplished a thing without such an extraordinary crew behind me."

"I couldn't agree more, Captain. Your people are without compare. If ever there was a captain and crew who deserved each other—and I mean that in the best possible way—it is *Dauntless* and you. No group of spacers has done more to stave off disaster in this war. And the more I review what happened out at Z-111, the more I'm convinced this time went well beyond the others."

"Well, sir, I'd have rated it more of a success if we'd managed to save the artifact. It was an astonishing find, and we blew it to atoms. I exceeded my authority. It wasn't my place to make such a decision."

"It was entirely your place." Striker's voice was firm. "Tyler…you did the only thing you could have done. I don't think it overstates the matter to say you saved the Confederation. As much as your grandfather did."

Barron nodded, looking uncomfortable. He'd always had trouble with praise. From most people, he considered it insincere…and in cases like this, where he knew it was genuine, it poked at the guilt he felt for his privilege in the navy. Serving with officers like Atara Travis, not to mention his encounter with Andi Lafarge, had reminded him that not all those who fought alongside him had shared his smoothly paved route to success. Barron knew he had served well, that he had done his grandfather's memory proud, but he wondered if he would have reached his rank with the energy to do all he had done if he had shared Travis's path.

"Thank you, sir. That means a lot." He hesitated. "With all due respect to others in the chain of command, sir, I believe we were fortunate that you got the top posting. I've only read a summary of the action at Grimaldi, but I feel comfortable in saying I don't think many other admirals would have had the stomach to stick it out until the end."

Striker nodded. "My thanks to you, Captain. I can think of no other officer whose words would mean as much."

Barron nodded again. There was nothing else to say.

"I have one other thing, Captain. A special order."

"Sir?"

"Well, I authorized a number of promotions for your people based on your preliminary reports. I'm sure more will follow, but there's been a bit of a problem with this first batch."

"I'm sorry Admiral…I'm not sure I follow. A problem?"

"Yes, Captain Barron, a problem. Every single one of them has been declined." Striker looked at Barron, an amused look on his face. "I must tell you, I'm not accustomed to having promotions thrown back in my face. Apparently, your people are concerned that any increase in their rank could force them out of their positions. Off *Dauntless*."

Barron was surprised. "I had no idea, sir." He was touched, but he had no intention of allowing his people to cripple their careers. "Sir, I will…"

"No need, Captain. That's where my order comes in. It exempts *Dauntless* from the normal rank guidelines…and it ensures that any of your people who wish to remain in their current assignments may do so, regardless of their rank."

"Thank you, sir." Barron felt a wave of relief. He knew he couldn't keep his crew together forever, but he wasn't ready to let them go, not yet. Not after the losses they had just suffered.

"My order takes care of the problem with all of your people. All except one."

Barron looked back across the table.

"Commander Travis, Tyler. Captain Travis, if she will allow me to promote her. She was offered her own ship…but she turned it down cold."

Barron leaned back in his chair. He felt a tightness in his stomach. He'd feared this for some time. He didn't want to lose Atara, and he had trouble imagining what *Dauntless* would be like without her. But he knew she deserved it. He couldn't think of another officer who rated her own ship more than Travis. "I'll talk to her, sir," he said, hoping he didn't sound as morose as he felt.

"Good," Striker said. "And now, perhaps the one good thing that came out of the fight at Grimaldi. The fleet's a wreck, but so is the enemy's. It's a virtual impossibility for either side to launch any kind of real offensive right now…and that allows us to leave a screening force and pull some damaged ships off the line. *Dauntless* is at the top of that list, Captain. We owe her overdue repairs, and we're finally going to pay that debt. The old girl's going to get a complete refit, from one end to the other. Commander Fritz's amazing patches and workarounds have carried her far enough. You won't even recognize your ship when you get her back…and in the meanwhile, you and your crew can take a nice long—well-deserved—rest. You're on extended shore leave, Captain, starting now. You and your entire crew. I'll need you around for another week or two for debriefings, but after that you can take off and go anywhere you want. Your time's your own for the next six months."

Barron took a deep breath. There had been a time he couldn't have imagined being away from duty for so long, but now he felt just how deep the fatigue ran in him. He'd never have been able to rest if he knew his comrades in the fleet were fighting hard on the front, but with the two sides having battled each other to exhaustion, that wouldn't be the case. And he needed some time away.

"Thank you, sir. I'm sure my people will appreciate the break."

"They've earned it, Captain."

"Sir…"

"Yes, Captain?"

"About Captain Lafarge…I'm not sure what her actions

prior to our…"

"Don't worry, Captain. I've already talked to Captain Lafarge. She is quite…something, isn't she?"

"Yes, sir…she is."

"I don't know what a civilian bureaucrat would have done in my position, Captain. I can imagine a politician calling her a smuggler and trying to prosecute. But the navy knows when it has a debt. Andromeda Lafarge probably saved the Confederation. If she hadn't gotten involved in the search for the artifact, it is likely the Union would have obtained it, with tragic consequences." He looked at Barron. "And from your report, she and her people aided your efforts considerably. I've authorized the Dannith shipyard to repair her vessel, Captain. A top quality job from top to bottom…on the navy. And I've agreed to an… honorarium…from the discretionary accounts. Not nearly as much as she wanted, mind you, but generous enough to compensate her people for their efforts."

Barron couldn't hold back his smile anymore. The thought of Andi negotiating with the top admiral in the navy was just too amusing. "Thank you, sir."

"It was only fair, Captain. Besides, I was afraid if I negotiated with her any longer, she'd walk out of there with my stars."

"She might have at that, sir." Barron inhaled deeply, struggling to force the grin from his face. "Thank you again, Admiral. For everything."

"No, Captain." Striker stood up and extended his hand. "Thank *you*."

Barron stood up and grasped the admiral's hand, and the two shook. Then he stepped back and snapped off a crisp salute.

"Go, Captain. You've got better things to do with your shore leave than stand here saluting me."

"Yes sir." He turned and slipped out the door.

*   *   *

"Atara, you know I want you here. You're the best first officer any captain could have. And my most trusted friend. I can't imagine the hole you'll leave on *Dauntless*. But you've fought tooth and nail for every step you've taken in your career. Can you really pass up the chance for your own ship? Everything you've been chasing for so many years?"

Travis sat on the far side of Barron's desk, as she had so many times, discussing so many topics. But she looked as uncomfortable as he'd ever seen her.

"Captain…"

"I think this is a talk between Tyler and Atara. I'll take my insignia off if that helps…" He smiled.

She sat there for a second, and then she laughed. "No, Tyler…that won't be necessary."

"So…?" He stared at her.

"I don't know. Yes, of course a command of my own is what I've pursued. But things change. I never imagined I'd find a place like this. Here, with you, with the crew…it's home. The first real home I've ever known."

"It is your home, Atara, and I hope you know I will always consider you family. I can't tell you how many times I've thought of this moment, knowing it was coming, even thinking of ways I could prevent it. But I could never stand in your way like that. You're one of the most capable officers I've ever known. No, *the* most capable. I don't doubt for a second that the admiralty lies in your future…but you have to command your own ship first, Atara. I want you on *Dauntless*…but the price for you to stay is just too high."

She shifted uncomfortably in her chair. "I know, sir. I know I have to command my own ship, that I will have to leave here one day." She looked up at him, and he saw something he'd never seen before. It was barely there, more of a glistening than anything else, but his eyes were fixed on it. A single tear, building up in the corner of Travis's eye.

"But not yet, Tyler. You have to trust me. I'm not ready… and I don't think *Dauntless* is ready for me to leave either. She'll have dozens of new systems after her refit…" Her voice became somber. "…and almost two hundred replacements. I need to stay. I need to help with that, to know that when I do leave, I'll leave *Dauntless* ready for whatever comes next. Do you understand that?"

Barron sighed, feeling guilty for the relief he felt. He wasn't ready for her to go either, but he couldn't help but feel it was selfish to try to keep her. "I do, Atara. But are you sure?"

"I'm sure, Tyler. I'm not going to destroy my career. I just need to stay for a while longer. And you're like brother to me. Our road together has a bit more to run. I'm as sure of that as I've ever been of anything."

"Okay...I'll tell Admiral Striker." He got up and walked around the desk. "I can't tell you how relieved I am, Atara. I didn't want you to go either."

She stood up slowly, facing him. Then he reached out and the two hugged. "One more tour together," he said softly.

"One more," she replied.

"Am I interrupting something?" Andi Lafarge stood by the open door.

"No," Travis said, smiling. "This guy here is like my brother... the brother I never had." She looked at Lafarge and then back at Barron, not even trying to disguise the grin on her face. "I will leave the two of you alone." She leaned toward Lafarge as she passed by and whispered, "Just try to have him back on *Dauntless* in six months...in something resembling working order." Travis paused for an instant, and then she slipped through the door and out into the hall.

Lafarge slid across the room, plopping right down into the chair next to Barron. "I heard you have six months of leave," she purred. "And also that your ship is laid up...just like mine." She looked up at him with a mischievous grin. "Whatever shall we do to pass the time?"

Also By Jay Allan

Marines (Crimson Worlds I)
The Cost of Victory (Crimson Worlds II)
A Little Rebellion (Crimson Worlds III)
The First Imperium (Crimson Worlds IV)
The Line Must Hold (Crimson Worlds V)
To Hell's Heart (Crimson Worlds VI)
The Shadow Legions(Crimson Worlds VII)
Even Legends Die (Crimson Worlds VIII)
The Fall (Crimson Worlds IX)
War Stories (Crimson World Prequels)
MERCS (Successors I)
The Prisoner of Eldaron (Successors II)
Into the Darkness (Refugees I)
Shadows of the Gods (Refugees II)
Revenge of the Ancients (Refugees III)
Winds of Vengeance (Refugees IV)
Shadow of Empire (Far Stars I)
Enemy in the Dark (Far Stars II)
Funeral Games (Far Stars III)
Blackhawk (Far Stars Legends I)
The Dragon's Banner
Gehenna Dawn (Portal Wars I)
The Ten Thousand (Portal Wars II)
Homefront (Portal Wars III)
Red Team Alpha (CW Adventures I)
Duel in the Dark (Blood on the Stars I)
Call to Arms (Blood on the Stars II)
Flames of Rebellion (Flames of Rebellion I)

www.jayallanbooks.com

Made in the USA
Columbia, SC
16 September 2017